IN THE
AFTER
LIGHT

ALEXANDRA BRACKEN

HYPERION

Los Angeles   New York

First Edition
1 3 5 7 9 10 8 6 4 2
G475-5664-5-14227

Printed in the United States of America

This book is set in Edlund
Designed by Marci Senders

ISBN 978-1-4231-5752-6

Reinforced binding

Visit www.hyperionteens.com

SUSTAINABLE FORESTRY INITIATIVE   Certified Sourcing
www.sfiprogram.org
SFI-00993

THIS LABEL APPLIES TO TEXT STOCK

For Merrilee, Emily, and the countless others around the world who have worked tirelessly to put this series into your hands, with my love and gratitude.

In our youth, our hearts were touched with fire.
—Oliver Wendell Holmes, Jr.

PROLOGUE

BLACK IS THE COLOR THAT IS NO COLOR AT ALL.

Black is the color of a child's still, empty bedroom. The heaviest hour of night—the one that traps you in your bunk, suffocating in another nightmare. It is a uniform stretched over the broad shoulders of an angry young man. Black is the mud, the lidless eye watching your every breath, the low vibrations of the fence that stretches up to tear at the sky.

It is a road. A forgotten night sky broken up by faded stars.

It is the barrel of a new gun, leveled at your heart.

The color of Chubs's hair, Liam's bruises, Zu's eyes.

Black is a promise of tomorrow, bled dry from lies and hate.

Betrayal.

I see it in the face of a broken compass, feel it in the numbing grip of grief.

I run, but it is my shadow. Chasing, devouring, polluting. It is the button that should never have been pushed, the door that shouldn't have opened, the dried blood that couldn't be washed away. It is the charred remains of buildings. The car hidden in the forest, waiting. It is the smoke.

1

It is the fire.
The spark.
Black is the color of memory.
It is our color.
The only one they'll use to tell our story.

ONE

THE SHADOWS GREW LONGER THE FARTHER I WALKED from the center of the city. I headed west, toward the sinking sun that set the remainder of the day on fire. I hated that about winter—night seemed to reach earlier and earlier into the afternoon. Los Angeles's smog-stained sky was painted with dark strokes of violet and ash.

Under normal circumstances, I would have been grateful for the additional cover as I navigated the easy grid of surface streets back to our current base. But with the debris from the attack, the installation of military stations and detainment camps, and the congestion of now-useless, abandoned cars fried by the electromagnetic pulse, the face of the city had been altered so dramatically that to go even a half mile through the wreckage was enough to become completely lost. Without the city's light pollution casting its usual foggy glow, if any of us scouted at night, we had to rely on distant lights from military convoys.

I cast a quick glance around, pressing a hand against my jacket pocket to make sure the flashlight and service pistol were still there; both were courtesy of one Private Morales, and would only

3

be used in absolute emergency. I wasn't letting anyone pick me up, spot me running through the dark. I had to get back to base.

An hour ago, Private Morales had had the unfortunate luck to cross into my path, coming off her patrol of the freeway alone. I'd been there since before sunrise, positioned behind an over-turned car, watching the elevated roadway shimmering like an electric current under a constant flood of artificial light. Every hour, I'd counted the number of tiny uniformed figures moving along the section nearest to me, weaving in and out of the trucks and Humvees lined up bumper to bumper like a secondary bar-rier. My muscles cramped, but I fought the urge to wait it out somewhere else.

It had been more than worth it. One soldier had been enough to arm me not only with the tools I needed to return to base safely, but also with the knowledge of how we could finally—*finally*—get the hell out of this damn city.

I looked back and forth twice before climbing over the fallen heap of brick that had once been the face of a bank branch, and let out a hiss of pain between my teeth as the side of my hand scraped on something jagged. I kicked the object—a metal C that had fallen from its logo—in irritation, and immediately regretted it. The clattering and grating noise bounced off the nearby build-ings, almost masking the faint voices and shuffling steps.

I threw myself into what was left of the building's interior, dropping down into a crouch behind the nearest stable wall.

"Clear!"

"Clear—"

Twisting around, I watched the progress of the soldiers moving along the other side of the street. I counted helmets—twelve—as they broke off to investigate the different smashed-glass

4

entryways of office buildings and stores. *Cover?* I looked around, quickly taking stock of the overturned, singed furniture, my body moving toward one of the dark wood desks and sliding beneath it. The scrape of loose debris against the outside sidewalk overpowered the sound of my own ragged breathing.

I stayed where I was, nose burning with the smell of smoke and ash and gasoline, tracking the voices until they faded. Anxiety kept a grip on my stomach as I edged my way out from under the desk and along the floor toward the entrance. I could still see the patrol unit weaving through the wreckage halfway down the avenue, but I couldn't wait, not even a few minutes longer.

When I'd dug through the soldier's memories, stitched together the information I needed, it felt like a block of cement had finally rolled off my chest. She'd shown me the gaps in the freeway's defenses as surely as if she'd handed me a map and marked them in thick, black strokes. After that, it had just been a matter of washing myself out of her memory.

I knew the former Children's League agents would be pissed that this had actually worked. Nothing they tried themselves had succeeded, and in the meantime, the hauls from their food scouting had dwindled. Cole had pushed and pushed them to let me try, but the other agents only agreed on the condition that I go alone—to avoid any additional "risks" of capture. We'd already lost two agents who'd been careless while walking out in the city.

I wasn't careless, but I *was* getting desperate. It was time to make a move now, or the military would starve us out of hiding.

The U.S. Army and National Guard had created a virtual barrier around downtown Los Angeles using the elaborate freeway system. The snaking cement monsters formed a tight circle around the inner city, choking us off from the outside world.

The 101 was to the north and east, the I-10 to the south, and the 110 to the west. We might have had a chance of escaping if we'd left immediately after climbing back up to the surface from the wreckage of HQ, but . . . there was that word that Chubs always used: *shell-shocked*. He said it was amazing any of us were capable of movement at all.

I should have. I should have forced us to go, instead of falling apart at the seams. I should have—if I hadn't been thinking about his face trapped down in the dark. I pressed the back of my hand against my eyes, steeling myself against the nausea and stabbing pain in my skull. *Think about anything else. Anything.* These headaches were unbearable; so much worse than the ones I used to have after trying to control my abilities.

I couldn't stop. I pushed through the hollow feeling in my legs to a steady jog. I felt the ache of exhaustion at the back of my throat, the heaviness of my eyelids, but adrenaline kept me moving, even as parts of me felt like they were on the verge of shutting down. I couldn't remember the last time I'd fallen into a deep enough sleep to escape the waking nightmare around us.

The roads were blistered with peeling asphalt, strewn with piles of cement the army had yet to clear. Here and there I passed bright dots of color—a red high heel, a purse, someone's bike, all dropped and forgotten. Some objects had blown out of nearby windows; the heat from the nearby blasts had charred them black. The wastefulness of the destruction was sickening.

As I ran across the next intersection, I stole a look up Olive Street, my eyes drawn to the glowing field of light that was Pershing Square three avenues over. The former park had been transformed into an internment camp; hastily thrown together, while the rubble of the city still smoldered. The poor people inside its fences had been working in the nearby buildings when President Gray launched his attack against the Children's League and the Federal Coalition, the small band of former politicians united against him. He'd supposedly retaliated because one or both parties had played a role in his most recent assassination attempt. We'd kept watch on each of these camps, searching for Cate and the others, watching as the numbers inside swelled as more and more civilians were picked up and held against their will.

But no Cate. If she and the agents who left HQ before the attack hadn't made it out of the city, they were hiding themselves so well that *we* couldn't find them—not even with our emergency contact procedures.

Another small military convoy—the buzz of radios and growling tires tipped me off two blocks in advance. I bit back a noise of frustration as I took cover behind the shell of an SUV until the soldiers passed me by, their boots kicking up a cloud of chalky gray dust. I stood up, brushed myself off, and started running.

We—the League, or whatever was left of us—moved locations every few days, never staying in one warehouse long. When we ventured out to find food and water, or went to watch the camps, if there was even a hint of suspicion someone could have followed us back—we moved. It was smart, there was no denying that, but I was starting to lose track of where we were at any given time.

The silence, thicker now that I had crossed into the eastern half of the city, was so much more unnerving than the symphony of machine-gun fire and weapons discharging that had filled the air close to Pershing Square. My hand clenched around my flashlight, but I still couldn't bring myself to take it out, even as my elbow scraped against the stucco wall I stumbled into. I glanced up at the sky. New moon. Of course.

A feeling of unease, the same one that had been perched on my shoulder whispering dark things in my ear for weeks, became a burning knife in my chest—sinking slowly, tearing everything in its path. I cleared my throat, trying to get the poisonous air out of my lungs. At the next intersection I forced myself to stop, and ducked into an old ATM alcove.

Take a breath, I ordered myself. *A real one.* I tried shaking out my arms and hands, but the heaviness remained. Closing my eyes, I listened to a distant helicopter slice through the air, moving at a furious pace. Instinct—insistent, baiting instinct—was nudging me to swing an early right on Bay Street, not stay on Alameda Street until I hit its intersection with Seventh Street. The latter was a more-direct route to our current base on Jesse Street and Santa Fe Avenue; the quickest way to give the others the details, form a plan, and *get out.*

But if someone were watching or tracking me, I'd be able to lose them on Seventh Street. My feet took charge and pushed me east toward the Los Angeles River.

I got a block and a half before I saw the shadows moving up Mateo Street toward Seventh Street. My punishing pace came to an abrupt stop—my hands flew out to catch myself against a mailbox before I spilled out into the middle of the street.

A sharp breath blew out of me. *Too close.* This is what happened when I didn't take the time to slow down and actually make sure the street was clear. I felt the echo of my racing pulse behind my temples and reached up to rub them. Something warm and sticky smeared against my forehead, but I just couldn't bring myself to care.

I kept my head and body low as I moved, trying to see which direction the troops were headed in now. They were already way too close to our base—if I doubled back, I might be able to out-run them to the warehouse and warn the others to bail.

But they had just . . . stopped.

At the corner of the intersection, they'd walked right up to the smashed-in facade of some kind of hardware store and stepped over the busted windows and into the building. I heard a laugh, voices—and my blood slowed to a crawl in my veins.

They weren't soldiers.

I moved up the street toward the store, running a hand along the side of the building until I reached the windows and dropped down into a crouch.

"—where did you find this?"

"Good shit, man!"

More laughter.

"Oh, God, I never thought I'd be so damn happy to see bagels—"

I looked over the ledge. Inside, three of our agents—Ferguson, Gates, and Sen—were hunkered down, a small spread of food in front of them. Gates, a former Navy SEAL, tore into a bag of potato chips so hard he nearly split it in half.

They have food. I couldn't get my head around it. *They're eating food here.* The disbelief was so numbing I had to work it through one thought at a time.

They aren't bringing the food back for the rest of us.

Was this what was happening each time a group went out?

9

The agents had been so insistent on going to scout for supplies themselves; I'd assumed it was because they were afraid if any of the kids got picked up, they'd immediately rat out the group's current location. But was this the real reason? So they'd get first dibs on whatever they turned up?

A cold, icy fury turned my fingers into claws. My broken nails cut into my palms; the sting of pain only added to the churning in my stomach.

"God, that's good," Sen said. She was a beast of a woman— tall, with muscles packed under taut, leathery skin. There was always this expression on her face like . . . like she knew where all the bodies were buried because she'd put them there herself. When she deigned to speak to any of us kids, it was to bark at us to shut up.

I waited through the silence that followed, anger flaring with each second.

"We should get back," Ferguson said, starting to rise.

"They're fine. Even if Stewart beats us back, Reynolds is there to make sure he's not shooting his mouth off again."

"I'm more worried about . . ."

"The leech?" Gates supplied, with a belly laugh. "She'll be the last one in. If she even makes it back."

My brows went right up at that. *Leech*. Me. That was a new one. I'd been called so many worse things, the only part I found offensive was the idea that I couldn't handle a trip back and forth across the city without getting caught.

"She's far more valuable than the others," Ferguson argued, "it's just a matter of—"

"It's not a matter of anything. She doesn't obey us, and it makes her a liability."

Liability. I pressed a fist against my mouth to keep the bile down. I knew how the League handled "liabilities." I also knew how *I* would handle any agent who tried.

Sen leaned back, bracing her hands on the tile. "The plan stays the same regardless."

"Good." Gates balled up the bag of chips he'd just demolished. "How much of this are we bringing back? I could go for another bagel . . ."

A tub of pretzel sticks and a bag of hot dog buns. That's what they were bringing back for seventeen kids and the handful of agents that had been stuck behind babysitting while the others went out to collect food and intel.

When they started to climb back onto their feet, I flattened myself against the building, waiting for them to step through the window and glance each way down the intersection. My hands were still clenched when I stood and started trailing them, keeping a good half block between us until the warehouse finally came into view.

Before they crossed that final street, Sen held a lighter up above her head, a single flame that the agent posted on the roof could see. There was a faint whistle in response—the signal to approach.

I ran, closing the last bit of distance before the woman could start climbing up the fire escape after the others.

"Agent Sen!" My voice was a harsh whisper.

The woman's head swung around, one hand on the ladder, the other reaching for the handgun tucked into the holster of her combat gear. It took me a moment to realize I'd had my own hand clenched around the gun in my jacket pocket the whole time I'd been stalking them down the street.

"What?" she snapped, waving to Gates and Ferguson to continue up the fire escape.

Not happy to see me, are you?

"I have to tell you something. . . . It's . . ." I hoped she'd think the trembling quality in my voice was fear, not anger on the verge of exploding. "I don't trust Cole with this."

That had her interested. Her teeth flashed in the dark.

"What is it?" she asked.

This time, I smiled. And when I slammed into her mind, I didn't care if it broke apart. I ripped through memories of bunks, training, HQ, agents, tossing the images aside faster than they could solidify in my mind. I felt her jerk, tremble under the force of my attack.

I knew when I had what I was looking for. She had imagined it so vividly, plotted it all out with a malicious efficiency that even I'd underestimated. Everything about the idea had an unnatural luster to it, like warmed wax. Cars dripped into the scene, faces I recognized as belonging to the kids upstairs were half-hidden by gags. Dust-colored military fatigues. Black uniforms. A trade.

I was gasping for air by the time I surfaced, unable to get oxygen into my chest deeply enough. I had just enough thought to twist her memory, to plant a false one in the place of the last few minutes. I didn't wait for her to recover, pushing past her to get to the ladder.

Cole—my mind was firing too fast, black fading into my vision. *I have to tell Cole.*

And I had to get away from the agent before I gave in to the terrifyingly real temptation to put a bullet in her right here and right now.

Because it wasn't enough for her to withhold food, to levy threats about leaving us behind if we weren't quieter, didn't move faster, didn't *keep up* with the rest of them. She wanted to be done with us once and for all—to hand our leashes off to the one group she thought could actually control us.

And she wanted the reward money we'd bring in to fund her next strike.

TWO

BY THE TIME I REACHED THE SECOND LEVEL OF THE warehouse, my chest was on fire and my head was a tangle of dark thoughts and dread. The fire escape rattled as Sen started climbing after me, and I couldn't get through the window— away from her—fast enough. Brushing aside the dark Ops jacket they'd hung up to block the weak interior light from the street, I slid my legs over the ledge and dropped inside.

My eyes frantically jumped from one flickering puddle of candlelight to another, skipping over the dark spaces in between. Every single kid seemed to be huddled in the far corner of the room, as if Gates and Ferguson had backed them into it in exchange for food.

No Cole, I thought, raking a hand back through my hair. *Dammit.* I needed him. He had to know—we had to figure this out.

"A little appreciation would go a long way," Gates sneered. It was like his words had disturbed a thick layer of dust in the silent room. Voices immediately floated up in quiet, quick thanks before the kids settled themselves back down again, eyes only on the floor or each other. I saw now what I hadn't wanted to admit

14

to myself before. In the end, all of the months—years—we'd spent training with the agents, and fighting alongside them . . . it all came to nothing the second they convinced themselves we were checks waiting to be cashed in.

I found the three faces I was looking for. Vida was back from her own scouting, a nasty cut marring her deep bronze skin, which Chubs was trying to bandage. Next to him was a black backpack. I bit my lip, trying to keep the relief I felt to myself. Inside was the research I'd rescued from Clancy's attempt to incinerate it—the sheets of graphs and charts and medical gibberish his mother had put together in her search for a cure for IAAN.

"Grannie, I swear to God, if you don't lay off the fucking *fussing*—" Vida hissed.

"Let me just disinfect it!" I heard him protest.

Liam sat with his back against the wall, knees up, arms resting on them. He was watching Gates out of the corner of his eye with the same hard expression he'd had ever since the attack. He didn't reach for the food, but simply passed it on to Chubs when it came into his hands.

The agents would turn them in, too. What if I hadn't seen those agents tonight—stopped and actually listened to what Sen and the others were saying? They were going to blindside us with it, set the deal up in advance over the next few days. There wouldn't have been time for me to do anything. Why did I think I could protect all of them? I couldn't even protect *one* kid, not when it mattered most. *Jude*—

Sen knocked against my shoulder as she swept into the room behind me. I barely felt it.

I was above ground, I knew it, but it didn't matter—right

now, I was in a tunnel, blindly squeezing my way through the collapsed walls threatening to crush us. Chased by distant screams, unseeing eyes, and the roar of cement splintering; earth pouring down, smothering everything in its path. The face floating in front of my closed eyes was freckled, his doe-brown eyes wide as he watched his own life end. I saw all of those things, and nothing stopped them. No good memory was strong enough to wipe away how I imagined it must have been. How Jude had slipped away forever in the dark.

I felt myself disconnect. Every nerve in my body lit up, every part inside of me was racing, picking up speed. The pressure inside of me built until I was sure I was going to be crushed by it, and the thought that everyone around me would witness it made everything ten times worse.

The touch at my waist was gentle enough that I didn't register it at first, but steady enough to turn me toward the door—strong enough, even, to keep me upright when my knees buckled at that first step.

Outside of the shrinking room, the hallway was at least ten degrees cooler. Quiet and dark enough that my skin didn't feel like it was bubbling up at the touch of fire in my veins. I only went a few steps down the hall, just enough to be out of the line of sight from the door, before I was carefully lowered down and maneuvered so my head was between my knees. Familiar hands slid the jacket off my shoulders, lifted my hair away from the sweat drenching the back of my neck.

"You're okay, darlin'," Liam's voice was saying. Something cool touched my neck—a bottle of cold water, maybe. "Just take a deep breath."

"I—I can't," I said between shallow gasps.

"Of course you can," he said calmly.

"I have to—" I brought my hands up, clawing at whatever cord was wrapped around my windpipe. Liam took them in one of his own, holding them flat against his chest.

"You don't have to do anything right now," he said softly. "Everything is okay."

It's not, you have no idea, I wanted to say. A sharp ache pierced my right temple, throbbing harder and harder with each passing second.

Touching him did help. I forced myself to match my breathing with the rise and fall of his chest. The cold air worked slowly to untangle the mess of thoughts knotting into a headache at the front of my skull. The pressure eased its grip enough for me to straighten and lean back against the wall.

Liam was still crouched down in front of me, blue eyes searching my face. The wrinkles in his brow smoothed out as he released a small breath of his own. He took the water bottle and poured some water on the bandana he'd pulled out of his back pocket. Slowly, tenderly, he wiped the blood and dirt from my hands and face. "Better?"

I nodded, taking the water bottle for a sip.

"What happened?" he asked. "Are you okay?

"I just . . ." I couldn't tell him. He and Chubs had been planning for days to find a way for us to slip away from the others when the time came to leave the city. What little hate he carried in him was aimed squarely at the agents. If he knew, he'd try to get us to leave tonight. Or, worse, he might accidentally tip the agents off. He'd never been able to guard his feelings the way

Cole did. They'd read him like the day's newspaper and dispose of him just as quickly to avoid him stirring up the other kids. "I just got . . . overwhelmed."

"Has it been happening a lot?" Liam sat cross-legged in front of me.

God. I didn't want to talk about these attacks, either. I couldn't, not even with him. Then I'd have to talk about Jude, about what happened, about everything we hadn't had the time to talk through before things went to hell. He seemed to sense that, at least.

"You've been gone all day," he said. "I was starting to get worried."

"It took a while to find someone I could use," I said. "I wasn't just out there running around being reckless."

"I didn't say you were," Liam said. "I just wish you had told me you were heading out."

"I didn't think I had to."

"You don't *have* to. I'm not your keeper. I was scared, okay?"

I said nothing. This was how it was between us now. Together, but not in the way that was important—the way we were only months ago. After I'd betrayed his trust so badly, I wasn't sure it could be like that again. And it didn't help that I could feel myself falling back on the only way I knew how to cope—wrestling with the thoughts inside of my head, trapping them there so they wouldn't infect anyone else. I'd carefully constructed this invisible wall between us, brick by brick, even as I hugged him, gripped his hand in mine, kissed him.

It was so selfish, I knew it was, to take even that much when I wasn't giving everything back to him . . . but I needed him here. I needed the presence of him at my back, at my side. I needed to see his face and hear his voice and know that he was safe and I could protect him. That was the only way to get through each day.

But it was impossible to clamp down or compartmentalize things around Liam. He was a talker. He felt things more deeply than anyone I'd ever met. He'd been trying to start these conversations with me for days. *You aren't responsible for what happened to Jude. About what happened in the safe house . . .*

"Ruby, seriously, what happened?" he asked, his hands loose around my wrists.

"Sorry," I whispered, because what else could I say? "I'm sorry. I didn't mean to be so . . . I didn't mean to bite your head off. Nothing's going on. I should have told you, but I had to leave in a hurry." *And I knew you'd try to tell me it was too dangerous and I didn't want to argue.* "But I got what we needed. I know how to get us out of here."

His lips compressed into a tight line as he studied me. Liam didn't seem satisfied in the least with that answer, but he was all too willing to drop the topic in favor of another one. "Does that mean we can finally talk about what comes next?"

"Cole isn't going to let us go." *Especially not you.*

"We could look for my parents—"

"Isn't it just as dangerous to drive around aimlessly, looking for your mom and Harry, as it is to stay with the others?" I asked. "This is our fight . . . what we wanted all along, remember? Cole made a deal with me that we'd actually focus on helping kids now—freeing the camps."

At least, it was what we had wanted while we were at East River. Liam had been the one behind the wheel then, steering us all in the direction of getting the kids out of the rehabilitation programs. Maybe it was foolish of me to hope that what had happened there wouldn't affect his dream. But sure enough, his eyes drifted over to the door down the hall that only Cole and I were allowed to enter, to the monster waiting inside.

"Cole says that now, and the agents might be playing nice for once," Liam said. "But how long before they're back to their own agendas?"

I tried not to wince. *Sooner than you think.* "This isn't the League anymore."

"Exactly. It could be worse."

"Not if we're here to keep it from becoming that," I said. "Can we at least give it a little while? See what happens? If things head south we can get out, I promise. If nothing else . . . I have to see if Cate and the others made it. If they did, they'll be waiting for us. She has the flash drive of Leda Corp's research on the cause of IAAN. If we can put that information together with the cure—we won't just be helping ourselves, we'll be helping *every* kid that comes after us."

He shook his head. "I don't want to make you feel like it was all for nothing, but what if there isn't anything useful in the pages you fished out of the fire? For all the sense we can make of them, we could shred them tonight and it still wouldn't make a difference to our lives. I don't want us to just . . . attach ourselves to the idea of them in the hope that one day down the road it'll make sense."

Objectively, I knew that what he was saying was true—but the words sparked such a fierce denial and fury in me, I almost pushed him away. I didn't need reality right now. I needed hope that I'd be able to look at the singed pages and see beyond the familiar words: *Project Snowfall. IAAN. The Professor.*

Giving up that last bit of hope would mean the fleeting moment of besting Clancy hadn't been a small moment of victory at all. It would mean, in the end, he had still won. He'd survived HQ's destruction, and the information he'd fought so hard to bury from us would be useless.

We needed this. *I* needed this. My family's faces bloomed in my mind, the sun at their backs. Just as quickly, the image was gone, replaced by another: Sam, the shadows of Cabin 27 hollowing her cheeks as she faded like a ghost. It became an endless parade of all of their faces—the ones I'd left behind the electric fence at Thurmond.

My fingers dug into the top of my thighs, twisting the fabric there until I was sure it would rip. The awful truth was, no matter how much I denied it to myself, there was crucial information missing. And the only person in possession of it was the one person Clancy had ensured we'd never find: his mother, Lillian Gray.

"I'm not giving up," Liam said, a fierceness in his voice. "If this doesn't work out, we'll find something that does."

I reached up to brush my fingers along his cheek, stroking the rough stubble growing in. He sighed but didn't argue.

"I don't want to fight," I said quietly. "I never want to fight with you."

"Then don't. It's that simple, darlin'." He leaned his forehead against mine. "But we have to decide these things together. The important stuff. Promise me."

"Promise," I whispered. "But we're going to the Ranch. We have to."

Before HQ was constructed, the League had operated out of Northern California, at a base that had been affectionately codenamed the Ranch. The location itself was fiercely guarded now—appropriate, given its status as a "last resort" base to fall back to in the event of an emergency. Only the senior agents—Cole included—had been around during that time, and actually knew how to find it.

If Cate had made it out, she'd be waiting there. I could see her in my mind, pacing along an empty hallway, as if expecting us to walk through the door at any moment. She wouldn't go against protocol. By now, she'd be out of her head with worry.

One thought slipped in, chasing out every hopeful one. *I'll have to tell her.*

Oh, God, why hadn't I thought about that? She wouldn't know—couldn't. *She trusted me. She told me to take care of him.* She had no idea that Jude . . .

I closed my eyes, focusing on the way Liam's hand was softly stroking up and down my spine.

"—the *hell* is this?" Sen's voice whipped out of the room, down the hall, slapping against our private bubble. "Stewart, you've done a lot of stupid shit—and I mean *a lot*—but this is—this is—"

"A stroke of genius?" Cole said, and I could practically hear the grin in his voice. "You're welcome."

I was on my feet before Liam could shoot me an exasperated look.

"Come on," I said, "something's going on."

"Yeah, yeah," Liam said, putting a hand against my lower back and steering me toward the room. "When is there not something going on with him?"

The agents had circled around the window so tightly, all I could see was Cole's black knit cap behind their heads. I glanced over to the kids, most of whom were standing, trying to see what was happening.

"Roo?"

My back straightened, and something gripped low in my stomach at the name. I turned toward the direction of Nico's voice.

"Yeah?"

"Is everything . . ." he looked at the agents. "Is everything okay?"

"What do you think?" I snapped. Nico flinched at my tone, which somehow only made me angrier. I didn't have an ounce of sympathy left for him. Sad, scared, traitorous Nico.

The Greens didn't know what to do with themselves once they realized there was no bringing back any of the electronics, and there was no way for the two Yellows we had left to spark them back to life. Nico spent most of his time sleeping, only acknowledging me and Vida with a few words here and there.

The pity I'd felt about the way Clancy had manipulated him had evaporated at the simple realization that if Nico had never fed Clancy the information about Project Snowfall and his mother's location—if he hadn't been stupid enough to ask the president's son to track us down—we would never have been in this situation. Jude would be alive, and we wouldn't be trapped in the hellhole that was Los Angeles.

"Ruby—" Liam started, his voice disapproving. I didn't care. I wasn't here to comfort the kid.

I held up my hand as Chubs and Vida cut through the agents between us, coming to stand next to us, but Chubs still let out a demanding, "Are you okay? Were you hurt?"

"No, Gran, she's dying. She's bleeding out at your feet." Vida rolled her eyes. "Did you get what you needed?"

"Yes—"

"Excuse me for showing concern for my *friend*," Chubs growled, whirling back on her. "I realize that's bound to be a foreign concept to any psychopath—"

"This psychopath sleeps less than three feet away from you," Vida reminded him, her voice all sweetness and light.

"Wow, we have such nice friends," Liam murmured. I'd already disengaged from the conversation. Cole glanced over, his brows raised in a silent question. I nodded, and he turned to look down—to the woman standing beside him.

She was middle-aged, olive-toned skin sagging with wrinkles and obvious strain. What must have once been an expensive navy dress had torn at the skirt seam, and her hair hung loosely from a bun, whole sections of it gray with either cement dust or age. Wide, dark eyes scanned the room, catching at the sight of the kids.

"Do you know who this is?" Cole demanded.

"A civilian who can now identify all of us and report back to the military," Sen shot back.

"My name is Anabel Cruz," the woman said, with a surprising amount of dignity for someone limping around in broken high heels.

"Christ, you meatheads," Cole said when he was greeted with blank looks. "One of California's senators? The Federal Coalition's international liaison? She worked on establishing contacts and negotiating possible support from other nations."

Sen didn't look impressed. She turned on Cole again, her hands on her hips. "Did you even bother trying to confirm her identity? If she was with the FC, why isn't she in one of the detainment camps?"

"I can speak to that myself," Senator Cruz said, eyes flashing.

24

"When the attacks began, I was meeting with Amplify outside of our headquarters."

"The underground news org?" Gates asked.

Liam turned to look at me, confused. I explained quietly, in as few words as I could. The group had been around for two years, maybe three. My take was that it was mostly a collection of reporters and editors who had landed on Gray's shit list for covering "dangerous" topics like riots and protests, and then had to go into hiding.

He opened his mouth, a spark of something in his eyes.

"Which, yes—" Cole looked at the other agents. "I realize it says something about her common sense, but—"

"Excuse me?" The senator crossed her arms over her chest.

"He means Amplify doesn't have a good track record of making their stories stick. They get seconds of glory here and there before Gray shuts them down," Sen said, assessing the woman again. "Online, on the social media sites that haven't been blocked yet, quick-and-dirty pamphlets. Their reach is too small. They're getting jack shit done."

This was clearly the one thing Cole and Sen were in agreement on.

"The reporter got trapped with her in the city," Cole told the others. "I was out doing the usual sweeps and heard the military storming a building nearby. They were tracking *him*, not her. Shot him on the spot, and probably would have done the same to her if she hadn't identified herself."

"So you swept in, saving the day." Sen rolled her eyes. The hatred I felt for the woman was starting to overwhelm my better judgment. I felt myself take another step forward. "And all you succeeded in doing was bringing in another mouth to feed."

"Speaking of—" Cole slid the stuffed backpack off his shoulder and tossed it to one of the Greens. "Found one of those juice shops with some decent produce still in their refrigerators. It's not a lot, but better than the crap we've been eating."

The girl looked like he'd just handed her a birthday cake he'd personally baked and frosted. Chubs was over there and unzipping it so quickly, I think he must have teleported. The others fell in behind him, thanking Cole, trying to pass a whole apple back to him.

"I'm good. Thanks, though." When he turned back to Sen, his smile was still there, broadening under her look of utter contempt. But I could see something dangerous in his stillness, the way he cocked his head to the right. It was like a match waiting to be struck against something just slightly rougher.

"I'm a little surprised, Sen. I would have thought you'd be ecstatic to have someone like this on the team. Once we get out of here, she'll be incredibly useful in helping us connect what we're doing to the rest of the world," he said finally, his tone light. "We're turning over a new leaf, aren't we?"

Yeah, well. Sen had no interest in connecting us to the world. She wanted to burn it down around us. Still, there had been a question buried in his words—a challenge. The longer this went on, the more the other agents began to shuffle their feet, steal glances at one another. Some of the Greens, the fast thinkers, were clearly reading into this more deeply than the others, who seemed content to chalk the familiar tension up to the usual frustrations.

He knows. Awareness prickled at the back of my mind. Cole might not have known the full details, but he must have had a sense they'd go back on their word to help us free the camps. He was baiting her, trying to get her to admit it in front of the kids.

"I'd be happy to discuss my ideas with you," Senator Cruz said. "Provided we have a way out of the city?"

The room's attention swung to me. "Yes—it's like we thought. They don't have enough manpower to be patrolling the streets *and* guarding so many miles of freeway. They've set up a few stretches that, at night, are just empty vehicles and floodlights."

I walked over to the driving map of Los Angeles we'd pinned to the wall after finding it in a nearby car. I pointed out the three spots I'd seen in the soldier's mind, proud of how steady my voice was as shadowy images started creeping in at the corner of my mind. PSFs. The red-stitched Psi symbols. Zip ties. Muzzle. Money. Guns. I couldn't look at any of the agents. Now that I knew what they really wanted, how they were going to repay me for getting their asses out of this city, a dark little voice at the back of my mind started whispering, *lie.* It wanted me to leave out a few key details. Let them brush close enough to danger to get bruised.

"Here," Cole said, passing me a pen. "Mark them for us."

Gates muttered something under his breath and I turned toward him, crossing my arms over my chest, meeting his gaze dead-on. He looked away immediately, playing it off as he wiped his mouth and nose against his sleeve. That flicker of fear I saw in his expression was better for my confidence than the steadying hand that Cole dropped on my head as he leaned over my shoulder to study the marks I made.

"I'm sure there are more," I said, "but these were the only ones I saw."

Cole glanced around the room, silently calculating how many there would be per group if we only had three potential exits.

Seventeen kids. Twenty-four agents, down twenty from the group that had come to liberate HQ. Five had died in the initial attack, and the rest had deserted. Eight groups of five or so. It was doable.

"It'll have to be quick and timed exactly right," Sen said. "It could be hundreds of miles before we reach an area the EMP didn't affect. All on foot."

"They had it marked on the map I saw," I said, uncapping the pen again and sketching out the area for them. Beverly Hills to the west, Monterey Park to the east, Glendale to the north, and Compton to the south. All in all, not a huge area. At least, much smaller than I'd expected.

"We'll assign teams tonight and head out in a few hours— three or four A.M.?"

"We need to talk our strategy through," Gates protested. "Gather supplies."

"No, what we need is to get the hell out of this city," Cole said, "as quickly as possible. The others are waiting for us at the Ranch."

I gripped his wrist, eyes flicking toward the door.

He gave me a slight nod before shifting his focus back onto the room. "Y'all need to hit the sack ASAP, because we're rolling out in a few hours. Yeah, that's right, Blair," he said, turning toward one of the younger Green girls who actually gasped. "That's what I like to hear. Excitement! We have a change of scenery coming our way."

"You can't make a decision like that without the rest of us having a say," Sen interrupted. "You don't make the call."

"You know what?" Cole said. "I think I just did. Anyone got a problem with that?"

The room was silent. The kids shook their heads, but the agents were a gallery of grim, tight expressions. No one spoke up, though.

"What about the people in the detention camps?" Senator Cruz asked, making her way over to us to study the map for herself. "We just leave them to their own fates? I'd rather stay here and—"

"Get yourself caught and put on one of those trials?" Cole cut in. "You said you were in the middle of a big negotiation with world leaders; why would you want to table that discussion when seeing it through will help *everyone*? Unless you were lying about it?"

"I wasn't lying," she shot back, dark eyes flashing. "Those people are my friends and colleagues. We've risked our lives trying to right this country."

"People will know what happened here," Cole promised. "They won't be left for long. I'm going to make sure of it, and you're going to help me."

The conversation shifted then, moving toward strategy, the right way to break the groups up and which surface-street routes to take up north.

"Everyone good?" Cole asked the clusters of kids, slowly working his way toward the door. His eyes jumped back to me as he continued, "Everyone get enough to eat?"

There was a chorus of *Yeah!*s. They were lying, of course. I wondered if they thought the truth would disappoint him, or if it would send him back out again. Even if you were to subtract Cole's ability to charm a cat into giving up its fur coat, he still would have won them over, by virtue of just acting like he cared.

"I still want in on the crazy eights tournament," he added, pointing at one of the Green boys as he passed. "I'm coming for that crown, Sean. Watch yourself."

He snorted. "Keep trying, old man. Let's see if you can keep up."

Cole mimed like he'd been shot clean through the heart. "A bunch of whippersnappers! I could teach you a thing or two about winning—"

"Or what the rest of us would call *cheating*," Liam called over from where he, Chubs, and Vida had posted themselves by the window, talking quietly with Nico and another Green. My eyes darted from their backs to their hands to their feet. *Where is it?*

"Which is why he always lost," Cole told the others with a wink.

The agents had migrated to the other side of the room to be closer to the map to, I assume, make their own plans. Whatever Senator Cruz was trying to tell them, they ignored her.

Where's the backpack? I circled back around the kids who were blocking me, searching the ground—and found it slung over Ferguson's shoulder. The temperature in my body shot up five degrees. And I knew, just like that, if I wanted the cure's research in my hands again, I was going to have to force them—I would need to compel each and every one of them to hand it over.

Cole reached the door to the hall and tilted his head. I waited a minute longer before following him. If the agents noticed, they just didn't care. I'd given them everything they needed to see their plan through, hadn't I?

The hallway was still a good ten degrees cooler than the room was; once I was outside of the dim glow escaping through the open door, I could barely see a few feet in front of me. I wished for a second that I had grabbed my stolen flashlight, but this seemed like a conversation best suited for shadows. Stripped of everything but its concrete and colorful piping, this building was like a tomb—even the air inside was stale.

I counted a hundred paces off in my head, sure I was nearing the end of the hall, when a hand reached out of the darkness and grabbed me. I was pulled inside a small, tight space—a closet? My heart was still fluttering when the door clicked shut behind me.

"So, Gem . . ." Cole began. "Busy night, huh?"

The only way I'd been able to keep myself mostly together these past two weeks had been to screw a lid down over every terrifying impulse of emotion that tried to bubble up. Now, though, I'd been shaken so badly that it was only a matter of time before I exploded. I just wished it wasn't now, and that it didn't come in the form of gasping tears. I couldn't get a word out.

"Gem—Jesus." Cole put a hand on my shoulder, steadying me as he snapped his fingers. A flame flickered at the tip of them, filling the cramped space with light.

"I was coming back . . ." I managed to squeeze out. "I overheard Sen and the others. . . . They aren't going to—we aren't going to the Ranch. I looked in her head and . . . they're going to—they're going to—"

"Take it from the beginning," Cole said. "Go slow. Tell me everything you heard the agents say. What you saw."

I repeated it, word for word. I told them about how they were going to take one or two of us kids in each car with them, how they planned to wait until we were an hour or two outside of the city before subduing each kid. The exchange of flesh and bone for blood money. The guns they'd buy, the explosives they'd set—they were going after Gray where they assumed he'd be stupid enough to be: the newly rebuilt Washington, D.C.

Cole's expression was shuttered, closed off in a way that Liam never could manage. If I hadn't seen his hand spasm, I wouldn't have known he was furious until he spoke. For a long time, though, he said nothing at all. I felt a trickle of sweat run down my face and was tempted, for a moment, to open the door and let the cool air in.

Finally, he said, "I'll handle it."

"*We* will handle it. But you have to decide," I told him. "Right now. You can't keep running down the middle, trying to have a foot on both sides of the line. Decide if you're with us or you're with them."

"Of course I'm with you," he said sharply, looking pissed that I'd suggested otherwise. "You know I—this affects me, too. I made you a promise back in Los Angeles, didn't I? You trying to make me out to be a liar?"

"No, I just—" I sucked in a deep breath. "You won't tell the others what you are. You won't even tell *Liam*. You haven't looked at the cure research since that first night."

"Oh, gee, could it be because I'm trying not to draw attention to the fact that I have a personal investment in getting rid of certain delightful freak powers?" He let the flame go out for a moment and then relit it for emphasis. "I can't show interest in something without the other agents wondering *why*, or without them wanting it more, just because I do. It's a game I've had to play for years."

"This is *not* a game, no part of it is," I said. "They won't give the research back now."

"I am well aware of that, and I've taken precautions. Their names are Blair and Sara."

The two girls were Greens. With photographic memories. "You gave it to them to memorize?"

"I tested them. Had each reproduce a diagram and chart, and they nailed it. I think we should let the agents keep the backpack—it'll help sell what we're trying to do," he said. I kept my back straight and looked just past his head, where I wouldn't have to both listen to the Southern drawl and see that smile, the patented Stewart charm assault. "I have an idea, but I also have a feeling you aren't going to like it."

"Way to set it up for me."

"I'm serious now, Gem. This has to be between you and me, understand? It won't work otherwise. Promise me. It's the only way to get rid of them before they get rid of us."

Cole offered a hand, and I hesitated before taking it. I held it long enough to feel the natural, innate heat of him warm the air around us.

Clancy had told me once that there had to be a natural hierarchy of people with Psi abilities; that those with the most power should be leading the others, simply because there wasn't anyone else powerful enough to question them. And now, holding Cole's hand, I saw that was true, but for a different reason. We were the ones who saw the full spectrum of everything right and wrong with the abilities we'd been given; we'd been feared and hated, and we'd feared and hated ourselves. Neither of us wanted what we had; we'd never try to keep our powers or abuse our position for absolutely longer than we had to. And on a basic level, the ones with the most power had to be out front, if only because we'd have the best shot at protecting the others.

I squeezed his hand. A look of relief and gratitude passed over his features before he could steady them back into his usual look of arrogant nonchalance.

"What's our next step, then?" I asked. "How are we going to accomplish anything without trained forces? Where are we going to go?"

"*We* are going to the Ranch," Cole said. "*They* are going to Kansas HQ with the rest of the agents. They get to wash their hands of us, but they don't get the damn Ranch. That is *ours*."

"How are you going to manage that?" I said.

"Gem, the better question is: how long is it going to take you to convince them that the Ranch is . . . oh, run-down . . . stripped of anything useful . . . indefensible?"

Understanding froze me at my center. "You want me to influence them. There are over a dozen agents—"

"And you have three hours before we leave," Cole said, letting his flame go out again. "So I would suggest working fast."

THREE

In the scramble leading up to our departure, everyone had different tasks to attend to. Some were sent to relieve the others on watch; some packed up the spare gear we'd accumulated; others, like Liam and Chubs, divvied up the last bit of food between the different teams. I moved between the agents like an unexpected breeze, brushing up against their minds just as softly. Cole and I had decided the order I should work in to make the shift in plan seem the most natural. Which meant starting with Agent Sen.

I stood behind her, back-to-back, as she studied the map and made adjustments to the initial lists of who was driving with who. Having opened her mind once meant the second trip in was easier than fitting a key into a greased lock.

With each agent, I started to feel myself slowing down more and more, forced to fight through scenes of bleak violence, training, dreams. I'd spent six months with these people, but it took me less than two hours to finally understand the trajectory of their hatred—for Gray, for us, for everything that stood in their way. There was so much aching loss between them, they created a black hole that sucked one another in.

When I finished, I felt like a rock that had survived a landslide. Steady enough to go three doors down the hall to deal with Clancy Gray.

I nudged his side with my foot, a bit harder than I maybe needed to. "Wake up."

He groaned, eyes bleary as I shone the flashlight directly into his face. "If this chat doesn't involve cutting my hands free, a mirror, either of the Stewart brothers' messy and untimely deaths, or a clean pair of clothes, I'm not interested."

I hooked my heel over his arm, forcing him to roll onto his back. He glowered up at me through the dark fringe that hung over his eyes in spikes. The slime from the sewers he'd taken to escape HQ had faded from a sickly-looking black to a dry, crusty gray that flaked off him when he so much as cocked a brow.

"No food?" He snorted. "Using deprivation as torture is so . . . direct."

"This isn't torture," I said, rolling my eyes. At least not in the traditional sense. I don't know that Clancy was all that bothered that we kept him separate from the others, in a kind of solitary confinement. I think what bothered him was that he was being blocked from information, only able to catch snatches of conversation through the wall. That was Clancy Gray's perfect hell. That, and the filthy clothes that stuck to his skin in odd places.

I held up the sweatpants and T-shirt and dropped them onto his face. "I'm going to cut your hands and feet free, and I'm going to give you a rag and bucket of water to clean yourself up with, and then you're going to come quietly and do exactly as I say."

I used the small knife Cole had given me to cut the zip tie

around his ankles, ignoring the welts circling the skin there.

"What's going on?" he asked, sitting up. "What are you doing?"

"We're moving."

"Where?" Clancy asked, rubbing his wrists once they were free, too. "I heard there's an old meat locker a few blocks away. That would be an upgrade."

I turned my back as he stripped down, throwing the rag back over my shoulder in his general direction. I kept my eyes focused on the floor, listening to him scrub himself down.

"Of course it would be too much to ask for warm water," he groused. "I don't even get a blanket—"

He stopped moving. I heard the rag slop against the tile floor and glanced back over my shoulder, keeping my gaze above his bare shoulders. His eyes were narrowed at me, clearly working a thought through. "What's really going on?"

"We're moving," I repeated, fighting back the usual swell of disgust. He didn't get information. He didn't get anything, other than the little he didn't even deserve. When I didn't elaborate, I felt the tickling sensation at the back of my skull as his mind casually tried to bump up against mine, as if knocking to get in. I shut it down, picturing a door slamming in his face. He flinched at the force of it.

"You're going to trade me—turn me in," he said in a tight voice. "That's why you're getting me all cleaned up."

If it hadn't been so close to what the agents were planning for us, I would have tried torturing him with the possibility. As it was, I didn't have the stomach for it. "You'd like that, wouldn't you? Bend a few of the PSFs to your will, orchestrate an escape . . ."

"Wow, so you *are* still capable of speaking sentences that

contain more than three words," Clancy said, sliding the clean shirt over his head and dragging the sweatpants up, one leg at a time. He looked paler than I remembered—as thin and shadowed as the rest of us. "How are you still so angry? Don't tell me this is about that stupid kid."

I don't remember anything that happened after I landed the first punch on his jaw, only that when I came back to my senses, there were arms locked around my waist and I was still thrashing, trying to break free.

"Hey—*hey*! Cool it!" Cole released me and shoved me away from both him and Clancy. "You're better than that. Get a grip!"

I pressed a fist against my chest, gasping for breath. Clancy still had his arms up over his head when Cole lifted him onto his feet, dragged his hands behind his back, and fastened a new zip tie. He jammed an old pillowcase we'd been using as a hood down over him next, knotting it to ensure it'd stay on.

Without another word, he dragged me over to the door, anger drawing deep lines in his face. "I need you focused," he hissed. "We're going to be driving for hours and he'll be in the car with us the whole time. If he tries something, you have to be the one to shut it down."

I stared at Clancy, taking in the way he angled his head toward us. Who's to say he wasn't "trying something" right now on Cole? He'd controlled far more people in far worse circumstances—this would be nothing for him. I'd just assumed that physically separating him from the others would be enough to protect them, but what if it wasn't?

"So we're going for a car ride?" he called over.

I searched Cole's face for a hint of Clancy's influence, pushing down the bubble of fear in my chest. His eyes were sharp, not glassy, and there wasn't that blank quality to him. In fact, he was smirking.

"Isn't there a way to knock him out?" I murmured. It would be safer. For all of us.

"Only by force, and I'd rather not run the risk of accidentally giving him a traumatic brain injury." Then, louder, he added, "He'll be riding in the trunk. Tied up, gagged, helpless. Just the way I like him."

Clancy's head snapped in our direction. And if I didn't know him as well as I did, I could have sworn there was an edge of desperation to his voice. "Oh, there's no need for any of that . . ."

"You're not riding in the backseat," Cole said. "It's too risky. What if someone sees you, or you try to escape?"

Clancy scoffed. "And separate myself from the Project Snowfall research before I can get rid of it?"

Cole shot me a look, tongue caught between his teeth as he grinned. An unexpected bonus of showing it to the Greens—Clancy had no idea we'd taken the precaution of backing the research up, so to speak.

"Ah, now that does sound reasonable, doesn't it, Gem?"

I pulled him farther into the hallway, shutting the door behind us. "Maybe taking him with us *is* a bad idea. If he gets loose in the Ranch, he could ruin everything." I clenched my hands at my sides, trying to work through the revulsion, the memory of how stupid I had been to ever think I'd had Clancy under my control.

Some people came into the world and never once looked up to see the lives around them—they were so focused on what *they* wanted, what *they* needed. No one else mattered to them. They disconnected from sympathy and pity and guilt. Some people came into the world as monsters. I understood that now.

"Hey," Cole said quietly. "You think I don't want to strangle the life right out of him, too?"

"He has more faces than a pair of dice," I warned. "If something doesn't benefit him directly he won't play along. And if it *threatens* him—"

"He's no match for you, Gem."

"I wish that were the case." I shook my head.

"Let's focus on what he has to offer if we can get him in a place where he wants to work with us," Cole said. "The intel, the insight into how his father thinks, even his value as a potential trade."

"He's too unpredictable." Even if we turned him over to his father, there was still a good chance he could escape and cause even *more* havoc. Was it better that he came with us, if only so we could keep an eye on him?

"You keep forgetting that, in the end, we want the same thing he does," Cole said, clearly fighting the urge to roll his eyes. "We all want his father out of office."

"No," I said, glancing back in at the figure kneeling on the floor. "He wants his father ruined. There's a difference. The only question is if you're willing to risk being part of the fallout when he figures out how to do it."

I realized a second too late that re-securing Clancy's hands with a zip tie meant having to feed him myself. He glared and spat at me like a cat furious at having its claws clipped. My skin crawled. All in all, a thoroughly unpleasant experience for everyone.

Liam greeted my return to the other room with a sympathetic look and a bag of potato chips, patting the ground next to him. Half of the room looked dazed by the excessively early hour; the other half was pacing in anxious circles. The wind had picked up outside, screaming as it whipped around the edges of the warehouse and passed through the cracks in the roof. It made for an eerily appropriate soundtrack to the morning.

"Okay, I'll make this quick," Cole began. "We'll be splitting into teams and dividing ourselves between the three exit points. If the location you're assigned is compromised in any way—soldiers present, shady-looking folks hanging around, anything—head to the next-closest."

Just to the side of him, Sen wore a smug little smile as she surveyed the kids sitting on the floor. I almost smiled myself, a small thrill of control trickling through me. *Good riddance,* I thought.

"Once you have your assignment," Cole continued, "check it against the map for your car locations and the routes listed next to them. Team A is me, Ruby, Liam, Vida, Nico, our guest, and what's-his-face—the one in the prissy button-down."

Liam threw his hands up in exasperation.

Chubs only shrugged. "Better than Grannie. And, for the record, Chubs."

"Not Nico," I cut in. He couldn't be trusted to use his judgment around Clancy, and I couldn't be trusted not to make him pay if he slipped again.

I saw Nico disappear from the edge of my vision, fading to the back of the group. Liam's hand tightened around mine, but I refused to glance up and meet what I knew was a look of disappointment. He didn't understand.

"Fine," Cole said, "Nico, you'll go with Team D."

"Am I the guest?" I hadn't realized Senator Cruz was in the room until she spoke up.

"You're with Team C. Team A has our less-welcome guest."

He must have informed her of Clancy's presence, because her only response to that was a soft "Oh. I see."

He ran through the details of each route the teams would be taking upstate. All involved sticking to surface streets, which added on hours and wasted gas, but ensured a safer trip. There was a single moment of silence after he finished speaking, as if everyone needed a moment to absorb his words.

Cole pointed at me. "Go grab him."

"Once you have your group," he continued as I exited the room, "go, get the hell out of here. Good luck and take care of each other. We'll see you up north."

Clancy struggled to his feet as I entered the room, his hands bound, his head still tucked inside the pillowcase. "We're going *now*? What time is it?"

I pulled it off him for the moment. "Any sign of you messing with anyone—"

"—and I'm dead. God, you're as annoying as my old nanny. I *understand*," Clancy snapped. He turned around and nudged me with his bound hands. "This is going to be just as suspicious as the hood. If something happens, I might need to use my hands—"

"Nothing is going to happen," I said, hooking my hand around his arm and drawing him out into the hallway, then back into the room to avoid being trampled, as the different teams ran to the building's different exits.

"Ready?" Cole called to me from the window as I pulled Clancy into the room. Anabel Cruz was still standing there, huddled between the two agents that were responsible for her. At the sight of Clancy she froze. He smirked, taking her in from head to toe.

"Enough," I said. "Leave her alone or I'll push you out of the window."

"I'd like to request that honor," Liam said as he helped me up next. He glanced back toward Sen, and shot me a questioning look as the woman adjusted the straps of the backpack containing the cure research.

I put a reassuring hand on his arm, then turned back, gripping Clancy's shoulder to steady him as he swung his leg up over the frame. His shoe caught on something and he went tumbling out of my hands, landing headfirst on the fire escape in a disgruntled heap.

"I see I'll be afforded no dignity in this," he growled as he straightened up, awkwardly trying to adjust his shirt with his hands bound.

I leaned over the steps, tracking Cole's progress. He was already back on solid ground, a gun in his hands, surveying the nearby windows with a look of focused intensity I'd seen on Liam's face so many times. The wind was tearing at his hair, making his jacket billow out around him. It blew me forward a step.

"As far as Stewarts are concerned, he's probably the better choice. Handsome. The bad boy. Seems more your taste," Clancy reasoned, following my gaze.

Clearly he didn't understand my taste *at all.*

I didn't let myself look back to check on Vida, Chubs, and Liam until we were down on the street too, our backs pressed to the building.

"Anything?" I asked Cole.

He shook his head. "All clear."

We headed one block east to walk along the railroad tracks

lining the Los Angeles River. Our exit was approximately thirteen blocks north, but those would be thirteen dark, silent, and tense blocks. Already, I felt a shiver of anxiety run down my spine as I looked back, but it was too dark to see the group of kids trailing behind us. Cole had warned them to wait ten minutes before following us through the exit, just on the off chance that something went wrong and they'd need the buffer of distance to run.

Nice for them.

I kept my gaze ahead and my grip on Clancy's arm firm. His skin felt unbearably warm against my hand. The morning had the city in a chilly grip without the sun there to burn it away, but it was like none of it touched him. Like nothing could.

Cole's hand shot up as he halted us in place with a sharp intake of breath. Clancy, curious, leaned in over my shoulder to see what the issue was.

"Ah," he said, moving away. "Good luck with this one."

Our route took us under the 101 freeway, where it formed a bridge over the Los Angeles River and nearby rail tracks. From what I'd seen in the soldier's memories, the army had blocked off the tracks below with overturned train cargo cars and floodlights. On the freeway, there'd been two Humvees and more lights, pointing in toward us. And there they were—I counted them as we made our careful, silent approach. I didn't see the problem at all. Not until the first of three shadowy figures appeared on the ledge of the freeway's elevated road. Their arms were raised in a way that made me think they must have been peering through binoculars.

Cole dropped to his stomach on the tracks. I forced Clancy down with me. Chubs began to ask, "What's going on—?" but someone—Vida—muffled him.

Dammit, dammit, dammit, dammit. Fear rippled through me. How did I get this so wrong?

It was still pitch black outside, but we had already passed into the faint edge of the floodlights' glow. There was a low curse from Cole as he turned and motioned us back with his hands. Vida pulled out a handgun and shuffled back on her belly, dragging Chubs with her, a hand knotted in his shirt.

The wind kicked up the back of my jacket, exposing my bare skin to the chilling air. To our left, the tin-like sheets of metal lining the tracks were rattling as if they were on the verge of exploding. *Go slow,* I coached myself. *Don't panic. Go slow.* Sudden movements or loud noises would only draw the soldiers' attention—

There was a *crack*, like broken bone as a whole section of the wall's metal siding flew off, catching a burst of wind and flinging itself straight toward us. I ducked down, covering my free hand with my head, my brain already calculating how fast we'd have to get up and run once the sheet slammed into the tracks and started banging around.

But one pounding heartbeat . . . two . . . three . . . with the exception of the wind and my own heavy breathing, there was nothing but quiet. I lifted my head, catching Cole's shocked expression as it morphed into relief, and twisted around to see why.

Liam had a hand outstretched in the direction of the huge piece of siding. It was frozen in place where it had struck the ground on its first, dangerous bounce, and was still angled toward us. The rusted metal stood upright, shaking like a strained muscle, but otherwise still. His face was a stony mask of concentration. I'd seen him lift and throw things much heavier with his abilities, but the force of the wind, and our exposure to it, was warring with his control.

Chubs shifted, but Liam said, quietly, "I have it."

Cole snapped once to get my attention, pointing up at the freeway. The figures we had seen there, the soldiers, were moving again. The floodlights that were trained on us switched off, just as another military truck drove up alongside the two vehicles already posted there. It took me a moment to understand what was actually happening.

They're there to swap out the cars and lights. Not to patrol; not as lookouts.

One of the Humvees rumbled to life, made a wide turn across the empty freeway lanes, and sped west. I kept my eyes on the shrinking taillights before squinting up toward the floodlights again. No movement. Gone.

Cole had come to the same conclusion. He rose slowly onto his knees, then his feet, waving for us to do the same. Liam let out one last grunt, using his abilities to lift the metal siding up in an arc over us and throw it in the direction of the Los Angeles River's dry cement bed. He let his brother haul him to his feet, but pushed him away.

"For someone who sucks so bad at sports, those were some surprisingly decent reflexes."

"That must be *thank you* in a language I don't speak," Liam said, his jaw set as he turned to look ahead. "Can we get moving?"

Cole stared at him a moment longer, his face unreadable. "All right. Let's roll."

By the time we reached Glendale on foot, the sun was up and shining over us. The area, despite being outside of the de facto perimeter the military had set up, was still close enough to the damage to have prompted either an official or panic-induced evacuation. There wasn't a soul alive around us. Cole had gone ahead to scout the nearby streets just to be sure, but there was this feeling, an unnatural buzz along my skin, that prevented me from relaxing. I kept my head up, scanning every corner, the nearby roofs, even the horizon of Los Angeles's ruined skyline for its source. What started as a billowing thundercloud of unease was becoming sharper, taking on more distinct edges. I was afraid it wouldn't fully take shape until it was already raining down over us like knives.

The dusting of ash and soot out here had been washed into stagnant puddles by the rain a few nights before. I shook my head. It all just seemed . . . strange. The buildings weren't wearing any open wounds; were stained a faint gray, not the menacing black of the inner city. I stepped over the cement block marking a parking space, and squinted at the building—a locked-up grocery store.

"There—" Cole said, pointing at something past the small shopping center. A parking lot. With its tall streetlamps on and flickering.

"Thank God," Chubs said as we crossed from one parking lot into the next. He stared up at the lights like he'd never seen one before.

Liam was already moving toward the nearest dark blue sedan, pulling a bent, wire coat hanger from the black backpack slung over his shoulder. He jimmied the lock so quickly, Cole didn't even catch on until Liam bent over the driver's seat, pulling out wires from beneath the dashboard, trying to spark some life back into the engine by hot-wiring it.

"What?" Chubs called. "No minivan?"

"Whoa, whoa, whoa—" Cole said as the engine finally sputtered to life. He pulled Liam out and did something that killed the motor. "Christ, who the hell taught you that?"

"Who do you think?" Liam snapped, ripping his arm out of Cole's hand.

"Harry?" Cole let out a disbelieving laugh. "Don't they take away your halo if you teach an impressionable youth how to steal a car?"

Liam's look could have peeled the paint off the sedan. "Are you finished?"

"No, I'm just—" Cole was picking at a scab, I realized, and he didn't even know it. "Harry. Harry Boy-Scout-Troop-Leader Stewart taught you. Why?"

"Because he trusted me not to abuse it." Liam turned a bitter smile on him. "What, you didn't get a lesson?"

The look Cole shot back was even colder than Liam's words had been. The fingers on his right hand gave a small spasm before he could tuck his hand into the back pocket of his pants.

"God. Even Stewart family drama is boring," Clancy said sullenly. "I thought we were in a hurry?"

"We are." I turned to Liam. "Did that car have any gas in it?"

He nodded. "Enough to get us a hundred miles, I'd guess."

"Grand," Cole said, "except we're not taking that one. There's a tan SUV over there that has your name on it."

Liam turned, took one look at it, and shook his head. "It's a gas-guzzler. They're top-heavy and more likely to roll in an accident—"

His brother silenced him by holding up his hand and pressing his fingers together in such a condescending way, it pissed me off, too. "Are you planning on getting into an accident? Then shut the hell up and do what I tell you—"

"You don't get to make that call—"

"Yes I do! *I'm* in charge here, whether you like it or not. *I'm* the one that's been out in the field. *I'm* the one that's going to get us out of here. And *I'm* the one telling you to pick yourself a SUV in case we have to take it off the road."

Liam took a step forward. "If we have to go off-road, we're pretty much screwed anyway. I'd rather have a car that won't devour gas." He glanced my way, tilting his head in a silent *back me up.* I bit my lip, shaking my head. Not this fight. This one wasn't worth it. Cole was making quick strides back in our direction from a nearby red pickup truck, and nothing was going to turn him from it.

All those months ago, when it had just been the four of us in a minivan making our way along back roads, siphoning gas from other cars like vultures picking the last stringy pieces of meat off bones, we'd functioned on two simple principles: move fast, don't get seen. For better or worse, most of our decisions had been gut reactions, and I wasn't about to pretend we hadn't made some questionable choices, but it was the only way we knew how to live and survive—it was how all of us freak kids had to scrape by, whether it was to avoid camps or skip tracers. And looking at Cole now, at the irritation sweeping over his features, it was never more obvious to me that he knew almost nothing about what his brother's life had been like after Liam escaped the League's training program. He was one of us by technicality, but outside of witnessing the cruel treatment of the kids in Leda's psionic research program, he'd never been forced to adapt to our reality.

They'd already fought about the driving arrangements earlier that morning, saving us a little time now. I spared one last glance at the three figures piling into Cole's chosen SUV before tugging Clancy in the direction of the red truck Cole gestured to.

It felt strange to not have all of us piled into one car, but I understood Cole's reasoning immediately, even if Liam didn't. It was the same reason I'd basically had the sole pleasure of babysitting Clancy over the past two weeks, feeding him, and dealing with his wounded ego. If I drove, the other Orange had less of a chance of commandeering the car because I could block him out. If one of the others was driving, it would only be a matter of time before Clancy slid into their thoughts and took control. I could see it happening as clearly as if the kid had planted the scene in my mind.

I would have preferred Cole in the other car, too, but that had been non-negotiable. The fact that it was just as likely for Clancy to hijack his mind, and command him to use his gun or knife on me, hadn't seemed to occur to him.

The gas tank was half full and the engine already hot-wired and running. Cole had snapped Clancy's zip ties off and attached new ones, so his hands could both rest in his lap and be hooked through the seat belt, and his feet could be bound to one of the bars running under the seat. Cole pulled the pillowcase over the kid's head.

It was just a matter of taking a deep breath and shifting the truck out of park. I looked up one last time at the skeleton of a city caught in my rearview mirror and tightened my hands on the steering wheel.

We were finally leaving that terrible place, and what we'd buried there.

Twenty minutes of driving, however, made a few things crystal clear: the truck didn't have working air conditioning, its owner's body odor had been absorbed into the faux-leather seats, and, yes, my window was broken.

To my right, Clancy had bent over at the waist, and was either sleeping or trying to subtly rub the pillowcase against his legs to pull it off. Cole, just to his right, was scanning the passing streets. The early afternoon light stood out in sharp contrast to the dark smudges beneath his eyes. It was like now that he was still, not rushing around or barking out orders, his body had finally settled into its aches and exhaustion. He rolled his shoulders back against the press of the seat belt and grimaced.

Cole had shown me where we were headed on a map—a town called Lodi, a little ways south of Sacramento. If we'd been able to take the freeway, it would have been a straight shot up the coast, five hours max. Less than that, if flights and trains had still been operational, and Gray hadn't ordered ships to patrol the Pacific coast.

I looked back over my shoulder to the SUV behind us. Liam must have been waiting for it, because he lifted his hand in a reassuring wave. In the front passenger seat beside him, Chubs was going on and on about something, his hands waving to emphasize each word. The sight was familiar and comforting enough to almost chase away the strangeness of the city around us.

Burbank, California, had been, by all definitions, a city brimming with life and commotion. Its importance had only grown in recent years; so many media companies already had studios or headquarters there, and many of the others in nearby cities had moved as well, either through mergers or deals to share equipment. Seeing the city streets so silent and empty, I wondered if Gray had already swept in to shut the place down.

Where the hell is everyone? It was like driving through the worst of the economically ravaged towns back east. I half expected to see an old newspaper dramatically catch the breeze and fly across the street like a tumbleweed. I felt my pulse kick up; the same shadow I'd felt behind us in Los Angeles was back and growling in my head like thunder.

"I don't like this," Cole said, as if sensing my thoughts. "Make your next right—"

If I hadn't looked back into the rearview mirror to signal to Liam, I wouldn't have seen it at all. The SUV was there one moment, and gone the next—the sound the military Humvee made as it crashed into the Ford Explorer felt like someone took a bat to the back of my skull. I jerked the wheel as the other car rolled once, glass and rubber exploding in every direction as it righted itself again, rocking hard against the sidewalk.

I slammed my foot onto the brake pedal, sending the truck into a skid. Clancy choked as his seat belt snapped tight over his chest. He tried to brace himself with his bound hands against the dashboard.

"What?" he demanded. "What the hell was that?"

But it was Cole I should have been worried about.

I was still fighting with my seat belt when his face, rigid with shock, transformed. The sound that escaped his throat was too ragged, too strangled to be a scream. It didn't sound human at all.

He threw his door open, but didn't run toward the military vehicle or the two soldiers who were approaching the tan SUV with their weapons drawn. Cole took one step forward as I jumped down from the truck, and, with no other warning than his right hand tightening into a fist at his side, the Humvee burst into a ball of fire.

The wave of pressure that came off the small explosion sent me stumbling back against the truck. It blew out the windows of nearby buildings and the back windshield of our pickup. The two soldiers were thrown onto the street, tackled from behind by the force of it. Cole moved toward them, unnervingly calm. His pistol was drawn out of the holster at his side, aimed with his usual precision. One shot, delivered to the face of the young soldier closest to the SUV. The other found himself hauled up, his helmet ripped away, and Cole's fist slammed again and again into his face.

I couldn't watch, wouldn't—my heart was banging against my ribcage as I ran for the SUV. Shards of tinted glass from the windows crunched underfoot. The driver's-side doors had taken the brunt of the impact, but there was movement—Liam's wide eyes met mine through what was left of the windshield.

"Are you okay?" I called, wincing at the sound of one last gunshot piercing the air.

Liam was sitting straight up, his hands clenched in a death-like grip on the steering wheel. His face was drained of all color, save for the red mark stamped across the left side of his face, and the rapidly purpling bridge of his swelling nose. The deflated airbags hung limp in his lap.

"Oh my God," I gasped. "You guys—"

Chubs had already crawled into the back with Vida, and was squinting as he examined a gash across her temple. His dark skin had taken on an ashy quality.

The burning vehicle was eating up the fresh air around us,

sending wave after wave of shimmering heat against my back. The roar of it consuming the metal and glass forced me to shout around the smoke I was already half-choking on.

"Okay?" I called back to them. Vida gave me a thumbs-up, swallowing hard, as if she didn't trust herself to speak just yet. "Liam?"

My hands shook like crazy as I tried to work the handle on the front door, the enormous metal indentation popping and protesting. There was so much adrenaline running through me, it was amazing I didn't rip the whole thing off its hinges. "Liam? Liam, can you hear me?"

He turned toward me slowly, coming out of his stupor. "I told him it would roll."

I almost sobbed in relief as I reached through the window and kissed him. "You did."

"I *told* him."

"You did, I know you did," I said, low and soothing as I reached in to unbuckle his seat belt. "Are you hurt? Anything feel broken?"

"Shoulder. Hurts." He squeezed his eyes shut, bracing himself against the pain. "Chubs? Everyone . . ."

"We're okay," Chubs called, his voice surprisingly steady despite the congested tone it had taken on. When he turned toward us, I saw blood running down from his nostrils over his lips. "I think his shoulder is dislocated. Ruby, do you see my glasses? I lost them when the airbags inflated."

"What happened?" Vida asked, pointing at the fire. "How did—"

"Bullet to the gas tank—lucky shot," came Cole's voice behind me. They were either too muddled or too terrified to really think the improbability of it through.

Cole shouldered me out of the way to get to the door's handle himself. After a moment of hesitation, I ducked around to the passenger side, forced the stubborn door open, and knelt down. I felt along the carpet until my fingers brushed his glasses. Or what was left of them.

"Did you find them?" he asked. "What's wrong?"

I held the mangled frames and cracked-but-whole lenses up for Vida to see. In a rare moment of sympathy, she gave him a pat on the shoulder and said, "Yeah, she's got them, Gran."

The driver's-side door finally came open with a scream of metal against metal. Liam rolled, trying to get his left foot out from where it was pinned under the mangled dashboard. All the while, he clutched his left arm against his side, trying to keep it from being jostled.

"Dammit, you stupid kid," Cole said, emotions simmering just beneath the surface. His right hand twitched and jerked as he reached inside to help his brother. "Damn you—how hard is it to not get yourself killed on my watch?"

"Trying," Liam said, between gritted teeth. "Christ, that hurts."

"Give me your arm," Cole said, "this is going to suck, but—"

"Are you doing it?" Chubs was asking, "make sure you're in the proper position—"

I don't know what was worse: the sound of Liam's shoulder socket realigning, or his howl of pain that followed.

"We need to *move*," Vida said, kicking the SUV's back door open. "This piece of shit is totaled—we'll have to get into the bed of the truck, but standing around here crying over each other is going to get us shot, and fast."

"Glasses?" Chubs called, holding out his hand in what he must have thought was my direction. Vida took that hand and looped it through her arm, accepting the twisted wire frames from me. I stopped her, just for a second, to make sure that she really was okay. Banged-up, bruised, but not bleeding. What a goddamn miracle this was—

Clancy. I spun back around to face the truck, heart paralyzed for the instant it took to spot his dark outline through the truck's back window. *Shit.* This is how we'd lose him. Chaos. Carelessness. I'd panicked—my mind had just blanked out with terror and I'd run. I hadn't even thought to take the keys out of the ignition. If Cole hadn't bound his legs, he'd be in the wind by now.

Be better than this, I thought, my nails digging into the palms of my hands. *You have to be better than this.* The adrenaline was slow to leave my system; I couldn't keep from shaking, not entirely.

"You know, Grannie," Vida's voice drew my attention back toward them, "you have actually not sucked in this crisis."

"I can't see your face so I can't tell how sincere that was. . . ." Chubs said.

I slid the backpack fully onto my back, jogging around to where Cole was helping a limping Liam around the bodies of the downed soldiers, toward the truck. I couldn't bring myself to look at them or assess what Cole had done in his moment of rage. Liam braced his bad arm against his chest. I slid my hand around the small of his back to help steady him—but, really, to reassure myself he was fine. Alive.

Liam tilted his head toward me and said, "Kiss me again."

I did, soft and quick, right at the corner of his lips where there was a small white scar. Seeing my expression he added, "Saw my life flash before my eyes. Not enough kissing."

Cole snorted, but his whole body was still tense with anger he couldn't release. "Wow, kid. Unusually smooth for you."

We lifted Liam onto the flatbed, laying him out next to Chubs, who was clutching the broken remains of his glasses over his heart.

"Oh, damn," Liam said, seeing them. "I'm sorry, buddy."

"Prescription," he said in a low, mournful voice. "They were prescription lenses."

Cole yanked the sheet of electric-blue tarp out from under his brother and spread it over them.

"What are you doing?" Vida demanded, already trying to sit up.

"Stay down and stay covered. We're going to get as far as we can away from here and switch cars. Chances are they radioed this one in."

"I would like to register the fact that this fucking sucks," she said.

"Noted," he said, shutting the gate.

I climbed back up behind the wheel again, soaking in the vibrations from the running engine. Clancy had finally gotten his hood up and off him, and even though I didn't look over, I saw him watching me out of the corner of my eye. For the first time in weeks, the sullen irritation that had coated his every mood was gone, and he was . . . smiling. His gaze shifted away, over to Cole, who slammed his door shut hard enough to rock the whole vehicle. In his lap was what looked like a leather pouch, and a pistol that he must have taken off one of the soldiers. They both slid around as his hand continued to jerk, spasm, until he finally tucked it beneath his leg. The sight made my brain think *Mason. Red. Fire.* It plucked at loose threads at the back of my mind until I saw the pattern of how they were woven together.

The Reds at Thurmond had moved strangely; they lurched when others walked, jabbed when others waved. But I'd just assumed the awkward jerks were because of the restraints the PSFs kept them in.

But Mason . . . the kids in Nashville, they'd called him Twitch. Twitch, because of the way his whole body spasmed with its strange rhythm. I thought . . . I don't know that I'd even really thought about why; I'd just assumed it had something to do with the way he was trained, the way the government had broken his mind trying to mold him into the perfect soldier.

All of them, all of the Reds—they all must have had some version of this physical tic. And if I was able to recognize it after only being around a few of them, then how could someone who had been there—to make suggestions for and contribute to and witness the training—miss the signs?

"Clancy . . ." I started to say.

"This is too good," he said with a bark of laughter.

Cole stiffened, his face turning to stone. The fury burning his pale eyes softened, going out of focus. I knew that look.

I threw my mind at Clancy's, but it was like driving into a wall. I was thrown back, with a sting that zipped across my skull and turned into a pounding ache. We didn't have time for me to break the connection that way, before something would happen—before he'd turn Cole into his little action figure. I drew my elbow up and hit him right where Instructor Johnson had taught me—in the temple. Clancy's eyes rolled back and he slumped forward, knocking his forehead against the dashboard.

The wheels spun as I floored the gas pedal, trying to outrun the signal fire Cole had created. The smoke would be hard to miss for any helicopters or patrols. I didn't need to think about the consequences of Clancy knowing. I just needed to get us the hell out of here.

My temples were still pounding and my heart was still sputtering at an unnatural speed when I looked over and saw Cole rub his forehead. "What the fuck . . ." The words grew louder each time he repeated them, until he was roaring them. *"What the fuck?"*

I smelled smoke—saw how badly he shook. "Cole, listen to me—you have to calm down, okay? Calm down, it's okay—"

He fumbled with the leather case in his lap, ripping out a vial of clear liquid and a syringe. I tried to look between him and the road as he filled it, but missed my opportunity to stop him before he slammed the needle down into the back of Clancy's neck.

"Cole!"

"That'll keep the little shit under until the urge to beat his ass into next Tuesday passes," he growled. *"Shit.* That was nothing like the way you did it at HQ—*shit!"* He tossed the syringe and bottle back into the pouch and let them slide down the dashboard.

His hand was steady now, but his anxiety charged the air; it made me feel like I was sitting next to someone who was debating whether or not to light a fuse.

He turned back toward the window, watching the buildings around us blur—but I could see his face in the reflection there, and it said everything he couldn't. He hadn't been in control when the Humvee caught fire—not even remotely.

"What did he show you?"

"Myself."

"What do you mean?"

Cole leaned his forehead against the glass and shut his eyes. "It was a Red camp. Somewhere. What they did to the poor kids to train them. I saw how everyone must see us, if that makes any sense . . . it was just . . . it felt like I was being smothered with smoke. There was nothing in their expressions, but, for a second, I was scared shitless. It was like I was really there. They had me and I was next."

"I'm sorry," I said, unable to keep the tightness out of my voice. "I realized what was happening a second too late. I should have . . ."

"It's my fault he figured it out," Cole said sharply. "Don't take that blame, Gem, it's not yours to shoulder. You told me he was involved with Project Jamboree. I should have checked myself instead of acting like a monster, it's just—*dammit!*" He slammed his fist against the door. "I wasn't thinking at all. I just—it won. For a minute, it won."

His words wrapped around my heart like a fist. I knew that feeling. It didn't matter how much power you possessed, how useful your abilities were. They had a will of their own. If you weren't constantly on top of them, they found ways to crawl out from under you.

"Those kids, those Greens and Blues especially, it all comes to them so easily, doesn't it?" Cole said quietly. "Easier to control, easier to hide. It doesn't fuck up their lives the way it does for us. We have to be focused, otherwise we slip. And we can't slip."

Liam—and Chubs, and Vida, and all of them—hadn't been able to understand how much work went into controlling what I could do, so it didn't control me. Loosening my grip on the leash even for a second could mean hurting someone. Hurting myself.

"It feels like I'm always at the edge of it, and I can't . . . I can't step in, not without feeling so damn scared I'm going to ruin everything. I want to stop ruining every good thing that comes my way. I couldn't control it for a really long time—"

"And you think I can? Jesus. Half the time I feel it boiling me alive under my skin. It simmers and simmers and simmers until I finally release the pressure. It was like that even when I was a kid." Cole let out a faint, humorless laugh. "It wasn't . . . it wasn't like a voice or anything, not one that whispered to me. It was just this urge, I guess. It was like I was always standing too close to a fire and needed to just stick my hand in once, to see how hot it really was. I couldn't sleep at night. I thought for sure it was because my dad was actually the devil. Really, truly, the Prince of Darkness himself."

"Harry?" I asked, confused.

"No, bio dad. Harry's—"

"Right, forgot," I said.

"Lee talks about him a lot, then?" He didn't wait for me to confirm before continuing. "Yeah, our real dad . . . that man . . . dumb as a bag of hammers, mean as a snake. Not a good combination. I still fantasize about looking him up, breaking into the old house, and setting his whole world on fire."

"Liam only brought him up once," I said, trying not to pry no matter how much I wanted to. This was the one part of his life Liam wasn't willing to share, and as horrible as it was, it only made me want to pick at the scab more. "When he lost his temper."

"Good, hopefully that means he doesn't remember the half of it. The guy was—he was a monster. He was the devil himself when he got his temper up. Guess one of us was bound to be a chip off the old block. I used to wonder, you know, if the abilities we have are somehow dependent on something we already have inside us. I thought, this fire—this is his anger. This is my dad's rage."

I knew it wouldn't do anything, or at least reassurance had never done much when it was delivered to me, but I had to say it. I had to tell him. "You're *not* a monster."

"Don't monsters breathe fire? Don't they burn down kingdoms and countries?" Cole sent me a wry smile. "You call yourself that, too, don't you? No matter how many times others tell you it's not true, you've seen the proof. You can't trust yourself."

I settled back against my seat, wondering, for the very first time, if he wasn't just as desperate as the rest of us for a cure.

"This isn't about the camps for you . . . is it?" I asked. "It's about the cure."

His throat bobbed as he swallowed. "Got it on the first try. Feel free to think I'm an asshole."

"Why? Because you don't want to suffer like this?" I asked sharply. "Because you want to be normal?"

"What's 'normal'?" Cole asked. "Pretty sure none of us remember what that feels like."

"Fine," I pressed, "then because you want a life where you're free from all of this bullshit. I want the cure more than I want my next breath. I never used to. I never let myself think of the future, and now it's like a compulsion. I want that freedom so badly, and it seems like the more I strain to try and reach it, the further away it gets."

Cole rubbed his hand over his face, nodding. "I underestimate it sometimes . . . you forget, because you function, and each time you get kicked down you manage to pick yourself up. But now, it's starting to get harder, right?"

"Yes." It was the first time I'd admitted it. The word was as hollow as I felt.

"It's not that I don't think I won't be able to get up. It's that I'm afraid one day I'll just . . . explode. Combust. Take out everyone I care about because I can't stop myself from feeling so damn angry all the time." He pulled up his hand, holding it in front of his face, waiting for it to spasm again. When it didn't happen, his gaze shifted down to Clancy. "They keep them locked in these white rooms. Lights are on the whole time and there are voices. Voices that don't stop, that are constantly telling them shit like, *you're wrong, admit you're wrong so we can fix you*. They *hurt* the kids—they really hurt them, over and over. It was . . . I could barely stand to see it, and I wasn't the one getting beaten. Was that . . . real? Can he make stuff up?"

My hands tightened around the wheel. "He can plant any image he wants in your mind, but I think the truth is bad enough that he doesn't have to embellish it."

"I don't know what pisses me off more—what they did to the kids, or that they figured out how to contain the fire in them. Shit, Gem. How the hell . . ." He shook his head as if to clear it. "If he tells any of the others, if he tells *Liam*, what am I supposed to do? None of the kids will come within a hundred feet of me."

"He's not going to," I promised. "How much more of that stuff do you have?"

He unzipped the pouch. "Three more vials."

"Then he'll stay out until we get to the Ranch and we get him secured," I said. "We'll keep him separated at all times, and I'll be the one he interacts with."

"Killing him would be simpler." There was nothing heated or furious about his words, and maybe that was why they were so disarming. Just cold, ruthless pragmatism. It was unsettling how fast the switch flipped.

"Can't," I reminded him, recycling one of his own arguments, "he's the only one who knows where his mother is. You can't do anything to him, not until we find out where she is. I need the cure. Whatever it is, I need it. I hate him more than anything in the world, but I hate living this way more. I hate the idea of there not being an end to this."

Cole turned back toward the window, watching the buildings around us blur around us. "Then you and me, Gem, we'll have to figure out a way to stay one step ahead of our monsters."

I nodded; my throat was tight with the need to cry, with the surprise of finally having someone who understood—who struggled not just with everything and everyone around them, but with themselves.

"Are you sure this isn't a nightmare?" he asked quietly. "And that we won't just wake up?"

I stared ahead at the road, the way the dust blowing in from the desert covered it with a faint golden sheen even as gray clouds began to gather over us.

"Yes," I said after some time.

Because dreamers always wake up and leave their monsters behind.

FOUR

THE RAIN STARTED IN WITH A CLAP OF THUNDER JUST outside of Mojave, a small town situated at the base of the nearby mountains' craggy slopes. In the distance, over their jagged crowns, I could see the first hints of green.

"That Days Inn," Cole said, pointing to the small, two-story complex hugging the corner. "Pull in there. We need to get them another car, and we need to switch ours out."

The town had been drained of its life some time ago, that much was clear by the complete and total lack of upkeep of its businesses and homes. It was a sight I'd grown used to over the past year, to the point that I didn't feel the creeping sense of dread that came with seeing empty playgrounds, or fresh dirt in graveyards, or homes that had been chained and boarded up. So not even California, which had run independently from the rest of the nation under the Federal Coalition, had been immune to the new normal of economic strife that the rest of the country had been clawing through.

"People could be staying here," I said. "They would stake it as their territory—"

"Look at the cars here," Cole said, "the amount of dirt on them. They've been sitting here awhile. I haven't seen any movement through the hotel's windows or around the perimeter, have you? *Park.* Pull up right there, next to that gray Toyota."

I turned off the engine as he double-checked that Clancy was still out and still secured with zip ties. He went to inspect the other cars to find a working one with gas, and I jumped down from the driver's seat and all but ran around to the back to untie the tarp. The three of them sat up in unison, blinking against the dull light.

Cool rain streaked down my face and neck as I helped the others down from the back. The air was thick with that strange, wonderful, indescribable smell that was unique to storms in the desert.

"Hey," I said, my hands closing around Liam's arms to steady him as he slid down off the bed. "Are you all right?"

Liam nodded and squeezed my shoulder as he passed by. "Chubs—wait—dammit, buddy—" Without his glasses, the kid couldn't see a thing. Chubs caught his toe on a pothole in the pavement and went down before Liam could reach him. After he used his good arm to get his friend back on his feet, he led Chubs toward the edge of the motel's parking lot and they disappeared around the corner. By the lack of explanation and how quickly they were moving, I took a guess about what kind of business they were conducting.

"Was it as special up front as it was in the back?" Vida asked, hopping down next to me. Her joints popped as she stretched her arms and back.

"No one's killed each other," I said. "Was it terrible back there?"

"Nah," Vida said with a shrug. "A little uncomfortable and cold at some points. You took a sharp turn somewhere and Grannie copped a feel by mistake. He looks like he wants to die of shame each time I bring it up. Basically, I'm going to milk that shit for all it's worth."

"Do you have to?" I asked pointedly.

"Whatever. He was more pissed off by us playing a game of who could think up the worst nickname for him."

"Let me guess, you won?"

"It was Boy Scout, actually. I mean, come on. Even I couldn't top Chubby Chubby Choo Choo. I almost pissed my pants laughing."

I made a mental note to give Chubs a good, long hug before we set off again.

Glancing over to make sure the boys were making their way back toward us, a pop of color caught my eye. Shielding my eyes against the rain, I took a step toward the two small cement homes that were oddly positioned a short distance from the corner of the street. A crude array of graffiti marred the cracked cement wall that separated the side of the house from the nearby parking spaces.

"What?" Vida asked. "What's with that face?"

Most of the art wasn't really art at all, and a good portion hadn't been spray-painted. I wiped the rain from my face, tucking my wet hair out of the way. There were names scrawled there in permanent marker—a Henry, a Jayden, a Piper, and a Lizzy all written in great looping letters under a large, black, outlined circle with what looked like a crescent moon inside of it. Vida trailed me as I walked over to it to get a better look.

My eyes skimmed over the wall, vaguely aware of the steps

coming up behind us. One of the tags, this one done in blue spray paint, was fresh enough that the letters there—what looked like a K, L, Z, and H—were running, drooping down to the ground. I pressed my fingers against it, unsurprised that they came away sticky and stained.

"Oh. Wow." Liam let out a startled laugh, stepping up next to me to get a better look.

"Oh, wow, *what*?" Chubs asked.

"It's road code. Remember? At East River?"

I glanced at Chubs as his brow furrowed, clearly as confused as I felt. Liam had dived into camp life headfirst, befriending anyone and everyone, but I had kept mostly to Clancy, and Chubs had kept mostly to himself.

"Well," Liam said, undaunted, "it was the system they worked out for safe travel. We used it to mark how to get back after going out on supply runs, and it was taught to all of the kids who left and went out on their own."

He flattened his palm against the crescent moon. "I remember this one. This means that this is a safe place. To sleep. To rest. That kind of thing."

"And the names are what, kids who have passed through?" Vida asked.

"Yeah. They were supposed to do that in case they had to split up, or they were trying to leave a trail for another group to follow." The rain was coming down harder, forcing him to stop and wipe it off his face. "There are different ones for places to pick up food, where you can find supplies, a house of friendly people who might be willing to help you, and so on and so forth."

"Clancy thought of this?" I asked.

"Amazing, right?" Liam said. "I didn't know he was capable of thinking of anyone other than himself for two seconds without killing himself in disgust."

"Huh." Chubs held up one of his broken lenses and peered through it like a magnifying lens, ignoring Vida's snicker. "Kids actually made it all the way out here from Virginia?"

We did, I almost said. But our circumstances had been . . . different, to say the least.

"I bet . . ." He took my arm, leading me away from the others, walking to the corner where the house's fence met the fence running along the end of the parking lot. Down the street on the opposite corner was some kind of church. Painted there in bold, black strokes were two inverted Vs, one on top of the other like arrows, surrounded by a circle. "That's a directional marker to show them which road to take."

"Wow," I said, "I've been seeing those since we left Los Angeles. I had no idea—I just assumed it had something to do with road construction."

"What's funny is that I remember them from before—when we were driving through—" He hesitated. "Through Harrisonburg?"

I looked up at him, confused. But it hit me soon enough, and the question in his tone registered like the sharp ache of a repeat injury.

"We did drive through there . . . together, I mean? I'm not—I'm not remembering the wrong thing, am I?"

What killed me, almost more than the frustrated expression on his face, was that there was no accusation in his voice. I knew that what I had done to his memory had mostly been—undone,

I guess. But he still had moments of overlap between what had really happened, and the story I had planted in his mind. I'd overheard him asking Chubs for clarification a few times, but this was the first time I'd ever been so directly confronted with it. My whole chest ached. If I'd had the option of melting into a puddle and letting myself be carried down into the storm drain, I would have taken it.

"No," I managed to get out. "You've got it right. We drove through on the way to that Wal-Mart."

I started to turn back to the motel, but he caught my wrist. I braced myself for whatever he was about to say.

Which, apparently, was nothing. He looked down, his thumb stroking the soft skin on the inside of my wrist.

Finally, Liam said, "I remember the other motel—it looked almost exactly like this one, but the doors weren't red." He rubbed the back of his neck, a rueful grin on his face. "I acted like an idiot trying to give you a pair of socks."

In spite of myself, I smiled. "Yeah. What about serenading me with The Doors? *Come on baby, light my fire. . . .*"

"I probably would have put on a whole song-and-dance routine if you hadn't started laughing," he said. "That's how badly I wanted you to smile."

My heart hurt in a completely different way now. I rolled up onto my toes, pressing a soft kiss onto his cheek. There was a sharp whistle from the parking lot. Cole waved us back over from where he stood next to a compact white sedan. Liam rolled his eyes at the sight of it, but started toward the driver's side. Cole shook his head and pointed to Vida.

"She's driving." He cut Liam's protest off before he could get a word in. "No attitude. Your shoulder needs to rest. Trade off later."

"You're *such* an asshole! I'm *fine*—"

"Is this what they call brotherly love?" Chubs wondered aloud.

"Hey, this works for me," Vida said, ignoring him. "Maybe now we'll break forty miles an hour. Laters—try not to drive us directly into another military patrol, 'kay?"

"Be careful," I called after her, pointlessly.

"Ready, Gem?" Cole asked. Instead of heading back to the red truck, he turned me in the direction of a new, blue one. "I got us new wheels. Someone probably reported the red one. The Little Prince is already inside and secure."

I noticed he was already walking toward the passenger side. "Don't you want to drive?" I asked.

"Why? Do you need a break, or are you okay to go a few more hours? I could use a second to close my eyes. We can switch when it gets dark."

It startled me a little bit to see how quickly Cole crashed once we were driving again. One minute he was leaning his head against the window, telling me to take the next right and turn up my windshield wipers, and the next he was dead to the world.

I could do this. The truck was new enough to have an electronic compass on its display, and I really just needed to keep heading north until I started seeing signs for Lodi or Stockton.

But the only signs I was seeing now were the ones spray-painted onto the sides of buildings. Along walls. On marquees and storefronts in shopping centers. Once my eyes were open to them, I saw them everywhere. They dragged my eyes over to them again and again, screaming for my attention.

When I saw the next set in the distance, I felt a reckless thought sneak up on me. I hesitated, looking over at Cole, trying to weigh how angry he'd be. We were flying toward the road symbols, and if I didn't turn now, I might lose the trail completely—

Does it matter? You don't even know these kids. . . .

It did. Because I knew what it was like trying to survive on the road, and if they needed help, I wanted us to be the ones who gave it to them.

I made that first right turn when the arrows suddenly shifted. They took me away from the two highways that would have gotten me over and through the mountains to Oak Creek Road, which in another life might have been the scenic route to take through these parts. Another right turn, onto Tehachapi Willow Springs Road, which skirted the city of Tehachapi. All of the signs announcing the approaching city were marked with a large X with a small circle around the letter's center. The shape reminded me enough of a skull and crossbones that I didn't want to risk ignoring it.

It was up near an aquatics park that my mind started to go a bit soft. I caught my eyes closing and jerked back awake more than once. *Stop it,* I thought, *wake up wake up wake up.* Cole needed to finally be able to recharge after the two hellish weeks we'd had on the run in Los Angeles. I could handle this. I could at least stay awake until we had to stop again for gas.

The light dimmed with every minute that passed, the winter sun setting even earlier behind the silver storm clouds. In the gray-blue light, the cement sign for the recreation area seemed to glow, and the tags there seemed especially dark in comparison. The initials I saw gave my brain something to play with, at least, while I watched the road.

PGJR . . . Paul, George, John, and Ringo . . . parrot, giraffe, jaguar, rabbit . . . pistol, Glock, Jericho, rifle . . .

HBFB . . . Hazel, Bigwig, Fiver, Blackberry . . . hash browns, bacon, flapjacks, bran flakes . . . Harrisonburg, Bedford, Fairfax, Bristol . . .

Below that line of initials was another faint one. I slowed the truck, squinting through the sheet of rain at it. The downpour had nearly carried the letters away, but I could still see the faintest hint of KLZH.

Kia . . . Lexus . . . Z-something . . . Honda . . . Okay, that one didn't exactly work. *Kansas, Led Zeppelin, ZZ Top, The Hollies.* Damn, Z was hard—zebras, zoo, zero, zilch, and Zu. And that was it. That was all my brain had.

I yawned through my smile. *K-something, Liam, Zu, Hina.* Oh—Kylie, Kylie from East River, that worked. *Kylie, Liam, Zu, Hina.* Or even *Kylie, Lucy, Zu, and Hina—*

The air whooshed through the vents, louder now that my mind was completely still and silent. It filled my ears until my heart started banging against my ribcage, hard enough for the sound to reach my ears.

Kylie, Lucy, Zu, and Hina. My mind was singing out the names over and over again until I felt almost delirious. *Stop it.* I tried to move on, tried *kangaroo, lion, zebra, hyena,* but I couldn't shake the fizzing sensation in my blood.

If they were kids leaving that tag, then we couldn't have been far behind them. And if they knew how to follow the code, then they were . . . they had to be from East River, right? I'd only seen one group of kids actually leave East River, and that had been Zu's group.

Stop it, I thought, sucking down a long gulp of the air coming through the vents. I reached over to turn the heat up slightly, trying to drive out the chill. There were other kids, plenty of other kids, with those same first letters. And regardless of who the other girl had been, if it was Zu's group, then there should have been a T there for Talon, the teen boy who'd gone with them. I tried to call up each of their faces, but Kylie, Lucy, Talon, and Hina were blank. Weird how I could remember their hair, the way they'd worn their black bandanas, the sound of their voices, but not what any of them really looked like. My mind had blocked out so much of our time at East River as a defense against the pain, it all might as well have happened to a different person.

But Zu—I remembered everything about Zu, from the way her hair spiked up first thing in the morning to each freckle across her nose.

Out of the corner of my eye, I saw yet another code tag—two of them, on a sign with directions to the nearby freeway that was counting down the miles to the next city. One was the crescent moon in a circle, the other was a set of arrows, pointing right— east—not straight ahead like the others.

I switched the truck's headlights on, letting them flood the clusters of trees on either side of the road. I started to pull the truck over onto the shoulder, wishing I had some other way to talk to Liam and Chubs, but I stopped myself.

These past few days had been hard enough on Liam already. Giving him this thrill only to have it ripped away seemed especially cruel. Chubs could bear the disappointment, but Liam . . . I didn't want to see his face fall when it all turned out to be nothing. I'd already let him down so many times, in so many ways. I couldn't add this to the list.

But there was that small voice rising above the other thoughts, whispering, *what if it is her, though?*

Kylie, Lucy, Zu, and Hina. KLZH.

This was dangerous—this was letting myself think that sometimes life had the near-magical quality of working out. It could unfold in a way that's so much better and easier than what you could have imagined.

That paint—it'd been fresh enough to run under the insistent stroke of rain, hadn't it? They couldn't have been that far ahead. *Don't do this to yourself,* I thought. We were farther north than where Liam thought her uncle's home was, and the initials were still missing Talon's T. Maybe it was exhaustion, or desperation, or some kind of need to prove that life could sometimes be kind. Whatever it was, I couldn't ignore it.

What was the risk in following this trail through, just to see what was waiting for us at the end? What if this was the one chance we'd ever have of finding her?

Jude would have done it. With him, it wouldn't have even been a debate.

I still felt crazy taking the next right, and clearly the others felt the same way. Vida tapped the horn, a quiet question. It was a dark access road, not even paved. The truck settled into the mud, rolling through the fresh tracks left by another set of tires. The overgrown trees lining the road were gnarled and twisted into each other; I kept the truck moving fast enough to tear through them, snapping branches and ripping away leaves.

It was that noise, not the earlier, inquiring honk from the other car, that finally shook Cole out of his two-hour nap. I saw him tense, running his hands over his face once, twice, trying to clear up the disorientation brought on by such a deep sleep.

"You should have woken me up!" He squinted at the glowing

dashboard console. "Wait . . . where the hell are we? Why are we going east, not north?"

"I have a hunch," I said.

"Yeah, and I have a pain in my ass—and surprise, it's you," he said, glaring at me over Clancy's prone form. "What's this about?'

"I think—" The trees suddenly pulled back, and I saw that the road we'd come in on hadn't really been a road at all, but a long driveway up to what once must have been a gorgeous mountain home. The thing was massive—two stories, a double-wide garage. The face of the house was stone and wood, as if despite its hulking presence it was still meant to blend in.

"Still waiting on that answer," Cole said as I threw the car into park.

"I think there may be some kids hiding here," I said. "I just want to have a quick look around—I swear, I *swear* I'll be fast."

Cole set his jaw, and I wondered what kind of expression I had that ultimately made him nod and say, "Fine, but take Vida with you. You have two minutes."

The others had opened their doors, but only Liam had stepped out into the rain. "What's going on?" he called.

"I just need Vida for a second," I said. "No, just her. *Her.* It's a quick . . . thing."

Chubs groaned. "What kind of thing? A Ruby-walks-into-mortal-danger thing?"

I shut the door on any further questions, wincing as I saw the hopeful look Vida shot me as she walked over.

"Is this about . . . is it Cate?"

Her whole face was glowing with hope, almond eyes wide, full lips parted as if she was uncertain if she should smile. God—if

Cate hadn't made it, if she wasn't there waiting for us, I didn't think I'd be able to put Vida back together.

"I think there might be kids hiding out here."

That perked her right up. I saw her hand slide back into the pocket of her sweatshirt, reaching for the gun hidden there.

"All right, cool," she said. "How do you want to play this?"

The front door and the first-story windows were all boarded over—the back and side entrances were, too. Vida's initial excitement quickly faded as we trampled through the mud and tall grass in the dark, slipping and sliding our way around the house a second time. There were no ladders that I could see to help someone up to the second floor. No lights on, no sounds coming from inside the house. The odd, shadowy shape on the garage door took form the closer we got, stopped me dead in my tracks. It was a crude crescent moon, cut out of some kind of metal. Someone had hammered it up with a single nail.

Safe place. I took a deep breath and reached for the cold metal of the garage door handle. Vida hung back but brought her gun up, aiming—

At nothing at all.

No cars, no bags, no kids huddled on blankets. Aside from rows of gardening tools and trash cans, there was only trash. The bright wrappers were scattered in heaps around the dark space.

Vida dragged her boots through the trash, scattering it. Now that my eyes were adjusting to the light, I could see other signs that there'd been at least one person here recently. A small pile of blankets and an abandoned duffel bag.

"Come on," she said. "If anyone was here, they must have peaced out days ago."

"There were tracks in the mud on the drive in," I said, wondering if my words sounded more solid than my thoughts did. I started toward the door that led into the house, only to be stopped short by the sight of the padlock hanging from it.

Cole honked the horn, and it was the slap in the face I needed.

You are acting crazy, I thought. *Pull yourself together. There are more important things—*

No. No there weren't. Because the truth of it was, I would have walked here. I would have walked here all the way from Los Angeles, alone in the dark in the pouring rain, if it had meant finding Zu again. I wanted it that badly—I needed to know she was safe and that she was okay, and that I hadn't failed her the way I'd failed all of the others.

Even the part of me that had expected this felt sad and small and foolish as I followed Vida out. I was glad for the rain now; anything to hide the fact that one wrong word, one bad stray thought, would push me to tears.

Vida put her hands on her hips, surveying the dark line of trees that formed a high wall around the house. "This would be a good place to crash for a couple days. I saw the signs too, you know. And I think if you hadn't come and looked, it would have bugged the shit out of you forever."

"Sorry to drag you out here," I mumbled. Vida waved me off as she moved back toward the other car. Liam had left his door open, and the light inside gave me a clear view of two very concerned faces.

Vida stopped in her tracks, slowly bent down at the edge of the driveway, and picked something up—something white and filthy with mud. "Hey boo," she called, tossing it over to me. My fingers were shaking and slick with rain, but I somehow managed to catch it.

It was a small shoe, clearly kid-sized. The white fabric was nearly black with mud and grime, but the laces were still a rosy shade of pink, like not even dirt could put a damper on it. I studied it, running my fingers over the swirled stitching along its side.

Cole made it perfectly clear my hijacking of our drive was over. He'd taken my place behind the wheel, and was in the process of rolling down his window when I tossed the shoe back onto the ground and said, "I know, I know."

My whole body shook with how hard my teeth were chattering. Cole took pity on me and redirected the warm air blowing from the vents my way, but he didn't say a word, and I didn't offer to start the conversation, either.

That shoe . . . God, that shoe with those curling pink laces . . .

Vida swung the car around, taking the lead on the drive back out to the main road. Cole followed, fiddling with the radio as the truck's headlights cut through the trees and foliage. There was a flash of movement as some kind of animal darted away.

"All right," Cole said. "Do you have any idea where we are? Did you see a city name? Gem?"

My mind was fixed on the shoe, obsessing over the stitching, how it had felt warm despite the chilled air and rain, and those laces, those pink laces were like something out of—

I sucked in a gasp loud and sharp enough to startle Cole into hitting the brakes. "What? *What?*"

But I was already scrambling to unbuckle my seat belt,

already jumping back out into the rain, running back up toward the house.

I knew those laces. I had picked those shoes out because of them. I'd dug down deep into that bin at Wal-Mart because I knew she'd love them, I knew—

The gunshot that boomed out, echoing in the dark mountains around us, was the only thing that could have stopped me— and it did. My momentum carried me forward, my feet sliding through the mud as I threw up my hands in the air. Both cars had stopped; Cole used the open driver's-side door of the truck to try to stop Liam and Vida from blowing past him. What guns we had were drawn and pointed into the trees.

I took another small step forward. I wasn't thinking about skip tracers or PSFs or the National Guard or even the home's owners. I was thinking about how terrifying it would be for a kid hiding out in those woods, not knowing who was stalking around one of the few places they thought were safe.

They hadn't shot me dead yet. That was a good sign at least.

"Zu . . . ?" I called, raising my voice above the rain ruffling the trees.

No response.

"*Zu?*" I yelled, taking another step forward. "Suzume? Zu?"

The forest seemed to let out a long sigh around me, settling back down into the night. If someone was there, it wasn't her. She would have come.

Wouldn't she?

I felt a sharp twist of despair low in my gut as I started backing away. "Okay," I said. "Okay, I'm sorry—we're going."

Glancing back over my shoulder, I saw Cole lower his gun. I saw Liam come around the door to stand next to him, stretching a hand out in my direction, only to drop it back to his side. He took another step forward only to stop, his eyes flashing wide.

And when I turned back toward the woods, she was the only thing I saw.

A blur of white and pink and black burst out from the shelter of the trees, away from the pale arms that tried to snatch her shirt and haul her back. Gangly limbs slipped and slid through the mud, covering the space between us so quickly I barely had time to get my arms up.

Zu slammed into me with the kind of force that should have tilted the world onto its side. I fell back, taking her with me, letting out a noise that was halfway between a laugh and a sob as I wrapped my arms around her. She buried her face against my hair and all but wilted against me. Every limb in her body went lax, like she was molding herself to me.

The shot of pure, unwavering joy hit me like a bolt of lightning. It sang a sweet song in my head, warmed me down to my toes. I was so wrapped up in the feeling that it was a full minute before I realized how hard she was shaking, how cold she was to the touch. She was crying, small gasps of sound that didn't signal happiness. I set her back so I could see her face and she only gripped my sleeves harder, shaking her head.

"I think this is yours?" I said, holding up her shoe. She let me try to wipe the mud from her bare right foot before I slid it back on and tightened it. It must have fallen off as she ran toward those trees. They'd heard us coming and panicked.

"Zu?" Liam came toward us so fast he slid through the last few feet of mud, landing on the ground with us. "Zu?"

All she had to do was turn her head and the elation on his face faded to panicked concern. He took her hands when she reached out to him, studying every inch of her for bruises, cuts, anything to explain why she was looking at us like we were back from the dead, why she was holding onto us like we might vanish with her next breath.

"Is it her?" Chubs called desperately, stumbling toward us. "I can't see—"

"Here—slow your roll—" Vida turned back and retrieved him from behind the car door, guiding him around. He patted his front pocket, reaching in for one of the lenses.

"Hey, what's a girl like you doing in a place like this?" Liam asked, letting her small hands run over his wet hair, cup his face.

Chubs dropped to his knees, sending a spray of mud over all of us. He held out his arms in what he must have thought was her direction. "You're not alone, are you? You know what happens when you try to travel by yourself, there's—"

Zu tackled him to the ground. The mud smacked against his back at the same moment the air went out of him.

"Well . . . all right," he murmured, carefully tucking her against his shoulder. "You are freezing. We need a blanket before she goes into hypothermic—"

Zu reached up and put a hand over his mouth, making Liam laugh and laugh. The smile she offered back was trembling, small, but still there. I felt like crying myself, seeing it.

I studied her, trying to align this new vision with the image I had tucked safely away in my memory. Her hair had grown back in long enough to curl around her ears. Everything else about her had changed, too. She was taller, but thinner. Painfully thin. The skin on her cheeks had sunken in. And even in the dark, I could see the same was true for the others who came out from behind the trees. They stumbled toward us, blinking against the cars' lights. I counted twelve in all, different heights, different shapes, but all kids. All kids.

Kylie and Zu's cousin Hina came out of the trees next. It only took seeing Lucy for me to remember the dozens of times I'd taken food she'd spooned out at all of East River's meals. She made me think of fire smoke, of pine, of the sunset reflecting on the nearby lakes. And the three of them—all of the kids, really—looked at us like we were blinding them.

"I'm sorry," Kylie said. "I didn't realize it was you, otherwise I wouldn't have fired, we just . . . the skip tracers and the soldiers and everything—"

Behind me, I heard Cole let out a long sigh.

"We're going to need to find another car," he said. "Aren't we?"

FIVE

FOR ALL THE HOPE I HAD THAT WE'D FIND HER, I'M not sure I ever thought about what would actually happen to Zu if we did. But it became clear, from the moment Liam saw her, that it was the only thought running through his mind.

"I thought you'd be at her uncle's house," I said. "What happened? Why did you leave?"

"He wasn't there. We would have stayed anyway, but there was . . . an incident just after we got there," Kylie was explaining as we walked. The trees pulled back to reveal a small clearing, ringed with darkness. When they heard our cars coming, they'd smothered the fires, but the clearing was still filled with the smell of smoke.

"What kind of incident?" Liam asked.

"A bad one. There was a guy, turns out a good guy. He . . . never mind, it doesn't matter." Kylie shook her head of dark curls, smoothing down the front of her ripped shirt. "We've been moving from town to town since then. When I saw the trail of road code I picked it up, hoping we'd find some other kids, but they're not having an easy time of it, either."

I felt my eyes widen at the sight of the soaking-wet makeshift tents they'd strung up using bed sheets, and the old food cans and buckets they'd left out to catch water.

"You drove in, right?" Liam asked. "Where did you stash the car?"

"Behind the shed at the back of the house." Kylie tried to wring her shirt out, without much luck. The others standing around her had introduced themselves in a blur. I didn't recognize any of them. Lucy had been quick to specify that two of them, Tommy and Pat, had left East River a few months before we'd ever arrived. The other three members of their tribe had split when the going had gotten too rough for them, and they hadn't heard from them since. The other ten teenagers, all about fifteen, were strays they'd picked up as they moved across the country.

Tommy was as long and narrow as the tree flanking him, his shocking head of copper red hair mostly hidden under a beanie. Pat was about a head shorter, and walked and talked with a frantic, bumbling energy that made it almost impossible to keep up with him.

"Well . . ." Cole said, looking at the sad camp set up around us. "Y'all tried."

"I'm just wondering . . ." Lucy stepped out in front of us, her braided blond hair swinging over her shoulder. She was wearing an oversized 49ers sweatshirt and black leggings that were shredded at the knees. "What are you guys doing here? When did you leave East River?"

Oh, damn—of course they wouldn't know. They couldn't have found out. I glanced over to Liam, but he was looking down at where Zu clung to his hand.

"Save story time for later," Cole said. "Pack up whatever you guys want to bring with you."

"Wait, what?" Liam said. "Hold on—they don't even know what they're getting into."

Cole rolled his eyes and turned back to the other kids, clapping his hands together. "I'll break it down for you. We used to be part of a group called the Children's League. Then the president decided he wanted to destroy us, the Federal Coalition, and all of Los Angeles. Now we're heading up north to set up shop and figure out new, fun ways to kick his ass. Are there any questions?"

Tommy raised his hand. "They destroyed Los Angeles? Like, literally?"

"I don't think we speak figuratively anymore?" Cole said. "It's a flaming heap of rubble. You guys are welcome to park yourselves here, but the military has control of the borders and freeways, and they've likely got a new stranglehold on what gas and food is out there. Meaning life is about to get a hell of a lot harder if you don't find yourselves a safe place."

I think the kids were actually too shocked to cry. They traded stunned glances, clearly struggling to process this.

Starvation doesn't help much on that front, either, I thought, looking at the way the rain made Kylie's shirt cling to her sharp hip bones.

"And where we'd be going, that's a safe place?" Pat asked.

"Tell them the truth," Liam said sharply. "It may be a safe, secure location, but we're always going to have targets on our backs. You've never done anything just out of the goodness of your heart, so what's the catch, Cole? They come with us and they have to fight? They have to work for their food and beds?"

"Well, realistically, we'll probably all be in sleeping bags," Cole said, irritation simmering under each word, "but no, no catches. If they want to be trained, then we'll train them. If they want to fight, then who the hell am I to stop them? But I have a feeling they're just as invested in finding out what caused IAAN and learning more about this so-called cure. And I *also* have this here little feeling that they'll be hard-pressed to find another group willing to help them get back to their parents."

"Don't manipulate them into thinking this is—"

"This is what?" I asked quietly, pulling him aside. "A way for them to survive? Liam . . . I get it, fighting is dangerous, but this kind of life is dangerous, too, isn't it? Being sick and starved and constantly on the run? They don't have to stay at the Ranch forever. We can get them out once we figure out a safe system for it, if that's what they want."

He looked pained; if he had struggled with the idea of me being trapped with the League, what were the chances he would ever accept this for Zu? No matter how much he wanted to see the camps freed, to see a real cure out there, his first instinct was always going to be to take the road that was safest for the people he cared about the most.

"When all of this is over," I said, my eyes sliding over to where Cole was helping the other kids eagerly pack up their things, "we can go anywhere we want. Isn't that worth it? Having her come with us now is the only way we can guarantee she's safe. We can take care of her."

We should never have let her go in the first place.

He let out a rush of breath. "Hey Zu, how would you feel about helping us start a little war?"

She looked up at him, and over to me, her eyebrows drawn together as she considered this. Then Zu shrugged, like, *Sure. Got nothing better to do.*

"All right." Liam released the words on the tail end of a sigh, and I felt the tension escape my body with it. With one arm around my shoulder, and his other hand on Zu's, we started back through the trees to where the others were waiting. It was grounding, the familiarity of it—like I was finally tethered back to the world again. "All right."

By the time we made it back to the cars, Chubs and Vida were there, leaning against the side of the truck. But while Chubs was practically bouncing on the balls of his feet, firing off a hundred questions to Zu that he had no chance of getting answers to, Vida took one look at her, crossed her arms over her chest, and came toward us.

"Hey, Vi, this is—"

She didn't stop, not to let me finish, not to take Zu's hand when she held it out to shake. Vida's eyes flashed as they met mine, and the accusation there was as silent as it was baseless. Her jaw clenched with the venom she was clearly fighting to keep back. "Can we get out of this fucking dump now?"

And just like that, the feeling of security was gone. A sick unease crept in, tearing my attention in two. Half of me wanted to go after her into the woods and the other half, the louder, more demanding one, wanted to stay exactly where I was, happily caught up in my love for the three people around me. My heart was swollen with it as Zu wrapped her arms around Chubs's narrow waist again and he patted the top of her head in his usual awkward way.

Liam had turned to follow Vida's shape as it disappeared into the darkness. When he turned back, I saw the question there; my own confusion, reflected back.

But I had no idea why she was angry.

It was hours past midnight by the time we reached Lodi, and the moon was already beginning its downward glide toward the western horizon. I'd slept on and off for a total of four hours, but felt absolutely no better for it. Sticking to surface streets, winding up California's spine at a leisurely pace, had added an extra four hours to an already long trip—and the extra hour it took to find one more car, and enough gas to keep us all going, rounded it out to an even ten hours. We seemed to be caught in some kind of reality in which time was simultaneously stretching and shrinking; minutes flew by, but in endless numbers. The rushing tides of anxiety and fear washed in and out of me, and I caught myself sending up desperate, silent prayers that we'd find Cate and the others waiting for us. The day had already gone too well, and I knew better than to expect some kind of pattern to form. Life had the nasty habit of lifting me up just to throw me back down.

The town was more rural than I was expecting, at least the fringes of it. There were a number of barren fields that might once have been vineyards, but they'd been left to wither and die in the shadow of a series of long, silver warehouses.

"There it is," Cole said, lifting his hand from the wheel to point. I was surprised he could tell the difference between each, given that they looked identical to my eye, especially in the dark.

"Are they here?"

"We'll know in a second."

The sky had blossomed into pale lavender by the time we entered the edge of town, our little line of cars like a parade through the empty streets. Cole's mood was shifting again, ticking higher and lighter as the car slowed and turned into a used-car dealership. He guided the car into one of the empty, covered spaces—next to what was most definitely an old exterminator's van and an electrical company's truck.

Not a used-car dealership, I thought. *At least not anymore.*

"Okay, Gem." Cole took a deep breath and glanced up at the roof of the car, muttering something I couldn't hear. "You ready?"

"What about him?" I asked, nodding toward Clancy's limp form.

"Leave him for now. I just gave him another dose. I'll come back out for him after we make sure everything's secure."

It didn't seem like the best idea, but I was so tired I found myself nodding anyway, too tired to fight. Besides, the kid was still breathing low and even, bent over at the waist and out of sight. This time, I was the one to double-check that his hands and feet were still zip-tied. It was the last complete, coherent thought I seemed to have.

My whole body ached with exhaustion as I climbed out; I could taste it at the back of my throat, feel it in the watery consistency my eyes had taken on. Liam found me immediately and cast a questioning look in the direction of the truck. I waved him off and leaned into his arm when he wrapped it around me. I kept trying to count the kids off, starting each time with Zu and Hina, but I couldn't seem to get past ten without forgetting my place and needing to start again. Focusing on one thing, Chubs's voice as he fired question after question to Vida about the blurred shapes around him, helped keep me alert, but it still took my brain far too long to process why we were standing outside of some kind of bar, hovering at the door.

Liam followed my line of sight. "She didn't say a single thing to Zu," he said quietly. "I know she's not a cuddlebug, but is this normal? Because if it keeps going the way it is, I'm going to have a problem with it."

I looked over at Vida again. "It takes her a while to warm up. I'll talk to her."

Cole peered in through one of the windows, ignoring the unlit electric OPEN sign. Letting out a deep breath, he tested the door to Smiley's Pub. Locked.

"Is this a bar?" Chubs whispered behind me. "Are we allowed to go in? We're not twenty-one."

"Oh, Grannie." Vida sighed. "I can't even."

I looked through the front window. There was a lot of pale, polished wood, empty shelves behind the bar itself, and red vinyl wherever there was seating. Old classic-rock tour posters were tacked up between all of the pictures of bikini-clad women lounging on sports cars.

"Do we have to break in?" I asked Cole.

"Nah. I was just checking to see if they were still using the joint as a front. The entrance to the Ranch is behind the bar."

For a second, I was confused, thinking he meant behind the counter inside the bar. Instead, he stepped down from the curb and jutted his chin toward the small alley between Smiley's Pub and the empty store beside it. We fell in place behind him, stepping around garbage cans and empty, stacked crates until we reached a back door. Cole went right up to it and pressed six numbers into the electronic keypad there. It flashed, beeped, and the door popped open, revealing what looked like a typical back room. There were shelves along each wall, most of them bare.

"It's a long way down," Cole said over his shoulder. "Anyone afraid of heights? The dark? Nah, of course not. You guys are champs. Just be careful, you hear?"

Long way down. God—another underground tunnel? A long one, I'd bet, based on the fact that we were far enough away from the Ranch's main building that I hadn't been able to see it from out in front of Smiley's. We'd had a similar setup for accessing HQ down in Los Angeles. The entry point had been a parking garage, which brought you down via elevator to what we called the Tube. That tunnel had been so hellish in its sewer stink and mold-slick walls, you half expected to find the devil waiting for you at the other end of it.

To access the trap door that opened to the Ranch's tunnel, we all had to cram into the small bedroom set at the back of the bar, and lift the bed and rug that had been placed over it. A cold, stale burst of air rushed up to meet us as Cole kicked the door open.

"Cool," Tommy and Pat said, leaning to look down into the dimly lit space. Kylie made a face in Lucy's direction, but was the third one down after Cole. Most of the teens went next, too tired to really question what was happening or where they were being taken. It was worse for the younger kids. Zu and Hina were mirror images of complete and total fatigue. They swayed on their feet like they'd snuck a few glasses back at the bar, and they couldn't focus their eyes on Liam, even as he was helping to navigate them over the lip of the ladder. He and I both had to help Vida get a half-blind, incredibly grumpy Chubs down next. Then, it was his turn.

I knew it was irrational, the way that fear seemed to walk up behind me and press a blade to my throat. I knew that we were not under attack, that there were already kids down on the path and they were fine, that I'd have to walk it if I ever wanted to get to the Ranch. I knew all that. But I still couldn't move.

Liam caught my expression and brought a reassuring smile to his face. Even with all of those unspoken words between us, he could still read my every fear. One of his hands wove through my hair and cupped the side of my face as he kissed my temple.

"Different tunnel, different destination, different end," he promised. "Okay?"

I swallowed and forced myself to nod as he started down the ladder. The moment his head of pale hair disappeared, I felt my skin shrink back against my bones and my stomach flip. *Different end.* I turned the words over in my head. *An end.*

This was just the beginning of it.

I straightened, smoothing my ponytail back over my shoulder and took the first step. The second. The third. I tried not to think of the way the darkness seemed to well up around me, swallowing me down. At the exact moment I was sure I'd be climbing down forever, I finally found solid ground.

The rest of the morning took on a strange, almost unreal quality. The tunnel was lit by strings of Christmas lights, some of them blinking, some of them out completely, but only ever revealing a small section of path at a time. It was all stark, unforgiving cement. The low ceiling and narrow walls amplified each and every voice, carrying whispers and sighs back through the darkness like ghosts. I sucked in shallow breath after shallow breath, feeling the blood actually start to pound out a low beat behind my eyes. This really was the prototype for HQ in Los Angeles—on a much smaller scale, and partly aboveground if what Cole said was true, but similar enough to send a shudder through me.

My mind was playing catch and release with the sights and sounds around me, filtering everything through a milky lens. It made me feel almost like I was seeing it all happen through someone else's memories. The smell of sweat and damp clothes. A grunt of pain from Vida. Chubs's bleak, hopeless expression as he stared down the dark. Zu, passed out against Liam's back, her arms wrapped around his neck as he carried her in. We walked for so long, there were moments I forgot where we were heading.

Up ahead of us, Cole climbed up a half flight of stairs and banged on something metal—a large, rusted square that must have been a door. There were no handles facing into the tunnel. We'd need to be let in from the other side.

"What if no one's here?" I heard Chubs ask. I pretended, for the sake of my heart, that I hadn't heard him at all.

He pounded his fist against it for another minute before the kids behind him crowded at his back and started banging against it with him.

No one is here, I thought. *They didn't make it.*

I couldn't breathe. There was nowhere to go—the walls were so close on either side of me, the kids behind me were blocking my route out. I felt Liam wrap an arm around my shoulder, but the weight of it made my chest feel even tighter. My feet tripped over themselves, backward, just as there was a loud groan, and the pathway was flooded with light.

Cate?

I shielded my eyes, trying to make out who the figure was, when Cole sang out, "Hello, Dolly!"

"Oh my *God!*" There was a faint note of some kind of accent in her voice—maybe New York? New Jersey. "Hurry up, get in here—my God! We thought . . . we were worried we were going to have to go out and find you."

Liam guided us forward, up the stairs, into the light. I hadn't realized how cold I was until a delicate wave of warmth rolled over us. I stepped inside, blinking against the flood of fluorescent light overhead.

Dolly blew out an aggravated sigh, moving down the line of us, blinking as she reached where I was standing beside Liam. She glanced between him and Cole. "Oh, God, there's another one of you? How has the world survived this long?"

"Pure, dumb luck," Cole said. "Is everyone here?"

Dolly visibly hesitated. "Well . . . not exactly."

"Cate?" The word came out of Vida in a naked rush of hope.

"Conner's just fine. She's been worried sick about everyone."

Liam's arm tightened around me as he glanced down, his expression so sincerely thrilled on my behalf as I leaned into him that my faint smile was almost a reflex. It surprised me, though, that the first feeling to flood into the hole that fear had left in me wasn't elation or relief. Those came only on the heels of a sudden, sharp ache that radiated out from my core. *She doesn't know.* Cate had survived, made it up here in spite of fiercely skewed odds, and she'd been waiting. The only message Dolly would give her is that we were here; she wouldn't know about Jude. I would have to keep from throwing my arms around her and crying long enough to tell her. *She doesn't know anything.*

And now she would.

"What do you mean, not exactly?" Cole said, looking around. "Ten of you came to open the place, right? And Conner brought her dozen—"

Dolly's sneakers gave a faint squeak as she shifted uncomfortably. She was saved from having to answer by the sound of bare feet slapping against the tile. My heart jumped into my throat as a head of pale blond hair rounded the corner of the hall at full speed—Cate.

Vida launched herself toward her, tearing through the mass of kids that stood between them, nearly tackling them both to the ground.

"I'm sorry, I'm so sorry," Cate was saying, "we were just outside of the attack zone and couldn't get back in through all of the barricades that were set up—"

Cate looked past Vida's shoulder to where I stood, a relieved smile on her face as her eyes met mine. *Oh God, oh my God, she doesn't know*—I couldn't get the words to my mouth, couldn't move. Heat flooded beneath my skin, the sweat bringing the guilt and shame and anger and sadness up from every pore. And then she wasn't looking at either of us, but at the empty space at my other side. She was looking at the whole hall, her eyes tearing from one person to another, all the while holding Vida to her tighter. She was looking for him.

In the end, I didn't need to say anything at all. She had to have known, the first second she saw my face.

Liam's hand found mine, tightening around my fingers as he pulled me away, bringing me in close to his side. I pressed my face against his good shoulder, listening to his heart pound against my ear, trying to catch my breath and stop the rising tears.

"How about . . ." Dolly put a hand on Tommy's shoulder. "How about I show you guys where the bathrooms are and where you can sleep? All of the rooms are open. Just pick which one you'd like. We'll have to figure out sheets and blankets tomorrow, I'm sorry."

"What happened to the bedding?" Cole asked in a low voice.

"They took it." Dolly lifted a shoulder and shot a look from him to the kids and then back to him, and finally Cole stopped asking questions.

She led us down another bright white hall, the lights overhead bleaching out everyone's skin, making the dirt and grime that much more obvious. Pictures taped to the wall fluttered as so many bodies moved past them. The sharp smell of bleach. A large room, the size of a school's gym, wide open and littered with sleeping bags and bedding.

Rest, I thought. *I can finally stop.*

"Hey, Gem," Cole said. "Can you come with us for a bit? I want to debrief Cate so she has the full picture."

Liam's grip on me tightened and I almost said no—I didn't think I could handle being around Cate until I recharged. But he and I were in this together. And I wanted to know where the other agents were.

"I'll be there in a second," I told Liam. "Pick us out a good room."

"All right . . ." he began uncertainly, but followed the others downstairs with only one last look over his shoulder.

Cole motioned for me to follow him into the room just to the left of the tunnel's opening, but I held my ground a second longer, trying to get a better look at the place. And I was . . . unimpressed.

Back in Los Angeles, HQ had had a kind of ramshackle look to it, like someone had dug a deep hole, poured in some concrete, and brought in mismatched tile, desks, and tables to decorate it. The lighting and plumbing had been exposed overhead, and we'd never had reliable hot water. But the Ranch just looked like it had been forgotten. Despite the fact that the agents had been up here for at least a week, the floor was coated with clouds of gray dust and dirt. Door handles hung limp and broken. Paint was peeling off walls and the wood on several doors was splitting. Light bulbs were either out or missing completely, leaving random patches of the hallway in darkness. The ceiling tiles were crumbling into powder; whole chunks of the ceiling had fallen to the ground and had just been kicked aside. It was like they didn't care; a wave of anxiety went through me as I took it in. This was how you treated a place you had no intention of staying in. Owning.

"—is *bullshit! This is such fucking bullshit!*" Vida's voice called me to the room the others had entered. I stepped in and shut the door firmly behind me, nearly knocking into a wall of filing cabinets. The room was just large enough for a single desk, three chairs, and a few framed maps of the United States.

This must have been Alban's office, I thought, *while he was still here.* It wasn't nearly as crammed with random junk as his office had been at HQ, but certain touches, including the limp American flag hanging on the wall, were recognizably him.

"As soon as they were out of Los Angeles, Sen contacted the Ranch and told them they were heading to Kansas," Cole explained to me from where he was leaning against the front of the desk with Cate. She kept her face turned down, her arms crossed tightly over her chest, thoughts clearly somewhere else. Vida paced what little free space there was to move, her hands on her hips.

"And they all left," I finished. *Dammit.* Cole had been sure that the agents who'd left HQ with Cate to look for transportation for us were, if nothing else, loyal enough to Cate to want to stay and help us.

"And took pretty much everything that wasn't nailed down here with them, including most of the food," Cole said. I was surprised at how calm he seemed. "Cate and Dolly were going to come looking for us—apparently you really sold that we were going to Kansas. We're going to have to start from scratch in building this place up, but it's doable."

Cate's head shot up. "What do you mean, she 'sold' that?"

"You *knew*," Vida said, a scathing edge to her voice. "You sent them away?"

I held up my hands, refusing to press my back against the door and get as far from those furious looks as I could manage. "I did. I influenced them to go straight to Kansas, so that we could break off on our own somewhere outside of the state. I should have made sure they didn't contact the agents here before we could arrive, though."

"What the *hell*?" Vida seethed.

"I second that," Cate said, leveling Cole with a cold look. "Explain exactly what you were hoping to accomplish."

"Ah, well, how about trying to save the lives of all of these kids?" Cole shot back. He braced his hands on his knees. "You want to know what your pal Sen was planning? They were going to split the kids up between the cars, take them just far enough outside of Los Angeles to think they were safe, and then turn them in for the reward money."

If it were possible, Cate went even paler. Vida, finally, stopped pacing.

"You can't know that . . ." Cate began.

99

"I saw it in her mind," I said, letting the acid I felt in my stomach coat my words. "She had everything planned out to the minute. They wanted the money to be able to buy weapons and explosives on the black market. They want to go hit Washington, D.C.—they have no interest whatsoever in helping us free the camps."

"Our plan played out like we thought it would," Cole said, "Mostly. Don't get your panties in a twist, Conner. No one got hurt. It's a clean break. The fact that the other agents left does nothing but prove that our instincts on this were right. No one wants to help the kids. At least this way, we've got the Ranch and we've muddled them on what our plans are. If they're stopped or picked up by President Gray's friends, they'll give them wrong intel on us. This is the right base of operations for *us*, not them. It's quiet, we have working electricity and water, and, now, plenty of space to work."

"Yeah, and look at what we don't have!" Cate finally detonated. Her pale face flushed, and she was barely keeping a lid on her trembling anger. "You sent away trained professionals— the ones who could have conducted these camp hits you want to do, the ones who could have protected all of these kids! We should have spent time working to bring them over to our side, not manipulating them into thinking it was their idea to go. And how *dare* you make this kind of decision without even consulting me? I can't—" She shook her head, her eyes latching so fiercely onto mine that I had to look away. "Ruby, what is going *on*?"

"Give it a rest, Conner," Cole said, with an edge to his tone. "The plan is to train the kids to fight. To empower them."

"To empower yourself," Cate corrected sharply, and if Vida

hadn't been in the room, I have no idea what Cole would have said or done in response to that. His fist clenched at his side. "I get it, Cole . . . I do. But this wasn't the right way. They took the computer servers. I have *one* laptop, and only because I brought it into my quarters to do some work last night and hid it when they started talking about leaving. They'll lock us out of the system. What are we going to do then? You burnt this bridge without giving us a way to get back over."

The League had spent the better part of a decade building up a network of information on everything: whereabouts of former politicians, access into the skip tracer and PSF databases, building schematics, black site locations. I'd been counting on having access to it to proceed with any and all camp hits. If nothing else, we'd need the few known satellite photographs that had ever been snapped of some of the camps.

"The Greens can break into the League's network, that's not even a question," Cole said. "They're the ones that built it. And I took measures to ensure that we would be able to copy the research on the cure. My only question is, where is the flash drive of the information I stole from Leda Corp? With the study on what caused IAAN?"

Cate's jaw set as she looked away. Her throat bobbed as she swallowed, silent just long enough for a cold, gripping dread to come over me. "It's in the garbage. We weren't far enough outside of the city when the EMP went off. It was wiped clean by the pulse . . . I'm sorry. I wish—" She shook her head, stopping herself.

At that, I sat down heavily in one of the chairs, feeling more and more like I was passing through a long tunnel in the opposite direction from everyone else. I barely heard Cole's sarcastic "Oh, *wonderful*." Didn't register that Cate had stood and was already moving around me to get to the door.

"Where are you going?" Cole asked. "Let the kids sleep a little while longer."

"I'm not going to the kids," she said coldly. "I'm going after the other agents to fix this mess you've gotten us into. To get them to come back so we can work together on this."

The chill in her tone sank through me, down to my bones. I'd never seen her like this, or at least I'd never had the full force of her anger barreling toward me. But I was angry too—furious. She had left us, she hadn't been there when I needed her, and I'd done the best I could to help everyone survive.

"You want them to come back?" I asked. "Who? The ones that ditched you at the drop of a hat to go play terrorists, or the ones that wanted to hand us over to the PSFs?"

Cate couldn't even look at me. "I'm sure there's been a misunderstanding . . ."

"You're right," I said, "I misunderstood how in denial you are about who these agents are—"

"Ruby!" Vida snarled. "Shut the f—"

"I don't know how many times they have to prove it to you, but these agents have never cared about the League you joined, the one that actually cared about the kids who are still stuck in camps—who are still dying every day from something we're within an arm's length of finding a cure for. We don't need them! We don't need to have them taint what we're trying to do here! *Wake up!*"

"I am not interested in sending kids out to play soldier," Cate said.

"You didn't have a problem with that before," I said bitterly.

"You were supervised by trained agents who led the tact teams—"

"Right. You mean the agents who then turned around and started picking us off one at a time? How about Rob? The one who tried to kill both me and Vida in one 'accident.' Do you even know that he came after us? He *hunted* us. He put a muzzle on me!"

Vida was frozen in place, her face ashen. The instinct to protect Cate from any insult was clearly at war with the side of her that knew the truth. Cole reached out to put a hand on my shoulder, but I sidestepped him, waiting for Cate to look at me. Waiting for an answer.

"Dolly and I will leave first thing tomorrow," she said quietly. "The other agents only left a few hours ago. We can still catch up to them."

It felt like she'd slapped me across the face. "Fine. Then go."

"Good luck," Cole added, with only a trace of mockery in his voice.

Her pale eyes flicked down over me one last time before she went out of the room, letting the door slam open and shut behind her. Vida was fast on her heels; I watched them go through the windows lining the computer room until they finally disappeared. I couldn't stand it anymore and started after them.

Cole caught my arm and drew me back. "Let them cool off. They're just upset, but it had to play out this way."

"Did it?" The question escaped before I could stop it, the doubt trickling in through the cracks in my heart.

There was another loud groan of protest from the tunnel door—the sound got me on my feet, and both of us rushed out into the hallway. I was so sure that I'd see Cate charging down into the darkness, about to make good on her promise to leave, that the dirty, tired faces of the eight kids standing there hit me like a blow to the chest.

Each of them looked a little more terrified than the last. Senator Cruz brought up the rear, brushing away all of the hands that reached in to help her climb the last few steps. She glanced around, avoiding the assessing look from Dolly as she appeared to my left.

"Made it in record time!" Cole said, pounding each of them on the back in turn, earning a few smiles and even more relieved hugs. "Did you have any problems?"

"No, we were a little confused about the instructions you gave us on how to get down into the base from the pub, but once we saw the place we figured it out." Zach, a tall, tan-skinned leader from one of the League's Blue teams, seemed as unshakeable as ever. He dragged a hand back through his dark hair and surveyed the place.

If Zach looked relaxed now, confident, Nico had swung to the other side of the spectrum. He looked small and terrified, black hair standing up every which way, like he'd spent the last day running his hands back through it in dismay. Nico crossed his arms over his chest, cupping his elbows, breathing in deep. At least, until he saw Cate. She pushed toward him, shouldering her way through the other agents, but instead of flinging himself at her the way Vida had done, he reached up, covered his face with his hands, and began to weep.

It was the only word to describe the sounds coming from him. They rose over the excited chatter, smothered each and every question, sapped the laughter until it died down to a whisper. My guts twisted until I finally had to look away, and let gray static fill my ears instead. None of the other kids moved toward him, only Senator Cruz, who made it very clear with her expression what she thought of us for that. Her arms were around him even before Cate's.

I turned to Dolly and asked where to find the showers and the sleep rooms, grateful for the excuse to get away from the horrible sound of Nico crying, from Cate's disappointment, the others' unknowing excitement for a place that had been stripped to the point of being almost uninhabitable.

From what I could see, the Ranch was split along two hallways that ran parallel to each other and were connected by double doors at either end. The lower level had the same floor plan as the upper one did: two narrow, twin halls with over a dozen closed doors lining each of them. One hall the stairwell emptied into was little more than a series of bunk rooms to sleep in, the kitchen, and a laundry room. One of the doors had been left open and I glanced inside at the four bunk beds.

The voices in the next room were muffled, but I recognized Chubs's *"What?"* when it burst out of him. I crossed the last few feet to the door and gripped the door handle, wondering why they'd shut it at all.

"—she couldn't have just told us?" Vida was ranting. "Un-fucking-believable. If our lives were in danger, she shouldn't have dicked around with Cole. We should have been the first people she told!"

I leaned toward the door, pressing my forehead against it as I listened.

"She and Cole have been acting all buddy-buddy for a while," Chubs said. "I'm not surprised they pulled something like this."

"It doesn't make sense—" Liam's voice dropped low enough

that I couldn't hear it, but I was already backing away, blood pounding in my ears at the anger laced through their voices.

I made my way down the hall, to the linen closet that Dolly had mentioned. All of the towels had been claimed, but there was a soft, oversized black shirt tucked into a bag of street clothes the agents had missed when cleaning the joint out. I took that with me as I walked to the bathroom, grateful I wouldn't have to change back into all of my dirty clothes.

The morning took on an unreal quality as I stepped into one of the shower stalls, stripped, and stepped in before the water could warm. The water burst out of the rusted showerhead and hit my skin with a freezing slap, cooling me instantly, easing the prickling on my scalp. They'd installed pumps of soap and shampoo in each stall: big, industrial-sized containers that were already half-empty. I let my shoulders hunch as my gaze dropped down to the water swirling deep, down, away under my feet. I breathed. The patches of dirt that didn't wash away on my ribs and legs turned out to be bruises. I breathed. I breathed.

I just breathed.

SIX

I DON'T KNOW IF I ACTUALLY SLEPT, SO MUCH AS DIPPED in and out of unconsciousness. Flat on my back, my hands folded over my stomach, I listened to the sound of the Ranch waking up. Voices called up and down the hall to each other, asking about the laundry they'd put in, complaining about the lack of hot water in the showers, laughing—I closed my eyes at the sound of Vida calling for me.

Get up, I ordered myself. *You have to deal with this.*

I swung my legs over the side of the bunk, scrubbing my face, trying to smooth my hair back into a ponytail. By the time I switched on the lights and opened the door, Vida was already at the other end of the hall, doubling back when I stepped out.

"What's wrong?" I asked.

"Oh? Finally done getting your beauty sleep, boo?" she sniped. "They waited for you—they waited an hour for you and you didn't show! What? You're too fucking good to even say good-bye?"

Something cold coiled in my stomach. "Cate and Dolly left already?"

After everything that had happened over the past few months, I was surprised by how deeply that cut. Didn't stop to say good-bye, didn't stay to hear us explain it fully. Cate would rather try to blow up everything we'd accomplished in getting the agents to leave by begging them back. She'd sabotage this for us.

"It's almost three in the afternoon," Vida said.

I stared at her in disbelief. Some of the ice finally broke from her expression. She shook her head, muttering something under her breath that I pretended not to hear. "You were sleeping this whole time? You must have been more wrecked than I thought."

"Listen," I started, "about earlier . . ."

She held up a hand. "I get it. I just have one question—did you keep Sen's plan from me because you thought I'd knife the bitch in the kidney?"

"That might have been part of it," I admitted.

"Then you don't know me as well as you think," she said. "Because I would have gone straight for the heart. But . . . fair."

"Where is everyone?" I asked.

"Gran is lying around moping somewhere," Vida said. "Boy Scout is annoying the shit out of everyone in the kitchen."

"What? Why?" At her shrug I asked, "And Zu?"

All at once, her expression shuttered again. When she spoke, her voice could have cut the skin from my bones. "Do I look like I give a single shit where she is?"

"Vida," I said, "seriously—"

Whatever it was, she didn't want to talk about it. Vida was already backing away, heading toward the stairs.

"We need to talk about this," I said, starting after her. The look she shot back stopped me. That was the expression of some-one who wanted to be left alone.

"By the way, if you decide you fucking care, when Cate was walking down into the tunnel," Vida said, "she said something to me: tell Ruby playing with fire only gets you burned. That mean anything to you?"

"No," I said finally. "I have no idea."

Vida had been partly right. Liam *was* in the kitchen—only he was actually in the pantry, past the stoves and sinks, in the darkened back corner. He'd left the door wide open, likely to encourage some light inside other than the small flashlight he had clenched between his teeth. He was scribbling something down on a small flip notebook. I reached over to flick on the light switch, about to laugh at him for missing it, but . . . nothing. I tried it twice to be sure.

Liam took the flashlight out of his mouth and smiled. And just like that, the past few hours seemed to melt away into a murky puddle that I stepped clear of.

"Did you know this place needs thirty-six new light bulbs? Why in the world did they have to take the light bulbs, too?" Liam asked.

"Thirty-six is very exact," I said with a faint laugh. "Is that your best guess?"

He seemed confused. "No, I counted. I did a walkthrough with Kylie and Zu earlier. We also could use five new door locks, several gallons of laundry detergent, and about two dozen towels. And this—" Liam gestured to the sparse shelves in front of him. "This is pathetic. I have no idea how they even found this many cans of beets, but good *Lord*. What can you even do with them?"

"Well, there's fried beets, beet soup, pickled beets . . ."

"Ugh." He covered his ears and actually shuddered. "I'd rather take my chances with the stewed tomatoes."

"Is it really that bad?" I asked, stepping into the pantry with him. I didn't really need to ask—it was. Actually, it was worse. Aside from a few loaves of bread and deli slices in the refrigerator, we had mostly canned vegetables and junk food like pretzels and chips.

I leaned against him as Liam went on about trying to find pasta, cans of soup, and oatmeal, and closed my eyes. His chest was warm against my back, and I liked the way I could feel every animated word as it rumbled through him. He reached over and gave my hair a gentle tug. "I'm boring you, huh?"

"No, I'm sorry, I'm listening," I said. "You were talking about Lucy?"

"Yeah. She was one of the girls who kept track of the food at East River. I think she'll be able to give some insight into how to rotate supplies and what we should be looking for."

Right. We would need to set up some kind of team to handle supply runs, though there were already so few of us, I couldn't imagine Cole giving consent unless the situation was absolutely desperate. And I couldn't imagine him giving consent at all if Liam were the one going out.

"You're tired," he said, running a thumb under my eye. "Where did you disappear to? I tried waiting up for you, but passed out the second I lay down."

"I took a shower and was too tired to figure out which room you guys were in," I said, because how could I admit that I'd purposefully avoided the bunk room they chose? I didn't want to deal with the questions, not when my head felt as heavy as my heart.

After having it out with Cate, there just hadn't been any kind of fight left in me. "I found the first open bed and tried to sleep."

He reached up and pulled one of those small, individual servings of canned fruit off the shelf and popped the lid off before I could refuse. He continued his careful count of the shelves as I tipped the can into my mouth and downed the fruit. I saw each and every possible conversation play out across his features, every question he wanted to ask, and felt a prickle of anxiety with each silent second that ticked by.

"I don't want to ask this, but . . . you were going to tell us about the agents and what you did eventually, right? You wouldn't have just let us figure it out when only cars of kids showed up?"

"I should have told you guys as soon as we were out of the city," I said. "It just . . . slipped my mind with everything that happened."

"You could have told us before we left," he said gently.

"It had to happen fast," I said, "and if anyone showed a hint that they knew what was going on, it could have clued the agents in to what I was doing. We had to scramble."

"You and Cole."

"He knows the other agents better than any of us. I needed his input on how to make the suggestion feel real." *And if I had told you, you'd have tried to force us to leave.*

Sometimes—most of the time, actually—it was hard to think of us as having had any kind of separate lives before they converged. Our lives were so closely knit together that it was a compulsion to tell him everything, to hear his thoughts on it all, to see if they matched mine. I'd held back from him before, about what I was, what I had done to my parents, but somehow . . .

it wasn't that it felt worse, exactly, more like there was just this nagging, this unflinching sense that something wasn't clicking the way it had before. I'd interrupted some natural pattern in our lives. I bit my lip, watching his brows draw together the same way Cole's had as he concentrated.

"That's why you panicked, isn't it? You'd just found out about it . . ." Liam rubbed the back of his hand against his forehead. "Damn. So what's the plan now?"

"We'll all meet for dinner to talk through a plan for freeing some of the camps."

"Maybe not dinner, if this is all we have . . ." he started. "But I'll figure something out. Everything will be all right."

Liam draped an arm around my shoulders and pulled me in. I pressed my face against his shoulder and let out a shuddering breath. My arms locked around his waist.

This was right. Being close to him like this was *right*. For the first time all day my mind wasn't racing. Here in the dark, my pulse fluttering at his closeness, everything else seemed far away. He kissed my hair, my cheek, and I thought, *Can't lose this, can't lose this, too*—I couldn't tell him everything, not if I wanted him to benefit from what we were trying to do, not if I wanted to protect him. But we could have *this*, couldn't we?

"Do you trust me to keep you safe?" I asked. I knew it must have seemed like I pulled the question out of nowhere, but all of a sudden it felt vitally important. I could see that he'd been hurt by my not telling him about the agents.

"Darlin', if it were a choice between you and a hundred of Gray's finest, I'd pick you every time."

I caught him by surprise, rolling up onto my toes and kissing him full on the mouth.

My fingers were still gripping his shirt when I pulled back. My voice sounded low, rough to my ears. I had to fight for the words, and I was so self-conscious I wasn't sure I was ever going to pick the right ones. "I want to—"

The dazed look faded from his face as he watched me, waiting. *I want to . . .* I felt my face flush, but I couldn't tell if it was out of embarrassment or because of the images flashing through my mind. I'd never felt so awkward and tense. I'd kissed him before, *really* kissed him, but every time before had felt like it had been prompted by stress or urgency or anger, and each had been cut off by the demands of the world around us. This was really the first chance I'd had to think about him, all of him, slowly; to make a thorough study of him. The feel of his hands. The rasp of his stubble. The small, breathless sounds he made at the back of his throat.

We were in a *pantry* and there were kids working outside in the kitchen. The rational part of me knew the limits of this moment, but next time, if we were somewhere else, and if we had another moment to ourselves alone—what then? I felt a small tremor work through me, powered by equal parts panic and longing. I wouldn't know what to do. How not to mess it up.

Liam's hands covered mine as he leaned back against the shelves. Relief broke over me when I saw his smile. He understood. Of course he did. From the moment I'd met him, he'd known me better than I'd known myself.

When he spoke, his voice was sweet, but his expression was anything but. There was mischief in his eyes, a hungry look. There was a jolt low in my gut as I realized it was because of me. "Now, darlin', I just had myself a little thought."

"Did you?" I murmured, distracted by the way he reached up to run his thumb over my bottom lip.

"I did indeed. It being that you are seventeen and I'm eighteen, and we have every damn right to make out like teenagers. Like normal, happy, crazy kids." He hooked two fingers over the waistband of my jeans and tugged me closer. I loved his voice when he lowered it like that. His accent broadened, warmed like summer air in the minutes before a thunderstorm. It was the full-on Stewart charm assault, and I was totally helpless against it. "You want to hear the rules?"

My heart jackhammered as I nodded. That same hand slid around my hip, up under my shirt, and felt warm and perfect against my lower back. I closed my eyes as his lips just barely brushed mine. His touch made me feel brave. It pushed the uncertainty back until it couldn't reach me.

"The first one is you can't think too hard about it. The second is you say when you want to stop. The third is you do whatever feels good to you. The fourth is—"

"—you stop talking," I said, blindly reaching back to pull the door shut, "and kiss me?"

He was still chuckling as he complied, and then I was laughing, too, because of the bubbling nerves, because his happiness was infectious, and because that dumb first rule didn't matter at all. Liam was the only thought inside my head. He was the hundreds of wild feelings exploding inside my chest. He deepened the kiss and coaxed my lips open to his; I mimicked the stroke of his tongue and was rewarded with a small growl of approval.

Normal. Happy. Crazy. For him.

It was a half hour later, after hearing him call for me repeatedly from down the hall, that Cole finally strolled into the kitchen and started banging around in the large, beat-up refrigerator. It gave me a second to disentangle myself from Liam and pull myself back together before going out to meet him.

"The animal needs to be fed," Cole said, filling a paper cup with water. "Or did you forget about him?"

And just like that, the weightless, wonderful happiness evaporated under my feet and I crashed back down into reality.

"I never forget about Clancy." My words were sharpened by irritation. "Was I not supposed to trust you to take care of it?"

"No, you weren't," Liam called from the pantry.

Cole grinned. "He's going to have a bitch of a headache after the drugs we loaded him with. The kid was only starting to come around when I secured him in his little cage. Looked like he was mad enough to shit a brick."

"All right. Let's get it over with."

Rather than taking us back upstairs, Cole led the way down the hallway of the lower level, passing several bunk rooms before reaching a door marked FILE STORAGE. He pulled out a small key ring and passed it to me. The lock gave me some resistance as I slid the key in. I took a quick glance around to make sure no one was watching, and rattled the handle to make sure it would stay locked. We slipped inside. Cole reached up to tug on the string for the lone light bulb overhead.

There were those simple, utilitarian metal shelves, stuffed with random boxes and piles of paper—archived Ops files, supposedly, if you believed the lie that had been etched onto the door. It was convincing enough at first glance. My eyes roamed the library of folders and binders, all neatly lined up on the shelves, as Cole moved to the two shelves that were flush against the back wall.

"This one," he said. "With the red storage box. Give it a tug."

I reached over the top of the letter-size box. The dust on the lid had been recently disturbed by hands reaching to get to the hidden latch on the shelf's back support bar. My fingers curled around it and yanked up. There was a loud, satisfying click as the entire bookshelf swung out toward me. The automatic lights in the hallway beyond it clicked on, flooding the small storage room with blinding, ultra-white light.

It was a short walk down the bare hall to yet another locked door. Here, I had to insert the key and punch in an access code— 4-0-0-4-0-0-4—before the door sprang open with a hiss.

"I'll be here," he said quietly. "Signal if you need me."

Another part of the deal—he wanted someone to watch my back from behind the door when I came to bring the little pest food. My choices were him, Cate, or Vida, but I'd added Chubs to the list since he had always been resistant to Clancy's influence.

I stepped inside the second hall, letting Cole shut and lock the door behind me.

There were two holding cells in the hall, both of them about ten feet wide and four feet deep. Each had been outfitted with a cot, a plastic toilet, and a bucket of water for washing and brushing teeth. As cells went, these were certainly an upgrade from the damp, musty spaces that had been carved out for the interrogation block at HQ. Better lit, too—almost blinding with all the ultra-bright-white walls and the exposed fluorescent light bulbs overhead. Hardly up to Clancy Gray's usual standard of living, though he seemed comfortable enough sprawled out on the cot, his arm thrown over his eyes. Cole must have hosed him down before bringing him inside, changed him into clean sweats. It was more than he deserved.

He didn't stir as I moved toward the door. The metal flap built into it had another lock; I assumed my key would work on it, and was right. It squealed as it opened, but still, no response from our prisoner. I dropped the bag of food inside, set the glass of water on the small ledge on the other side, and took extra care in relocking it. Clancy waited until I had already turned to go to speak.

"Move-in going badly?" His voice was unsettlingly curious as he turned around to face me. "Your thoughts are so loud I can hear them through the glass."

It was irrational, but for a moment I was worried he meant that literally. But I could feel him when he was trying to poke around inside of my head. There was always a tingling rush that raced down the back of my skull and neck.

Clancy dragged his food over to his cot with his foot. He made a face as he pulled his sandwich apart. "What, there's no steak anywhere west of Texas? What is this meat?"

I started to roll my eyes, only to realize he was actually serious. "It's bologna."

He sniffed at it, his lip curled in disgust, then rewrapped it in the plastic it'd come in. "I think I'd rather starve."

"Be my guest."

"In any case," Clancy said, ignoring this, "I'm disappointed by your lack of smugness. I would have thought you'd be in here first thing, gloating about being reunited with your little flash drive again. What's got your mood so sour?"

"I'm looking at him."

He let out a light laugh. "I overestimated how much you'd be able to figure out in these first few hours. Does the flash drive even work, or was it erased by the EMP? How are those crispy research pages you rescued from the fire? You probably haven't even found out what they're doing to Thurmond yet, have you?"

An invisible hand seemed to wrap around my throat, forcing me to lean forward. *Thurmond?* What was happening at Thurmond that would have him looking so damn gleeful at my blank look?

Don't say it, I commanded myself, fighting against the panic that spiraled up inside me at that one word. *Don't react.*

Clancy tore off a piece of the sandwich's bread and popped it into his mouth. When I didn't demand answers, the corner of his mouth lifted into a smirk.

"If you want to know, you'll have to look and see for yourself." He tapped his temple—a challenge or an invitation?

"I know you're angry," he began, "about the way it all went down in Los Angeles—"

Thurmond, I kept thinking. That word was an infection—exactly as he'd hoped, if I had to guess. *He's been trapped with us for weeks, there's no way he could have new information*—unless it wasn't new information at all, just a card he'd been holding on to, waiting for the exact right moment to play it.

It took me a few seconds too long to answer. "*Angry* doesn't begin to cover it."

He nodded. "One day, though . . . one day months or even years from now, maybe you'll see that destroying that research was a selfless act, not a selfish one."

"Selfless?" I whirled back toward the glass wall, cutting off my own retreat to the door. "Taking away the chance for kids to survive and never face the change? Robbing them of their only real chance to be reunited with their families and returned home is *selfless*?"

"Is that what you want? I thought liberating Thurmond in

time would take precedence," Clancy said, inspecting one of the grapes. "Are these organic?"

I spun on my heel, crossing the distance between his cell and the door as quickly as I could without running.

"Ruby—listen to me. The cure is another way to control us, take decisions out of our hands. What happened when you brought the research here? Have they even let you see it? Do you know where it is right now?"

My fingers curled into fists at my side.

"It's not some magic bandage that's going to heal all wounds. It's not going to erase the stigma of what we are in their minds. If there aren't side effects, they'll always be waiting, watching, praying that we don't relapse. Tell me," he said, drawing his legs up, crossing them on his cot. I watched, silently, as his fingers drummed against his knees. "Does knowing there's a cure change the way the agents here treat you?"

Silence stretched between us. He smiled. "What they're trying to do here isn't about you at all. They may have told you things to get you to come along, to surrender your trust to them, but they won't see their promises through. Not even Stewart."

"The only person I have to worry about not trusting is you."

"Whatever you're trying to accomplish by being here," he said in a low voice, "bring all the kids you can to back you up. They're the ones that'll follow and trust you, not any of the adults. You'll be lucky if they ever see you as anything other than a useful weapon."

"Because it's so easy to find kids in hiding scattered around the country?"

"I can help you track down the tribes roaming around. You

can train them, teach them to defend themselves. We're heading toward the endgame, and if you don't find them, they're going to be collateral damage in the war."

I gritted my teeth, but he was talking again before I could fire off any retort. "Forget the adults, Ruby. Make sure you're out in front of the kids. Make them love you, and you'll have their loyalty forever."

"*Make* them love me," I said, my anger coming back in a surge.

"Not everything at East River was fake," he said coolly.

But everything that had been important—every memory I had of that place—was tainted by the creeping black touch of his mind. Just the thought of the way he had studied me across the camp fire . . . the way he'd slid right through every one of my last mental defenses . . . the way those kids, the Cubbies, had looked at him in total adoration. A shudder ripped down my spine. The room had grown too small and too cold for me to keep standing there and listen to every last trace of bullshit he wanted to spew.

I turned back to the door, unlocking it, and made sure I switched the lights back off. And still, Clancy's voice floated to me through the darkness. He contaminated the air, made it sound like he was everywhere at once.

"When you're ready to be in charge and actually *do something*, let me know. I'll be here, waiting."

And judging by the last look I'd had at his face, that was exactly where he wanted to be.

SEVEN

Cole didn't say a word to me until we were back out in the hall, with several doors between us and the president's son. Even then, he seemed distracted, pale brows furrowed, arms crossed over his chest.

"Could you hear what he was saying?" I asked.

He nodded. "Through the small grate under the observation window."

"Before the attack, did you hear any intelligence chatter about Thurmond?" I asked. "Were there any rumors floating around HQ?"

"I was hoping you'd have some idea of what he was talking about," Cole said as we headed down the hallway. "I'll look into it."

I was headed to the large former rec room just to the left of the stairwell for dinner, but he was clearly escaping into Alban's old office. I caught his wrist as he brushed by me. "When are we going to firm up a plan for the camps?"

"Not tonight," he said. "We're still waiting on two more cars, and I want to try making a few calls to old supply contacts. Outfitting this place has to be priority number one. No one is going

to believe we can do anything if we can't even get the kids clean clothes and a few warm meals. I asked some of the Greens to start thinking about how they would stage a camp assault. In the meantime, take a breather. We'll be working soon enough."

I returned his wave as he crossed through the doors connecting the hallways, and followed the smell of spaghetti sauce into the rec room. Someone had assembled folding tables and chairs in neat lines, brought in a small radio, and propped it on the scuffed-up pool table the agents had oh-so-graciously left behind. Next to that were two large pots with serving utensils, and a dismally small stack of paper plates.

It had taken me a few hours to notice that the Ranch was reassembling itself into something that seemed kind of . . . clean. The silent downstairs halls were punctuated by the banging of washers and dryers, which seemed to be going at all hours of the day. I finally saw that the floor tiles were more white than yellow. And when I went to splash some water on my face in the bathroom, there were no drizzles of rust-stained water streaking across my skin. I smelled bleach. Detergent. It was almost . . . homey.

I passed by two sheets of paper tacked onto the door, stopping to examine them. I recognized the handwriting immediately as Liam's, but it took me a moment to understand what the charts were, why there were stubs of pencils attached to each one with string. They were sign-up sheets, divided up by chore: laundry, cleaning, organizing, food preparation. Under each of these headers were the names of kids. Everyone had to help, but they could choose their chore. That was Liam's style.

I spotted Liam, Chubs, Vida, and Zu sitting at their own table, heads bent close together. Vida saw me first and instantly shut up, pulling back and casually picking up her fork again. I finished spooning some pasta onto my plate and moved toward them.

"What's going on?" I asked, taking the open seat and turning to poke Liam's side. "I saw the chore charts—you should have told me earlier so I could have signed up for something."

Liam glanced up from his notebook. When he moved his hand, I saw a string of numbers—equations he seemed to be untangling. "It's all right. You're busy with other things."

Other things that were, unfortunately, not spending time with him alone in the pantry.

"What's this?" I asked, leaning over to get a better look at what he was doing.

He shot me a rueful smile. "Trying to figure out when, exactly, we're going to run out of food. I've been looking at the nearby towns, and I think I have a few we could hit for supplies where there's minimum contact with the population."

"Cole said he's handling it," I said.

He snorted.

Something about that rankled me. "It's too dangerous to leave the Ranch right now. He'll take care of it."

Zu turned to study me, her expression troubled. I pointed to her plate of pasta, but she still didn't touch it.

"*We* could go out," Liam pressed. "You, me, Vi. Hell, I'd bet Kylie would come—it'll be like old times."

Zu reached across the table, gripping his forearm, holding it down against the table. She kept shaking her head, eyes wide. He wasn't allowed to go. She wasn't going to let him leave. And secretly, I was glad she was the one telling him so, because I was right there with her. I wanted him here, where he was tucked safely out of harm's way.

"I've done it a hundred times," he told her softly. "What's got you like this?"

She released his arm, shrinking back in a way that was very unlike her. I started to ask her what was wrong, only to be interrupted by a frustrated groan.

"Oh, *never mind*! I'm not even hungry," Chubs exploded, shoving his plate away from him. There was more sauce down the front of his shirt than there was left on his plate. It turns out it's fairly difficult to get a fork full of slippery noodles up to your mouth when you were missing the *eye* part of hand-eye coordination.

When Vida didn't go in for the kill on that one, I shot a sideways glance in her direction. The whole room vibrated with happy chatter, laughter. Which made Vida's silence that much more unnerving.

"You shouldn't have thrown the old lenses away. They weren't cracked that badly."

"What was I supposed to do?" Chubs snapped. "Tape them to my face? Walk around holding one up to my eye like a magnifying glass?"

"Wouldn't that have been better than sulking around and blindly bumping into things?" I asked. He'd gone off earlier and pitched them into a trash can in hopeless frustration. I'd fished them out and brought them back to the sleeping room for when he calmed down and started thinking rationally again. "We can ask Cole about getting glasses added to our supplies list," I said.

"The lenses are prescription," Chubs said sharply. "I don't have the information, even if he could get them made. Reading glasses aren't strong enough, and they give me a headache when I wear them too long—"

Vida slid something across the table, never once looking up from her plate of pasta. Chubs must have thought it was some kind of utensil, otherwise I have no idea why he didn't immediately snatch the glasses up.

The frames were about the same size and shape that his old ones had been. The lenses stuck out, not by any means a perfect fit, but close enough. I opened them and slid them onto his face and Chubs practically reared back in surprise, patting them in disbelief.

"Wait—what—this—these are—"

"Don't lose your shit," Vida said, casually raking her fork through her spaghetti. "Dolly had an extra pair of reading glasses and helped me switch out the lenses for yours. They look just as stupid as the other ones did, but you can at least see, yeah?"

Chubs and I both stared at her, stunned.

"Vi . . ." I began.

"What?" Her pitch rose slightly on the word, coming out as a bark. More insecure than angry. "I got tired of being his seeing-eye dog. It made me feel like an asshole for laughing every time he tripped or walked into something—and I don't like feeling like an asshole all the time, okay?"

"It's so hard to go against our nature—" Chubs started.

"He means thank you," I said, cutting him off. "That was really thoughtful, Vi."

"Yeah, well." God, she *was* embarrassed. I took another bite to hide my smile. "I didn't save the starving children of Africa or anything. He breaks this pair, he's SOL."

"Wait, *what*?" Liam's startled voice broke clean through our conversation. He slid the paper Zu had been scribbling messages on closer to him. "Are you sure? I mean, *positive*? Why didn't you tell me before?

Zu reached across the table and took the paper back out of his hands. He was too impatient to let her finish writing the words out and awkwardly leaned across the table, his eyes scanning the words as fast as she could put them down.

I thought you would leave to find them. I'm sorry.

"Oh, man," he said, dropping a hand on her head. "I wouldn't have. I won't. You don't have to be sorry, I get it. But are you sure? It just seems like such a coincidence—"

He stilled suddenly, looking a little sick to his stomach at whatever she wrote down next. "That sounds like her . . . But how did it even happen? What were you doing in Arizona?"

Chubs waved a hand in front of his friend's face. "Care to share?"

"Zu . . ." Liam pressed a fist to the base of his throat and rubbed it for a moment. "Apparently on the way over to California, Zu crossed paths with my mom. . . . I've been trying to figure out where they've been in hiding."

Zu was still pale, watching Liam closely, like she didn't quite believe him. I sat back, the flicker of concern turning into an all-out flame. Before, we'd always made it a priority to keep the four of us together as a unit. It was rare for us to split off, and even then, no one was really ever left alone. I could understand the rush of feeling that came with being back together, wanting to make up for lost time. But this desperation I saw in her, the way she always seemed to be tracking us, making sure we were still there, made my heart feel like it was tearing itself into pieces.

What had happened to her? Zu wasn't normally scared or even all that anxious as a person—at least, she hadn't been.

Someone had done this to her, exposed every last nerve. Left her wide open and raw.

"Because they caught heat from Gray's lapdogs after you broke your stupid ass out of that camp?" Vida asked, with her usual sensitivity.

"Why Arizona?" I asked. "Or, I guess a random choice is a good a choice as any?"

Zu was furiously scribbling something down, looking up only to shoot an exasperated look at us when we crowded over her. Liam put his hands up. "At your leisure, ma'am."

When she did finish, it wasn't at all what I was expecting. And judging by how Liam's face lost the remainder of its color, it wasn't what he was expecting, either.

They're hiding kids in their house—protecting them. She used the name you gave me, Della Goodkind, but I knew it was her because she looks and talks like you. I told her you were safe.

"Oh, God," Chubs said when I spun the paper his way. "Why am I not surprised? Your whole family fell from the crazy tree and hit every damn branch on the way down."

Zu knocked her pencil against the end of his nose in reproach before continuing in her big, looping handwriting. *It was just for a few minutes, but she was really nice.*

Liam was like a starving kid stumbling across someone's picnic basket. "Did she say anything else? Was Harry there with her? You said she's been helping kids, but did she ask you if you wanted to stay? Or any of the other girls? Is that what happened to Talon?"

"Which of those questions did you want answered first?" Chubs asked. "Because I think you just crammed ten into two seconds."

Zu shrank back against her chair. The pencil rolled off the table and into her lap as her eyes drifted down to where her fingers were busy rolling up the hem of her shirt.

"Kylie said Talon didn't make it to California," I said carefully. "Did someone hurt him? Did he . . . ?"

"Did the kid croak?" There was a steel-cut edge to Vida's voice. "Oh, I'm sorry. Am I supposed to act like the rest of them and treat you like you're a baby? You need me to coat everything in cotton candy? Or can you be a big girl?"

Liam flushed with anger. "Enough—"

"You have no idea what you're even talking about!" Chubs growled.

"That's not fair—" I began.

The only one who didn't seem bothered by it—who didn't seem to be showing much of any emotion—was Zu. She stared at Vida for a moment, meeting her hard gaze with one of her own. Then she returned to her sheet and began to write quickly again. Both Liam and Chubs were silently fuming in Vida's direction.

Zu held up the paper again, this time angling it so even Vida could read the words there. *We got run down by skip tracers and he died when we crashed. A friend helped me get to California when I got separated from the others.*

I let out a soft sigh and closed my eyes, desperately trying not to picture it. God . . . Talon. No one deserved that.

"Friend?" Chubs pressed. "Another kid?"

She shook her head, but didn't elaborate.

"An adult? An *adult* drove you?" Liam ran both hands over his face. "Oh my God, I'm scaring the crap out of myself picturing this. We never should have split up. Never. Never. Oh my God. Weren't you scared he was going to turn you in?"

Zu was so still, so pale, I wasn't sure she was breathing. She looked up toward the ceiling, blinking rapidly, like she was trying to fight off rising tears.

"She's a good judge of character," I said, putting an arm around her shoulders. Still so small. Little bird bones, made that much sharper by hunger and stress.

"And you came to that conclusion how, exactly?" Chubs asked, pushing his glasses up. "Based on the fact that she let you into the van instead of locking you out?"

"Exactly," Liam said. "I seem to recall *someone* trying to vote her out."

"Yeah!" I said. "Thanks a lot. Trying to dump me off on some random road . . ."

"Excuse me for trying to look out for the group!" Chubs huffed.

Zu started to write something down, but Vida ripped the paper out of her hands, held it in front of her face, and tore it straight down the middle. "If you want to say something, fucking *say* it."

Her chair screeched as she shoved herself back from the table, and swiped her plate from it. I saw the strain of keeping it together in how stiffly she held her neck up and her shoulders back. For one strange second, all I could think about were those old cartoons they used to show on the weekend, the way they'd show a spark burning its way up the fuse of a pile of dynamite.

I should have known better than to follow her.

"Vi," I called, and had to jog to catch up to her. She was stalking down the hall, all lean muscles and furious power, down the stairs to the lower level. Where was she even going? "Vida!"

I grabbed her arm, but she threw me off—hard enough that

I hit the nearby wall. A burst of pain rocketed through my shoulder, but I didn't back down. Her top lip had been curled into a snarl, but the second she registered what she'd done, it lost most of its ugliness.

"You're gonna want to walk away," she told me, and for the first time I realized she probably didn't know where she was headed, either. She was just trying to get away from that room. From us.

"Not like this," I said. "What's going on? Talk to me."

Vida turned and started down the hall again, only to spin back on her heels. I had misdiagnosed the situation—badly.

"Jesus Christ, you can't let anything sit, can you?" she snapped. "You can't ever just let anyone be to work their shit out. Hilarious, seeing how you can't even handle your own crap."

"I'll try to work on caring less," I said. Zach was coming down the hall toward us, his eyes looking everywhere but at the corner we'd drawn ourselves into. I turned my back on him at the same moment Vida did. She waited until his footsteps faded before releasing a harsh breath.

"You know, I really thought you and me—" Her voice choked off. When she laughed, there was a strained quality to it. "Never mind. What do you even care?"

"You just told me I care too much and now I don't care enough?" I said. "Which is it?"

"Both—neither! Jesus, what does it matter?" she snapped, running her hands back through her short hair. The ends were still bleached, with only the barest hint of blue still clinging to the strands. "I'm happy for you, oh-so-fucking happy for you that you get to have this beautiful reunion with your *real* friends. You get to stay with these people and shoot the breeze about how great it was when it was just the four of you. You get to have all of your stupid inside jokes. But what I can't stand—what makes me sick—is how you—"

"Is how I *what?*" It was a struggle to keep my voice down. "What else? Lay it on me. Come on. Clearly something else is pissing you off if you're picking fights with a girl who's clearly been through hell and back. I can't fix it if you won't tell me what's going on!"

The spark finally hit the pile of dynamite, but the explosion wasn't what I was expecting. Vida's expression shattered, and she ripped air into her lungs with short, jagged breaths. "You just replaced him—in your head, you just traded Jude for that little girl, like he was nothing, like we were nothing to you! I get it, okay? But don't—don't pretend to act like you give a shit when you clearly don't!"

She was crying, really crying, and I was so stunned by it that I just stood there. She spun away from me, anger and humiliation coming off her in waves, backing herself farther into the corner.

You just replaced him.

Like we were nothing to you.

Was that really what she thought? A deep, echoing pain ripped through me. That I'd never . . . that I'd never cared about them? That I wasn't committed? I was cold to them in the beginning, I know I was, but it had only been to protect myself. Letting people in, dropping the walls from around your heart—I couldn't risk being vulnerable like that in the League, not when I needed to survive.

It had seemed crucial to learn to bury every feeling, good or bad, at Thurmond—to fold every wild emotion back before it got away from me and someone wearing black noticed. There, if you

131

were still, you were mostly invisible; if you couldn't be provoked and punished, you were left alone. I'd fallen right back into that strategy at the League, functioning from moment to moment, Op to Op, lesson to lesson, numbing every stray feeling to avoid exploding with how unfair it all was, how terrifying, and how crushing. So no one, even for a second, would question my loyalty to their cause. For a long time, it had been the only way I had of protecting myself from the world and everyone in it.

But Jude . . . Jude had burrowed right in, either oblivious to what I was doing, or trying in spite of it.

Did she blame me for all of this? If she had been Leader, would any of this have ever happened? Would we all . . . I closed my eyes, trying to black out the images that stormed in my mind. Jude on the ground. Jude suffocating on his own blood. Jude's broken back, twisted legs. The look in his eyes, like he was begging me to help him—to kill him and end the suffering.

That damn nightmare. Chubs told me again and again that it would have been instantaneous . . . that his . . . why was it so hard to say the word "death"? He'd *died*, not passed away. Jude hadn't passed anywhere. He hadn't slipped away. He'd died. His life was over. There would never be another word from him; he'd come to an end the way all stories eventually did. He wasn't in a better place. He wasn't with me. Jude was buried with all of his hopes under cement and dirt and ash.

"God," Vida raged, her voice raw, "even now, you can't even fucking deny it, can you? Just leave me alone—go away before I—"

"You think I don't know that it was my fault? That if I had kept him close . . . if I hadn't let him come at all . . ." I told her quietly. "I imagine how it was for him, how in the end, he must have suffocated under all that weight. I wonder how much pain he must have been in, and if Chubs is lying to my face every time he swears it would have been too quick for him to feel anything. My mind keeps circling back to it, over and over. He must have been so scared—it was so dark down there, wasn't it? And he just fell behind. Do you think he realized it? That he was waiting for us to come back and . . ." I knew I was babbling, but I couldn't stop myself. ". . . he shouldn't have been out at all . . . he was only fifteen, he was only fifteen . . ."

Vida backed against the wall, sliding down it, openly sobbing, both hands pressed to her face. "It was my fault, why don't you fucking see that? I was in the back, you weren't even close to him! I should have heard him, I should have made him walk in front of me, but I was so damn scared I wasn't thinking at all!"

"No—Vi, no." I crouched down in front of her. "It was so loud down there—"

This wasn't her fault at all. I felt a fierce surge of protectiveness go through me at the thought of anyone else walking by and seeing her so vulnerable. Later, when she pulled herself back together, it would make her mortification about this that much worse. I rearranged myself as I sat down, trying to block the view of her from anyone coming down the hall. When I reached out to her, she didn't stop me.

"You and Cate, you won't even say his name," she said, "I want to talk about him, but you keep trying to box him up and put him away."

"I know you think I don't care." My chest felt unbearably tight. "It's just . . . if I don't hold these things in, I feel like I'll dissolve. But you, all of you . . . the only thing I've ever wanted was to keep us all together and safe, and I can't ever manage to do that."

"Them, you mean." Vida hugged her knees to her chest. "I get it. They're your people."

"And you're not?" I asked. "There's no ranking of who I care about most. I couldn't do it even if I tried."

"Well if the building was on fire, who would you save first?"

"Vida!"

She rolled her eyes, wiping her face. "Oh, calm down, boo. I was just kidding. Obviously it wouldn't be me. I can take care of my own damn business."

"I know," I said. "I don't know who I'd try to save first, but if I had to pick someone to back me up on the rescue, there wouldn't be any question."

She shrugged and after a while said quietly, "The thought of going back into that room makes me . . . I know this is going to make me sound like I'm on crack, but I keep walking into rooms and I keep looking for him like he's going to be there. It's like a punch to the goddamn throat when I catch myself."

"I do that, too," I said. "I keep waiting for him to come around each corner."

"It is a stupid, fucking awful place I'm in," she said, "to be jealous of that little girl and you and all of them, that you get to all be together when it's never going to be that way again for us. You can't even *look* at Nico—God, Ruby, what's it going to take for you to stop punishing him? When do you start listening to his apologies?"

"When I have a chance of believing them."

She gave me a hard look. "Jude was his only friend. Nothing

you could do to him is worse than what he's doing to himself. Cate's not going to be able to pull him back from this again. This is worse than when they first brought him into HQ, after he got out of that research program where they did all of that shitty experimenting on him."

I took a deep breath. "I'm sorry I left you to tell Cate alone . . ."

"No," she said, holding up a finger, "be sorry that you've been too chickenshit to really talk to her about it. I don't understand—I don't get why everyone I care about is in fucking pieces and none of you will even try to help each other because it hurts too much to face it head-on. Jude would never have let this happen. He wouldn't have. He was the best of us."

It was amazing, you know, how Jude had pinned us all down, how deeply he had read into who we were and what we wanted. There were people in the world whose purpose seemed to be to serve as points of connection. They opened us up to each other, and to ourselves. What was it that he had told me? That he didn't want to just know someone's face, but their shadow, too?

"He was." There would never be another person like him. There was the loss I felt, and the loss that the rest of the world would never realize. Both sat like stones on top of my chest.

"I'm not good at huggy shit," Vida warned. "But if you want to talk like this again . . . I'm there. Okay?"

"Okay." And I don't know why that moment about did me in, when every moment before had been just as gutting. I leaned my shoulder and head against the wall. Maybe because I knew how proud of us he would have been for coming this far, and saying this much.

"Talk to Nico, please," Vida said. "Don't make me beg. Don't treat him like he's not even goddamn human."

"I think I hate him," I whispered.

"He made a mistake. We all did."

I leaned back on my hands, fingers curling against the cold tile.

"Did they mess with her?" Vida asked suddenly, holding out an arm to stop me. While she didn't whisper the question, the fact she wasn't asking directly in front of Zu seemed to indicate some newfound sensitivity. "Scramble some eggs up here or something?"

Or not.

"No," I said quietly, watching as Liam settled in next to her, running a hand over her hair. "She doesn't want to talk, so we don't make her. It's her decision."

Vida nodded, absorbing this. "Must have seen some shit then. Some real bad shit."

"Stop pushing her on it, okay? She's had every other choice taken away from her. She at least gets to choose what she wants to say, and when she says it."

I turned at the sound of soft footsteps padding up behind us. Zu hung back, her hands tucked into her pockets until Vida waved her toward us. She waited until Zu was looking at her before saying, "My bad, Z. I shouldn't have gone bitch on you. We cool?"

Some of the strain on the girl's face faded. She stuck her hand out to shake, but Vida gave her a little fist bump instead.

"All right," I said, forcing my stiff body up off the floor. "Should we go back? The boys are probably wondering where we are."

"Let 'em wonder," Vida said. "We've got some catching up to do."

EIGHT

THE HALLWAY WAS WASHED OUT IN A FAMILIAR SHADE of red, one that seemed to glow in an unsettling way. It grew brighter, pulsing as I took another step forward, glancing at the framed photos that lined each side of the otherwise bare walls around me. There were faces there I recognized, I remembered: that young agent who'd been killed escaping custody after an Op gone wrong. The woman who'd been picked up just as she was going to meet a contact—shoved into a dark van, and never heard from again.

I ran my hand under the photos, counting them off in twos, then threes. Dead. This is where the League marked the lives it'd sacrificed, and remembered the bodies that would never get graves. So many—so many men and women who'd died before I ever joined up. Almost eight years of death.

My fingers stilled under the unsmiling face of Blake Johnson. He looked . . . small. Young. It might have been because he was surrounded by older faces, or maybe the shot had been taken when the League first brought him in. That had to be it. He had looked so much more grown-up when he'd gone out on the Op that'd killed him, hadn't he? Why was there such a difference between the face of a fourteen-year-old and a sixteen-year-old?

Something warm and wet hit my toes. A thin line of black liquid, like ink, was gathering there, soaking my skin. Staining it. That tiny rivulet was the product of four separate, winding streams sliding down the tiled hall. My hand knocked against the next picture as I braced myself, and there was a sharp, white-hot pain in my palm that finally forced me to look up. The last dozen pictures were cracked, their frames hammered together with what looked like twisted pieces of metal and shards of glass.

The red light burned brighter, dimmed, and burned again. Over and over. I raised a hand to shield my eyes, but it was only an EXIT sign. At the next swell of light, I saw the black ink had a source, a growing pool. I saw it wasn't black ink at all.

The figure was facedown, both arms and legs twisted at a strange angle. It was a—it was a boy, all thin limbs. Big hands, big feet, as if he hadn't quite grown into them yet. Puppy paws, Cate had called them once. The light faded over him again as I rushed forward, and brightened just enough for me to see it was Jude.

The blood was everywhere, streaking his face, his hands, his broken back. I was screaming, screaming, screaming, because his eyes were open, his mouth was turned down into the pool of it, but his lips were moving. He shook, his body giving those last involuntary jerks—

Two hands clamped down on my upper arms, ripping me out of that hallway and into another. No—*oh God*—he needed help, I needed to help him—

My mind came awake with a surge, so quickly I thought I

was actually going to be sick. I spun, my legs disappearing under me, but someone held me up. My teeth knocked together as I was shaken back into reality.

"Easy—easy!" Southern—Liam? No, Cole. His anxious face came into focus. The lights overhead were pure, unwavering white, with more light from small windows at either end of the hall. I focused on the pane of glass behind his head, where I could see a variety of weights, treadmills, and mats. *Gym.* Cole's face was beaded with sweat, his skin was flushed, because he'd been in the gym. But I hadn't walked here. I hadn't come to find him. I hadn't left—

Cole drew me forward into the training room. The air conditioning was running at full throttle, instantly cooling the patches of sweat on my back and under my arms. He lowered me down onto one of the benches and disappeared for a second, returning with a small towel and a paper cup of water.

I hadn't realized I was shaking until I tried to drink. Cole took my left hand and pressed the towel against my palm. I looked down, surprised to find streaks of fresh blood running down my wrist, into the crook of my elbow. It was all over my jeans and shirt.

I jumped up, or at least tried to. My mind narrowed in on the image of Jude, the way the red light had turned his blood black. But this was—this wasn't his blood, was it? This wasn't HQ. This wasn't Los Angeles.

We had left Jude in Los Angeles.

"Do you know where you are?" Cole asked, crouching down in front of me. He waited for me to nod before continuing. "I'm sorry to wake you up the way I did, I know you're not supposed to, but I saw you pass by and then you started screaming. I didn't realize you had those kinds of pipes, kid."

I barely heard him. "I was . . . sleepwalking?"

"Seems like it," he said, not unkindly. "What did you cut your hand on?"

I shrugged, my throat aching. "What time is it?"

"It's about five in the morning." The lines around Cole's mouth were so much more pronounced. Now that the flush was fading from his face, the shadows were returning—under his eyes, under his high cheekbones, the new beard growth along his jaw. "You made off with about five hours of sleep."

"More than you," I pointed out.

"Yeah, well, I decided to try running from my nightmares instead of diving into them headfirst." The screen on the treadmill he'd been using was still flashing, paused. "Got too much adrenaline. Too many thoughts knocking around my skull. Energy to burn."

I finally came back fully into the present when my ears picked up the soft voice of a broadcaster coming from the TV bolted to the wall. The room's smell flooded my nose: plastic, sweat, and metal finally driving out the stench of blood.

Cole gave me a shrewd look, studying me for a moment with a look like he recognized something in me I didn't necessarily know was there myself. Unlike Cate, unlike Liam, unlike Chubs—unlike Jude—he simply let what had happened drop at our feet. There was no pressing about how I was feeling or what I'd seen, and that was exactly what I wanted. To push it behind me and leave it there.

He pulled the towel away from my palm, inspecting the cut.

"Looks pretty shallow," he announced, rising to his feet.

"Already healing. It'll probably sting like a bitch for a while, though." Finished with me, he lifted his shirt to wipe the sweat from his face, giving me a flash of toned skin I hadn't asked for.

I looked away. "Are you here every morning?"

"All two days we've been here," he said, amused. "Trying to get my ass back in shape. It's been a while since I trained. Helps, too, to get the . . ." He made a vague gesture with his hand. "To blow off steam."

"I miss it," I heard myself say, "feeling strong. I just feel like we know where we're going. You and me. But I can't shake the feeling that I'm just spinning and spinning and spinning waiting to get there. And *dammit*—the research on the cause of IAAN, I can't get over what a goddamn waste it is that, after everything, we can't even have *that*. I used to be able to handle things. I'm not . . ." I lifted my hand. "Obviously that's not the case these days."

"Yeah, and what are you going to do about it?" Cole tucked his arms against his chest. "You recognize the problem, how are you going to fix it? Stop thinking about the flash drive, the cause. Don't waste your energy on regret or self-pity. If that road is closed to us, we'll focus on figuring out the cure. So, again, tell me: what are you going to do about it?"

"Train," I said. "We'll have to train all of the kids. We're going to need them to be able to fight."

"You're not training anyone until you get yourself in shape."

"Was that an offer?"

A slow smile spread across his face. "Why? Think your monster can keep up with mine?"

I thought mine could run circles around his. Tie his into knots.

"There's no simple fix, if that's what you're thinking," Cole said, tilting his head toward the treadmill. "I get strong and I get fast, so if I can't fight the monsters off, at least I can run them out of my head for a little while. When was the last time you trained seriously?"

"Before . . ." Jesus, when was the last time? A week before I left to find Liam? The training at HQ had been brutal at first, the very definition of an uphill battle—one that was fought with limp, weak limbs. I'd had blisters on my feet and the heels of my palms, and the endless string of bruises had made me look like I'd been in a major car accident. The pain had flared and pulled and twisted me, like it was reshaping my body to its own standards.

Most of the kids had been in the program long enough to hone their bodies for Ops at the same time they were trying to sharpen their Psi skills. It meant weightlifting and cardio every other day, with self-defense, kickboxing, and weapons training thrown into the mix for variety. When you're working that hard, you're focusing on every movement your body is making, trying to train each and every muscle to be as sharp as a knife. You get out of your head for a little while.

There had been a window of time when it had all come together for me—I'd been strong, mentally and physically, and more than a little driven to see each Op through. And somehow, in the process of looking for Liam, I'd managed to lose that piece of myself. I'd let the doubt back in, the insecurity. I'd lost control of myself.

"I want to be pushed harder than the instructors worked us," I told him. "I can't keep falling apart and waiting for everyone around me to put the broken pieces back together. I want to take care of everyone."

Cole held up his hands. "I get it."

"You don't," I said, hating the edge of desperation in my voice. "It's like every time I turn a corner, I find myself right back in that tunnel with all the walls collapsing, and it feels like—"

"No." Cole stood. "We're not going to sit around, holding hands, and use the Cate Conner method of coping—art therapy with finger painting." He crossed the room in two long strides and dug through a blue plastic bin to retrieve an old, worn pair of sparring gloves. He tossed them my way.

Cole crossed his arms but didn't relax his posture in the slightest. I slid them on without hesitation or consideration for my hand and was rewarded with a nod of approval that warmed me at my center. If I was ready, he was ready.

He pulled out a pair of gloves for himself. There was a stretch of black mats on the far side of the room, and I crossed over to them. Plastic, sweat, rubber—it was a familiar smell. I took in a deep breath of it and set my stance, letting my weight sink into what little give the mats offered.

"Just so you know," Cole said, knocking his gloved hands together as he turned around, "getting strong means taking hits. A lot of them. You ever act like it's too much, or you can't get your ass off the ground, then this is over."

"Fine," I said. "As long as you don't pull back because you think I can't take it."

He snorted. "And Gem? One last thing. You don't tell anyone what we're doing. Not Conner, not Vida, not Lee, not any of them."

Who the hell cared if we trained together?

"Let's see if you can actually hit me first," I taunted, but his eyes were still grave, darkened by something I didn't understand. "Are you embarrassed or something?"

"Let's just say, I doubt they'd approve of this method of

coping," he said, one foot sliding back, his hands up to guard his face. His voice was so quiet, I almost didn't hear it. "They don't burn, do they? Not like us."

His fist flew out and clipped the side of my temple. I staggered back, but stayed on my feet. Anger—at myself for not paying attention, at the flash of pain—flooded through me. His lips twisted into a smile as I threw an arm out toward him, and he stopped, correcting the motion, forcing me to do it again and again until I landed the hit the exact way he wanted me to. Cole gave a playful punch to my shoulder, and was still grinning when he lashed a foot out and I caught it with mine. He bounced back, driving another hit to my center.

Minutes flew by, and I seemed to move with them. My body's muscles remembered how to fight, even if my heart had bowed out of the game. A hot rush of exhilaration went through me as I blocked a blow and landed a hit square in his stomach. His breath escaped in half a laugh, half a gasp of pain. By the time he remembered he was supposed to be teaching me, we were already flat on our backs on the mats, trying to catch our breath.

No, I thought, reaching up to wipe the sweat-slick hair out of my eyes. *Not like us.*

Hours later, with my muscles like jelly and the fog of my nightmare cleared from my mind, we gathered in the rec room to officially begin planning the camp hits.

I surveyed our group, including one last, newly arrived car, which had rolled in while I was rinsing off in the showers after training with Cole. The kids, all four of them, were valiantly fighting through their exhaustion, explaining that they'd been held up by car problems, when Cole strolled in behind me and gave me a gentle push forward, toward the circle of kids sitting on the floor. I reared back slightly, confused, but his smile was encouraging. "It's just what we talked about, remember? Give them the rundown."

"Shouldn't you—"

"No, it should be you." He nudged me toward them again, ignoring the narrow expression on Chubs's face. "Go get 'em, Gem."

Make them love you. . . . I shook my head, ignoring the purr of Clancy's voice in my ear. Zu scooted back and motioned for Hina and Tommy to do the same, opening the circle.

"So this . . ." I began, only to catch myself. Suddenly, it wasn't about the faces that were there, but the ones that weren't. I turned to Chubs, who was plucking at a hole in his jeans, the perfect picture of forced nonchalance. "Where's Liam? And Kylie . . . and James?"

"They must be in the bathroom," he managed to squeeze out, his voice unnaturally high. Then, all of a sudden, no one could look at me. Not even Zu.

You didn't, Liam, I thought, fighting against the steady rise of panic. *Tell me you didn't rush out to get supplies without even taking a weapon to protect yourself.*

"They left," a small voice whispered. I looked around but didn't catch who it had come from.

"Who left?" Cole said, catching the tail end of this. "One of—"

I knew the moment that he spotted who, exactly, was missing. He went still, his expression controlled and blank. It was the look of someone just before they calmly and methodically stabbed someone.

"Why did they leave?" I asked.

145

"So we would have something to eat today!" Chubs snapped.

"Where did they go?" I had to keep myself from shouting, from reaching over and shaking him as hard as I could.

"The next town over," Lucy said. "They promised they'd be back in an hour."

"Did they." Cole ground the words out. "Well. If they get their asses killed, that'll at least bring the average IQ of this place up. Do *not*"—he addressed the whole group now—"go outside until you've had the training you need to survive, and until we're stocked with weapons. I'm going to take care of everything, and we're going to take care of each other, but you have to listen to what I tell you, otherwise this won't work. All right, guys?"

Several nods. Several affirmative noises.

"Okay," I said. *Dammit, Liam. What were you thinking?* "All right." I forced my mind to click back onto the right track. "The first thing you need to know is that the flash drive containing the research Cole stole from Leda Corp, about whatever caused IAAN, was wiped by the EMP."

Vida must have told Chubs and Zu this, because they didn't look nearly as rattled as the others did. Seeing their faces, a sharp stab of hopelessness hit me at my center. I pushed past it again, aware of Cole's eyes on my back.

"There's no way to get it back?" Tommy asked.

"No," Nico said. "We've tried everything. The files are gone."

"We still have the research on the *cure*, though," I said quickly. The Greens had copied it down again and uploaded it into our lone laptop. All fifteen indecipherable pages of it. "And we'll work from there. But in the meantime, I think we should move forward with freeing the camps—it's the right thing to do, and our strongest strategy to hold Gray accountable for what's happened to us.

But I—we—" I motioned back to Cole, "there's no way we can do this alone. So I have to ask, are you guys with us? It's okay if you're afraid, or you don't want to participate in the Ops. It really is, and it's nothing to be ashamed of. There's so much to do here that you'll still be a part of it. Or, once it's a little safer, we can find a way for you to go home to your parents."

I waited until they were nodding, or had voiced their consent. "The best way to do this, then, is to think through a potential plan for a camp hit together. Can we break up into smaller groups, maybe four or five kids each, and just start thinking about how we could pull something like this off—it doesn't matter if it seems crazy, or if we don't have the materials we need now. Just be creative and we'll run from there."

I let them divvy themselves up, and was proud of the way they mixed the old League teams and the new arrivals we'd picked up along with Zu. Cole slapped a hand on my shoulder, grinning his approval, as he began making his rounds. I smiled back, feeling light enough to jump from the floor to the rafters above.

And just like that, the sensation was gone. A silent, heavy presence came up behind me, falling over me like a shadow. I didn't need to turn to know it was Chubs. Irritation crept in the longer he punished me with that oppressive silence. I turned away, watching Vida perched like a queen in the middle of a group containing Tommy, Pat, and two other League kids. They crowned her with praise and wonder and adoration for a good three minutes before she deigned to give her input to their proposal.

"When are you going to start looping us in on these things earlier?" Chubs finally asked. "It feels like you're springing things on us because you know we'll disagree with something."

I blew out the breath I'd been holding through my nostrils,

returning his hard stare with one of my own. "It sounds like the real issue here is that you don't trust me to make good calls without you."

Cole had warned me this would happen—he'd told me that I had too many voices weighing in on my choices, and that was why I never felt fully secure in making them. They'd told me over and over that they trusted me, that they had faith. Clearly that wasn't actually the case.

"Why did you let Liam go out?" I demanded. "He wasn't even armed."

He threw his hands up into the air. "They're freaking Blues! Oh my God, Ruby, you have to—look, never mind, it's not—"

"I have to what?"

Chubs gave me a narrow look, one I turned right back on him.

"Okay, look," he said, beginning with a deep breath. "However you want to define what's between you and Lee, that's none of my business. And, honestly, it's stressful trying to keep up with the circles you run around each other. It *becomes* my business when one of my best friends starts treating the other the way you've been treating him lately."

"What do you mean?"

"Holding him at arm's length. You're just . . . here, but not here, you know?" he said. "Even when you're with us, you're not even really present. You zone out, you dodge topics, you *hold back*. And every once in a while you'll just . . . disappear. Is there something else you're not telling us?"

"You've been so busy picking apart everything I do, but you don't seem to have any idea what that is. I'm *disappearing*?" I said. "Try *training*, to make sure I don't make an ass out of myself getting these kids in shape. Try *planning*, to make sure no one gets hurt or killed. Try dealing with Clancy, because no one else can."

My voice had dropped to a furious whisper and the force of it had clearly stunned him. He reached out, taking my shoulder, his expression going soft as mine went hard. I hated the way he was studying me.

"I just want you to talk to us," he said. "I know it can't be like before, but I miss it. I miss . . ." Chubs shook his head. "I didn't mean to jump down your throat."

"Well, you did," I said with a sigh.

"Because you needed to hear it from someone," Chubs said. "From my perspective, you've thrown your hat in with the Asshole Brother—which, fine. But don't forget who's been pushing for these camp hits to happen basically from the second we arrived at East River. Don't you remember? Liam thought he had it all figured out and was all Lee-like because he was working and making a difference and seeing some kind of result in the kids around him. You have to let him *do* something, Ruby. What I want to know is, are you upset that Liam went out without getting your permission?"

I shook my head in disbelief, thoughts as tangled as my feelings. "Because it's dangerous! Because he could be captured or killed! And I can't—" The words choked off and I was surprised by the rush of emotion that slammed into me. Frustration, anger, and, above all, fear. "I can't lose another person. . . ."

Chubs let out a long breath and tucked me into his arms, giving me his usual awkward-but-caring pats. I pressed my hands against his back, holding him tighter, remembering the rush of elation I'd felt when I'd seen him for the first time in months and finally known that he'd survived. The texture of the memory had changed, becoming like a fading sunbeam. He wasn't saying any of this to be accusatory or cruel; he just wanted us to be safe and together, but he wasn't thinking that far into the future. Chubs's whole focus was on our little circle, but mine couldn't be, not anymore. I had fight against that instinct and consider *everyone*.

"He's just one person, I know, but he's *our* person," he said, like he'd read my thoughts. "And, the truth is, I think we need to be focused on Zu. We have to try to get the full story out of her about what happened to that guy she was traveling with. I don't think it's going to be as simple as waiting until she's ready to talk about it."

I nodded, leaning back against the wall, watching her as she sat between Hina and Lucy. Her eyes were focused on the floor, her hands folded neatly in her lap, her legs tucked under her.

"It wasn't a mistake to bring them here, was it?" I asked. "The young ones? I won't let them fight, but I can't shake the feeling that this is going to hurt them in ways I can't see yet."

"We can't protect them from this, not if we're determined to give them a choice. That's what this is really about, isn't it? Giving them and the next wave of kids a shot at a better life than what we had. To come out of hiding."

Yes—that was it exactly. The freedom that came hand-in-hand with being able to make choices about our lives once our abilities were gone. The freedom to live where we wanted to, with whomever we wanted to, and to not be scared of every passing shadow. For kids not to grow up with the fear that one day they might not wake from their sleep, or that they'd blink out like a light bulb in the middle of an otherwise normal day.

I knew, just as Cole did, that the only way we were going to come out of the other side of this successfully was through force. A real fight. But the cost . . . I looked around again, taking in the sight of their animated faces, and tried to absorb their faint chatter and laughter to ease the grip of fear around my ribs. I couldn't have both, could I? I couldn't get my battle without acknowledging that there was a damn decent chance that not all of these kids would live to benefit from winning.

"I want it so bad, Ruby. I want to go home, see my parents, and walk around my neighborhood in broad daylight. I want to go to *school*, so even if they hold my abilities over me, they can't deny me things because I'm not educated. That's enough for me. I know it's not going to be easy, and I know I'm going to be lucky to make it through alive, but it's worth it, if I can just have that." Chubs was quiet for a moment before saying, quietly, "Everything will be worth it, and we're going to be around to see it."

"That's not very Team Reality of you."

His smile matched mine. "Screw Team Reality—I'm leaving to join Team Sanity."

An hour later, Liam and the others appeared at the entrance to the tunnel, each dragging in a large cardboard box or plastic tub. Their voices carried down the long pathway, bubbling over with excitement. Clearly they didn't know what was waiting for them at the other end.

Liam appeared first, his face and hands covered in a fine layer of dust, his hair hopelessly mussed by the growling windstorm outside. The sight of him, tousled and laughing and looking so happy, made me forget why I'd been so angry in the first place.

It didn't have the same effect on his brother.

Cole was on his feet, bracing his shoulder against the wall to the right of the entrance. He hadn't said a word, but his breathing had grown harsher over the last hour. Even with his arms crossed over his chest, he couldn't hide the way his fingers on his right hand were convulsing every few minutes. It was one spark away from explosion, I saw that clear enough.

And still, I wasn't fast enough jumping up to my feet.

Liam had a half second of joy to see me sitting there, and then Cole had him. His arm shot out, gripping him by the front of his shirt and whirling him around to slam him up against the wall. The box in Liam's hands crashed to the ground, sending the cans and bags inside skidding in every direction. A bright red box of Lucky Charms cereal slid right over to me, stopping just short of my feet.

"Jesus *Christ*—" Liam choked out, but Cole was already hauling him away, into Alban's old office. I caught the door before it was kicked shut in my face. Liam was practically thrown into the large, scuffed desk.

"What the *hell* is your problem?" Liam gasped, still winded. Cole had a few inches on his brother, but Liam's anger seemed to stretch his spine and even out the difference. They never looked more alike than they did right then, seconds away from ripping each other's heads off.

"My 'problem'? Try finding out a kid's gone out to get himself and two other kids killed! Are you really that stupid?" Cole rounded on him, cutting a furious hand through the air. "I hope it was worth it. I hope you got to feel good about pretending to be a hero again, because you just jeopardized the whole operation!

Someone could have followed you back to us—someone could be monitoring the building right now!"

Liam's temper finally broke over him. He shoved Cole back against the empty bookshelf behind him and pinned him there with an arm barred across his chest. "Play the hero? You mean what you've been doing this whole damn time? Walking around, barking out orders like you have *any* right to lead these kids. Like you know how they feel or what they've been through?"

Cole let out a derisive laugh and for a moment, I really thought he'd tell his brother his secret, if only to throw it all back in Liam's face. Get the shocked and horrified reaction he'd been afraid of for so long.

"I got it done," spat Liam. "We weren't followed, no one ever saw us. I've done this a hundred times, in a hell of a lot worse places, and each time I got it done—which I would have *told* you if you'd treated me like I was capable of doing something besides sitting around with my thumb up my ass, waiting for someone to take care of me!"

He was right. Of anyone here, he had the most experience doing this kind of hit. The security team at East River had kept everyone fed and stocked with medicine and clothes simply by preying on truck shipments along a nearby highway.

"Why are you acting like you actually care?" Liam pressed, his voice edged with frustration. "You ignore my existence for years, going around thinking—"

"You have no idea what I'm thinking," Cole snarled, finally throwing him off. "You want to know? Really? I'll tell you—it was *how am I going to tell Mom another one of her kids is dead?*"

The words seemed to suck every last trace of air out of the

room. The color in Liam's face drained, and his clenched jaw went utterly slack.

"You made me tell her, remember that? You couldn't stop crying, couldn't even leave Claire's room. I had to go downstairs and stop her, because she was already making her sandwich and getting her lunch bag ready for school."

I pressed a hand over my mouth; the image was too painful for me to even bring to mind. Liam stumbled back, blindly bumping into the desk. His hand caught the edge of it, and it was enough to keep him upright. I saw his face, stricken, only for a moment. It disappeared again behind his hands. "Sorry—God, I'm sorry, I didn't think—I just wanted to *do* something—"

After seeing so many varying shades of his anger, I was surprised to see that Cole could turn his voice and face so frighteningly cold. "The only reason you're here is because I don't know where the hell Mom and Harry have holed up, and I can't ship you straight to them—*what?*"

Liam had always been an easy read; every thought that passed through his mind at some point or another registered on his face. It had been so easy, even for a damaged girl terrified out of her mind, to trust that what he said, he meant—that when he offered something to you, it was only with the purest intention of wanting to give it to you, no catches, no takebacks, no favors. I used to wonder how painful it would be to have a heart that felt things so deeply, even the most secret of things could never fully be contained.

I just wished like hell he hadn't looked up at the mention of their parents. Because the moment Cole saw his face, he knew. And so did I.

Liam didn't tell Cole, I thought, unable to understand it. Liam

154

and Cole had both known their mother and stepfather had assumed fake names, Della and Jim Goodkind, when they went into hiding and left their home in North Carolina, but searching online and through phone books had brought up dead end after dead end. Cole should have been the first person he told after Zu told us how she'd met their mother. Liam should have stood up from the table and gone to find his brother immediately—

"You know!" This time Cole did hit him, the icy demeanor shattering as he landed a blow on Liam's chin. "You lied to my goddamn face! *Where are they?*"

"Cut it out!" I shouted. "Stop it, both of you!"

Liam lurched toward him. I saw his arm pull back, the glint in Cole's eyes, and shot forward. I slid between them just as Liam threw his punch, barely blocking it before it collided with Cole's stomach. There was a single instant he seemed to strain against it, still struggling to land the hit—and then he came back to himself, to the moment. I saw it happen; the anguish and resentment released with a sharp inhalation and a horrified look. I had to grab a fistful of his shirt to prevent his immediate instinct toward a panicked escape. The other hand was thrown out toward Cole, to warn him off moving.

"Oh my God," Liam said hoarsely, "why did you—that was so stupid—"

I unclenched my fingers, sliding my hand around to his back as I stepped in close to his side. He was still breathing hard, fighting to keep his emotions from boiling over again. I should have realized how quickly shame would work its way through him. He wasn't a fighter, not by nature. Dammit—the thought of hurting anyone he cared about would do far more damage to him than Cole's fist ever could have.

"Liam should be quartermaster," I said.

Cole crossed his arms over his chest. "That's—"

"A great idea," I said. "You're welcome. He does know where your parents are, and will happily fill you in on the details now."

"As a trade?" Cole shook his head, giving his brother a dubious look. "Do you even know what a quartermaster is?"

"Of course I do," Liam said between gritted teeth. "I know you try to forget, but I was part of the League for a few months."

"It's not a trade," I said. "It's because he'll do the best job out of anyone here. It's a role that needs to be filled, fast. It's because you're brothers and you love each other, and should respect each other's capabilities and focus your energy on the actual fight in front of us, not each other. Am I wrong?"

"Gem, it has never been more obvious than now that you're an only child. The joys of siblinghood have never played well with logic."

It was a huge job to track our supplies and bear the responsibility for figuring out how to bring new ones in; I would have stopped to second-guess the decision if I hadn't seen with my own eyes that he could manage it.

"Cole," I said softly, making Liam tense all over again. "He's already been doing it."

"It's not a matter of whether or not he can do it, but if he deserves it," Cole fired back. "He disobeyed a direct order not to leave the premises and he acted without permission."

"Oh, right, I forgot, you elected yourself leader," Liam said, and the ugliness in his voice made me actually cringe. "So glad we got a vote on that. What, were you afraid someone would question why you had any qualifications for the job? What you knew about us and our lives? Or was that another decision the two of you made and kept from the rest of us, hoping we'd all just nod and trail behind you like little mice?"

I stepped away from him, stung more by his tone than his words. Cole had the opposite response—he came closer, stepping right up into his brother's face. To his credit, Liam didn't flinch. Not until Cole said, "My qualifications? Try not getting a hundred and five kids killed with a naively planned and poorly executed escape attempt from a camp that wasn't even that bad in the first place."

"Out of line," I warned Cole, feeling my own temper flare now. "The fact that you consider *any* camp to be 'not even that bad' shows you have no idea what you're talking about. The two of you—"

"You want to punish me," Liam cut me off, pushing me back from where I'd stepped between them. A wash of furious red worked its way up his neck to his face. Both he and his voice were shaking. "Fine. Name it. If you want to throw your weight around, just do it. I'm done with you wasting my time."

I sent a sharp look of warning to Cole, but he was already saying, "Clean the bathrooms. With bleach."

I'd seen Cole wear a smirk countless times at this point, but I'd never seen it on Liam's face. That baiting, haughty look. "It's already done."

"Clear out the backup in the sewage system."

"Already done."

"Laundry. A month. By yourself."

"You let them steal all of the sheets and towels," Liam said, "in case you managed to forget."

Cole released a loud breath through his nostrils, his eyes narrowing. Something clearly clicked, because his mouth tensed into a tight-lipped smile. "Then you can clean out and organize the garage."

I whirled back toward him, confused. "The what?"

He didn't say anything else, just strode to the door and held it open. I caught Liam watching my reaction out of the corner of my eye as he went first, but the only thing I saw as we followed Cole downstairs was his back. He kept two steps ahead of me the entire time and didn't once turn to make sure I was still there. The unnerved feeling I had expanded into confusion as we moved through the kitchen; I could see my pale face reflected in the stainless steel surfaces as we passed by the sinks, stove, oven, and finally the pantry, until we hit the wall of metal shelves used to store pots, pans, and baking sheets.

The muscles in Cole's arms flexed as he dragged the shelves away from the wall. The metal protested against the linoleum they'd used to tile the floor, but once the shelves were set aside, I had a clear view of what it had been hiding.

"Really?" I said, exasperated. "Another hidden door?"

Liam finally looked at me, brows lifting. "There are others?"

"It's not *hidden*," Cole said, stepping into the dark hall. He felt along the wall until the lights flickered on, revealing yet another damp, concrete tunnel. "We stopped using the space and just . . . left it alone. I'm thinking this will be our emergency exit. It'll be important to make sure the kids know where it is."

"What was it used for before?" I asked, more to fill the silence than anything. I was walking between them, eyes tracking Cole's powerful, purposeful strides forward, the way his wide shoulders moved beneath his shirt. My mind was on Liam, though, the way frustration seemed to pour off him, clouding the air around us.

He trailed behind me now, and I felt his eyes working over me as clearly as if he'd reached out and tugged my braid. Our shuffling steps and breathing echoed around us, and somehow were amplified by an unpleasant feeling that the two of them were one scathing word away from slamming each other up against the wall and beating one another senseless.

"We used it to run Op simulations, which is one reason it needs to be cleared out—any strike against a camp has to be worked through and choreographed," Cole explained. "Then it became a kind of storage unit for all the crap we acquired over the years."

"Fantastic," Liam muttered. "I don't suppose there's anything actually useful in there?"

Cole shrugged. "Guess you're going to find out, baby brother."

In response, Liam only grunted.

I reached back, slowing my steps, suddenly unable to escape the thought that it was me he was angriest at—that Liam would feel like I hadn't stood up for him enough upstairs, that not telling him about Cole's and my plan had hurt him more deeply than I'd expected. I reached back for his hand, wanting the security of his touch, to comfort him, apologize, to just . . . be, and be with him next to me. I hadn't even looked to see that he was okay; he was mentally banged up now, but I hadn't checked for bruises, bumps, cuts.

And . . . nothing. My hand hung in the cold air. Nothing. God, he *was* mad, furious maybe. A painful knot formed in my chest and I pulled my hand back, drawing it closer to my side in a last-ditch effort to protect myself from the raw feeling of rejection.

Liam caught my fingers, but instead of weaving his through mine, he pressed a kiss there and crossed the last two steps between us so we could walk next to each other. He looped an arm over my shoulder and didn't pull away when I stepped in closer to his side. I ran my hand along his back, up and down, up and down, until I felt the tight muscles there ease. When he looked down at me, his expression had softened enough that I felt the sudden urge to stand on my toes and press a soft, quick kiss to his jaw. So I did. He ducked his head, trying to hide his little, pleased smile. It was the first time I felt myself relax since he came strolling back in through the tunnel.

We're okay, I thought. *This is okay.*

In total, it was about a five-minute walk from one door to the other. Stairs waited for us at the other end, and I realized with a start that we were heading back aboveground. The door waiting at the top of the stairs looked to have been hammered out of solid metal, and though the door hadn't been locked, Cole still had to drive his shoulder into it in order to get it unstuck from its frame. He stumbled in with the force of his momentum.

The smirk on Liam's face fell away the moment we stepped inside.

It was clear we were standing in one of the nearby ware-houses—one of the many identical long, white buildings that seemed a dime a dozen in this part of Lodi. It looked to be roughly the same dimensions as the Ranch, but one level, and decidedly less livable—concrete, metal rafters. Windows lined the top of the wall, coated in dust and darkened by blackout sheets. The lights hanging from the rafters sputtered to life, illuminating the towering mounds of junk piled up around us.

There were no walls or offices, let alone heat or insulation from

160

what I could tell; it was simply an unfinished garage. There were a few actual cars inside—their stripped-down bodies, really, and all of them propped up on lifts. Liam walked toward the nearest one, crouching down to inspect the engine and innards on the floor beneath it. All of the tires and hubcaps seemed to be lining the loading-dock door, which had been secured several times over by metal chains and locks. For the most part, though, it was a bizarre assortment of things: broken bed frames, sleeping bags, bags of screws and nails. I moved to open one of the nearby garbage bags, half afraid of what I'd find inside, but it was only crumpled old clothes they'd probably ripped off from a donation drop-off.

The smell in here was vaguely sour, tinged with exhaust and oil. Dust flew thick and heavy, forcing me to wave it away from my face in order to breathe. There didn't seem to be any rhyme or reason to how the League had stacked and sorted. I felt the first spark of temper hit me and turned to find Cole walking across the building.

Liam stood, his hands on his hips, eyes lit with something I didn't understand. He didn't seem daunted in the slightest now that the initial shock had worn off. There was an eagerness in its place. Somehow, he was seeing something I wasn't—some sort of potential.

I mostly just saw red.

"This is a huge job!" I called after his brother. *"Cole!* He's not going to do it by himself."

"Obviously," Cole hollered back. "He's allowed to take some of the younger kids who won't be training. His bosom buddy—the one that always looks like he's got a bug up his ass."

I started after him. "They're not going to do this for you overnight—we should *all* be helping—!"

A clatter of metal against the concrete made me look back. Liam had moved on from the car to a nearby pile of bikes that were tangled together like brambles. He picked through frames and spokes and wheels, working carefully, trying to get down to whatever he'd seen under them. I stepped over a downed floor lamp to help him. I saw a flash of silver, then my fingers brushed against a tire. Liam let out a breathless laugh, working twice as fast now, his smile practically contagious.

"What is it?" I asked as we hauled it upright. "A dirt bike?"

He was vibrating with excitement, his hands flying over its sleek body, brushing away the dirt and dust. "Oh, man," he breathed out. "She's a beauty, isn't she?"

"I'll take your word for it. . . ." I said.

It looked like a hybrid of a dirt bike and a motorcycle. Apparently I wasn't that far off, because Liam explained, talking fast, "It's a dual-sport motorcycle. It has the capabilities of a dirt bike for off-roading, but see? It has mirrors and a speedometer for streets. It looks like it's a . . . yeah, a Suzuki. *Wow.* I'm kinda freaking out—"

"I know." I laughed. "I can tell. Do you think it'll actually run?"

Liam was inspecting it with reverent hands, stroking its every inch. "It looks like it's in decent shape. They beat the hell out of it, didn't treat her nice. Might be an easy fix." He looked up and saw my expression. "What?"

"Do you actually know how to ride?"

"Do I know how to ride?" Liam scoffed, leaning over the bike's seat so his face was inches from mine. His pale blue eyes were electric with his excitement; they sent a charge through me, dissolving the rest of the world into peaceful, quiet static. That last bit of distance must have been as unbearable to him as it was to me, because his fingers came down over where my hands rested on the busted leather seat. I felt his touch spread over my skin like late-afternoon sunshine. His lips skimmed my cheek, his breath warm against my ear as he said in low, honeyed tones, "Not only can I ride, darlin', but I can give you a few pointers—"

"Hey, Hell's Angels!" Cole barked. "I didn't bring you in here to shop around for yourselves! Get your asses over here!"

Liam's expression clouded over as he pulled back, the fluttering excitement vanishing like a candle blown out with a single breath. I must have looked as disappointed as I felt, letting out a small sound of irritation, because just like that he was smiling again as he tucked a loose strand of hair back over my ear. A softer, smaller smile than before, but one meant for me. It warmed me down to my bones.

After a moment of making sure the kickstand would hold the dirtbike up, he used his shirt to wipe the grime from his hands. I took the hand he offered, giving it a squeeze. With one last glance over his shoulder at his find, we made our way to where Cole stood in front of a towering stack of pallets. We were right behind him when I finally made the connection and realized what we were looking at.

I'd seen cardboard boxes like this before, and recognized the phrasing printed along the outside: 10 x 24 HOURS RATIONS GP NATO/ OTAN APPROVED.

"What are we looking at, exactly?" Liam asked.

"Humanitarian rations," I said, cutting Cole off. I felt hollow at the sight. "Do you know what country they're from?"

"You've seen these before?" Cole asked, brows raised. "The government has this stuff under lock and key. They didn't take any of this crap to HQ, either."

163

"It was in . . ." I released Liam's hand, stepping closer to the boxes so I wouldn't have to see his face as I said, "It was when we were in Nashville. The military was housing food and medical supplies in an old airport hangar."

The raid was like a night tide in my memory. It constantly seeped up from the darkest corners of my mind to catch me off guard, lay me low. Liam, so pale as he struggled to breathe. The knife in my back. Jude's quiet bravery as he stepped out in front of all of us and sent electricity shooting toward the soldiers. Losing sight of the others. Rob. The muzzle. Blood on a broken windshield.

I turned my back on the boxes and pallets, but forced myself to stand still until the crushing weight lifted off my chest and I could breathe again. It was getting harder to outrun its reach.

"Okay," Liam said finally, "but where did *this* stuff come from? And how old is it?"

"A few years, but most of this stuff is nonperishable. Meant to last. I just forgot it was here until I saw an inventory list in the office." Cole pulled a small knife out of his back pocket and flicked the blade out. He gutted the box, letting the red, individually wrapped packages of food spill out at our feet. There was a simple image of a man bringing food to his mouth and a Chinese flag. "We heard rumors that the government was trying to hide humanitarian aid other countries were air-dropping—that whole 'we're America, we can do it ourselves, everyone else has abandoned us' bullshit. This load was left somewhere in Nevada."

"You never used them?" I asked.

"Never had to," Cole said. "We had food suppliers. Alban wanted it as evidence of how Gray was working against the public, but nothing ever came from it. This building is filled with half-baked ideas, lost trains of thought."

164

He shut his eyes, rubbing his forehead with the back of his hand. I saw the way his grim expression seemed to twist with pain in the second before he turned to Liam. "If you get this place in order, then, fine, consider yourself quartermaster. You can figure out a way to bring in supplies."

"Supplies meaning food, cleaning supplies, sundries," Liam said. "If you're thinking that I have a way of getting you guns—"

"No shit, kid," Cole interrupted. "We're going to have to work Senator Cruz's connections for gas, weapons, and the mountain of ammunition we'll need."

"Exactly how much do you think that'll be?" Liam asked, alarmed. "We're fighting, what? One or two key battles? Not a whole damn war."

"You worry your pretty little head about breakfast, lunch, and dinner," Cole fired back. "Let the big kids do the hard thinking."

I sent him a withering look he ignored, and he stooped to pick up one of the daily ration packs from the ground. He tossed it from hand to hand, his forehead creased in thought. "But it doesn't solve the bigger issue we have now. Based on the plans that are coming out of that room, we're going to need a lot more bodies working with us. Another two dozen kids at least for a camp hit. If you have any bright ideas on how to find 'em, I'm all ears."

A tired kind of resignation wove in and out of my thoughts, overriding the worst of my reservations. I must have sighed, because both of the Stewarts turned to me, mirror images of interest.

"Actually," I said, my voice betraying the unsettling certainty working its way through me, "I think I do."

NINE

WITH THE KIDS OCCUPIED WITH THEIR PLANNING, IT wasn't difficult to slip downstairs unnoticed. I didn't need to look over my shoulder again and again to ensure that no one was watching as I unlocked the door of the old file storage room and stepped inside.

It was how quickly my hand shot up to find the light fixture's cord dangling overhead, the way the darkness seemed to settle over my skin, that made me stop myself. My breathing sounded harsh to my ears, and it was the strangest sensation—feeling my body slip into panic while my mind sat far back, at a cool, reserved distance. My heart galloped, pounding out a beat that was too fast, too hard. Sounds that weren't there filled my ears, the world rolled up under me. Wasn't it just the way of the dark that with one sense gone, the others were amplified? The dark made small prickles of anxiety stretch and reshape to suit its needs, to trap you there, paralyzed. No wonder Jude had been so terrified of shadows.

In a space this small, it was easy to imagine there was no escape. The rational part of me knew that there was nothing to be afraid of. There were two doors, two outs, but the only way through the darkness was to lean into it and just *move*. I could tell myself a thousand times, but each time my whole self would feel the shock of it all over again—because the dark was where things were lost. It devoured everything good.

This is not Los Angeles. I pressed back against the memory of dust and smoke.

This is not the tunnel. I pressed back against Jude's face, his pleading voice.

This is now. I pressed and pressed and pressed.

I stayed there as long as I could physically stand it before tugging on the cord. The pale yellow light flooded the air around me, revealing the clouds of loose dust kicked up from the barren shelves. Rising, falling, spinning. I focused on that, until my breathing evened back out, and there was nothing to be afraid of besides the monster on the other side of the door.

It didn't matter how long I needed to refocus and steel myself; it was time well spent. Going in with scattered, distracted thoughts would be like walking into the room and handing Clancy Gray a loaded gun. And this time, I hadn't brought Cole back up with me.

He was flat on his back on the cot again, throwing something—a plastic sandwich bag crumpled into a ball—up into the air; catching it, throwing, catching, throwing, catching, all while whistling the cheeriest little tune. At the sound of the door's lock clicking back into place, he caught it one last time and craned his neck to look at me.

"I have a theory I'd like to have confirmed," he said. "The agents who were here left, didn't they?"

"They're around," I lied.

"Strange, then, that I haven't heard *them*. Just the kids." He pointed to the air vent above him by way of explanation. "They must have been gone before you even arrived. And the others—what, they abandoned you? Just didn't show up?"

My silence must have been confirmation enough.

"That's fantastic news." His voice was so genuine, so excited. "You're better off without them. Is the plan still to attack the camps? Did you find the information on Thurmond?"

There it was again. He kept dropping the same little bomb, waiting for me to pick it up, to agonize over it. I crossed my arms over my chest to hide the way my hands couldn't seem to stop trembling. *What about it? What's happening?*

"Clancy. You really want to pretend we're on the same team?"

"Aren't I basically the mascot?" he said, his mouth curving in an imitation of a smile. "Try to avoid insulting me if you're coming in here looking for me to do you a favor. Don't think for a second I don't know that you need me to help you track down more kids for your adorable little brigade. If you want the information, you'll have to retrieve it yourself."

My patience had been worn down to the width of dental floss in the span of two minutes. Clancy Gray got off on driving people to the edge and watching them throw themselves over, though, so I wasn't going to give him the pleasure. "Where did you leave the files? Colorado? Back in Virginia?"

"Not files, and closer than you think," he said, raising his eyebrows. "Come on, don't play dumb. You know exactly what I mean."

I did.

"You really are sick in the head," I told him. "You're just going to block me out. Is that how you're going to make yourself feel better about all of this? By watching me embarrass myself?"

"You seemed to manage breaking into my memories just fine in Colorado. And in that Los Angeles rathole you called HQ. Why no confidence now?" he taunted. I knew him better than he thought I did—*I'm bored*, is what he was really saying. *Entertain me.*

"I'm surprised you have confidence left," I said, "considering what happened in Los Angeles. I really loved seeing all of those precious memories of you and your mom. You were kind of a cry-baby, weren't you?"

His brows drew together, assessing. For a moment, I wished I hadn't brought up Lillian Gray; it was too early to signal to him that I had an interest in her, too early to so much as hint she was on my mind. I needed a strategy if I was going to try to suss out her location and what, precisely, her son had done to her.

I kept my expression neutral, my breathing even. *You've done it before, Ruby.* It was always easier to slide into someone's mind after I'd already created a path there. But both times, I'd had to catch him by surprise to do it—I'd been so damn furious in each case that if my hit had been physical and not mental, I was half-convinced I could have taken out a cement wall.

He blinked and I let the invisible hands unfurl at the back of my mind; by the time his dark, thick lashes were rising again and his gaze met mine, their nails had turned to hooks, waiting to latch on—

The block from Clancy felt like I'd slammed face-first into the glass wall between us. I cringed, fighting with everything I had not to bring a hand up to rub at the center of the pain right between my eyes. A dull headache flared to an outright, piercing throb.

"You're rusty," he said, surprised. "That was borderline pathetic. When was the last time you tried this?"

Shut up, I thought, trying to keep my pride in check.

Would you rather we talked like this? His voice bled through my mind, his lips never so much as twitching. He'd done this to me once before, at East River, as a friendly challenge—the sensation of it was exactly the same. It felt like there were a thousand moths trapped beneath my skin, their wings brushing and beating until I had the urge to scratch them out by force.

I *was* rusty, but there was a difference between being down and being out. Clancy had to constantly feed his confidence with moments like this in order to support the weight of his ego. I'd been counting on that trademark smugness, his unwillingness to accept that he was anything less than the most powerful person in the room. *Come on, asshole. . . .*

I wanted him to really believe, even for a moment, that my abilities weren't just like a muscle I hadn't flexed in weeks—I wanted him to think I was hopeless.

I shook my head, forcing what I hoped was a frustrated, upset expression onto my face. I had the advantage of him already assuming that his blow would be lethal to my own pride. I could see it in his face: he thought he was torturing me by forcing me to use my abilities, and he was enjoying the struggle, relishing the sight of me trying and failing.

That was one way to feel powerful while locked up behind three inches of bulletproof glass, I guess.

My abilities were practically purring inside my skull in anticipation. It took strength I didn't know I had not to laugh, to hold that look of fury and annoyance. I just needed a single moment of him being thrown off balance. Just one, but it was like finding a way to land a hit on a guy standing behind a cinder-block wall. As with any fistfight, though, however unfairly stacked it was in one corner, there were tricks. Dirty cheats.

I wasn't above it. Not by a long shot.

"Sorry, couldn't resist. Ready to go again?" Clancy crossed his arms over his chest, glaring at me from behind the glass. "My only request is that you actually pretend to try."

When he smiled again, I smiled right back.

This time I threw my abilities at him like a fist, aiming for the blank white curtain he threw up again to guard his thoughts. I slowed my assault, letting him sweep that same curtain forward to maneuver me right back out of his headspace. His own power brushed against mine like the soft stroke of knuckles against a cheek.

I reached over and unlocked the door to his cell, propping it open with my foot. Clancy jerked back, startled, and that great white nothing that had masked everything working behind his eyes lifted, just enough for me to slide into the twisting hallways of his mind. The colors were suddenly vivid as jewels—pristine emerald lawns, a home perched next to a sapphire sea, a flowing amethyst evening gown, camera flashes like the sun striking the surface of a diamond, dissolving the world in flashes of pure light.

I worked faster than I ever thought I'd be able to, flipping through each memory as I stepped back and shut the door to his cell again, flipping the heavy lock. The win was short-lived. Clancy's memories and thoughts had always passed through my mind like thunderclouds—expansive, brimming with darkness, and always on the edge of bursting. Now they were overly bright and crisp—still, too, like I was flipping through a stack of photographs, not trying to navigate the winding, endless paths that each memory sent me on. I felt myself coasting, carried along by a firm grip. Someone else was at the wheel.

The cell, detention hall—they were ripped back from the

edge of my vision in one sharp tug. A layer of reality gone, just like that. And in its place was an old, familiar scene.

Clancy's back was to me as I stepped toward him, letting the room solidify around us. Dark wood, everywhere. Shelves that blossomed with books and files. A TV appeared in the corner and burst to life with a flash of silent color. A desk appeared in front of where Clancy sat, his hands poised in the air until the laptop appeared beneath his moving fingers, papers growing up from the surface of his desk in neat white stacks.

He must have left the window open. The white curtain he used to separate his bed from the rest of the office fluttered at my back, and the memory was clear enough for the sound of the kids at the fire pit below to drift up to my ears. A soft breeze brought in the damp, earthy scent of the nearby trees.

I shuddered. We were at East River.

The memory was moving now, throwing me forward with a lurch, but it was only at half speed. I stepped up behind where Clancy was working, dividing his attention between his father's face on the TV set and the laptop in front of him.

I sucked in a sharp breath, and even though the rational part of my mind knew that none of this was real—I wasn't here, and Clancy wasn't actually here—I still couldn't bring myself to touch him, not even to lean over his shoulder.

How is he doing this? This wasn't a memory—it was something else entirely. It was walking onto a stage after a play had already begun. I'd crossed whatever barrier had kept me an observer, not a participant.

He took a deep breath, unbuttoning the collar of his shirt with one hand, typing in a web address . . . a password . . .

The Clancy sitting in front of me sank down in his chair, tilting his head back so he was looking up, almost like he was looking right at me—

"Did you get that?" he asked.

I shot out of his mind, dropping the connection before he could—he could—I don't know, seal me in? Was that even possible? Could he—

The lights crackled back to life in the hallway, burning my eyes with the sudden intensity. I knew my head was still tripping, still locked in that initial panic, because all I could smell was that pine—the distant campfire smoke.

He'd moved back to the bed, reclaiming his makeshift ball. And it was so strange—once the memory cleared and the ground felt solid under my feet again, I wasn't scared or even pissed off that he'd managed to wrest control away from me in the end. I was . . . curious. I'd never experienced him walking me through a memory in that way—at East River, he'd shown me memories of himself that he'd stitched together, but this was so . . . *different*. I had no idea that was even a possibility for us. The throbbing ache behind my eyes had disappeared, and, for the first time, the dive into his head didn't leave me exhausted or disoriented. I was still riding on that initial high of overcoming his barrier, just for a second.

"See you tomorrow, Ruby," Clancy said, tossing the plastic wrapper back up into the air. And as I walked out, clearly dismissed from his presence, I had the strangest feeling of lightness spreading through my chest, sparking and trembling and glowing. I'd held back the monster for too long, apparently. It needed to be let out, to stretch its legs, to remember how good the control felt.

I remembered now how good being in control felt.

I think I might have even enjoyed it.

There was one laptop left in HQ, and despite the number of Greens salivating to get a turn on it, their unspoken code of honor seemed to dictate that the kid Cate entrusted it to got ownership of it. Or at least first dibs.

So, at any hour of the day, you could find Nico working at the desk in the center of the otherwise empty computer room. Sometimes there was a small cluster gathered around him, crowding in over his shoulders and pointing at the screen, typing something in for him if he so much as leaned back.

"Those kids make vultures look like fluffy yellow chicks," Cole said as we stood outside, watching them through the long glass window. "If he were to fall over dead, would they just push the body out of the seat and use it as a footrest, do you think?"

I snorted. "They're bored. If we don't give them something to work on, they're going to start taking the electronic locks off the door to try turning them into cell phones."

"Yeah, well, Conner is the one that's supposed to be wrangling them. You and I sure as hell don't have the patience for . . ." A Green girl let out a squeal as Nico surrendered the laptop to her. ". . . this."

I had somehow managed to get through the day without letting my thoughts turn back to Cate and that expression on her face when she'd realized what Cole and I had done.

"Has she checked in yet?" I asked.

Cole rocked back on his heels, a crease forming between his brows. "Nope."

"She should have listened to us." I hadn't realized the words were out of my mouth until Cole dropped a comforting hand on my head.

"Mark my words, Gem. Conner will come crawling back tomorrow, tail tucked between her legs when they reject her. This'll be good for her. Everyone needs reality to punch them in the face every once in a while. Keeps you on guard."

But that was just it. I didn't want her knocked down like that. My anger had shallow roots. It had hurt me when she left; I didn't have enough pride to act like it hadn't. But I could understand her decision, that instinctive need she always had to mend fractures and soothe jagged edges. Cate couldn't understand that the others would gladly abandon us, use us, hurt us, because she'd never once considered it herself.

To have that be our first and only conversation since we'd arrived at the Ranch—that was quietly killing me. I'd let her down so horrifically in Los Angeles, betrayed every last trace of trust she'd put in my ability to protect our team. I should have forced myself to say something to her before she left, any small conversation to start working my way back to her. Maybe it was too late now, and I'd missed my chance of trying to make things right between us.

That single, poisonous thought made me feel like I'd been turned inside out, dragged against the ground. I just didn't know what to say, how an apology could ever be enough for her to forgive me. How do you pour the weight you feel crushing your chest into two little words? *I'm sorry, I'm sorry, I'm sorry, I'm sorry. . . .*

I'm sorry wasn't enough. Not for losing him. It echoed hollowly in the space he'd left behind. *I'm sorry* didn't balance out all of the things he could have, and would have, been.

Cole gave a friendly wave to one of the Green girls, Erica, who glanced over. She went bright pink and ducked back down, blocked from sight by Nico. The ghostly blue light from the computer screen gave him the look of a half-frozen corpse. The lines of his face seemed deeper, harsher, the longer he concentrated.

"I don't think this is a good idea to have him access Clancy's server," I said quietly. "His judgment is impaired where Clancy's concerned."

"Your reservations have been noted, Gem. But he's our man on this. I'm willing to bet on him—Nico has the most to prove. He won't let you or Cate down again, not if he can help it."

"The *if he can help it* part is the problem."

"Hey now. You got to plead Lee's case. I get to do the same for Nico, and it's your turn to deal."

"Liam didn't give confidential information about the organization to the enemy's son, the same person who then not only betrayed us and him, but also possibly destroyed our one shot at a cure." I turned my back on the scene in front of me, leaning against the glass.

"Right, but if he hadn't involved Clancy, if you hadn't been tricked into coming back, we wouldn't even know a cure existed."

I stared at him, momentarily speechless.

"Didn't think about it that way, did you?" Cole shrugged. "The loss . . . it opens a hole you in, a goddamn black hole at the center of your world. It sucks in your thoughts before you even have time to stop and examine them, and it's always hungry for more. It doesn't hurt any less to weigh what you lost against what you gained, does it?"

I shook my head. After a moment, I kicked myself off the

wall, holding out the piece of paper I'd used to write down the server and password information I'd seen in Clancy's mind. Cole took it wordlessly, glancing down at my scrawl.

"Hey, Ruby," he said quietly. "The thing is . . . what they don't tell you about forgiveness is this—you don't give it for the other person's sake, but your own."

"Who'd you steal that one from?" I asked.

"That one's courtesy of having lived and learned."

I rolled my eyes. "Oh, I'm sure—"

My mind couldn't finish the thought. It was there, then gone, just like the shadows that passed in his eyes. The recovery was just as quick—Cole's eyes jumped from me to the floor, and then the smile he forced onto his face was actually painful to witness. After a moment, he shrugged, his arms coming up and crossing over his chest. He was daring me to say something about it, and the longer I didn't, the harder it was for him to stand there, stand still. I saw the moment that vulnerability welled to the surface inside of him. The uncertainty of the moment made him look young, like a boy standing there waiting for some kind of punishment to be delivered.

"Who did you have to forgive?" I asked. It wasn't my business, I knew that, but his reaction had left my chest hollow. I wanted to know; I wanted him to tell me, to ease some of the weight of whatever-it-was off him, just for a second.

"It's not—listen, it doesn't matter, just—just think about it?" He fumbled for the words, raking his hand back through his cropped hair. There were so many possible answers to my question: his parents for not seeing what he was, Liam for giving him a hard time, the remnants of the League for turning their backs on him. I knew about all of that, and the fact he wouldn't say, wouldn't so much as look at me, told me it had to be something and someone else. It had to be much worse than what I'd imagined.

Cole had become so good at slipping into the armor of charm he always wore that I'd let myself be distracted enough to miss the signs of real turmoil beneath. He didn't trust anyone with the truth of exactly how deep the pain cut, did he? Maybe in time, he could confide in me, and I could be for him what Liam and the others had been to me. They hadn't let the grip of Thurmond, of what I was, drag me back into a small, lonely existence.

"All right," I said, taking the paper back from him and pushing him into the room. "Come on."

Nico had to look up and then look again for his mind to accept that I was the one standing in front of him.

"Can you download the files from this server?" I asked.

He stared at me long enough that I felt an itch to fidget.

"Yeah, sure, no problem," Nico mumbled, taking the paper.

The Greens had backed away from his chair to make room for us, but edged closer in curiosity as Nico brought up a series of screens. The strange code that formed the computer's language began to scroll by.

"Hey, guys," Cole said, in his best buddy-buddy voice. "Can one of you go grab the senator from her quarters and send her our way? The rest of you would absolutely be my heroes if you went and helped poor Lucy scrape together dinner."

They were too smart not to figure out they were being dismissed, but none of them seemed to care. On the screen, a window popped up, and a half dozen folders appeared.

"What was that for?" I asked when the last Green had slipped out and shut the door behind him. Cole silently pointed down at Nico, who'd gone so still in his chair, it wasn't clear if he was breathing. His shoulders sank, rolled down and forward, like he wanted nothing more than to curl his ends together like an old piece of paper and disappear.

"Nico, my man," Cole said, with that same casual voice. "Do you think you could go—"

"I'm not going to go." I had to strain my ears to hear him.

"Maybe you could—"

"I'm not going to go," Nico said, firmly, and clicked on the first of the file folders. It was only when the bigger folder opened that I saw the label: THURMOND.

There were maybe fifty files total inside of it—a mixture of videos, photos, and scanned documents. Nico navigated across the screen, releasing his breath harshly. The cursor hovered over one of the images.

Somehow, even before he opened it, a part of me knew what face would appear on the screen. He had always seemed younger than he actually was, but the image of Nico as a boy, an actual young child, drove into me with all the gentleness of a spike. His dark hair had been shaved down to black fuzz, and his normally rich, tan skin was the color of cement powder. It contrasted sharply with his dark, expressionless eyes, and the scars still healing along his scalp.

Oh God, I thought, a sick feeling slamming into me. *Oh God . . .*

Nico at seventeen stared at the child like he was a stranger. This was the hell he'd had to climb out of, and he wasn't running from it. He wasn't even turning his back on it. A slow, grudging respect pooled inside of me as I watched him hold it together when I felt like I was one wrong image away from shattering.

Thurmond. This was Nico at Thurmond. The camp's early years had been dedicated to researching the cause of IAAN, but had expanded as the years went on. Before I ever set foot there, Leda Corp had taken over that branch of research and moved those original test subjects—kids—to their facility in Philadelphia. Cole had been in deep cover at Leda, trying to turn up valuable intel on the research they'd done on the kids, and it had been Cole who had managed to ultimately extract Nico by secretly supplying the method of doing so to Alban. After Clancy had gotten himself out of Thurmond and left all of the other kids behind.

"You okay?" Cole dragged one of the nearby chairs over so he was right beside him. After a moment, I did the same from the other side. "You don't have to see this," Cole added. "Ruby and I can go through the files."

"These are . . . *his*, aren't they?"

Cole and I exchanged a look. He nodded.

"If he has the files on the Thurmond testing program," Nico said, "he might have some information on here about the cause of IAAN. Or, at least, what they ruled out. This is . . ." Nico took a shuddering breath in and released it before closing the photo and moving out of that folder entirely, back to the full list. "It's good. If we get something out of it, it's good."

Senator Cruz stuck her head in, and Cole waved her over, giving up his seat as he quickly explained what we were looking at.

"My God," she breathed out, leaning closer as Nico opened the folder labeled FEDERAL COALITION. Her discomfort grew exponentially when he pulled open the document with her name. There were hundreds, literally hundreds, of profiles spread out among the folders: PSFs, men and women in President Gray's inner circle, Children's League agents, Alban, and kids—including myself, Liam, and Chubs. In the latter case, he'd clearly pulled the original files from the PSF and skip tracer networks and expanded on them with his own new section: *observations*.

His observations of me: *Indecisive when making a decision that affects only her. More confident in dealing with others close to her to the point of being overly protective. No real vices—doesn't enjoy sweet foods, enjoys older music (related to memories of father). Allows herself one unrealistic hope of finding her grandmother. Desperation for closeness and intimacy means response to overtures of friendship. Tease out thread of physical attraction. Gullible, not vindictive, forgives too easily . . .*

My jaw set in irritation and embarrassment at the less than flattering assessment. Forgives too easily? We'd see about that.

"Here, that's the one, TRIBES," I said. "Open that one."

"Tribes?" Senator Cruz asked.

"That's what Clancy called the groups of kids who left East River—the safe haven . . . well, not really a safe haven in the end, but that was his claim. Whenever a group of kids left, he'd send them off with supplies." And the road code to communicate safe routes to each other. I'd wondered, more than once, how many of these "tribes" had left East River together before we arrived there, and now I had my answer: twelve, most in groups of five or six.

The grid was divided into columns by group, with dates and locations listed under each header. I had Nico scroll across until he found the listing for Zu's group. There were two updates beneath it: one in Colorado, one in California. The last update was a month ago.

He knew where she was. Or, at least, that she had made it out west. I gripped my hands together behind my back to keep from giving into the urge to punch the screen. He'd known, that whole time I'd felt hopeless about ever finding her again.

"How did he get these updates?" Cole asked. "This is gold, but only if the information is good."

"He told me once . . ." Nico started to say. I felt, rather than saw, his eyes dart to me for a moment. His voice was soft again when he continued. "There was a number that they could call and leave status messages. Or ask for help. He said he sometimes helped one group find another if they were feeling scared to be out on their own in smaller numbers. He knew everything."

I didn't doubt that. There was so much information here, we'd have to spend the next few days weeding through it. Our cursory glance through had turned up absolutely nothing about Lillian, not that I'd expected it to.

"Can you go back to the Thurmond folder?" I asked. Out of the corner of my eye, I saw Senator Cruz press a hand against her mouth and start to rise.

"All of the camps . . . are they all like that?" she asked.

"It's sort of like comparing rotten apples," Cole said, and I knew he was assessing her reaction the same way I was. "They're all bad, but some of them make the others look appetizing."

"What's the most recent file in the folder?" I asked Nico. "Can you tell?"

"Yeah, it's this one. . . ."

"The fire evacuation plan?" Senator Cruz clarified. We'd already looked through the document, seen the maps marked with the order in which the PSFs and camp controllers would clear out the cabins in the event of an emergency. The other files were on PSF personnel, and materials on the research conducted in what I knew was called the Infirmary. None of which featured Clancy himself, of course. If evidence had existed, he would have found a way to destroy it rather than let anyone see him so powerless.

"Clancy kept dropping hints that there was something going on. . . ."

"And you're sure he wasn't just baiting you to get a rise out of you?" Senator Cruz patted my shoulder. "His father loves playing that game with people."

Nico was just about to close the file's window when Cole sucked in a sharp breath and said, "Wait. Scroll back up."

Cole's eyes narrowed and his hand came up to rub along his unshaved jaw. I looked between him and the screen several times, trying to see whatever it was he was seeing.

"Damn," Cole said softly.

I felt something heavy drag down my stomach. "What?"

"They're moving kids *out* of the camp in this scenario, but if there were a fire, then why not move the kids to the inner rings until it's contained? Or why not herd the kids to the boundaries of the camp? The thing is like a mile wide, right? And why only account for one scenario? What happens if the fire is in the Mess, or the work facility? We just *assumed* it was an emergency plan based on a bunch of arrows and numbers, but there's nothing on here to indicate that that's what it is."

"If it's not an emergency action plan, then what is it?" I asked.

"I think it *was* an evacuation plan, in the event of the camp's location being compromised or if Gray was taken out or over-thrown. But look—"

I leaned forward. He was pointing to the small text at the top

183

of the page. The word AMENDED was listed next to December 10th of the previous year. The date struck through beside it was from almost five years earlier.

Cole took control of the mouse and scrolled down again, "They've labeled this with the operational name Cardinal. And here—I thought the numbers next to each cabin referred to how quickly by the minute the PSFs needed to reach them, but three-zero-one could be March first, couldn't it?"

"Wait—" I said, "wait, what does it mean, then?"

"It means that they're not evacuating the camp," Nico said, his voice small, "they're moving the kids out, four cabins each day."

"Am I wrong in assuming that the only reason they'd move the kids out is if they were closing the camp?" Senator Cruz asked.

"There was another file labeled Cardinal," Cole said. "Yeah, that one, the list of the small camps."

"And the PSF personnel transfer list," I said. "Oh my God."

I pressed my hands against my face and forced myself to remember to breathe. The room was shrinking around me, tightening and tightening around my shoulders as the possibility solidified into something real. *They're closing the camp.*

"Sweetheart, are you all right?" Senator Cruz asked. "I don't understand—isn't it a good thing? From what you've told me about the conditions in the camp . . ."

"If you look at it that way, it is a blessing," Cole said. "But razing the camp likely also means moving or shredding all of the hard-copy records on site, not to mention, the camp can't serve as evidence of the cruelty of the rehab program. The camp is . . . a powerful symbol. It's the oldest, the largest, and, I'm going to venture a guess here, really sets the bar for abuse and mistreatment."

"Separating the kids . . . the cabins . . ." My throat was dry.

Most of them had been together for almost ten years. They were each other's families. And they wanted to take even that from them?

"All right, so that's one camp out of contention." Senator Cruz leaned back against her seat and folded her hands in her lap. "What are the other potential big hits?"

"There is no other big hit," Cole said. "We're still going after Thurmond. It's our endgame."

I looked up. Shock must have registered on my face, because confusion spread across Cole's. "Really, Gem? I must have said it ten times this morning. *Thurmond, no matter what.* What's with that look?"

I moved back through my day, trying to remember. It must have been after we finished training . . . or before Liam and the others had returned? The whole morning had a strange, glossy sheen to it, as if exhaustion was clouding my memories like steam on a mirror.

As if tracking my thoughts, Cole said, "Damn, kid. We need to get you more sleep."

"Is five weeks enough time to pull something like this off?" Concern creased Senator Cruz's face.

"We'll make it work," Cole said simply.

"You asked them to write up proposals for a mission, correct?" Senator Cruz asked. "I don't mean to be insulting, but how in the world are these children supposed to come up with plans for a successful military operation and then execute it?"

"We received training," I told her, "to do exactly that. At least those of us who were with the League. We need to have time to work with the other kids—bring more in, make sure they can function under pressure."

Cole reached for the small stack of papers he'd collected from the groups and passed them to her. "I'm impressed with some of their imaginations. There's a lot of good stuff here. The Greens really put the best of the League to shame with some of this—I definitely wasn't expecting to get statistical probabilities of success, or . . ." He squinted at the page he held. "Christ, I don't even know what that word means. In any case, before we hit Thurmond, we'll have to do a test run on a smaller camp first, make sure the plan is viable."

The senator sat up a little straighter. "Any camp?"

"Preferably one on this coast, but yeah, sure. We'll try to match a smaller camp with the layout of Thurmond, get an experience as close as possible to the real deal."

"Nevada?"

Cole leaned against the desk, his eyes lighting up with excitement. "Are you thinking of Oasis?"

Oasis? The League had kept a map of the United States posted on one of the hallways, all of the known camps, big and small, marked with thumbtacks. I closed my eyes, trying to picture the pastel spread of states, moving east to west. It was . . . in the northeast corner of the state. Remote.

Nico didn't break his gaze from the laptop's screen. "That's the one with the children from the Federal Coalition."

Senator Cruz nodded, swallowing hard, and brought up a hand to rub against her throat. She looked at some point past us, at the clock on the wall maybe. "My daughter Rosa is one of them. I put her in hiding with her grandmother, but . . . Gray was determined. He hired men specifically to find our children. To make an example of all of us. I know of at least ten other Federal Coalition officials who believe their children were taken there.

Knew of. *God*. Is there a chance any of those people are still alive in the detainment camps? Will they ever get to see their children again?"

"Sure," Cole said, not sounding entirely convinced himself. "There's always a chance, right? But regardless of whether or not their parents are still alive and kicking, they'll have a place with us. A chance to fight, if they want it. Lord knows they don't have anything else to go back to in Los Angeles."

Nico shoved his chair back and stood, his hands coming up to clutch at his elbows. His eyes were darting around, creating a scattered path across the room, trying to land on everything but us. "I'm going to . . . I'm going to go . . . shower . . ."

He couldn't have left the room faster if it had been on fire. I wondered if he even felt the sharp stab of pain as his hip checked one of the desks and sent him stumbling forward.

I took a step to follow him out but caught myself. Cole raised his brows, his eyes sliding over to meet mine in a silent question. I shook my head. *No.* I wasn't going to go after him. I could feel guilty about forcing him to relive that time in his life for a few minutes, but I wasn't going to comfort him or try to shield him from his own horrific memories of Los Angeles. How could I, when part of me was glad that he was just as miserable over it as I was?

You didn't drop the bombs on the city, I thought.

But neither had he. Nico hadn't planned the attack carried out by the military; he hadn't been responsible for the agents overthrowing Alban in a bloody midnight coup that fractured the League forever; he hadn't—

I pressed the heel of my palm against my forehead. I didn't want to think about this now. It was like prodding a swollen, angry blister that hadn't popped yet. I needed to focus on Thurmond, on the fact that, apparently, we had less than two months to not only gather supplies, but find additional kids, train them, figure out transportation, get to Nevada, get back from Nevada—the impossibility of it rose over me. A mountain that only stretched higher and higher into the sky the closer I got to it.

"We'll meet with everyone tonight to settle the plan," Cole was saying. "We'll clarify the goal we're working toward, focus everyone's energy. In the meantime . . ."

"Yes, yes, of course. I'll make contact with the Canadians, see what they might be willing to do for us about ammunition and gas." Senator Cruz ran a comforting hand down my arm, then squeezed my hand. I barely felt it.

"You are the queen of my heart, Madam Senator," Cole informed her, with a devastatingly handsome smile.

"Oasis," she reminded him, heading toward the door.

"We'll meet in here at seven sharp," Cole said. "I'll have a plan ready for you."

She paused, turning back to look at him. It was there and gone faster than a blink, but I saw the moment she let herself hope. "Thank you."

I waited until she was gone before leaning forward and resting my head against one of the empty desks. Closing my eyes didn't make the headache any better. In fact, the glassy film over my thoughts thickened as I turned my mind back in the direction of Thurmond. I felt myself sit up, suddenly flooded with images of men in black uniforms tearing the camp down before I could do it, destroying every last piece of evidence before the world could see what had really happened there.

"—em? Ruby?" Cole was waving at me from further down the row of computers, an odd expression on his face. "Are you okay?"

"Yeah," I said, rubbing at my irritated eyes. "Why?"

"You just . . . were staring around the room, but you didn't—"

I was alert again, at least, pulling myself out of the slow, dulled, shapeless thoughts I'd sunken into. "I'm fine," I interrupted him. "So the plans—the ones the kids made? You've read them?"

"Yeah," he said, slipping into Nico's seat in front of the laptop and clicking around. "They're not bad, but I seem to remember a better one."

"Whose?"

"*Yours,*" he said pointedly. "You put together a whole plan for hitting Thurmond, remember? Gave it to Alban behind Conner's back."

I had, hadn't I? Three months ago might as well have been three years ago at this point. When they'd taken my plan and twisted it, wanting to use it to arm kids with explosive devices and send them into camps, it'd been like they'd cut off my legs at the knees. They'd turned a dream into a nightmare.

"This thing about Thurmond . . . it sucks. I know that's a crappy word to express the magnitude of how terrible it is, but it just plain *sucks* and we're going to have to work harder and faster now. We have until the beginning of March to get our act together. It would help to have a fully formed plan to run with so we can jump into action—the one you spent months thinking through."

Cole picked up a small notepad he'd tucked into the folder of handwritten plans from the other kids and tossed it to me. "Here. Write it out—everything you remember from your original idea.

I'll work on combining everyone's ideas into something cohesive and realistic for tonight's meeting."

I found a pen in one of the desk drawers at the front of the computer room and sat down to write. The first words were halting, and I was self-conscious of the loops and uneven lines of my terrible handwriting. The longer I wrote, the easier it felt—the words came trickling back slowly, like they didn't fully trust that this time it would be different. That this was worth getting my hopes up for, all over again.

This is different. One kid enters the camp ahead of the assault with a tiny camera installed on a pair of glasses, so images of the interior of the camp can be relayed back to headquarters and the Op strategy can be mapped out. *Cole promised this would happen.* We take their own transportation in, blindside the PSFs and camp controllers, subdue them without killing them. *If you can't believe in this, then neither will they.* We'll leave one camp controller free under my influence, to report back in status updates until we're all away.

It took up ten whole sheets, front and back, and my writing got more and more illegible as excitement started fizzing in my blood again and I could see each of these moments unfolding with perfect clarity. By the end, my hand was cramped and I felt drained, but my head was clear. I did feel better. Calm, at least, which wasn't nothing.

I stood up and turned back toward where he was still sitting. Every now and again, I heard voices and sounds coming from his direction, and the part of my brain that wasn't distracted by my work knew that he was watching the videos we'd downloaded. The crying, the soft begging, the questions that never had answers. They were the kinds of things I'd learned to tune out at Thurmond for my own self-preservation. I don't know what it would have done to me to have nightmares every single night.

The light from the screen flashed across his face, thrown onto the wall behind him. I lingered by my desk, caught by his bleak expression. Moving a few steps back, I was able to see what he was watching reflected in the windows lining the wall. Fire streaked across the screen. Cole glowed orange, red, gold, as the light from the video bathed him in deadly color. And just like that, my small slice of peace was gone, washed out by sudden, cold understanding. The hair on the back of my neck prickled.

The video zoomed in on the face of a young boy, no more than thirteen, strapped to some kind of metal post. He was panting hard, thrashing against the restraints that trapped his arms against his sides. There were small electrodes dotting his shaved head, ringing his scalp with a crown of wires. Revulsion rose in me, bile burning its way up my throat. I pressed a hand against my face and had to work up the courage to watch the terrible truth of it.

Cole glanced at me once as I stood behind him, then turned back to the screen. It was as much of an invitation as I was going to get. He started the video again from the beginning, and it was that much worse to hear the Red's guttural sounds and screaming mixed with the scientist's calm, dry notations to the camera.

"They were testing the kid to see what kind of emotional response triggers his abilities," Cole said, staring at the last, frozen close-up of the boy's face, streaming with sweat and tears. "Trying to map the way his mind processed it."

"Ruby," he said, turning so his face was in profile, "after

tonight . . . after we have our Op strategy . . . I want you to do everything in your power to find Lillian Gray. *Everything.* Do you understand?"

"Yes," I said, finally finding the words as he started the video over again. "I do."

TEN

I LEFT THE COMPUTER LAB IN ANOTHER GLASSY DAZE, walking and walking with nothing but the images of all of those kids trapped inside of my head. Burns. Surgeries. Blood being drawn. Questions. So many variations of *What's happening?* And *Why are you doing this?*

Even if my mind was checked out, my body at least knew where it wanted to go. This whole day had passed like a year spent underwater. I just wanted to go to sleep for a little while, and try surfacing again later.

The others had claimed one of the empty bunk rooms on the lower level—I had my own creaky bed and everything. Truthfully, though, I would have curled up in the corner of one of the halls on the cold tile, as long as it meant shutting my eyes for a little while.

Someone clearly had the same idea. The overhead light was off, but a smaller, desk-sized one was on, perched on top of the crappy little dresser on the other side of the room. I hadn't realized how badly I wanted to see him until he was there, and a little glow lit at my center. Liam was sprawled across one of the bottom

bunks on his stomach, his face turned away, his hands tucked up under the folded sweatshirt he was using as a pillow. His hair and back were still damp from the shower he must have taken.

"Hey," I said, coming toward him. A small test of sorts to gauge his mood. If he wanted to be left alone, I'd turn and go without a second's hesitation. Instead, his shoulders, then the rest of his body, visibly relaxed. I dropped my knee on the free space at the edge of the bare mattress. His hand automatically moved to hook his arm around it.

"Hey yourself," Liam mumbled. He didn't sound sleepy, but he did sound wrung-out. "Time for dinner?"

"Not yet. How's the garage looking?"

"Getting there. You can see half of the floor now. That's an improvement, right?" he said, finally lifting his head and turning toward me. "Present for you."

I followed his gaze over to the dresser, where there was a square of clear plastic to the left of the lamp. I picked it up and laughed—it was a CD case, The Beach Boys' *Pet Sounds*. I popped it open, smiling at the liner notes and disc inside.

"It's like our song is following us everywhere," he said.

He meant "Wouldn't It Be Nice," the opening track. I smiled. "Our song?"

"*Wouldn't it be nice if we were older . . .*" His soft voice trailed off into a hum. "I figured you could use some pleasant background music to drown out the sounds of you and Cole beating the shit out of each other, if it's going to be an every-morning kind of thing."

The warmth at my center evaporated. I closed the case, pressing it against my chest. "How did you know?"

"The two of you were the only ones that showed up to

breakfast with new bruises. It's not that hard to put two and two together." He finally looked up at me. "Please . . . please be careful. The thought of him hitting you, pushing you around . . . it just makes me want to *kill* him."

"It's just sparring. I have to train."

"And you couldn't ask Vida?"

I felt myself heat up. "Are you . . . implying something?"

I didn't want to explain this to him. I shouldn't have to explain. It had nothing to do with him. I started to pull back, but his hand reached out again and caught mine.

"No, dammit, of course not. I'm sorry. That's not the reason." He closed his eyes and sighed. "I found it in the car they'd stripped, its glove box. I brought it because it made me think of you."

I reached over, placing it on top of the nearest dresser.

"Sorry. I've got a real knot in my tail today," he said, turning those blue eyes up on me again. I felt frustration retract its claws from my stomach. "And I know you can take care of yourself, but it still drives me crazy to think about it. I guess I'm being a hypocrite, considering how close I came to hitting you this morning."

He'd spent the whole day hauling junk around, trying to put it into some kind of order—and that was after having his brother read him the riot act. Of course he was entitled to be short with me.

I sat down on the edge of the bed. "You didn't hurt me. Hey—I mean it. Not even close. I wouldn't have jumped in if I didn't know I could block you." I picked up his hand, folding his thumb toward his palm and the other four fingers over it. "Plus, you had your fist like this—and that's a good way to break your thumb."

I pressed my lips to his knuckles to show I was just teasing. Finally—*finally*—I was rewarded with a smile.

His soft cotton shirt had ridden up his back slightly, exposing a sliver of skin. I wanted to touch it, so I did. I dragged his shirt up that much farther as I worked my fingers up and down his back in soft strokes.

"Feels nice," he whispered. "Will you stay? I don't want to see anyone but you for a while."

He moved back toward the wall, a silent invitation to slide into the small bunk beside him. It felt so good and easy now; I knew exactly how we fit together, as if we'd been cut from the same pattern.

"You okay?" I asked, fingers worrying the front of his shirt. Liam wrapped an arm around my waist, drawing me closer. Everything that came out of the laundry practically reeked of detergent and bleach, including the shirt he wore, but underneath it all was this scent that was all warm skin and evergreens and mint toothpaste. And that was Liam.

The scent had a drugging effect on my system. I took in one steadying breath after another.

"Just dog-tired, darlin'."

The silence that followed was the first true spell of calm I'd experienced in months. It was the dim, shadowed light, the steady rise and fall of his chest against my cheek, his warmth pressed against mine. All of these things conspired against me; one moment I was awake, Liam's fingers carefully stroking the loose hair back out of my face, the next I was slipping into a slow, sweet doze.

The soft kiss was the only thing to bring me out of it.

"Dinner time," he said, his own voice sounding rough from sleep. "They just shouted down the hall."

And yet, neither of us moved.

"What did you do today?" he asked after a while. "I didn't even ask . . ."

"Are you sure you want to know?"

He leaned back at that, the focus in his eyes sharpening.

"I got us into Clancy's private collection of files. Besides a list of the different tribes and their last known locations, it basically was a digital scrapbook of nightmares."

"How did you get access?"

Now it was my turn to fix him with a look. "The usual way."

I watched his reaction carefully, already feeling the words settle between us, add to that space. They were an unwelcome reminder. *This is what I do. This is who I am.*

He took it in stride. "Was there anything about the cure on there?"

"A bit about the testing they did at Thurmond to find the cause. But . . . it turns out that they're going to close Thurmond down at the end of March."

"Oh, damn," he said, "I'm sorry."

"Cole still wants to plan a hit."

"Well . . . I guess two months is better than two weeks," he said. "We'll figure it out. But can I ask you something, and can I get an honest answer out of you?"

I bristled a bit at that.

"This quartermaster thing you suggested, me being in charge of supplies . . . is it a consolation prize?"

"What do you mean?"

"Is this a way to keep me here? Keep me behind, I mean. When things get rolling with the camps, am I going to be left waiting here, hoping everybody comes back in one piece?"

"You mean, exactly what we're all going to be doing while you're out looking for supplies?" I said. "No. And for what it's worth, Cole was only panicking because you didn't tell him where you were going. It was the same for me—you were just gone. I know you can fight if you have to, but I don't know that he does."

"He has no idea what I've been through . . . what I've had to do. He acts like I don't even know how to use a gun." His hands bunched up the back of my shirt. "I do, though. Harry taught me before I left home. I just don't want to shoot one unless I have to."

"That's the way it should be," I told him. "Sometimes I can't believe that this happened to us, and I wonder when it became so natural to pick up a gun and act like it's nothing. I have to teach the other kids how to shoot, and I have no idea how I'm going to do it. I don't know how to show them how absurd and terrible it is that they even have to learn."

"Maybe it doesn't have to be that way," he said, quietly. "Maybe we don't have to actually show up with guns blazing."

I'm not sure I could have been more surprised if he'd suggested we should just go straight to the top and assassinate Gray. I'd based my camp liberation plan on the one he and the others had come up with at East River. And both involved considerable use of force.

"No, it has to be a real fight," I said. "They have to take us seriously. The thing is . . . what I can't get over is, how the kids will take it. What'll happen if they find themselves in the position to kill and pull the trigger. We can train them to steady their nerves and we can give them targets to practice with, but it feels like forcing them to drink poison that'll never leave their system. I know it's a sacrifice and that they'll be the ones choosing to make it, but I worry about the cost. I'm afraid of what we'll be at the end of the road."

Look at what it's done to us. Zu's crying face the other night floated to the forefront of my mind, only to be replaced by the memory of Chubs's confession about the requirements of becoming a skip tracer; him being shot; Liam's battered face—all of these were linked in my mind now. They'd never fade, not even in the afterlight of all of this.

"I think they understand more than you'd think," he said, tracing a finger along the edge of my ear. "The kids who aren't League have been out there running—for *years*. No one is innocent here. They want it just as bad as we do. We'll figure out a way to keep them as safe as possible. We'll take care of them."

"Is that enough?"

"It will be." Liam's kiss was unbearably tender. "I missed this. Us talking, I mean."

A bolt of guilt shot through me at his words, at how content he sounded.

"Everything else seems crazy," Liam said, one hand threading through my loose hair, "Let's just stay here, you and me, and not let anyone or anything else in for a while, okay?"

This was the danger of him. In an instant, he could lift everything off my shoulders and set it aside. He became the answer to every doubt and lingering question. My world refocused, settling on him—beautiful, perfect him. I didn't have to think about what I'd done, what would happen to us even five minutes from now.

Maybe he would never forgive me, not fully, but there was

no thinking in this. If I couldn't bare every secret to him, unload everything in my heart, at least I could be close to him this way. He wanted comfort, and so did I.

I nodded and brushed my lips as soft as a breath just behind his ear. The response was instant—a shudder ran through him and it became a challenge to get that response from him again and again. He rolled over on top of me and I shifted to draw my legs around his. He pressed down to capture my mouth and I froze at the friction between us.

Liam pulled back, bracing his elbows on either side of my head, his brows drawing together as he studied my face. I felt myself flood with color, the way it spread down my throat, across my chest. It wasn't the first time I'd felt how much he wanted me, but here, in this room, on this bed—it felt like more of a decision that needed to be made. One I wasn't ready for.

"It doesn't have to be anything more than this," he said, softly. "I don't want you to think it has to be. This is actually pretty damn great." Fingers skimmed against my ribcage, ran along the edge of my sports bra. Every last ounce of his attention focused on my lips again. "But if . . . when I went out, I made sure to get . . ." The words were flustered, tangled up in one another, but I understood his meaning and it sent a small, growing spiral of happiness through me. He wanted this enough that he'd thought ahead; he would take the necessary precautions. "Days, weeks, years from now . . . when you're ready, so am I. Okay?"

I wondered if he could feel how quickly he'd dialed up my heartbeat with only a few words. I was close enough to see the pulse at the base of his throat, if the trembling in his hands hadn't already spoken for him.

I wrapped my arms around his waist, drawing him down to me again.

"What am I going to do with you?" I asked, only half joking.

That tiny smile grew as he lowered his face toward mine. "Oh, you could try out a thing or two . . ."

"Like what kinds of things?" I teased, pulling back as he came forward. He made a small, impatient noise. "Things that'll get us in trouble?"

"You *are* trouble," he said. "Capital T and everything—"

I pulled him down, cutting his laughter off before it had the chance to start. My kiss eased off under his touch, becoming slower, a sweet kind of lazy. It made me feel, for the first time in my life, that I actually had time. We could take that soft pace. Explore.

"Can we not go to dinner every night?" I asked as his lips left mine and started to work toward my throat.

"Okay," he whispered, "works for me."

I didn't feel shy or clumsy when my hands slid under his shirt again and began to draw it up, off. I heard him whisper my name, the sound of it breathy and raw, and it was like a hit of a drug to my system. I wanted to hear it again. Again and again and again and again . . .

There was a tentative knock on the door.

Liam pulled back, breathing hard. It was hard to tell which looked more wild—his hair or his eyes.

Don't make a sound, I thought, *they'll go away . . .*

They seemed to. I let out a soft sigh as Liam settled back down over me, blocking the rest of the room with his broad shoulders.

Then, the door cracked open.

Liam shot up so fast, he nailed his head against the top bunk and actually half tripped, half fell onto the ground. Cold air hit my skin and I looked down, realizing that at some point, my own shirt had mysteriously vanished, only to reappear on the other end of the bunk's thin mattress.

"Hang on!" Liam barked. "Just a sec!"

I shoved the thing back over my head just as he bent to scoop his up off the floor. A small piece of folded paper fell out of his back pocket, fluttering to the ground softly. He stumbled over himself to get to the door before it could open the rest of the way, catching it in his hand. Liam filled the doorway with his body, preventing whoever was there from looking or coming in.

"Hey sorry," came the timid voice, "but the showerhead is going crazy. Do you think you could fix it?"

Liam's whole posture relaxed. "Now's not really a great time . . ."

"The whole bathroom is flooding and, I'm really sorry, I didn't mean for it to happen—"

"It's okay," Liam said, glancing back at me. His face was a portrait of apology. He held up one finger, motioning for me to wait.

As soon as the door shut behind him, I set my mind to remaking his bed, refolding the top blanket one or both of us had managed to kick off at some point. My heel brushed something warm—something that wasn't the cold tile.

I bent down, retrieving the piece of paper that had fallen out of Liam's pocket. It had been folded over once into a smaller square, but it had opened as it hit the ground. My eyes were already taking in the neat letters carefully printed there before I could spare a thought to it being wrong.

Your name is Liam Stewart. You are eighteen years old. Your parents are Harry and Grace Stewart. Cole is your brother and Claire was your sister. You were in a camp, Caledonia, but you broke out. East River did burn. You were lost. You're in Lodi by choice because you want to stay with Chubs, Zu, and Ruby. You want to be here, helping them. Do not go, even if they tell you to. DO NOT GO! Ruby can take your memories, but what you feel is the truth. You love her, you love her, you love her.

I read the words again, and a third time trying to make sense of them. Because the words were ones I knew, I recognized I was reading sentences, but my mind disengaged. It up and left the picture before my heart could make the connection.

Ruby can take your memories . . .

It was a note to himself—to a future self, one he apparently was so sure would fall victim to my mind again. This was a cheat sheet. Security; because, clearly my word wasn't going to cut it. I could promise him over and over again that I'd never touch his mind again, but it meant nothing. I had done it once. The trust between us was already broken.

I went cold to the core. The shock of it—jumping from his warm touch to this—it was too much. I was the ash brushed aside after the fire had finally been blown out. *You are so stupid, so stupid, so stupid. He doesn't trust you, no matter what he says.*

"Stop." The world broke me out of the free fall I dropped into, and all at once the sensation of falling, sinking eased. I said the word again, forcing my heart down out of my throat, stilling my thoughts. I said it again, and one more time, until my voice sounded like my own again, not some dry rasp.

I paced the length of the room, trying to stop the torrent of thoughts shooting through my mind. Quick steps were moving down the hall, bare feet slapping against the tile. I panicked, shoving the note inside of the CD case just as Liam swept back into the room.

He was drenched in random places—his left shoulder, down his right side, the back of his sweats, the fabric below his knees—and the expression on his face was the resigned look of someone nominated for sainthood against his will.

I plastered a smile on my face, holding my breath in the hope it would keep me from crying. Just seeing his face was enough to start unraveling the binding I had wrapped around the hurt.

"Soooo," he said, wiping his damp hair off his face, "apparently I have to stop telling people I know a little bit about plumbing. Because *a little bit* is how to twist the knob to get the water to turn on and off—what? I look that pathetic?"

"No—no, not at all," I said.

"What's wrong?" He took a step toward me. "Your voice sounds—"

"I just realized it's almost seven," I said. "Cole wants us upstairs to talk through the plan for the camps. We should—we should go."

His brow creased but he stood back from the door, opening it for me. Just as I passed, he caught my shoulder and turned me back toward him. A droplet of water worked its way down from his hair, mapping out a trail on his cheek, over his jaw, down his throat as he swallowed hard. I couldn't meet his eyes as he studied me, and managed not to cringe as he leaned forward and pressed a sweet kiss to my cheek.

The others were only just starting to mill into the computer room, joining the Greens who were rearranging the desks out of their usual, tidy rows and dragging them against the walls so they lined the room instead. Nico had reclaimed the laptop and was sitting at one of the desks along the rear wall, his back toward us. Everyone else faced the old, marker-stained white board and the map of the United States taped up next to it on the opposite end of the room.

Chubs was standing in front of the map, pushing in small red pins as Vida read something—city names?—off a printed list.

"Nicely done with the brain voodoo, boo," she said when she saw us. "Consider your ass forgiven for not coming down to help us haul shit around the garage."

Chubs glanced back over his shoulder, one hand still splayed out on the map. "If we're going to try picking some of these groups up, we have four good options. There are at least ten kids in Wyoming alone."

"If they haven't already moved on," Liam pointed out.

"Now who's Mr. Doom and Gloom?" Chubs shot back.

Whatever Liam was about to say was preempted by his brother sweeping into the room like a tornado of energy, a visibly pleased Senator Cruz at his side. The rare glimpse of happiness on her features made her look ten years younger. She smiled when she caught my gaze, giving a small, affirmative nod.

She'd done it, then. She'd managed to secure some supplies for us.

Zu, Hina, and Kylie were the last to appear in the doorway, and carefully made their way through the field of kids on the floor to come sit beside us.

"Okay," Cole said, clapping his hands together. "So. Thank y'all for all of your ingenious planning and scheming. I reviewed everything, and I think we've landed on a winning strategy."

He walked back toward the white boards, picking up one of the markers. A blue line was drawn down the middle of the board. At the top of one half he wrote, THURMOND. On the other, OASIS.

Without any other preamble, he started in. "We're going to be making two hits: one, Oasis, is in Nevada. It'll serve as a kind of test run for our big hit on Thurmond in five weeks' time. In addition to getting those poor kids out, think of Oasis as an opportunity to work out the kinks in our strategy."

I crossed my legs and rested my elbows on my knees, hands gripped in front of me. Calm. Something in my mind clicked into place at the familiarity of this—being debriefed on an upcoming Op. The other League kids, Vida included, appeared to feel the same way, leaning into the moment when everyone else seemed to edge back, unsure.

"One or two volunteers will enter Oasis ahead of the actual hit." He turned to face the cluster of Greens sitting together. "We're going to need to install a small camera in the frames of someone's glasses, and it can relay back to us here. We need to get a sense of the compound's layout to fine-tune our timing."

"Why glasses?" Senator Cruz asked. "Won't those be taken when they're brought into the camp, too?"

"No, they're considered essential items," I piped up. "They're probably the only things that won't be taken."

If Liam recognized that that had been lifted from his original plans at East River, he didn't show it. He sat with his legs sprawled out in front of him, leaning back on his hands. He watched his brother with wariness.

"The catch is, the kids who volunteer can't have been previously in a camp. PSF policy dictates that kids be returned to the

206

original camp they were processed through, and Oasis is a relatively new camp. There is absolutely *no* pressure to participate. Like I said, this is purely volunteer."

Zu glanced between Liam and Chubs, but it was Vida who smoothed a tuft of her hair down in silent reassurance.

"That aspect of the plan won't be necessary for Thurmond, as we have three people who have been inside of the camp and are intimately familiar with its layout. The other difference between this and the big hit is what we're doing with the kids we free. From what intel we have"—otherwise known as what intel Clancy let us have—"Oasis has approximately fifty kids, all of whom I'd like to have return with us. Depending on how willing they are to fight, we can ask them to join us in the Thurmond hit, or we can slowly return them back to their parents, a few kids at a time."

"Are we still going to go out and try to round up the tribes of kids?" Chubs asked, jerking his thumb back toward the map.

Cole nodded. "We'll start sending out cars once we have supplies. We need as much manpower as possible if we're going to pull this off ourselves."

He moved through the other parts of the plan quickly; they were sketchy at best until we had actual images from inside of the camp's walls. It would be a small team, no more than ten of us, armed but with the order to avoid a firefight if we could. With only fifty kids, there would be maybe twelve PSFs there at most, and one or two camp controllers. We would pose as a military convoy bringing in the weekly supplies; I would be out in front, of course, because I'd have the job of influencing one of the camp controllers. He or she would continue to report that everything in the camp was fine while we drove the kids out using the camp's own transportation, whether it be SUVs, trucks, or a bus.

The kids were silent, processing this, until Liam finally said, "Fifty kids is a hell of a lot different than three thousand kids."

"Better to run this through on a scaled model," Cole said, smiling but somehow not smiling.

"Okay, that may be true, but other than giving us practice, and rescuing a small group of kids, what is this going to accomplish?"

Cole put his hands on his hips, one brow raised. "That's not enough for you? Really?"

"No, I mean—" Liam ran an agitated hand back through his hair. "The plan is good, but couldn't it serve as something else, too? Are we going to release the photos or video that's taken so people can actually see what conditions are like in there?"

A few kids murmured in agreement, including Lucy, who added, "I like that idea a lot. People should have the opportunity to see what it's really like."

"Do you have the means to do that without Gray tracing their source, swooping in, and blowing this place sky high?"

Liam's face was still hard, but I could sense him retreating under Cole's look.

"Whose plan was this?" Chubs asked. "I read through all of them, and I don't recognize it. . . ."

Cole's jaw set, just for a moment. "It's a combination of a number of them. I pulled the best elements from each."

Actually, it was the exact plan I had handed him, and he knew it. I faced the front of the room, refusing to turn when I felt Chubs's gaze fall on me. There was no reason to fuel the fire by pointing it out to them.

"Senator?" Cole motioned for her to step up.

"Ah, yes," she said, "I was able to secure a promise of supplies from my contacts in Canada. Food, gasoline, technology, and a limited supply of guns. The issue is that they refuse to bring them across the border into California. They want to bring them in by boat to Gold Beach, Oregon. Is that doable?"

Liam spoke up before Cole did. "I just need a map and a car, both of which I can find around here."

"And at least three kids as backup," Cole amended. "Kylie, Zach, and Vida."

"And me—" The words were only just out of my mouth when there was a bang at the other end of the room. I turned around in time to see Nico stumble backward and trip over the chair he'd been sitting in. He pressed both hands against his mouth as his knees gave out under him. The noise that escaped him was a high, keening moan.

I was up and moving toward him before I could stop myself, gripping his arms to steady him and stop his rocking. "What? What is it?"

By then, Cole and the rest of the room had already surrounded the laptop, blocking my view of whatever was on the screen.

"Cate," Nico cried, "*Cate*. Ruby, they took her—they took *Cate*."

Gasps flew up around me like a flock of birds. I released my grip on Nico and pushed to the front of the kids, who folded against each other to create a path for me. Vida was gripping the laptop, had lifted it off the desk, and it was only because Chubs was there to grab her arms that she didn't get to slam it down against the hard surface.

"You *son of a bitch!*" she spat at Cole. "This is on you, asshole! God dammit—*dammit*—" Chubs wrapped both arms over her chest, pinning her arms to her side as she lashed out with her feet, not caring who she kicked. She thrashed around, trying to headbutt him off, and only succeeding in knocking his glasses off his face. Zu rushed to pick them up before they could be trampled.

The video on the screen was looping on the homepage of a news site, fuzzy and shaky, as if it had been shot from a distance. A long line of men and women with black hoods and bound hands and legs were lying on the side of a highway, with smoking car wreckage nearby. They were loaded onto the back of a military truck one at a time, overseen by soldiers armed with assault rifles that reflected the late afternoon light. The headline running beneath the pictures was *Children's League Agents Captured in Colorado.*

My head throbbed as I watched it play through again, searching for her, trying to see what made Vida and Nico certain. Nearly all of the prisoners were dressed in black sweats or Op gear, the same things they had left the Ranch in—some were easy enough to identify. Sen's long braid. Instructor Johnson's imposing height.

Maybe she hadn't reached the other agents in time to try to turn them back—maybe she was the one who had recorded the video, and was safely on her way back to us—maybe she—

Cole paused the video on a shot of the prisoners lining up at the truck, and pointed to a smaller figure at the end. I leaned forward, bringing my face close to the screen. When he moved his finger, I saw the traces of white-blond hair escaping from beneath the hood. The figure was standing calmly despite the awkward angle at which they'd bound her arms. The other agents bucked and bumped the soldiers, hassling them even on their way into imprisonment. Cole unpaused the video and she walked forward, head down, not so much as shrugging off the touch of the soldiers who lifted her into the back of the truck.

No.

I felt a painful crack down my center. The shapes and faces around me seemed to blur as I stepped back, wrapping my arms around myself. Blood pounded through my veins, making my legs feel light, my head lighter. I couldn't calm the sensation, couldn't get the jitters out of my nerves long enough to think a whole, coherent thought. *Cate.*

She left.

I let her go.

They'll kill her, they'll execute her as a traitor, I let her go, and now they have her—they have *Cate*—I heard Nico's crying and felt the pressure build behind my own eyes, a pain that spread to cover my whole face.

"What does the AMP watermark mean?" Liam was asking. "It's in the upper right-hand corner of the video."

"That's short for Amplify," Senator Cruz answered. "They're an underground news outlet. Gray must be livid. They've shown he hasn't successfully stamped out the League in the Los Angeles attacks like he promised."

"Do they collect information? How do they distribute it?" Liam pressed. "Do you have any contacts there?"

"Well, yes, but—"

"But it doesn't matter, Lee," Cole cut in.

"Look at this," Liam said, gesturing toward the laptop. "They got the video to a major online news outlet. They convinced them to run it, knowing that Gray could come after this company, too. *This* is what we should be focused on, not fighting." Kids were nodding now, whispering. "We don't need guns, we need to get people information—information about camp locations, what the conditions are like there. Amplify could help us get the word out, and then the parents will want to do something to help the kids themselves. They'll go to the camps, stage protests—"

"*Liam!*" Cole barked. "Pay attention to what's important here. New organizations cannot be trusted, no matter how *underground* they claim to be. They'll sell you out in a second if it means attaching their name to a good story. You want to know why I won't contact them? Because I don't want to risk the lives of everyone here by accidentally or intentionally revealing our location. We can do this ourselves. *End of discussion.*"

Liam stood his ground, color washing up from his throat to his face as his temper rose. Cole squared off against him, looking as furious as I'd ever seen him.

"We have to go after them," Vida was saying. "Where is the nearest prison bunker to where they were picked up? Would they fly them east? They'd have to keep them alive, they'd want to interrogate them, right? We can put our ear to the ground, stage an Op—"

"We can't do that, Vida, and you know it," Cole said. He leaned back against the desk, his arms crossed over his chest. Still, I saw how his hand gave a small jerk, and how he pressed his arms closer to his body to try to hide it. His face was painted with fury, lined with sympathy. The words didn't make sense to me, not in the context of his expression.

"What the *fuck*—"

"Hey—*hey!* You think I don't want to go after my friend? You think I want her to go through this? No one deserves this, least of all Cate. It's too late to do anything. You're right, they're probably going to try to bring them in for interrogation, but once they have them underground, they're gone. They've disappeared. We're not ever—" He swallowed. "We're not going to see any of those people alive again."

Vida let out a scream of frustration. "We got your ass out! We got you out of one of those prisons—"

"With a fully armed, well-trained tactical team," Cole said, "and even then there were casualties. Even if we find where they've brought them, do you honestly think Cate could live with herself knowing that any of you were hurt trying to get her out? This is why we had that rule in the League. If you're caught, we can't come for you."

"Yeah, unless it's *you*," she snarled.

Because Alban thought he might still have the flash drive of information from Leda, the one that was now worthless. Because of what he really was. I looked over at him, silently willing him to just *tell* them so they'd understand.

"You're always bragging about those crazy-ass missions you went on," she said, her voice taking on a pleading tone. Vida slumped, her furious energy sapped to the point that Chubs was holding her up on her feet. "Why not this one? Why?"

"Because this one wouldn't be crazy, it'd be suicidal," Cole said. "And the fastest, best way we have of getting her and the others out is to see our plan through. It's to get Gray out of office."

"Talk to Harry," Liam said. "He has contacts in the different branches of the military. He can recommend someone to talk to."

Cole looked like he wanted to argue with that, like the idea of asking his stepfather for help repulsed him, but he held his tongue. "The bigger concern we have now is deciding whether to stay here or go. Any one of them could compromise our location."

"You said that your plan was to trick them into thinking we were going, too," Chubs said. "That we weren't coming here at all."

"Right." Cole hesitated. "But Conner knew that we were staying."

"Oh, *fuck you!*" Vida yelled, finally breaking out of Chubs's hold. "Fuck you, Stewart! You think she'd give us up?"

"Having experienced their interrogation methods firsthand, darlin'," Cole said, his voice venomous, "I would say that is an unfortunate possibility."

"She won't." The others turned to look at me, and I wondered if I looked as flushed and crazed as I felt. "Cate would die before she'd tell them." And that was the problem, wasn't it? She would let them kill her. She would sacrifice herself before she'd ever let them hurt us. A scream bubbled up in my chest as Liam reached over, trying to wrap an arm around me. I shrugged him off, pulling away from his touch. I didn't want to be near anyone right now. The room was suffocating, got smaller and smaller and smaller as more people turned to stare.

I have to get out of here. Now. Right now, before the black swelling in my vision overtook everything. I couldn't get air into my chest, not with so many people around me.

The air in the hallway was cool, at least. I wanted to go, just *go*, but I couldn't take the tunnel out, and I couldn't keep pacing the downstairs halls like an insane person. Without a thought, without remembering getting there, I was upstairs, pushing through the double doors separating the halls, and I was in the training room.

I got on the nearest treadmill, blood rushing loud enough in my ears to drown out the electronic beeps as I turned up the speed and began to run. The levels flew by, and still I kept my finger on the up arrow until it felt like I was flying. My feet struck the belt in time with the bruising pace of my heart. *She's gone, she's gone, she's gone just like Jude, you told her to leave, you sent her away, they'll kill her—*

I lost time, I lost my head, I lost everything and ran.

My arms pumped that much harder at my sides, as if they could keep dragging me forward when my legs started to give out. The air conditioning sent chills shooting down my back, cooling the sweat dripping from my face. I was only getting air to my lungs in long, harsh gasps, each breath sobbing in and out of me.

There was a blur of black in the corner of my vision, a streak in front of my eyes. I pitched forward as the belt snapped to a stop under me, barely catching myself on the arms of the treadmill. Once my legs stopped moving, they seemed to dissolve under me. I couldn't put weight on my ankles, let alone straighten my knees.

There were sounds to my right, murmurs that became words, words that finally took on meaning. I rolled onto my back, raising my hands to cover my face as I dragged in one breath after another. My hands were pulled away. A face swam in my vision. Blond hair, square jaw, blue eyes—*Liam.*

"Okay, easy does it. Come on, Gem, that's enough."

Cole. He caught me by the arms and forced me upright, sliding me forward to sit up at the edge of the machine. Sweat stung my eyes, tasted like salt on my lips.

"I told her to leave," I said hoarsely. "It's my fault."

"It's not your fault," he said softly. He pushed the hair sticking to my forehead out of the way. "She made the choice to leave. She was doing what she thought was right, just like you and me."

"I can't lose her, too," I told him.

"I know," he said. "She'll make it, though. You're right, she won't give us up. Of course she won't. Conner is smart, she'll figure out a way to survive and get back to her kids. That's how she is."

She and Jude and who else? Who else would I have to lose before this was over?

"Kansas HQ is probably already on this," he said quietly. "We don't have the means to go get her, but they do. It's a lot of agents to lose, and good ones at that. I'll see if I can find out if they have something planned."

He turned us slightly to the right, reorienting my line of sight toward the door, where there were at least ten kids watching his progress, varying degrees of worry on their faces. I tried to take a step, but now that my muscles were still, it was like they had seized up.

"You gotta stand up and walk, Gem," he said quietly, turning his back on them. "You have to walk out of here. Not just for them, but for yourself. Come on. You have to walk out of here on your own two feet."

So I did. Each step made my feet scream in pain where they rubbed up against the edge of the tennis shoes. I looked down to where bright red stains were spreading across the white cotton socks.

I kept my hand on Cole's shoulder, trying to hide how heavily I was leaning on him as we made a left down the hall instead of heading right to go downstairs, where the bunk rooms were. I didn't have the energy to protest as he opened the door to Cate's old room and turned the lights on.

I managed to stay vertical until the small bed was in arm's reach; by then, my knees had had enough. Leaning forward, I tried to untie the shoelaces but my hands were shaking so badly

Cole had to tease the knots out for me. He clucked his tongue at the sight of the socks as I peeled them off, but said nothing.

"I ruined it, didn't I?" I asked. "The other kids won't trust me."

Cole shook his head. "All they saw was someone upset over losing someone they love. No harm, no foul, as the saying goes. Will you cut yourself some slack before you literally run yourself into the ground? Take care of yourself so you can help me take care of them, all right? That's the deal, and it starts tonight, right now—with you staying here and sleeping for at least seven hours."

"But Clancy—"

"I can deliver the Little Prince's meal for one night," he said. "Do you honestly think you could handle him right now if he tried to take you on?"

"Take someone with you," I said. "Have them watch from behind the door to make sure he doesn't try anything."

"I'll ask Vida."

"Chubs would be better."

"You got it."

I spread my legs out on the bed in front of me as he stood up, too tired to argue, too tired to do much beside watch him go. Just as he turned out the lights, I said, "Tomorrow. I'm going to find Lillian Gray tomorrow. I'm going to take care of it." Of everyone. And when this was over, I'd be the one to go find Cate. I'd save her the same way she saved me.

"Atta girl. I have no doubt." He stopped in the doorway, turning back. "There's someone waiting for you. Do you want me to let her in?"

I nodded.

It was Zu. Cole shut the door behind him, and I could just

make out the edges of her dark shape, outlined by the faint glow bleeding into the room from under the door. She pulled the thin top sheet up over me, finishing with a kiss to my forehead.

And that—not the video, not imagining what they would do to Cate as a prisoner—that tender kiss was what brought the tears to the surface.

"I'm sorry," I whispered. "I didn't mean to make you worry. She took care of me . . . and I never treated her as well as I should have, and now she's gone, and doesn't know that I'm sorry. They could kill her. . . ."

I felt her hand around mine, squeezing in reassurance. *I know, I know.* She used her other hand to smooth the hair away from my face.

"You lost someone," I said, my voice sounding rough to my own ears. "The guy who helped you get to California. Will you tell me about him? Not what happened to him, not if you don't want to talk about it, but what he was like as a person. Would that be okay?"

My eyes had adjusted to the darkness well enough to see her nod, even if I couldn't read her expression.

"What was his name?"

Zu picked up the same small notebook she'd been toting around for weeks. I closed my eyes, listening to the faint scratch of her pencil against the paper, only opening them when she tapped my shoulder with it. She reached over and switched on the light on the dresser so I could read it: GABE.

In the single second before she turned the light off, I saw tears caught in her lashes. The expression on her face knifed clean through my heart. I would have done anything, *anything*, to take the weight of that pain off her shoulders before it crushed her into dust. But I knew better; there was no real relief from it. You just had to be willing to let the people around you serve as supports, and take their share of it when it seemed too much, too heavy, to hold on your own.

I shifted back on the narrow mattress, giving her room to crawl in next to me. Zu was all elbows and knees. Growing, stretching up in height, the way everyone seemed to right before they crossed that strange, ambiguous line into being a teenager. An almost-adult.

But the way she cried, the way she wrapped her arms around me and buried her warm, wet face against my neck—that was a kid. That was a kid who'd already lived a hard life and was being asked to take on more.

"I know," I said quietly. "I know."

The darkness rose and fell over me like a cold wave. I shut my eyes, relishing the simple fact that my mind was like a blank sheet, drained of all thoughts. But hours later, no matter how still I forced myself to be, I couldn't shake the rush of sensation in my legs—the feeling that they were still running.

ELEVEN

I WOKE UP THE NEXT MORNING LOOKING FOR A FIGHT. Muscles ached that I didn't know I had, and my feet screamed bloody murder when I slid my tennis shoes back on. All the sleep had done was process my stifling sadness into pure, unflinching anger. I had energy to burn. I opened the door and shut it behind me as quietly as I could, so as not to wake up Zu.

The manual clock in the hallway said 4:45 A.M. It would be another hour before anyone else was up and ready for the day. Plenty of time to work out the lightning zipping through my body, and return to some state of calm.

The light in the gym was already on, and my whole body tensed in anticipation when I saw who was running on the treadmill, taking quick, confident strides. Cole must have seen me out of the corner of his eye, but he kept running and didn't acknowledge me until I was standing right next to the machine and its whirring belt.

"Not in the mood, Gem." His voice was flat, edged with warning.

"Too bad," I said, walking over to retrieve two pairs of gloves. "I am."

I waited for him. Gloves on my hands, stretching, trying to warm my body up for this. Finally, after a good five minutes, he let out a grunt and hit the STOP button on the machine. Cole scooped up the gloves from the floor, his face flushed from the run, his eyes overly bright. I had half a second to drop back into a fighting stance before his knee rose up toward my stomach; I jumped back, but was caught by yet another obvious swing he made to my sternum. That, at least, sent the thoughts shooting out of me, along with every last ounce of air in my lungs. It was a distraction—he had me pinned against his chest in the space of a single heartbeat.

I twisted out from under his arm, trying to use the momentum to flip him over onto his back. Like that was ever going to happen. The best I got was a stomp to his instep. He didn't back off, though, not the way he normally would have. I felt the temperature in the room spike dramatically, and then—

He pulled back, letting me drop onto the floor with a sound of disgust. *No.* The word shot through my mind as he turned his back to me and started to remove his gloves. The sparring may have started as a way to release some of the heat that was boiling me alive from the inside out, but my head had hooked into the rush of it in a way I hadn't expected. I needed more. I needed to get the black thoughts of Cate and Jude and what was waiting for us at the end of all of this out of me. And that required sweating or bleeding it out.

I lowered my head and charged toward him. I saw his expression darken in the mirror in front of him just before he slammed into it. This time, momentum actually did its job, sending us both sprawling back onto the edge of the mat. Without a single word, Cole dragged me by my neck further onto the mat, and then he showed me just how pissed off he really was.

Trying to roll or kick him off did nothing. He had me pinned beneath him, his whole crushing weight settled on my chest. One hand pinned mine over my head, and the other arm came across my neck, applying just the right amount of pressure there to dwindle my oxygen supply down to nothing.

He eased up on my windpipe, but not by much. I thrashed under him, knees kicking up to try to hit his lower back. His skin seemed tight against his skull, his face set with fury.

I choked in a shallow breath, but he didn't pull back—my mind was floating away from my body, drifting into that same pool of black forming in my eyes.

"Cole—" I choked out. "Stop—"

He didn't hear me. Wherever he'd gone inside, I wasn't going to be able to touch him. And I knew that the only way out of this was *in*.

I drove into his mind like I was throwing a punch. I should have landed the hit and bounced back out, let it register like an electrical shock to his system. But his thoughts had hooks; they caught my mind, dragging it back down, drowning me in the scene melting into place around me. Light swirled around me, bending into shadows that became a small kitchen paneled in dark wood. There was dim, warm light coming through the curtains that masked the window above the sink. I smelled something burning—food. The trail of gray floating around me was smoke drifting from the closed oven door. Pots and pans popped up on the stove, appearing one at a time. The faint sizzling sound came from the brown sauce that had boiled over the lip of the metal pan.

A woman appeared in front of me, wearing a simple blue dress. I had a low vantage point from the floor, I couldn't see anything besides her long blond hair and the hands that kept pushing me back, back, back. A surge of anger flooded me and I saw, rather than felt, my own arms up, straining to reach for something—for—

The man was the last to materialize, facing the woman. His face was in shadows, but there was something familiar about it, the shape of the nose, the set of the jaw—I knew this face, I'd seen two younger versions of it. He had gone a shade past red and was screaming, screaming, sweat and fury pouring off him, clouding the room, making everything feel slow and heavy. My gaze shifted down, taking in his dark, wrinkled polo shirt, the squirming toddler he held like a sack in one arm, slowly going pink in the face as he cried, trying to wriggle free, reaching for my arms. His hair was lighter, curling at the ends. The first sound that broke through the muffled din of the memory was his piercing wail of terror as the man picked up the steaming iron from the board and brought it up near his face, as if he was going to press its tip against the baby's cheek.

The woman in front of me fell onto her knees, begging. "Put him down, please, I'll fix it, I'll fix it, it'll be all right, don't you know I love you? I won't have anyone over again, I promise. Just—please give him to me, please give him to me—"

The iron was lowered, set back down on the board, singing the shirt left there, waiting to be smoothed out. The man's expression transformed, a sickening look of triumph crossing it as he shifted the sobbing boy, holding him under his other arm. He reached out to touch the woman, to stroke her face. The man was so fixated on her bowed head that he didn't see the skillet she'd pulled off a nearby low shelf, not until she stood and swung it up in a clean arc toward his face.

The baby fell to the floor and I rushed toward him, the sound of gurgling and pain and metal striking flesh and bone drowned out by his hysterical tears. I turned his soft weight over and picked him up. There was a cut at the corner of his lips, where one of his new teeth had caught the tender skin. It was bleeding profusely, but the boy stilled and quieted, looking up into my face with these wide eyes, rimmed with big tears. His thumb slid into his mouth as I tried to wipe the blood away. He didn't start bawling again until he saw the woman, his mother, crying too, reaching down to pick him up and clutch him to her chest.

She snatched up my hand and dragged me away from the man's prone form on the floor, the mess of his blood on the black-and-white checkered tile. He shuddered and coughed and we only moved faster, toward the door. She swiped her purse off the counter, then doubled back for the keys when she realized they'd fallen out.

The door led to a garage, and the light that flooded the cramped, dark space dissolved the memory once and for all.

I surfaced at the exact moment the weight came off my chest. I was breathing, coughing, choking on the flood of air that filled it. I rolled onto my side, curling into as small a protective ball as I could. It was several agonizing minutes before fear released its claws from me.

The small, breathy sobs I heard weren't my own. I propped myself up on my elbow, looking for the source.

Cole sat at the edge of the mat, his back to me as he hunched over his knees, struggling to master his breathing. The section of the mirror in front of him was a spiderweb of cracks, stained with blood. I forced my feet under me and stood on shaking legs, taking one halting step toward him, and then another. He clutched his right hand to his chest, ignoring the way it bled onto his shirt. I walked to the towel rack and returned with a small cloth, pulling his hand toward me so I could clean the blood away. His skin was hot, boiling to the touch as he shook.

"Fuck," he breathed out. "I'm sorry—we shouldn't do this anymore. *Fuck.*"

"Okay," I said softly, and stayed anyway.

I was in the bathroom, still dripping from my shower, when I heard Chubs's voice carry down the hallway. With one last glance to make sure my hoodie covered the worst of the new bruising on my neck, I dashed out of the room, calling after him.

He spun on his heel, clearly relieved. "There you are. You missed the others—they had to leave. Apparently it's an eight-hour drive to Gold Beach and the idiots want to do it in one day."

"They found a truck to carry the supplies?" I asked.

"Yeah, which you would have discovered for yourself, had you made an appearance at breakfast—ah, sorry, that came out wrong. I didn't get to tell you last night, but I'm sorry about Agent Conner. I want to tell you everything will be all right, but I'm afraid you'll punch me."

It was the first faint smile I'd managed all day. "Was Vi okay about going?"

He let out a long sigh, deflating somewhat. "She was trying

to find you last night to run ideas by you, but it's probably for the best she didn't. She had a million ideas of how the two of you could sneak off to find Agent Conner."

There it was, the now-daily sensation of being the biggest asshole in the world. I hadn't even tried to talk to her about this last night. I'd promised her that we would talk about these things, work through them together, and what had I done? Gone off alone to run my head clear.

"Are we still going to talk to Clancy?" he asked.

"Wait—how did you—?" I didn't remember mentioning it to him, but that was exactly why I'd come out to catch him.

"We talked about this yesterday afternoon, when you were going to lie down for a while," he said.

I gave him a look that must have registered how blank my mind felt. "We did?"

"Uh, we did. For at least ten minutes. You nodded. That's generally a sign that you, you know, understand and agree."

"Oh . . . you're right. Sorry."

"You are exhausted," he said, poking my forehead. "Impaired judgment and forgetfulness are both symptoms."

I nodded, giving him that. "Do you mind coming now? I have a feeling this might take a while."

"And miss the chance to spend another day hauling around filthy, broken crap? Lead on."

Cole hadn't had the thought, or likely the time, to prepare Clancy's meals for the day. I listened to Chubs complain about Vida and Vida's language and how Vida's "reckless history with firearms" was going to get us all killed as I did my best not to take Clancy's water bottle, dump it out, and fill it with bleach.

The pantry had been nothing but bones a week ago, but the

humanitarian rations had managed to flesh it out to the point that it was starting to look like a healthy stash. I glanced at the clipboard posted outside of its door, feeling a faint smile stretch across my lips at Liam's neat, careful notes about what we'd already used, and what was on the menu for the rest of the week. Food allergies were noted at the very bottom of the chart—of course. Leave it to Liam to be thoughtful enough to kill himself to try to find almond milk and gluten-free pasta for the two whole kids that needed it.

"Ready?" Chubs asked once we were standing in the file room. I punched in the code, bringing him into the small hallway that connected it to the cells. The door at the other end of the hall had a small window he could observe us through.

"You have to stay here the whole time," I said. "You can't come in. I know you think he can't affect you, but I'd rather not test the theory."

"Hell no, I'm not coming in. If he takes over your head, I'm going to lock you both in there together and go get help." He shot me a sharp look. "That's not allowed to happen. Make sure you don't put me in that position."

I nodded. "One more thing. No matter what happens, I don't want you giving Liam specifics of what I'm going to do. Good or bad. Promise me."

"What exactly are you planning on doing? Using your body to get him to talk instead of your—wow, I can't even finish that sentence, my brain is already trying to purge it."

My fingers tightened around the sack of food. "*Nothing* like that. I'd just rather not have this serve as a reminder of how far I can go."

"Ruby . . ."

I pushed by him, stepping through the door and shutting it firmly behind me. I glanced back over my shoulder and met his gaze through the glass. Then he stepped back, just out of my line of sight.

"Taking time out of your busy schedule of sitting around, doing nothing to come for a quick visit? I'm honored." Clancy sat in the middle of his cot reading, back against the wall. Blanket and pillow were neatly stowed beside him, both requests previously granted by Cole in the vain, stupid hope it might butter the kid up to be more loose-lipped. As I opened the door's flap to throw his brown-bag meals in, Clancy flipped to the next page in his book, marked it, and set the book down on top of the pillow.

He might as well have thrown the copy of *Watership Down* at my face.

"Oh," he said, all innocence. "Have you read it? Stewart brought it in for me since I've been such a good boy. I was hoping for *War and Peace*, but beggars can't be choosers, et cetera et cetera."

It was an old edition of the book—the cover was wrinkled by mistreatment and there were ancient-looking library stickers on its spine. The pages had yellowed, curved under too many rough grips. But I had a feeling if I brought it up to my nose, it would have that scent—that one indescribable fragrance that no amount of cleaning could ever scrub from libraries and bookstores. A few more books had been stacked neatly beneath the cot—battered copies of *To Kill a Mockingbird*, *Sons and Lovers*, a book called *A Farewell to Arms*. And a copy of a blue book—*Tiffany's Table Manners for Teenagers*—that had been torn to shreds and tossed across the cell.

Typical Cole. I wondered who he'd picked to watch his back last night.

"What did you give him for it?"

"Some crumbs of information he was desperate for." Clancy glanced inside the bag as he sauntered back over to his cot. He combed his dark hair back off his forehead, grabbing the book again. "It's only by virtue of everyone's sheer stupidity here that they haven't figured out what he is. He telegraphs it so obviously. Gets *so* pathetic when he asks about them—"

"Why that book?" I interrupted, well aware that Chubs was listening. My mind was jumping from memory to memory, trying to remember when I had told him about loving the book. The way he was holding it, pressed against his chest, made me want to go in there and rip it out of his hands before he tainted that, too.

"I remembered you mentioned it at East River," he said, sensing the unasked questions. "You said it was your favorite book."

"Funny, I don't remember it ever coming up."

Clancy returned my tight-lipped smile. "Must have been one of our more private conversations, then."

Private conversations? That's how he rationalized all of those invasive lessons, when I let my guard down and let him inside my mind—all on the grounds of him trying to "teach" me how to control my abilities?

"'. . . your people cannot rule the world, for I will not have it so. All the world will be your enemy, Prince with a Thousand Enemies,'" he read, "'and whenever they catch you, they will kill you. But first they must catch you, digger, listener, runner, prince with the swift warning. Be cunning and full of tricks and your people shall never be destroyed.'" He snapped the book shut and leaned back against the wall. "Never thought I'd find a story about rabbits fascinating, but even they have their appeal, apparently."

"Do you even understand what you just read?" I asked, angry all over again. In the story, the lines had been spoken by Lord Frith, the rabbits' god. He was addressing El-ahrairah, a prince of his kind, who'd let his warren's population spiral out of control, too proud of their strength. In retaliation for his arrogance, Lord Frith turned the other animals of the forest into the rabbits' enemies and natural predators. But, at the same moment, he had gifted them with the traits and skills they'd need to have a fighting chance of survival.

Leave it to Clancy to mentally cast himself as the hero in every story.

"I do, though I think I prefer this one to make my point: *A rabbit who does not know when a gift has made him safe is poorer than a slug, even though he may think otherwise himself.*"

I shook my head. "Stop. Just stop. This is low, even for you."

"Oh, believe me, this isn't even close to how low I'm willing to sink to get you to understand what I've been trying to tell you."

"The issue isn't that I don't understand, it's that I don't agree."

"I know," he said, "God, do I know that. There have been so many times I wished you could—that you hadn't let them crush you the way they did at Thurmond. You're so unkind to yourself, and you can't even differentiate the actual truth from the warped version of it that they fed to you."

I was so sick of these speeches that if I hadn't come in here with a purpose, I would have left before he could get started. But this was my price of admission. I had to listen to his bullshit excuses for why he treated everyone around him with as much thought as the grass beneath his shoes.

"Never once, in the whole time I've known you, have you ever referred to what we can do as a gift. You snarl and snap your teeth if the word *gifted* is so much as whispered in your direction. There's a stubbornness in you I just don't understand, no matter how much thought I put toward it. I can't imagine how exhausting it must be to use your . . . what do you call them? *Abilities.* You punish yourself if you fail to control them, and you punish yourself if you succeed. One of the things I find most fascinating about you is that you're somehow able to mentally separate your gift from yourself—like it's a whole separate entity that you can beat back into submission."

He stood up and came toward me, his arms crossed over his chest in a mirror of my pose. The air conditioning clicked on overhead, breathing out a hiss of cold air. The chill stroked its icy fingers over my bare arms, my neck, my cheeks. It was a caress. For a moment I was sure I was standing somewhere else, the smell of evergreen and spice filling my nose.

"Stop it." I didn't know how he was doing it, but I wasn't the same Ruby I'd been at East River. I wasn't blind to his tricks; this is how he consistently wormed his way into my head, by unsettling me.

His eyebrows rose. "I'm not doing anything."

I let out a small noise of disgust, and made a show of starting to turn back toward the door, testing how desperate he was for me to stay. How hard it would be to play this little plan of mine out.

"Don't you wonder why it's so easy for Blues to control what they can do?" he called. "It's because each time they move something, it's a natural manifestation of their will—something they want to happen. It never turns off for the Greens, because their gift is like a net over their minds; they see it as their mind working and nothing more."

Whereas, for someone like Zu, a Yellow, or me, or even Cole—we had to know we could turn it off, and completely, otherwise we'd destroy everything and everyone around us. We used our minds like weapons clenched tightly in our fists, struggling to return them back to their holsters without injuring ourselves in the process.

"It must be torture for you to be around those three Blues constantly, to have them tell you everything will be all right and that you can control what you do—and then see them lift a finger and have it work perfectly. You spent six years at Thurmond, scared to so much as breathe the wrong way in case it made them give you a second look. You know what they'll do if they ever catch you and bring you back to that camp. They'll keep you there long enough to run their tests and confirm what they already know. You saw how quickly and quietly they took the Reds, Oranges, and Yellows out. The Reds, they went to Project Jamboree. The Yellows, to one of the new camps built specifically to keep their abilities at bay. But what happened to the Oranges? Where did those kids go?"

My throat had closed up on itself. What little courage I had left was draining out of me as fast as the familiar dread was rolling in.

"Do you want me to tell you?" he asked, his voice quiet as he leaned his shoulder against the glass.

I surprised myself with a breathless, "Yes."

"Some of them went to Leda's research program, the one that Nico and I were brought into after they closed the first one at Thurmond," Clancy said. "The others, if you believe the word of some of the PSFs stationed there at the time, are two miles north of the camp, buried a few hundred feet away from the railroad tracks."

"Why?" *Why kill them, why waste their lives, why do it like they were animals that needed to be put down, why—why them—*

"Because they couldn't be controlled. Period. It was the neatest, easiest solution to their headache. And because they also knew, if the kids were to ever be released from the camps, they could explain it simply by saying that IAAN was the root of it, that they were susceptible to a non-existent second wave of the disease. Our gift manifests in few enough kids that it won't raise many, if *any*, red flags."

The birth rate was low enough these days—few people would take the risk of a child being claimed by IAAN—that it seemed impossible to guess.

His dark eyes slid toward me. "I've seen the military orders—the explanations for how to do it 'humanely' so the child only registers the smallest amount of pain. I've never been able to reach any of them in time to save them."

"You don't save anyone," I said bitterly. "You only help yourself."

"Listen to me!" he snapped, striking a palm against the glass. "You are your abilities and they are you. I can't put it to you more plainly. Do you know why I hate this cure? It's a statement that *what we are* is inherently wrong. It's a punishment for something that isn't our fault—all because they can't control their fear about what we can do, any more than they can control their resentment that there are people out there stronger and more powerful than they are. They want to strip you of yourself—your ability to protect and enforce your right to make decisions about your life.

Your own body. Mark my words: in the end, it won't be a choice. They'll decide this for you."

"The cure is not a *punishment* if it saves the lives of the kids born after us. They should *never* have to experience what we went through. Did you ever stop and think about them before you tried to burn the research?"

"Of course I did! But this cure you keep talking about? It's not a *cure*—it's a painful, invasive procedure that only helps the kids who have gone through the change. It doesn't do a damn thing for the others who were never going to survive."

"Try again," I said. "I've gotten much better at detecting your bullshit."

He ran an angry hand back through his dark hair in frustration. "You need to be focusing your energy on finding out the cause—it isn't a virus, that much Leda figured out. It has to be something in the environment, something that was tainted . . ."

Whether or not he realized it now, he'd walked right into the trap I'd hoped he would. I needed him to be talking and thinking about the cure. It would naturally lead to thoughts of his mother—what he had done to her, where we could find her.

"Now isn't the time to change yourself to fit into the world," Clancy said, his voice raw with whatever thoughts were storming beneath his skin. "You should be changing the world to accept you. To let you exist as you are, without being cut open and damaged."

This was it—I felt the opening in the conversation as though the air had parted around us. He'd always been able to get what he wanted out of me by plucking and plucking and plucking at painful memories until I was too distraught or emotional to ward his advances off. I knew he was capable of losing his temper—I'd seen it too many times to think it was a rare occurrence—but I didn't want anger. I wanted anguish, the kind I had seen on Nico's face the instant he opened the photo of his younger self. When he reconnected with what they had done to him, Clancy would be as malleable as wet sand in my hands.

"If everything you say is true—that the cure is cruel and will change us—prove it."

That brought him up short. "How?"

"Show me. Prove it to me that it's as terrible as you say. I have absolutely zero reason to take your word for it, considering your stellar record of telling the truth."

The look of hope on his face turned sour. "Years of research and information isn't enough for you? I already gave you everything I had."

"Yes, on Thurmond. On the Leda research program. Not about this."

"Ah." Clancy began to pace, running his fingers along the glass wall separating us. "So you want to see for yourself? If you can't take my word, how can you trust my memory? Even those can be faked, as you yourself know."

"I can tell the difference," I said, realizing with a shock of awareness that I actually *could*.

The memory from the other day. The one he'd used to show me how to log into his server and pull all of those files. It had felt different because it *was* different. It was pure imagination on his part. That was why I'd been able to step into it, interact as myself with what was happening rather than reenact what had happened as the person I was reading. There'd been a different texture to the whole experience.

"You did figure it out. Well done." Clancy sounded pleased.

"Memory and imagination are two different beasts, processed and handled in different ways by the mind. All of those times you replaced someone's memories, planted an idea in their head—you didn't realize you were doing several different things at once, did you?"

Was I? Until now, I'd taken everything I could do in stride, done what had felt natural. Maybe it was pointless because hopefully I'd one day be rid of them and the terror they held for me, but . . . shouldn't I at least make more of an effort to understand exactly what I was doing and how?

"You're stalling," I reminded him.

"No, just waiting for you," he said quietly. "If you want to see it, if this is the only way to prove it to you, then . . . it's fine."

I tested his defenses with a brush of my mind against his. But he was waiting, and the moment I closed my eyes and tried to touch his mind with mine, it was like he'd reached out a hand to guide me in. I was pulled through the gauzy layers of stained memories, catching a face here, a sound there. Clancy possessed a highly organized mind. It was like running down a winding hallway of windows, each offering a tantalizing look inside. Or walking down the aisle of a library, searching for the right book, and only glimpsing the other titles as you quickly passed.

The images began to smear, dripping down like ink on a wet page. The colors morphed and merged and then, with the force of a blow to the chest, settled. I was thrown into a memory so solid I could feel the cold, metal table biting at my already stiff skin. Blinking several times to clear the halo of light around my vision, I felt myself try to strain up, only to be jerked back down by the black straps pinning my wrists and ankles. There were no layers of fabric covering me, not even a blanket—only wires and electrodes, exploding out of my head and chest like a bursting cocoon.

The men and women in white coats swarmed the table I'd been laid out on, their voices buzzing around my head. They pulled wires off my skull, replaced them with new ones, touched everywhere—everywhere—forced my eyelids open roughly to shine a blinding light there. I could hear their quiet jokes and murmurs, see the outlines of their smiles behind their paper masks.

He had shown me a memory like this once, back when we were at East River. It had been horrifying to watch, even more so to realize that it was taking place in a part of the Infirmary I recognized by sight. But the simple truth was, the stronger the memory—the stronger the feelings associated with it—the clearer everything became. I knew now that when I heard something, smelled something, felt something in a memory, it was because it had been burnt so deeply into that person's mind, it had left a scar.

This wasn't a memory about the cure research—that had been under his mother's control, far away from him. This was what they had done at *Thurmond*, before he'd been able to get himself out. They were studying him like a specimen, the way they had studied that Red. Nico.

A plastic mask was lowered onto my face, and sickly sweet air came flooding into my lungs. The overload of sensation dampened at the first touch of drugs to my system.

He'd told me once that they kept the kids sedated but awake during procedures, so the machines could better monitor their normal brain functions and map the way the Psi abilities rippled through them. Thurmond's blue tiles echoed the machines' screeching, making it sound like they were everywhere, all of them drawing in closer, waiting for their turn. I couldn't swallow around my dry, heavy tongue; saliva dripped past cracked, swollen lips into the muzzle they'd secured over my head.

The jolt of fire came without warning, zigzagging down my spinal column, a ripping sensation that left me breathless with pain. It was—it was like a static shock had been cranked up to a thousand levels higher. I couldn't control myself as my body seized up, relaxed; seized; relaxed.

"Try it again, this time—" A stocky researcher let out a cry of disgust, jumping back from the table. The stench of bleach was replaced by piss and blood and burnt flesh. I would have emptied my stomach, too, if there'd been anything in it. In that moment, I would have given anything to have choked on my own vomit and died. Humiliation seared through me as one of the researchers waved a nurse over to clean me up so they could start again.

I'm going to kill you—I'm going to kill you, all of you— The words were lost as my brain was overloaded with a crackling sheet of pure, burning white.

My gaze dropped from the U-shaped fluorescent light over me before its glow overtook the room and blinded me completely. I was surrounded by white coats and clipboards again, the clatter of metal instruments against metal trays, the goddamn *beep, beep, beep* of a heartbeat that wouldn't give out. The woman in front of me stepped to the side, flicking something on—music, the Beatles, singing, *I want to hold your hand, I want to hold your hand*, their bright voices perfectly in sync with the cheerful music.

One researcher began to sing along, off-key, as another bolt of white-hot lightning tore through my skull.

When my vision cleared, the black at the edges retreating, my body was still throbbing, but it was dark around me, sweetly dark, and the surface under me was cloth, not steel. *Done.*

"—will give a good report of progress—"

"—carefully adjusting treatment—in good hands—treatment—working—"

The stocky, balding doctor shook hands with a man in a jacket . . . what color was that? *Not-blue . . . not-blue . . .* Panic rose up, gripping my brain as it grasped for the word. The man in the jacket pulled his mask away. *I see beard. I see nose. All familiar. Head hurts—no name, only face. Face next to Father. Phone. Report. Report me to him. Help. Help. Help.*

Lift hand—lift hand—trying. No go, not without—without me. Words broke and crumbled in my mind, leaving sounds. Letters. *Tongue stuck. Arms stuck. Pain—burning, everything burning—*

A small shape appeared, the cot next to mine groaned. He came forward now. It was safe. *Nico. Nico, help.*

A cold cloth on my face, cleaning. My hands. Neck. *Careful. Careful, Nico.* Aching head, soft touches, soft fingertips. *Nice.* I was lifted, arms put into sleeves, shirt down over my head. Held. *Warm heart.* Dark eyes burning. *Safe.* "It's okay. I'm here." Cup to lips. *Water.* Metal to lips—*not-fork . . . not-fork . . . what is . . . spoon. Spoon. Sweet. Meal.*

Nico. Ni-co-las.

Crying.

Warm Nico.

Crying—

TWELVE

I RIPPED MYSELF OUT OF THE MEMORY, SHOVING AGAINST it. The exit was worse than the entry. I couldn't tell which direction I was going, couldn't navigate. Forward meant seeing that horrible moment again, Nico's shaved head and gaunt body, the heart-wrenching expression I recognized on his face. I didn't want to see it again, but I couldn't escape it, the simple truth. So I went the other way, only to find it was like passing through a field of barbed wire backward. No matter which way I tried to pull out of the memory, I was cut up, I was in pain.

When I came to, safely back inside of my own mind, I was on my knees, my forehead resting against the glass. I gulped down one breath after another.

"Was that enough for you?" Clancy snarled. His skin had taken on a clammy quality, and he was trembling, shaking almost. "Are you satisfied?"

I don't know how I did it. I don't. I just disconnected my mind from everything I'd seen, scrubbed every ounce of feeling from my voice. "No."

He wheeled back around.

"I already knew what the Thurmond testing was like." *Oh God—oh my God.* I felt like I was going to throw up all over again. What they'd done to his mind, even temporarily . . . "You're supposed to be proving to me the cure itself is cruel."

"She adapted the cure *from* that research! *From* the shocks. You think I don't know what you're really trying to do?" he said. "That I'd be stupid enough to show you the actual cure procedure or where my mother is—"

He knows. He knows where she is.

He stalked over to his cot. There was enough of a link still left between our minds for me to be momentarily stunned by the resentment billowing through him. He needed to stop, I wanted him to stop—I stilled completely and reached deep into his mind, letting the intention steer me past his memories altogether into the part of his mind that was sparking with heat and drive.

He froze: muscles, limbs, expression like stone. Clancy didn't move until I did, and then it was only as a mirror of my actions. It was like plucking strings; each touch against this part of his mind produced a different response in him. I arranged him like I would an action figure, ignoring the pressure of his own mind trying to fight me off.

This is it—this is what he felt each time he played with one of us. Lightheaded, dizzy with the possibilities.

I wasn't where I needed to be, not really—somehow, I needed to redirect myself back into his memories, only I didn't know how to remove myself from this part of his mind. It was dark, and gripping—

Mirror. The word sprang into my ears. Clancy's voice, assertive, forcing me to listen—he knew I couldn't get out on my own, and he must have been afraid of what damage I could do inside him if he was actively trying to help me. *Mirror minds.*

I understood.

My own thoughts shifted; I squeezed my eyes shut, hands clenched at my sides, as I forced the memory of me walking into the room to rise to the surface. I pulled free from the dark, feeling every bit like I was being physically dragged back by the hair. I was in the hallway again, watching as one by one the windows into his memories were slammed shut. I only had a second, just one, before he recovered—

"Lillian," I said, "mother—"

The trick worked the way it always had. Hearing the words redirected his thoughts, drawing up the one memory he'd been thinking of most recently—the one he wanted to protect.

I knew what I was looking for, having seen a glimpse of the memory before. At the first appearance of the beautiful woman, her face framed by blond hair, a plea on her lips, I dove in, driving harder than I ever had before. Lillian Gray's lab took shape around me—objects clicking into place like a puzzle. She'd tried to trick her son in order to bring him in to perform the procedure. She'd leaked her location in Georgia, knowing he'd be able to find her—and he did. I tugged harder on the image, forcing it to pass faster. Her hands were up, pacifying, the words *Calm down, it's going to be okay* tumbling out of her. I remembered the splatter of blood on the lapel of her white lab coat, how she'd ended up begging *Clancy, no, please Clancy* from the floor as he set the world around her on fire, trashed her machines.

What I hadn't seen was the way he gripped her neck between his hands. I could actually feel her racing pulse beneath my fingers at the slightest pressure. Oh God—he was going to—

But instead, my hands drifted up, gripping either side of her face. There were no words to describe what I saw next—reading a mind within a mind, an explosion of memories within a memory. The heat at my back was unbearable, but I was working, holding her still as I twisted, bent, broke every thought the woman had.

A gunshot broke the connection, pain tearing across my right shoulder. I turned away from the woman's blank face, letting her crumple to the floor, as two dark figures burst through the door. The glass around her caught the winking light of the fire. The strange, entrancing beauty of it was the last thing I remembered before I ran.

I was thrown out of his head so hard that I fell back, cracking my skull against the wall behind me. Clancy was on the floor, as far away from me as he could get. His face was turned into the wall, his whole body heaving for breath. The cot was on its side, a barrier between us.

"Get out," he snarled. *"Get out!"*

This time, I ran. My hands fumbled with the first lock, Clancy screaming those two words at me the whole time. The door opened from the other side and I collided with the person there, struggling to get out of their grip as the door was kicked shut behind me.

"It's me, it's just me—" Chubs hauled me down the short hall, into the old file closet. I clung to his arm, my mind a mess of thoughts and feelings that weren't even mine.

My legs gave out before we were in the hall. He jammed the key into the lock and turned it, stopping only long enough to rattle it once to make sure it was secure.

"Ruby?" he said, his face splitting into two, three, four . . . We walked briskly toward the end of the hallway, me leaning on him the whole time, trembling with the effort it took to stay vertical. He opened one of the bunk room doors and pulled me inside.

I slid down the nearest wall, trying to purge the sound of Clancy's voice with each exhale. Chubs crouched down in front of me, watching me intently. How much of that had he heard? How much of what he'd seen had he actually understood?

You out-Clancyed Clancy. I never even thought there was a chance I could do that with my abilities. To beat him, I'd managed to become him. And even with all of my promises to do whatever it took to find out about Lillian, I'd somehow never imagined . . . *this.* That I was capable of it.

Don't think about it. I had what I'd come for. I got the confirmation I needed.

"She's still with the League," I said before he could ask me the question I saw in his face. "They came and took her away at the end."

"The First Lady? He definitely didn't kill her, then?"

I shook my head. "He did something much worse."

By the time I went looking for him, Cole was already gone. Senator Cruz delivered the news when I passed her in the upper-level hallway.

"He went to meet with a friend who's still associated with the League to see if they have information about the agents who were arrested," she said. "He told me to tell you not to worry and that he'd be back tonight."

Of course he hadn't taken a burner phone with him—there was no way to contact him to see if he could pump information about Lillian Gray's whereabouts from this same "friend."

If she was still with the League, where were they keeping her? She'd been running her research near Georgia HQ with only a few agents assigned for her protection. Would they have brought her to Kansas HQ with the others when they closed the other location?

I passed by the gym and did a double take at the sight of Zu, Tommy, Pat, and a number of the others trying to fuss around with the exercise machines.

"Sorry," Pat ventured, stepping away from the weights. "We were just . . . doing nothing. And we wanted to do something. Since, you know, we're going—me and Tommy."

"Going?" I repeated.

Tommy popped up next to him, bright red hair glowing under the bare lights overhead. "We volunteered. For Oasis. Sorry, we voted after you, um, left."

Ah. I looked at the two of them, sizing them up. When Tommy squirmed under the scrutiny, Pat smacked his side to get him to stop, forcing his chin up higher. I smiled.

"Do you want to learn some self-defense?" I asked.

I'm not sure if their reaction could have been more enthusiastic if I'd offered candy. The other kids abandoned the machines, darting over to the mats, where I instructed them to line up. I led them through stretches, taught them how to break out of different holds someone might have on them, and demonstrated—repeatedly—how to flip someone over your shoulder if you weren't a Blue. And hours later, when we were finished, I couldn't say who was happier with how the day had turned out—me, or them.

Finally, Cole announced his arrival with three bangs against the tunnel door. I came barreling out of Alban's old office, abandoning the ancient Op files I'd been looking through, and unlocked it. He gave a guarded, uncertain smile as he came up the stairs.

"The others are back, too," he said. "I told them to bring everything around to the garage's loading dock. Can you gather up the kids to help haul the stuff in? I'll go ahead and cut the chain so we can get the damn door open—"

"Cole," I said sharply as he started to walk away.

He shuffled to a stop, turning his head slightly. "I'm sorry, Gem. They're looking for the agents, but they don't know either. Liam must have contacted Harry behind my back, because he got in touch with me this morning to say he'd ask around. He's ex-Special Forces and still has a number of buddies in different branches of the military and government."

The mention of his stepfather brought a flash of the memory I'd seen in Cole's mind, and pain stirred in me. The man from his memory, his biological father, smiling down at their mother that way . . .

"Okay," I said quietly. "Thanks for trying."

He let out a shuddering breath and forced himself to shrug. "You . . . okay?"

"Yeah," I said. "Let me go get the others. I'll meet you down there."

Cold night air filled the warehouse with a crisp, clean scent that reached us in the tunnel. The door at the other end was already open, waiting for us. But the moment I stepped through, I stopped dead in my tracks.

The whole place looked as though they'd power-washed it for hours on end. They hadn't been able to actually remove the junk from the building—it might have attracted too much unwanted attention—but they'd somehow fit everything together, using the four walls as the frame of a puzzle. They'd lined up all of the shelving units, made some new shelves out of the broken bunks, and created a workstation with the tools they'd found. The car lift and frame were still at the center of the expansive space, but it looked like they were piecing even *that* back together. Someone had outfitted it with wheels, at least.

Two large SUVs and one white van had come up the loading ramp and were parked inside. I jogged over to Liam and Vida as they used their abilities to lift boxes out of the trunks and set them aside.

Liam looked up as I came over, a familiar smile on his face. He waved the group coming in behind me over. "We're organizing by type. Set computers and electronics over there—"

There was an actual, blissful sigh from one of the Greens, which made him chuckle.

"Food and water goes here. There should be a few bags of clothes, bedding—no, no, leave the stuff in the white van," he said, jogging over to shut the door. "It's—Cole's going to take care of that stuff."

Meaning, I'd guess, weapons for our locker.

Vida was . . . blank. Her expression didn't so much as flicker with annoyance as Chubs pelted her with a series of endless questions. I wasn't sure she was even aware of what she was doing, there was that much of a visible, numb disconnect.

Zu came to stand beside me, her dark gaze meeting mine in question. I wanted to tell her not to worry about this, that I was coming to see the heavier your heart got, the stronger you had to be to keep carrying it around. But the truth was, all I wanted to do was risk a punch in the face and hug Vida. So, I tried.

And she let me.

Her arms stayed down around her sides, pinned there by my tight grip. Slowly, her hands rose and pressed against my back. I smelled dust and the salt of ocean water on her skin, mingling with the exhaust from the cars, and I wished like hell I had thought to volunteer to go instead, so she could have had the day to recover.

"We are going to fucking get her back," Vida said fiercely. "I will burn Gray's house down over his head. If she's not all right, I'm going to rip out his heart and eat it."

I nodded.

"You really shouldn't eat raw meat," Chubs said somewhere beside us. "It can carry pathogens—"

We both turned to him slowly. He lowered the computer box he'd been holding down to the ground and backed away.

"The Canadians came through, didn't they?" Senator Cruz looked around at the haul, strolling between the piles.

"What are they going to want for this stuff?" one of the kids asked.

"Don't worry about it," Senator Cruz said. "The reparations are still quite a ways off yet. This is what we'd call a favor. Oh— did they not provide gas?"

"They sent a fuel tank," Liam said. "We hid it behind the bar, since it wouldn't fit through this loading dock. I also did not, um, feel super comfortable having a ton of explosive material in here."

"Fair point," Senator Cruz said with a faint laugh.

"They seem really invested in this. We established a drop site so they can bring things down when they find openings. They gave me this—" He pulled a sleek silver phone out of his pocket. "To make contact when the supplies are ready."

"Spray paint?" Chubs asked. "Did you remember to grab that?"

"What for?" I asked.

"When we send the cars out to pick up the tribes," Liam explained, using his hands to add emphasis, "they're going to mark the safe routes they take with the road code. That way, we can get back in one piece *and* there's a chance other kids we don't know about will catch on and follow the route in."

That smile on his face had always been contagious. I bit the inside of my lip; he was looking at me like I was the best damn thing he'd ever seen.

Ruby can take your memories . . .

"Great idea," I said, glancing away.

"Yeah . . ." His voice faltered. "Thanks?"

The kids were only too happy to cart the load off into the Ranch. Cole stood at the back door of the white van, leaning against it as he watched the progress the kids were making around him.

"Wait—" I said, catching Chubs and Liam by the backs of their shirts before they could follow Zu and Hina to the tunnel. "We need to talk about something."

Cole and Vida must have picked up on the nerves in my voice because they came around into our huddle.

"I . . . dealt with Clancy today," I said. "To find out where his mother is."

Cole straightened. "And?"

"She'd been working out of some facility in Georgia, protected by the agents from the HQ there. They seem to have gotten her out in time. Her lab burnt down, though."

"Damn, girl," Vida said softly. "You're sure?"

"Positive. And I doubt they would have let her out of their sight."

"You think they're hiding her in Kansas," Cole said.

"It makes sense, doesn't it? It's League procedure that when the organization is under attack, remaining forces and resources fall back to a central, safe location. I don't know that they would risk keeping her in an external location anymore after what happened with Clancy, and I don't think she's the kind of prisoner they would have cut loose . . ."

"Would they trade her?" Vida interrupted. "A prisoner exchange?"

"The First Lady?" Cole said. "Not even for a hundred agents. I just don't understand why they wouldn't have used her before now—they aren't exactly shy about using hostages to make demands."

"Well . . . they might not want to put her in front of a camera," I said.

"Explain."

"Clancy tampered with her mind. Really tampered with it."

"Brain voodoo?" Vida clarified. "Awesome. So much for getting any answers."

"You want to go get her." Liam's voice was quiet, and I could hear the hint of unhappiness in it that went unspoken. "You think you can fix whatever he did."

I nodded.

"You mean you want to send an extraction team into a secure facility, manned by a hundred trained ex-soldiers who specialize in torture and terror . . . because you have a theory," Cole said.

"If she's not there, then at least we'll find answers about where she is," I said. "It'll be a quick in-and-out. It's not like we don't know where Kansas HQ is. Two of us could go, survey the situation. If it seems too dangerous, we'll back off. It's worth the risk. If we find her and I can fix her, we'll have answers about the cure. If not, then . . . we'll have someone to trade for Cate."

Vida's interest in the Op shot way up at that. "Promise me that we'll eventually trade her for Cate, and I'm in. You and me, we can do this. It's nothing we haven't done a dozen times before."

Chubs groaned, putting a distressed hand to his face. "Don't tell us that. That makes it worse."

"It can't be Ruby," Cole said, "she's needed here. To deal with *it*."

I opened my mouth to protest.

"Wait—wait, wait, wait—" Liam interrupted, "slow down. A few hours ago you were worried about Agent Conner revealing the location of the Ranch, but what if they spill their guts about Kansas HQ? What if they've already packed up and left?"

"Then we'll follow their trail," Vida said. "Though I'll put a hundred bucks on the smug assholes feeling too invincible and secure to beat a hasty retreat. They're still there—a hundred bucks."

I turned to Cole. "If anyone is going in to bring him food, it's going to have to be you. I can pretty much guarantee he's not going to want to see my face for a while."

Cole looked intrigued by this, but ultimately shook his head. "No, you're needed here. If not for that, then to lead the camp hit."

"It would just be for a few days," I protested.

"No. I mean it."

The others shifted uncomfortably as Cole and I stared each other down.

"I'd offer, but I told the others I'd start organizing a search for the tribes," Liam said, running a hand back over his shaggy hair.

"I want to go out and try to find Olivia's group myself. I think I have an idea of where they are."

"Really?" I asked. Olivia and Brett and all of the other kids we'd met at Nashville had some experience with fighting. They'd be invaluable if they were willing to help.

Chubs straightened his windbreaker, zipping it up with a startling amount of conviction. "I'll go with Vida."

There was a moment of total and complete silence.

"Uh, no thanks," Vida said. "Pretty sure it would be more helpful to bring a dish towel."

"I still have my skip tracer credentials—it's just a matter of stopping somewhere to get a new ID made," he said, more to her than the others.

"You? You were a skip tracer?" Cole started to laugh, only to realize the rest of us weren't. "Wow, okay then. Why not? Continue."

"I can access their network and GPS system to make sure we steer clear of them." He swiveled toward Vida. "Also, screw you—maybe you can be all stealthy and break into their building to get the woman out, but I can get us there *and* back safely. I did this for months and never got a second glance from anyone, including PSFs."

"Probably because your ugly-ass face blinded them on the first look," she muttered.

"Really? Ugly jokes?" he hissed. "Don't tell me you've finally emptied out your arsenal of wit."

Liam stepped between them, blocking their view of each other—and still they kept slugging words to each other under their breath.

"Look, Vida, I'm happy to agree to the trade you want, but

the odds of pulling this off really aren't that great, kid," Cole said. "I can't even begin to predict what would happen if they caught you. How would you even play it?"

"By saying I was sick to death of how chickenshit everyone here is, and that I was ready to take an actual risk if it meant a huge payoff," she said, pointedly. "The 'payoff' in their minds being that I want to enlist with them."

"That's actually pretty plausible," I offered.

To Vida, this wasn't about getting the cure; her investment was a hundred percent in the fact that this was a real avenue to getting Cate back. I wish I could have had her confidence. I wish I could have let myself believe that they'd keep her alive long enough to matter, but what was the point? It was easier to feel the numbness of certainty than live along the burning edge of hope.

"All right, Vida. All right. You can go, as long as you take Skippy the skip tracer here with you. Unnecessary risks aren't an option. Do you understand?"

I almost told him that the two of them had pretty much opposite definitions of "unnecessary risks," but kept my mouth shut. I didn't like the idea of either of them being out of my sight for that long, let alone what could happen along the way. But if we were going to take a big risk, it needed to be for something like this.

"You got it," Vida said. "If you think I'm going to blow any chance to get Cate back then you must be smoking the good stuff."

"Darlin', I wish."

Cole, Liam, and I worked silently, hauling in one crate of weapons at a time. For once, I was grateful for the uneasy silence; no matter how unbearable the tension was, another fight would have been infinitely worse. There was a moment when I'd leaned forward to pick up a rifle and place it up on its proper rack in the weapons locker, and my sweatshirt had gaped. Liam had reached over and pulled the fabric down out of the way. He didn't comment on the bruise on the side of my neck, only smoothed the collar back up and turned away. When we were finished, he was the first one out of the room, disappearing through the double doors, heading, if I had to guess, back to the garage.

I followed the route he'd taken, stopping to check our bunk room first. Most of the kids had checked out for the night, but the door to our room was open; only Chubs was inside, passed out on his bed with all the lights on, a book resting across his chest. I smiled and reached for the light switch when I noticed the colorful, small box on Vida's bed.

It took less than thirty seconds to figure out where she'd gone. The top of the hair dye box had been ripped straight off, meaning one thing.

The ventilation in the bathrooms was bad enough that we had to prop both of the doors partly open to keep the spaces from feeling like the South in late summer. The steam had been thick enough to make me light-headed.

"That's okay, you know," Vida was saying, "but Z, that's a really shitty way to live."

I paused outside of the door, one hand pressed against it as I leaned forward, catching the one-sided conversation.

"Yeah, but doesn't it bother you?" she continued. "Aren't there things that are important enough to say—I know you can write it out, don't get me wrong, but how are you ever really going to get this shit off your chest if you can't talk it through? I mean, look, Z, you know I feel you, but the only person that's being hurt with this silence is you. Don't give them that power. Don't let them trap you into never saying anything. There are people worth remembering, speaking up for. You're important. You deserve to speak and have people shut the hell up and listen to you. You're smarter than ninety percent of our population."

I closed my eyes, pulling back to lean against the wall.

"Oh, girl, I get scared, too," Vida said. "I'm always a little scared when I go out on an Op. Not, like, shit-my-pants scared, but I'm afraid of what could happen to the others if I screw up or don't cover them well enough. Our friend Roo owes me about five years of my life back." She paused, likely waiting for Zu to write something. "Thing is, though, fear is worthless. It stops you when you need to keep moving most. And it only exists inside of your head. You can hate yourself for being scared, but that's still letting it control your life. Aren't you tired of that same old shit? It's just going to keep dragging you down."

There was another pause; long enough that I started to open the door again.

"People come in and out of our lives all the time," Vida said, her voice tight. "They can promise that they'll be right back, but you might never see them again. We got a good unit here, and you know why it's so strong? Because we chose it. We made it. My sister, she wasn't like your parents, but she still left me. The bitch called in my location for a reward, but I won't let her win. I won't give her the satisfaction of not letting myself trust anyone ever again. She didn't choose me, and now I'm choosing a different family."

I waited until Vida was back to humming a little song before slipping inside.

"Hey girl, what's doing?" Vida glanced over.

For once, the smell of bleach wasn't coming from the cleaning products we used to scrub out the showers, but from the thick cream Vida had combed through her short hair. There was an old ratty towel over her shoulders to catch the gooey mixture before it hit her sports bra. For a second, I couldn't see anything other than the scar tissue on her shoulders from the burns she'd gotten in Nashville, fighting Mason. It made my stomach go sour.

Zu sat perched on the counter next to her, swinging her legs back and forth, little white socks bobbing up and down through the air. She held up two different boxes in her hands for me to see—one blue, one red—then gestured toward Vida.

"I made Boy Scout stop on our way back from Oregon," Vida explained, taking the towel from her shoulders and wrapping it around Zu's much smaller ones. "Glad I did, too. Had to get my war paint on to go into battle tomorrow."

I gave her a look in the mirror.

"Fine. My carefully planned, reasonably cautious reconnaissance mission." Vida cocked a brow. "You sure you and me can't just sneak out tonight?"

"Chubs is useful," I reminded her. "Please try not to kill him."

"Yeah, yeah, we'll see. All I'm saying is, accidents happen."

Before I could even think of questioning it, she used her gloved fingers to scoop some of the product out from the cup she'd mixed it in and made a thin stripe of it in Zu's hair.

"Uh . . ." My mind blanked, cutting quickly to how Liam—and, worse, Chubs—would react to this development.

Zu glanced back in the mirror and made an impatient gesture, like, *more!* Vida shook her head. "Start with that and see if you like it first. Did you decide which color?"

"She'd rather have pink," I said. Zu whipped around to look at Vida again, her eyes wide with the possibility.

Vida cocked her head to the side, looking at the two boxes. "I could try mixing a separate batch and using a little less of the red dye than I normally would. Might not work, but it's worth a shot."

Zu nodded eagerly, flashing me a big smile.

"Charlie Boy's going to kill me," Vida sang out, leaning back against the counter. "But we don't give a damn what boys think, do we, girlfriend?"

I laughed, startled. "Charlie Boy?"

"Well—I mean, his name is Charles, right?" Vida said quickly, glaring at me in the mirror's reflection. "How is Chubs any better?"

"Good point," I said. "Well . . . I'll leave you guys to it. . . ."

"Where's the fire, boo?" Vida asked, hopping up on the counter next to Zu. "Stay awhile. It seems like we haven't seen your face around much."

I hesitated, knowing that I still needed to find Liam, but how could I say no when for the first time in days, Zu looked like her old self? When I'd missed seeing their faces, too?

"All right," I said, reaching for the bowl of dye. "Let's see if we can get you the perfect shade of pink. . . ."

THIRTEEN

A<small>FTER LYING AWAKE FOR THREE HOURS IN THE DARK,</small> counting Chubs's snores, waiting for Liam to come back, I finally pushed myself up off the stiff mattress and headed for the hallway. I wouldn't bother him, but I just . . . needed to make sure he was where I thought he was.

The music flowing down the tunnel to the garage was a pretty good hint I was on the right track. The Rolling Stones. Mick Jagger was crooning about wild horses, the promise in his voice stopping me just outside of the door.

I thought of the CD he'd brought in for me, the note that was still hidden inside, and felt caught between the need to go in, and the need to walk back to the bunk room, slide under a blanket, and disappear.

There were a few kids lingering around the space. One was working at the table along the opposite wall, her back hiding whatever it was she was doing. The others were playing cards on a blanket they'd spread out over the floor. It was strange to me that they were down here instead of using the chairs and tables in the big room upstairs, where it had to be at least twenty degrees warmer.

I stepped forward, wrapping my arms around my center to try to trap some warmth in. There was a sticky pull at the bottom of my shoes. I glanced at the ground and immediately jumped away. A large, white crescent moon. Someone must have painted it there earlier in the night.

Liam had his back to me as he crouched down, working on the motorbike he'd found. Its gray shell of grime had been polished away, and the silver accents and black panels gleamed under his care. It looked like he'd just brought it home from the store.

He stood up suddenly, reaching for a piece of foam, and started to wrap it over the bike's seat to cover the gashes in the leather.

"I like what you've done with the place!" I had to shout over Mick Jagger to be heard. The radio stood a foot away from my feet, and somehow I had the feeling that I didn't have the right to turn it off. You listened to music this loudly to drown out everyone and everything, letting the rhythm and beats flow around you like a shield.

Liam spun around, startled. His white shirt was spotted with oil and dust, and somehow, clearly without realizing it, he'd managed to wipe some of it across his forehead and cheek. It was disarming how good he looked to me, how much I wanted to go straight toward him, take his face in between my hands and kiss him and kiss him and kiss him until that carefree smile was back. It made me forget everything that had happened between the start of this and now. My mind was still on blown-out tires, socks, and the Beach Boys, even as he said, "What's wrong?"

"Nothing," I managed. "I just . . . I was worried when you didn't show up for lights out. I wanted to . . ."

"Make sure I didn't run away? Really?" He started to turn back to his bike but stopped midway, pressing his hand to his forehead. "Oh, damn. I did do that, didn't I? That was . . . not Nashville, right?"

The small bubble of contented memory popped around me. "It was Oklahoma, at the national park."

"Right. Right. That's the last foggy part. Right before you . . ." He waved a hand through the air. "Sorry. We need a clock in here."

My eyes drifted over his profile, the line of his jaw, and I thought with crushing certainty, *I'm not wanted here.*

"Okay, well," I said, forcing a horrible brightness into my voice. "Okay . . . I'm just going to . . . get going. . . ."

My throat was aching by the time I finally got the words out, and I had a feeling they didn't make sense, either. *Stupid, so stupid.* I'd wanted distance, hadn't I? I hadn't wanted to talk to him about everything—and now it was like I'd forgotten how to talk to him entirely.

I got a step away when the music got quieter and he called out, "I'm thinking of calling her Lovely Rita. What do you think?"

In spite of everything, I felt myself smile. "Like the Beatles song?"

He was leaning against the motorbike's seat, his legs out in front of him, his arms crossed over his chest. I made a mental amendment—*this* was the best thing I'd ever seen. This was the first time Liam had looked like Liam in months, from his wild, kept-running-his-hands-through-it hair to the way his jeans were slung low on his hips.

"Fits, right?" he said, offering the smallest, sweetest little smile.

"Isn't Rita a meter maid?" I asked, walking back over to him, my heart thrumming in my chest. Liam was watching me so intently, I almost tripped over my own careless feet. The warmth that pooled at my center threatened to spark when his arms slid forward, his hands turned up, toward me.

I stepped into the circle of them and leaned against his shoulder.

"Yeah," he said, quietly, "but she's so lovely."

My hands slid up along his back, and I was relieved that it was as hot to the touch as I felt. I wanted to ask him about the drive up, what the people they made contact with had been like, but it seemed enough to just be held, to feel him kiss my hair, my cheek.

I leaned back, looking up at his face. One his hands moved, sliding into the back pocket of my jeans; he was still watching me when I reached up and tried to thumb some of the oil off his face.

"Damn," he said, chuckling, "how much of a mess am I right now?"

You are perfect. My fingers and eyes shifted down, to the pale scar at the right corner of his mouth, and felt the first touch of something dark and insistent pressing at the back of my mind.

"How did you get this scar?" I asked. I just needed to hear it from him, to confirm what I'd seen locked inside Cole's mind. "I never asked you."

"It's a good thing you didn't," he said, reaching up to catch my hand and hold it in his. "There's not a good story to it. I've had it forever. Cole told me I got it when he pushed me off his bed."

I closed my eyes, let out a soft breath. And when he kissed me, I let it chase the truth away.

"Cole said you called Harry to help find where they brought

Cate," I said. "Thank you—thank you so much. I know you're trying to keep them out of this."

Liam laughed. "Like I could ever keep Harry *or* Mom from getting themselves in trouble. Zu's story pretty much proved that."

"You got to talk to them?"

"Yeah, I used one of the extra burner phones," he said. "It was amazing to hear their voices. It felt like it had been forever since the last time."

I ran a hand up and down his arm. I was thrilled for him—honestly thrilled beyond anything I thought possible. Enough, at least, to ignore the small pang of jealousy in the corner of my heart that was still bruised.

"I was worried he wouldn't accept Harry's help," Liam continued. "The two of them have knocked heads since day one."

"Why is that?" I asked. If he hated his biological father the way I knew he did, then why push back so hard against Harry?

He shrugged. "Cole used to act out a lot when we were kids, and Mom didn't have the heart to discipline him after everything that happened with our bio dad, so Harry had to do it. And you know, he's a great, loving, super funny guy, but he can be strict. He spent years in the military."

"And Cole has never liked being told what to do," I finished. That, and I was sure that once the change came over him and he developed terrifying abilities he had to fight to control, he spent most of his childhood angry and afraid of being found out. I swallowed hard at the thought, unable to speak. If he'd just *tell* Liam . . .

"I think he was—I'm not sure this is going to make sense, but I don't know that Cole ever let himself trust Harry. He remembers more of what it was like when our father was around, and he feels protective of Mom, which I do get. But it's like he's waiting for Harry to let us down. To hurt us. And Harry never would. I think he joined the League just to spite Harry, actually."

"Maybe working together now will help Cole learn to trust him?" I offered.

"That's what Harry's hoping. For the record, I hope so too." Liam pressed a kiss to my hair again before pulling back. "All right. I'm tuckered out—"

I wasn't tired in the slightest anymore, and I had a feeling he wasn't either, not really. I kissed the scar at the corner of his lips, running my hands up his neck and burying them in his hair. His pale blue eyes seemed to darken as he leaned down to meet me halfway.

Someone coughed behind us.

And coughed again.

Liam said something uncharacteristically vulgar under his breath as he pulled back, his face flushed and his eyes a bit too wild. "Yeah?"

It was the girl who'd been working at the table—she was a Blue who'd come in with Zu's ragtag group. Elizabeth. That was her name. Liza.

"I finished, but I'm not sure it looks . . . I think it might look more like a white banana?" She held up a black helmet for the two of us to inspect. Painted along one side was what looked to my eye like a crescent moon. Liam's arms tensed around my waist.

"It looks great," he said.

"Well *you* know what it's supposed to be, but what if she can't?" Liza said.

"She?" I repeated.

"Our contact," Liam said quickly, "Senator Cruz's, I mean.

When I go to pick up supplies, she wanted something to identify me."

"But won't you be driving a car or truck?" I asked. "Not the bike?"

He hesitated, standing up and away from the bike. I saw the effort of his concentration as he turned a smiling face back on me. "Sometimes the bike, depending on the situation. We'll paint one of the doors of the trucks, too."

I don't know what it was, exactly. The odd tone of his voice; the way Liza all but bolted, her face pale; how quick he was to take my hand and start guiding us back toward the tunnel. Every thought that passed through his head had always registered on Liam's face, good or bad. Seeing his carefully blank face, half-hidden by the shadows in the tunnel, I pieced together the realization.

He was keeping secrets, too.

Vida and Chubs left the next morning, long before the sun came up. Liam, Zu, and I were all there to see them off at the tunnel's entrance. Regardless of whether or not we'd been planning on it, the two of them had been bickering so loudly from the moment the alarm on Liam's watch went off that none of us had any chance of falling back asleep. Nico and Cole showed up a few minutes later, both pale and drained with an exhaustion that hadn't come with waking up at that ungodly hour, but staying awake to meet it. It set me on edge the way they wouldn't make eye contact with any of us. When I asked Cole what was going on, he only said, "We'll talk about it after."

As Vida went over the map one last time with Liam and Cole, I pulled Chubs aside and walked him a short ways down the hall. I could see him fighting inside himself for some composure; Chubs was so ruled by his head, by logic, that he didn't have a coping mechanism for when powerful emotions threatened his careful process. I don't think he was afraid for himself, so much as afraid of what could happen while they were gone.

"Don't do anything stupid," he started. "Be safe. Make sure that you seek out proper medical attention—"

"Isn't that the lecture I'm supposed to be giving you?" I asked.

"Yo, no time to chat and hug it out," Vida called. "Let's get cracking."

Chubs held up a finger to signal to the others that we needed a minute. Vida let out an impatient snort, then turned a very different finger in his direction.

"I have no doubt you guys are going to pull this off," I began, "but how are you going to get through it without one of you strangling the other?"

"Well, we're pretty evenly matched," he said reasonably. "She has the brawn, I have the brains. Either both of us will come back, or neither of us will because we'll have clawed each other's throats out."

"Don't even joke about it," I whispered.

"I have to joke about it, otherwise I'll probably start crying." Chubs's face suddenly looked as drawn as I felt.

"You don't have to go if you don't want to," I said quickly. "It's not too late."

"Isn't it? Besides, I have to pull my weight, too." He shrugged with a nonchalance that looked unnatural on him. His voice sounded strained, filtered through a lump in his throat.

"You and Vida will both be fine," I said, planting both hands on his shoulders and forcing him to look down and meet my gaze.

"You have everything under control. You'll both be careful, and quick, and back in one piece."

Chubs turned back toward Vida, who was the only person I knew who could make pacing look like prowling.

"Well," he amended with a long-suffering look, "hopefully no more than two pieces."

Despite what Vida had said, she waited patiently as Chubs knelt to talk to Zu and gave Liam a good pounding on the back. Cole unlocked the door, letting a draft of cold air into the hallway, and stood back as Chubs took the first few steps down.

As much faith as I had in them, I did have to fight off the urge to throw myself in front of the tunnel out and block their path. I pressed a hand against my chest, trying to stamp the feeling of panic out. But Zu had no such reservations. She bolted out of Liam's grip and pushed past Cole, who was shutting the door after them. By the time we caught up to them, she was gripping their packs, her heels digging into the unfinished floor, crying in that silent, heartbreaking way. Crying harder than I'd ever seen; she shook her head, her lips moving with silent pleas. Chubs looked back at us, startled.

Zu had been the toughest of our group in many ways, the one quickest to bounce back after terror or sadness knocked her flat. Whatever walls she'd built up to keep the feelings from cresting, they weren't high enough now to stop the desperate fear. And it devastated me. My throat ached with the need to cry, too.

Vida dropped her pack and knelt down in front of her. "Hey girl, none of that. It's like what we talked about, yeah?"

Zu pressed her face against Chubs's backpack.

"What happened to you with that guy—the one who drove

you to California, that was some—" I saw her catch herself, modify her word choice—"that was some messed-up stuff, and I'm sorry, I'm really sorry that it happened to him. But me and Charlie Boy? We're coming back. None of us are going to leave you here alone. We take care of our family, right?"

I didn't realize Liam still had a hand on my shoulder until it tightened. His face was ashen.

That calmed Zu down, at least enough to release her grip on Chubs and turn toward Vida fully.

"You can trust me, Z. I won't let you down. Okay?"

She nodded, scrubbing at her face with her sleeve. Vida held up her fist for a bump, but Zu one-upped her, wrapping her bony arms around the older girl's neck. Vida said something too low for any of the rest of us to hear, but when Zu pulled back she was nodding, a look of fierce determination on her face. With no other warning she turned and hugged Chubs, too, looking back to point a finger toward Vida as if to say, *Be nice.*

"I told you," Vida said as she stood. "I keep my promises."

Liam stepped forward to guide Zu back into the hallway so she didn't have to watch the door shut and lock behind them. I saw her straighten herself out, her fists clenching at her sides and her chin lifting up—the same way I'd seen Vida prep herself for battle.

"Let's go get something to eat, okay?" Liam said. He looked back over his shoulder. "Coming?"

I shook my head. "Have to shower and take care of a few things. I'll catch up with you later."

Liam waved and started walking with Zu back down the hall, heading to the kitchen in the lower level.

"Okay, what's going on?" I asked before either Cole or Nico could speak. "What happened last night?"

"It's easier to show you." Cole started past me, heading the same way his brother had taken, toward the stairs. I followed him silently, watching Nico watch the floor, my stomach clenching. It was getting too hard to pretend like I didn't care.

It was the first time I'd been down in the computer room since the supplies had come in last night. Where there had once been only one laptop, there were now five desktops. Another three silver laptops were spaced out along the desks, which were still pushed against the walls, leaving an empty space at the center of the room for planning. I spotted a printer and a scanner near the old laptop. Nico had picked a seat at the far back corner of the room, as usual. Cole brushed aside printouts of indecipherable code from one of the nearby seats and offered it to me.

Nico keyed in some kind of a password and brought up a window of more code.

"Somehow this doesn't feel 'easier,'" I said. "What are we looking at?"

"This is our server log," Nico said. "It seemed like it was lagging last night, so I was trying to troubleshoot what the issue was. This right here—" He pointed to the screen. "That means someone sent one of the files saved there, transferring it via FTP to another encrypted server."

"What file?" I asked.

"It was one of the videos from the Thurmond testing," Cole said.

"But there's more," Nico scrolled up. "There are gaps in the server's activity log, all between the hours of midnight and four A.M. on two other days."

"It's not because no one was awake to use the computers?" I asked.

Nico shook his head. "We've been leaving the computers on overnight to transfer everything to remote backup servers in case ours fail. There would have been huge spikes of activity—but look."

The huge spikes of activity were there, beginning at eleven o'clock in the evening, but abruptly cutting off at two in the morning, only to resume four hours later, right around the time Nico or another Green would first roll in to start the day's work.

"Is there really no way to tell who did it?" I asked, squinting at the screen.

"It was a Green," Nico said.

"It *might* have been a Green," Cole said.

"No," Nico insisted, "it had to have been a Green. How many kids actually know how to erase server activity?"

"Okay," I said. That made sense, unfortunately. "But if they went to such great lengths to hide the other instances, would they have left this blip for someone to find?"

Nico shrugged. "Maybe they were interrupted? Or they were in such a hurry they didn't have time?"

Cole asked another question that disappeared beneath the rush of blood in my ears as I stared at the screen, blinking to clear the blurriness that turned it into nothing more than a glowing square.

". . . think?" Cole touched my shoulder to get my attention, making me jump.

"Sorry," I said quickly, avoiding their stares. "I'm tired. What did you just ask?"

"My theory is one of the computers just glitched, or there's a problem with the server," Cole said, his eyes soft with concern.

"Occam's razor," Nico said. "Make the fewest assumptions. The simplest solution is usually the right one."

"I don't know anything about a razor, but who the hell would kids be sending the intel to?" Cole asked. "Who'd be stupid enough to try to sell information at the risk of getting their asses caught and hauled into a camp?"

"Could it be someone from Kansas HQ accessing files remotely?" I asked Nico.

He shook his head. "It's someone here."

Damn. I shared a look with Cole.

"I want to believe it's a one-off thing," he said, "but keep digging. Let me know if they try anything again, okay?"

There was a knock on the windows running along the side of the room—Kylie, dressed in all black, her hair tied into a poofy bun. "Ah," Cole said. "That'll be the groups leaving this morning to try to track down those tribes in Montana. You two figure the camera situation out, okay?"

"Wait," I said, "They're leaving this morning? Where did the cars come from?"

"They're taking the SUVs Lee rounded up for yesterday's haul," he said, stretching as he stood. I followed him to the door, listening to him rattle off instructions about training and which weapons to pull from the locker for training the next day, but when I reached the door, I didn't follow him out into the hall.

I stepped back into the computer room and caught sight of the white board out of the corner of my eye. Someone, likely Cole, had started scribbling information on it—coordinates, camp populations, number of PSFs assigned, anything and everything the League might have had in its files. Peppered through were details from Clancy's documents—I saw tidbits about the camp controllers tossed in like afterthoughts.

The basic outline of the Oasis plan was there, too. I found my name written next to *influence camp controller in charge of communications.*

"You don't have to stay," Nico said. "I can do this myself."

"I know." I picked up the dry erase marker from the ledge, and started to fill in additional information about Thurmond, fleshing out sections of the plan where I could.

"It was your strategy," Nico said over the warm purring of the machines around us. "Right? It seemed like you."

"What do you mean?"

"A little reckless. Smart, but not giving attention to the details."

"Really," I said dryly, turning back to face him.

He kept his back to me the whole time, shoulders bunched up with tension. I'd really been a monster to him, hadn't I? There seemed to be a five-foot radius around me that Nico was too frightened to cross. I fought to keep from cringing at the thought of how badly I'd mistreated him.

"How would you do it?" I jerked my chin in the direction of the blank space under the word *Thurmond*, trying to ignore the way it seemed to be taunting the both of us.

He stared at me and sixty full seconds of awkwardness passed before he took a tentative step closer. "It doesn't matter what I think."

"You said I wasn't paying attention to the details," I prompted. "What did you mean by that?"

Nico looked down at the floor, running his shoes over the

tile. I had a fleeting thought of how Vida used to call the Greens "squeakers" because of the way they all seemed to shuffle their feet as they walked. "The Oasis plan is okay," he said finally. "The way we have it now makes sense. Based on the size of the camp, there'll only be two or three camp controllers, and it'll be easy for you to figure out who is in charge of security and sending the status updates to their network. It won't work that way at Thurmond."

I watched him wring his hands, still unable to look at me. "There's going to be, what, two dozen camp controllers in the Control Tower? That was the estimate in . . . in Clancy's files. Its position at the center of the camp means that anyone forcing their way in through the gate is going to have to fight through all of the rings of cabins to get to it to subdue the PSFs and controllers inside, and by then the camp controllers will have called for reinforcements. Even if you found a way to subdue all of them, it would still be too late. All they'd have to do is turn on the White Noise and we'd be done. The power generator and backup generator are all on the camp premises, and I have a feeling cutting the power would automatically trigger an alarm on the military's network."

In the space of two minutes, he'd managed to chisel my confidence down to dust. "So we'll need a bigger attack force. One that can work faster, get them in and out."

"Liam's idea about trying to get the parents to storm the camp might work," he offered, "but its success depends half on us being able to inspire civilians to revolt and come after the camps, and half on whether or not the PSFs would fire on civilians or figure out some other way to deter them."

"He has an actual plan?" I asked.

"Not in the technical definition of the word. I just heard some kids asking him about what he would do." Nico shrugged. "His option isn't perfect, either."

"Is there a third option?" I asked.

Finally Nico stood up and, with tentative, halting steps, walked beside me. I tried to offer him the marker, but he didn't take it. "Are you sure you want to know?"

"Try me."

"The only way I can think of to disable the camp controller's access to the camp's systems—not even disable or disarm the system itself, but lock them out and keep the system running so no one outside notices anything amiss—is to install a Trojan horse program in their system and control it remotely. They'll be so disoriented that the tactical team will have an easier time of it."

"Is that something we could upload into their server?" The League had given us a limited education on technology and the way viruses worked, but this was out of my depth.

"No, the programs don't install automatically like a virus. Someone has to install it," he said. "And with all of the security safeguards in place, I don't think one of them would carelessly download any kind of email attachment."

"So someone would have to go into Thurmond and install it before the assault," I said. "But the camp has been closed to new kids for years."

"They take escaped kids back into the camp they were originally processed in," Nico said quietly. "I already started coding the Trojan horse. Cole told me to . . ."

I held up a hand to cut him off. "Cole approved this already?"

He nodded, eyes wide. "He said he'd talk to you about it. I can have it ready in a week. They'll be powerless to stop it once the program is installed."

I felt every last drop of blood drain out of my head in horror.

"*No,*" I said, horrified. "*No way—*"

"I meant me," Nico said quickly. "Not you. I could bring the Trojan horse program in on a flash drive, the same way we're bringing the cameras into Oasis. Glasses frames. Have you seen them?" Nico crossed the room, retrieving a pair of glasses with black plastic frames.

I had to lean against the desk to stay vertical. "Nico—*no.*"

"It's already installed—right there," he said, ignoring me and pointing to one of two shiny silver screws that looked like they were holding the frames together. "This is the camera, and this is just a screw the frames don't need. We had to make them seem as real as possible. Tommy said they're fine, so he'll get this pair. For Thurmond, maybe I could take one of the thicker frames— break up one of the arms that hooks behind the ear and replace a piece of it with a small flash drive? It's either that or embedding it under my skin, but they still do strip searches, don't they? The cut would be too obvious."

"Nico!" I interrupted. "Listen to me! *No.* There's no way in hell you're going back in there! Even if they brought you back into the camp, how would you get yourself into the Control Tower to upload it? You haven't been there since the camp changed. They don't just let you walk around unsupervised. Every move you make in there is choreographed down to the minute. And it's the most fortified building in the camp."

He paused, trying to think this through. "I'd need to observe the schedules of the PSFs, figure out a moment I could slip away.

It doesn't matter if they catch me in the end, not really. It would be okay . . . I would get to . . . there's not anyone left for me now that Cate's gone. And this is how I could make it right." His voice dropped to a whisper. "This is how I could make it right for Jude."

I stood straight up at that, whirling around to face him fully. "Throwing yourself into danger . . . throwing your life away . . . what would Jude say about that? What would Cate say? I haven't been a good friend to you these past few weeks, but Nico, I swear to God—please, I forgive you, I do, I understand what happened and I'm sorry I treated you the way I did. I've been up in my own head too much, and it was hard for me to see things clearly. But please *listen* to me—"

"It's okay." Nico's voice was hoarse.

"It's not!" It wasn't. It wasn't even remotely all right how I'd been acting—blaming him for everything, hating him because I couldn't function if all of my energy went into hating myself. I tried to think of what Jude would say and do in this situation. Or even Cate, all those times she'd had to talk the kid out of a manic fit about some conspiracy.

"We can't change what happened in Los Angeles. I was angry—I was so damn angry that he just . . . slipped away, and I couldn't save him. I should have talked to you, should have *helped* you, or at least tried to understand what you'd done. I let everyone down, but it was easier to blame you. It hurt less. But the truth is, I knew what Clancy was capable of. I should have tried to confirm some other way that what he said was true. And you know what? Jude would have wanted to go anyway, even if I said no."

"He was my best friend," Nico choked out.

"I know. But . . . it's different with Clancy, isn't it?" I said quietly. "Rules don't apply when you love someone. And that's how it was with Clancy, right? It's not like how you loved Jude, or the way I love Chubs."

I'd known it the moment I saw his face in Clancy's memory. The tortured expression and the ragged sobs were only part of it. It was the way Nico had held the other boy, how he'd fed him and cleaned him with every ounce of tenderness he had in him. *You see it in others,* I thought, *when you recognize it in yourself.*

"You trusted him, and he took your words and twisted them for his own ends," I said. "I was so angry with you for believing him, for giving him everything you did. But I know firsthand that people are capable of doing things for the people they love that they never would have considered before."

Nico buried his face in his hands, letting out a shuddering breath.

"I didn't mean to ruin everything," he whispered. "I trusted him. All the intel I gave him, he swore he was using to help us and I thought . . ."

"You thought that he would help keep us away and safe, didn't you?" I finished for him. "I know. It sounds to me like maybe you fell into my pattern for a while there."

"I don't know why—I knew it was wrong, that it was bad, but he was good. When I knew him, he was good and he helped me. And I just extrapolated it would apply to everyone else. The only reason you were there was because I forecast the results incorrectly. I didn't factor all of his behavioral outliers in." His voice became so small, I had to lean in that much closer to hear him. "He wasn't always the way he is now. They broke something in him."

"I'm sorry," I said. "For not letting you explain. For acting the way I did and not being there for you."

"I have to fix this," he said, voice ragged, "I have to make things right. I can't—I can't stop thinking about all of the other outcomes we could have had. Vida said if you hadn't been there we wouldn't have had the cure, but we don't have it, do we? It was for nothing."

It was a punch to the gut. I felt tears spring to my eyes and fought to hold them back. The pain in him was unending. His life was tragedy upon tragedy upon tragedy. And I'd ignored him, punished him. Vida hadn't made any real attempt. Cate had left altogether. He didn't have anyone to help him through this. We'd stranded him out in a dark sea without so much as a life vest.

"We can make it right," I said, taking him by the shoulders. "You've done so much already, but there's still so much left. We'll figure out another way."

"You have no logical reason to trust me," Nico said.

"You may have noticed this about me, but I've never been good at listening to logic."

"That's true," he agreed. "It's not your pattern. Jude liked that. He said you knew when it was okay to break the rules to help people. He said you were like a superhero because you always tried to do good things even if the odds were bad."

"Jude's pattern was exaggeration," I said, hoping he didn't catch the hitch in my voice.

Nico nodded, his jet-black hair falling forward into his face. He looked sick to me—sick in body, mind, and heart. The pallor of his usually golden-brown skin made it look like his ghost had already up and left his body. "Jude never made logical decisions, but he tried."

He tried. He tried so hard, at everything, with everyone.

"Ruby, what does the future look like?" Nico asked. "I can't picture it. I try all the time, but I can't imagine it. Jude said it looked like an open road just after a rainstorm."

I turned back toward the board, eyes tracing those eight letters, trying to take their power away; change them from a place, a name, to just another word. Certain memories trap you; you relive their thousand tiny details. The damp, cool spring air, swinging between snow flurries and light rain. The hum of the electric fence. The way Sam used to let out a small sigh each morning we left the cabin. I remembered the path to the Factory the way you never forgot the story behind a scar. The black mud would splatter over my shoes, momentarily hiding the numbers written there. 3285. Not a name.

You learned to look up, craning your neck back to gaze over the razor wire curled around the top of the fence. Otherwise, it was too easy to forget that there was a world beyond the rusting metal pen they'd thrown all of us animals into.

"I see it in colors," I said. "A deep blue, fading into golds and reds—like fire on a horizon. Afterlight. It's a sky that wants you to guess if the sun is about to rise or set."

Nico shook his head. "I think I like Jude's better."

"Me too," I said softly. "Me too."

FOURTEEN

AFTER LEAVING NICO TO HIS WORK, I HEADED TO THE upper level, barely keeping a lid on the fury ripping through me. It didn't matter, not even for a second, that Senator Cruz was in Alban's old office with Cole and they were having a serious, quiet discussion. I let myself explode into the room.

Senator Cruz leapt to her feet and pressed a hand to her chest. Cole only leaned back in his seat.

"He told you," Cole said, his voice flat.

"Yes, he told me!" I snapped. "How could you authorize—"

"Shut the door—*Ruby*!" Cole slammed a hand down on the desk, cutting off my tirade before it could even really begin. The way his voice immediately softened, the pained quality of it, brought me up short. "Shut the door."

I kicked it shut behind me, crossing my arms over my chest.

"It is a *death sentence* to send that kid into Thurmond," I told him. "He won't be able to handle it, and even if he could, who's to say they'll take him to the camp and not back into Leda's testing program?"

"The one he was in was closed shortly after I got the flash drive out," Cole said.

"Like there aren't others?" I said.

"You were fine with sending Tommy and Pat into Oasis," Senator Cruz reminded me. *She knew about this, too.*

"I'm not *fine* with it. I don't *like* it. But they're functioning as eyes and ears only, and we'll have them out within two days. Nico won't be able to get away to install the program, and even if by some miracle he does, he won't be able to get away from the Control Tower once it's complete."

"Then, what do you suggest?" Cole asked. "Really, I'm all ears."

I thought of Zu's reaction to Vida and Chubs leaving, the pale shock that had wrapped its icy hands over her. If Nico was right, and this was the only way, then it . . . I took a deep breath in, my fingers curling into fists. Wouldn't it have to be me? Nico was too fragile right now. Being back there would destroy him. But I could—if it helped the people I loved, if it helped every kid that came after us—I could accept that it was the role I was meant to play in this.

They'll kill you, I thought. Clancy had already confirmed what they had done to the other Oranges. *You would have to convince them again—make them think you're Green.* I shook my head, trying to clear the thoughts. Last resort. This was a last resort plan.

"I think we need to consider Liam's ideas," I said. "Maybe we should go more indirect. Use the media. Get the parents involved. If we take Gray's image down, shake up that last bit of trust people have in him, we can dismantle his government that way. The international community can't ignore evidence of abuse and wrongdoing for long. They'll step in—"

"Sweetheart, they've been ignoring evidence for years," Senator Cruz said. "They tried to drop aid into the country and it backfired. Gray threatened to shoot their planes out of the sky if they crossed into our airspace again. I've tried and tried."

"We just have to get them the right proof," I said. "We can use Lillian Gray's words about the cure and whatever she knows about what caused IAAN to prove it's safe for them to travel in, and help overthrow Gray. Haven't there been peacekeeping forces formed in the past?"

"We have a deal. Oasis for supplies," Senator Cruz said sharply, turning to look at Cole. "Are you reneging?"

"No, I promise you, that's not what we're doing," he said, both hands out and placating. "It's natural to have cold feet before an Op like this. Can I speak to Ruby alone for a few minutes?"

Senator Cruz rose stiffly, casting an unhappy glance in my direction as she exited the room and pulled the door firmly shut behind her.

"Talk to me, Gem," Cole said. "Tell me what's going on in that head of yours."

"We should keep the plan for Oasis, but I think we need to rethink our approach to Thurmond. Nico won't be able to handle the strain, and we have no guarantee he'd even be brought in. We don't have to be the League—default on a straightforward assault."

Cole let out a humorless laugh, rocking back in his chair again. "Do you know why that became the general strategy? It wasn't always that way. Alban tried for years to release the truth about Gray and the quality of life in the camps. He tried propaganda, straight-up emotional manipulation. And what messages did get through fell flat. It wasn't that people didn't care. It was that their heads were already in Gray's game, and he told them, time and time and time again, that if they took their kids out of his camps, they would die. For what Liam's suggesting to work, it's not just about getting the parents there, it's making them willing to come. And if you don't think the PSFs wouldn't open fire on civilians, you are dead wrong, Ruby. Dead wrong."

"There hasn't been a situation like this before, though," I said. "You can't know for sure."

The metal banged and screeched as Cole reached into the bottom drawer of the desk and slammed it shut again. He stood up and began slapping down sheets of paper across the empty desk, one at a time, lining them up in neat rows, a gruesome echo of the pictures' contents.

They were—all of those pictures were of kids in those thin, color-coded camp uniforms, black Psi ID numbers across their backs. Some of their eyes were open, but more often than not, they weren't. Some were bloodied, their faces swollen. A few looked like they were just sleeping.

The only thing they had in common was the long, empty ditch at their feet.

"Where did you get these?" I whispered.

"Amplify released them a few days ago," Cole said. "I don't think I need to tell you that these aren't doctored, no matter how hard Gray's cronies try to spin it on the news shows."

I shook my head, feeling like I was about to crawl out of my own skin. I would have backed away if there was room to move. As it was, the walls were folding in over my head, falling down over me, crushing, crushing, crushing.

I had to get out of this room. My palms were drenched in

sweat, too slick to open the door. Cole grabbed my arm and forced me to stand in front of the desk, forced me to look down at the photos and *see* them, absorb the blood, the bone, the vacant eyes.

"These are the people we're dealing with," he said. "*This* is reality. These are people who won't hesitate to kill anyone who interferes with their orders. This is what hesitation has cost us. This is why we have to fight. Revolutions are won with blood, not words. These photos have been out for days, and what have they done to get people involved—angry enough to stand up and protest? Nothing. Ruby, even *this* isn't enough. They all think they're fake."

"Let me go!" I struggled out of his grip, the floor rising and rolling under me. That face, I knew that face—the girl in green—

"No one is going to fight for us, Ruby—*we* have to fight. We have to end this. Match force with force. Every second we waste circling back and debating the same shit is a second we could be saving these kids from something like this. What do you think sparked this? They were beaten to death. Was it because they tried to escape? They were caught in the middle of a fight? Did some PSF snap? Does it *matter*?"

Oh my God, I was going to be sick. I pressed my fists against my eyes, trying to remember how it was I usually went about breathing. "These pictures are from Thurmond—this is *Thurmond*. That girl—that girl in green—"

Cole's grip on me tightened. I had the vague sense that he was the only reason I was still standing on my feet.

"I know her. Her name is . . . was . . . Ashley. She was one of the older girls in my . . ."

"In your cabin?" Cole finished. "Are you sure? Maybe you should take another look."

I did and it changed nothing. I lived with those girls for years, I knew their faces better than I knew my own. Ashley had been at Thurmond for over a year before I showed up, and she took care of us like you'd think a big sister would. She was nice. She was . . .

Dead.

"Okay," Cole said quietly. "I'm sorry. I believe you. I'm so sorry. I wouldn't have showed them to you at all if I'd known. The source that sold them to Amplify didn't identify which camp they're from."

Jesus—that ditch. The realization thundered down around me. They were putting them in that ditch? That was what they got? After everything—*this*?

Too late.

This was Thurmond. This was *real*. We weren't going fast enough. I hadn't been able to get to them in time. A swell of bile rose up in me, and I ripped myself out of Cole's grip, collapsing onto my knees. I barely got my face into the trash can before I could throw up everything in my stomach.

When I came back to the moment, Cole was holding my hair back with one hand, rubbing a circle across my shoulder blades with the other. I braced my arms against the plastic container and gave in to the sting of tears.

"Did the source say what happened?" I used the tissue he handed me to wipe my mouth. I felt lightheaded, like I was slipping out of the moment, and fought against the pull.

"They issued a statement saying one of the PSFs stationed there snuck a cell phone into the camp and snapped the photos. Ruby . . . I think—I don't want to believe this, but it seems like too much of a coincidence that this happened and they're closing the camp. There are over three thousand kids there and the other camps are small and crowded. Is it possible they're trying to reduce the population of kids before the move?"

"They've killed kids before," I said. "The ones who tried to escape . . . the Oranges. Reds who wouldn't let themselves be controlled. If this has happened once, it'll happen again. They're going to keep doing this. We're sitting around, waiting to get one useful piece of information, and they're *dying*. This can't just be about evidence. Not for Thurmond. We need to get those kids out *now*."

I saw the future with sharp clarity and it wasn't a road, it wasn't a sky, it wasn't anything that beautiful. It was electricity singing through metal chain-link and bars. It was mud and rain and a thousand days bleeding into a stream of black.

Cole must have sensed it, seen it reflected in my face, because he leaned back and finally let me go.

"We're going to need actual fighters for the Thurmond hit," I said. "Trained soldiers to go in first."

"Agreed," Cole said, looking away. "Harry . . . Harry offered to help us fight. I wasn't going to say yes. I hate the idea of owing him anything, but we don't have any time to waste now. Nico is right. The only way to shut down the camp's defenses is by attacking them from within. I'll see if I can try to bribe one of the PSFs—someone has to know *someone* there—"

"No," I said, my voice calm. "It has to be me. I have to be the one who goes back. A PSF can flip, take a bribe, tip the camp controllers off to what we're doing. If it has to be done, I'm going to do it myself."

"The others will never agree to it," Cole said quietly, but he didn't disagree. He didn't want to stop me.

"I know," I said, "that's why we aren't going to tell them until we have to."

Over the next week, the face of the Ranch seemed to change.

Kylie and the other driver who had gone out looking for tribes returned victorious, even as Liam set out to find Olivia twice and came back empty-handed both times. If he was frustrated by the wasted time and gas, he didn't show it—a part of me wondered if he used the time to get away from all of this for a few hours, taking Lovely Rita in the direction of the rising sun and returning in time for the sun to set.

The new recruits were willing enough; the group of five Blues that had come back—Isabelle, Maria, Adam, Colin, and Gav— had all served on East River's watch and, in theory, knew how to use weapons. The issue was, after months spent in the wilds of Utah looking like they'd survived a meteor apocalypse, they only took orders from Gav—who didn't particularly enjoy taking orders from anyone, least of all an "adult shithead" like Cole. He complained about the cramped sleeping conditions, the plain, basic food we ate, the smell of the shampoo—like he was some kind of connoisseur of floral notes in fragrance. Gav was stocky, had a ruddy complexion, and seemed mean enough to want to fight, but only if we begged him.

The Saga of Gav the Asshole ended when Cole hauled him up by the arm from dinner, dragged him into the shooting range, and locked the door behind them. Five minutes and a muffled gunshot later, Gav came out a team player, and Cole looking far less like he wanted to set the kid's hair on fire.

The other tribe was a group of Greens, who spent days circling the various computers that the resident Greens now seemed

chained to night and day, if only to keep the new hands from
tampering with their settings. Only one of the girls, Mila, offered
to join the tactical team, but I had to work with her each morning
to get her to understand what each hand signal meant so she'd be
able to follow my commands.

The third group that arrived, two days after Mila's, found *us*.
And we knew them.

Nico had spotted the three teens looking around Smiley's,
clearly drawn to the crescent moon that we'd painted on the now-
defunct bar's door. Kylie and Liam had all but run for the tunnel
door to greet them. It wasn't until I saw their interaction on the
computer screen, the way Liam pounded the back of one of the
guys with shaggy dark hair and tan skin, that I recognized him.

"Friends of yours?" Cole asked, coming out of the office as the
five them came up through the tunnel laughing, practically talking over each other to get answers.

"You remember Mike," Liam said, gesturing to the kid in the
Cubs baseball hat. He was thinner than I remembered—a good
ten pounds lighter from stress and the strain of the road, likely—
but I knew him by the wary look he cast in my direction. The kid
gave me a stiff nod, then turned to accept a bear hug from Lucy.

Cole let out a faint whistle at that. "Not a fan of yours, I
take it."

"The feeling is mutual," I assured him. Mike hadn't liked me
or trusted me, and had never really wanted to take the blindfold
off his eyes about Clancy.

"That's Ollie and Gonzo over there, they're brothers," Liam
continued, pointing to the two teens standing off to the side.
One—Gonzo, I think—had his hand on a makeshift knife made
out of a glass shard, a stick, and fabric. "They were on watch

287

with me. You guys hungry? I think dinner should just about be ready. ..."

I caught his arm before he led the group away. "You can't tell them about Clancy."

"I already did," he told me in a thin voice. "And they don't care as long as he stays locked up."

"If they try to find him—"

"They won't," Liam said, pulling his arm away. "They're not here for him."

I wanted to ask him what, exactly, he meant by that, but he was already gone, jogging to catch up to the others. Zu, who'd been idling nearby in the hall, had come to stand beside me, looking up at me in question.

"I'll tell you later," I promised her. Because we didn't have time. I didn't have time to think about Liam, let alone constantly seek him out in the garage where he kept to himself.

The morning after the Greens perfected the cameras embedded in the glasses, two and a half weeks before March first, Kylie and drove Tommy and Pat out of California. They wound their way down surface streets and access roads until they reached Elko, Nevada, the closest town to Oasis that was more than a few houses baking in the desert sun. The boys spent the next few days hanging out at the fringes of town, appearing, disappearing, causing just enough suspicion for some money-hungry soul to call them in for a reward. There was a close call, during which it seemed like the PSFs who collected them were going to take them out of state, up to the camp in Wyoming, but they changed course at the last moment.

Their glasses captured everything. We had a front row seat as the kids were driven up through the desert, as they were processed into Oasis, as they walked through the hallways with their many doors, as they were brought into their rooms, as the PSFs roughed them up a little to show off, slapping Tommy hard enough to knock the glasses off his face. We charted meal times, lights out, rotations, and compared the personnel lists on the PSF network to the faces we saw.

After one day, we'd already seen the entirety of the premises. The camp was a two-story building, shrouded from outside eyes by a tall electric fence and canopied tarps, both to keep out the sun and to block any views of the yard from above.

We knew that the weekly supplies came at four-thirty every Friday morning. The loud engines and tires chewing gravel and dirt announced their arrival.

"The batteries in the cameras will run out soon," Nico warned.

"Is everything saved and downloaded somewhere?" Liam asked, standing behind him, next to a clearly impressed Senator Cruz.

Nico turned around in his chair. "Yeah, but why?"

Liam glanced toward the floor. "In case we need to refer back to it when we figure out planning and timing."

"There's nothing left to do, then," Cole said, "but practice. And wait."

Four days of waiting.

Four days of basic self-defense training.

Four days of reminding the kids to keep the safety catch on the guns until they were ready to fire, to brace themselves when they needed to, and to use their abilities before they'd think about firing.

And now, day three of the run-through. The first day had been simple enough—most of the kids in this group, the East

River kids at least, had experienced overpowering a large truck in a highway setting. They'd had to do it any number of times to steal supplies and food. The trick was reminding them repeatedly that they couldn't destroy the truck in the process.

I adjusted the strap on my tactical helmet, tightening until I felt it dig into the soft skin beneath my jaw as I crouched down, breathing in the clean, cool February air. It was my first time outside in what felt like a month, and we'd only been allowed to position ourselves outside of the garage's loading dock door.

It had taken us nearly half a day to clear out space in the garage, temporarily moving the cars, Liam's bike, and the bigger pieces of furniture and crates outside. I saw him lean back, as if checking to make sure they were all still on the other side of the building where we'd left them. I'd had a hard time putting a finger on his mood today. It seemed to shift by the minute.

The kids behind me were a cluster of disordered black fatigues. Each piece had been found, collected, and pulled by Liam and others running the supplies specifically because they were close to the fatigues worn by the PSFs. The look was pulled together with the assault rifles in their hands. Everyone had spent hours of the last three days in the makeshift shooting range we'd set up. The rapid firing of the bullets had steeled my nerves more than I'd expected; lacing up black combat boots, adjusting holsters and utility belts, had made me feel like I was stepping back into a shell I'd abandoned when I'd split with the League. It was a good fit—steadying, at least. I felt my feet fixed firmly to the ground with the added weight of the necessities of combat.

Liam put a hand on my shoulder to steady himself as he adjusted the strap on his rifle, and for the tenth time today I felt my chest tighten, my hands clench around my own gun. To think

I'd believed being in the Children's League would destroy him, ruin every good part of him. The only person dragging him into this firefight was me.

"Begin!"

We came at the door in a rush of overeager energy, pouring through the opening. I felt the lick of adrenaline against my heart, counting off the timing in my head. The two Blues in front of me, Josh and Sarah, raised their rifle sights to their eyes and stepped into the makeshift hallway we'd constructed out of pallets, simulating the layout of the lower-level hall we'd seen. They swept their hands out toward Zu and Hina, who were pretending to be the PSFs posted at either end of the hall standing guard, and the girls made a dramatic show of pretending they were thrown back. Liam actually laughed behind me, which set my teeth on edge.

"Stop!" Cole called from his perch atop one of the ladders. "Girls! You have to take this seriously, otherwise I'm subbing you out. There's not enough time for us to be dicking around, not when it could mean this team not getting their timing down. Got it?"

Zu and Hina wilted at his sharp words, but nodded.

"Go from the top," Cole said. "Everyone reset—but this time, Liam, switch places with Zach—yeah, you'll be behind Ruby. Lucy, hop out—you too, Mila. Sorry, ladies. You're not right for this Op. I want Gonzo and Ollie to take their place."

Liam opened his mouth but caught himself. I gave him a quick nod, letting him know it was all right. Cole had been making these switches and substitutions for the past two days, trying to get the best chemistry in the group. We were getting there, but the birthing process had been painful and I was feeling each day passing like a strike to the back of the head.

I would have given anything for Vida to be here next to me. I checked in with Nico every single day to see if he'd gotten another status update from them, but the last contact they'd made had been to let us know they had safely arrived in Kansas.

"Begin!" And the dance started all over again.

We moved into the garage two at a time—Gav, at my left, grunted as he dropped down to his knee. He pretended to cover Josh and Sarah, as they pretended to zip-tie Zu's and Hina's hands and feet.

"Remember," Cole was shouting, his hands cupped around his mouth, "the point is to be as silent and fast as possible. Do not fire unless your life depends on it. Get the PSFs down silently so they can't alert the camp controllers!"

Zach and I bolted forward, him covering me as I ducked into a gap between two pallets meant to represent the Control Room. I reached a hand out toward Lucy, who was now posing as the camp controller at the helm of the camp's security. She took a generous step back, her eyes widening in what I thought was real alarm. My stomach clenched.

Zach went through the motions of restraining the other kid posing as a camp controller. Then we were at the back of the pack, joining the others as they hit the other end of the hall, and we mimed going up a flight of stairs. Liam said something under his breath that made Mike, Gonzo, Ollie, and Sarah burst into laughter.

"Stop!" Cole called. "Lee, you're out. You too, Mike."

Liam swung around, a look of total disbelief on his face. "Excuse me?"

"You," Cole repeated slowly, as if Liam's hearing had been the problem, "are *out.*"

"What the hell for?" Liam spun toward me, gesturing with his hands, asking me for something I had no intention of giving him. The minute the words had left Cole's lips, relief had flooded my system. Liam's expression changed abruptly, darkening as he shook his head and twisted back around in the direction of his brother.

"*Why?* I've done everything you asked—both me and Mike have experience hitting trucks. So *why?*"

The kids around us began to shuffle their feet and look away, the tension swiftly moving from awkward to painful.

"Because," Cole said, jumping down from the ladder, "I decided twelve is too many—you guys are practically tripping over each other. We need to be in and out faster and quieter. If you take this personally, you're an idiot."

"That's bullshit," Liam said, his hands on his hips. "You just want me out of this."

"Well, your attitude isn't doing you any favors either, baby brother," he said, holding out his hand. "Your helmet and gun. You go cool off somewhere. Mike, I need you as another PSF—third door on the right, yes, you got it—"

Liam ripped the gun strap off his shoulder, pushing it into his brother's chest, and unbuckled the helmet, letting it fall to the floor. He turned on his heel and strode toward the garage's tunnel door, his body rigid with stiff, furious lines.

I held up one finger to Cole, not waiting to get a negative response from him, and followed Liam out. He was already a good ten feet into the tunnel before I caught sight of him and called, "*Hey!*"

He stopped, but didn't turn around. I unclipped my own

helmet and approached slowly, recognizing the red staining the back of his neck, the way his hands were clenched into fists—the veins stood out in his forearms, he had such a tight grip.

"Liam," I said softly. "Look at me."

"What?" he said, plucking at his fatigues. "Did you need me to hand over these, too?"

"I want you to calm down," I said. "I'm sorry—but you know it has to be this way."

"And which way is that?" he asked. "The one where you stand there silently and let me get dismissed like a kid being sent to time-out?"

I let out a sound of frustration. "We have to listen to him. There has to be some kind of order here—structure. Otherwise this whole thing will fall apart."

Liam stared at me, disbelief fading into a humorless smile. "I get it," he said as he started walking again. "Believe me, Ruby, I get it."

By the time we filed back into the Ranch six hours later, he was long gone. Zu was waiting for me in the bunk room, a folded piece of paper clutched in her hands. She watched me as I read it, her eyes making my heart ache.

Finding Liv. Good luck.

I wasn't upset. I was furious.

"He left without taking any kind of backup—*again*," I said, pulling my shirt up over my head and kicking off my fatigues. Zu had already changed into the oversized shirt and boxers she slept in. "Didn't he?"

She nodded, then held up her notebook with the message, *What's going on?* She flipped the page. *Why are you acting like idiots?*

"Did Chubs tell you to ask me that?"

Zu went back to the first page, underlining the first question twice. *What's going on?*

"Just a disagreement," I assured her, the little lie already gnawing at me. I pulled the worn shirt and sweats on and sat down next to her on my bunk. "Looks like it's just you and me tonight."

I lay down on my back and she followed suit. I was grateful for the warmth of her next to me, her presence, which always seemed to sweeten sour situations. I'd spent the rest of the simulation feeling like someone was walking over my grave. I still couldn't shake the feeling.

She picked up her pen and notebook again and wrote, *Are you okay?*

"I've been better," I admitted.

You keep going to your bad place, she added. *I have one, too. I get trapped there if I stay too long.*

I shifted so I could wrap an arm around her shoulders and draw her in closer.

You don't have to go there alone. She paused, as if collecting her thoughts. *Do you remember, right before I left East River, I said I had something to tell you, but I didn't know how?*

"I do." Thinking about that day was like raking nails down over my heart.

It wasn't really that I didn't know how—I wanted the words to be better. More beautiful, I guess. But Lee told me it doesn't matter, sometimes simplest is best. She turned the page, scribbling the words down quickly. The sound of the pen against the paper was strangely soothing. *It doesn't matter what you do, it won't ever change how we feel about you. I'm proud to be your friend.*

I stared at her, swallowing the knot in my throat. "Thank you. I feel the same way about you. The luckiest day of my life was when I met you. You saw how scared I was—"

It wasn't because you were scared, Zu wrote, then added quickly, *maybe a little, but do you know how I knew we could trust you?*

I shook my head, fascinated by this insight into her judgment.

When the people following you, looking for you, started to get really close, you were going to run again, not hide behind Betty. It was because you didn't want them to accidentally find me either, right?

"That's right."

She put out her hands as if to say, *well, there you go.* She picked up her pen again. *That meant you were never going to purposefully put us in danger. That you were a good person.*

"That's an awfully big assumption," I said. "It could have just been me panicking, not thinking at all."

Zu gave a little shrug. *Better to risk helping someone than regret what you could have done. Lee said that.*

"That sounds like him," I said dryly. And that was the exact reason Chubs and I had to be so vigilant about every new kid we crossed paths with.

Are you and Lee fighting about the memory thing?

Ah. So he or one of the others had told her.

"Not exactly." But then, what were we doing, exactly? Not being friends to each other. Not being whatever it was we had been. "It's complicated. After what I did to him, it's been nothing but complicated. And I accept full responsibility, but . . ."

Zu, as always, zeroed in on the root of the situation. *Do you think he doesn't forgive you?*

Reluctantly I reached around her, pulling out the Beach Boys CD case from the dresser drawer. The paper was soft and beginning to tear at the center from how many times I'd opened and read it and refolded it again. I don't know why I felt like I had to keep rereading it every night, punishing myself with it.

Zu read it, the crease between her dark eyebrows deepening. She clearly recognized his handwriting, but when she looked up, I saw confusion, not understanding.

"What?"

She wrote, *What does this prove?*

"The fact that he felt like he had to write this is a pretty big clue he thinks I'll do it again—take his memories, I mean. Send him away."

Zu calmly folded the note back up and then reached up to smack me in the nose with it with her patented *are you serious?* look.

Seeing I still wasn't getting it, she picked up her notebook and pen again. *OR—he wrote it because he was scared someone else would make you do it, like his brother. He says he wants to stay. This means he wants to stay, with you, with us, even knowing what happened. Did you even ask him about it? Does he know you took it?* She gave me a very different look now. *You shouldn't take things that don't belong to you.*

"I haven't talked to him about it," I admitted.

Did you miss this? She pointed to the last line.

I shook my head, swallowing hard. "I saw."

Zu studied me for a moment, dark eyes penetrating, flickering with understanding. *Do you feel like you don't deserve it?*

"I think he . . . I think he deserves better than the best I could offer him." It was the first time I'd admitted it out loud, and somehow putting it into the open only added to the weight of truth. I felt sick, lightheaded. *He deserves better than me.*

She looked torn between kicking me and hugging me, but settled on the latter. Too late, I'd realized how this would affect her—how someone already so panicked and afraid would react to seeing the people she thought of as her rocks crumbling.

When he comes back you have to talk to him, okay?

"Okay," I said, not as certain as she was that he'd *want* to talk to me.

If you go to the bad place again, she said simply, *tell one of us so we can help you back out.*

"I don't mean to be such a burden," I whispered. *All I ever wanted to do was protect you.*

It's not a burden if people are willing to carry it, she pointed out and, having made her final point, let herself drift to sleep. I rolled onto my side and tried to do the same.

It must have taken at some point because then I was dreaming, walking the damp, dark hallways of HQ, taking the path to Alban's cluttered office, eyes tracking the exposed light bulbs overhead. The next moment, I was in a different hallway, cold tile under my feet, small hands fisted in my shirt.

I jerked back, my mind ripping out of the foggy haze of sleep, scrambling away from Zu's terrified look. The lights in the lower-level hallway were switched off, as they always were after midnight. She stood in contrast to the shadows, worry overtaking confusion on her features. Her brow creased as she stepped toward me tentatively, reaching for the hand I'd pressed over my heart, trying to steady it.

"Sorry," I told her, "sorry—sleepwalking—stress—it's—" I couldn't get my tongue around the right words, but she seemed to understand. Zu took me firmly in hand and walked me back toward our room, never once letting me stumble. My head felt light enough to drift away, and when I climbed back into bed, I banged my clumsy knees against the metal frame. The last thing I was aware of was Zu stroking my hair, smoothing it again and again until the pain pounding in my skull eased, and I was able to breathe normally again.

In the earliest hours of the next morning, the Op team and I set off for the open desert of Nevada.

FIFTEEN

I KEPT MY BELLY DOWN FLAT AGAINST THE WASH, IGNOR-
ing the tinge of pain in the muscles of my lower back. It seemed
wrong for the desert to be so damn cold, but I guess without
the sun, and without the benefit of thick-leaved trees and brush,
there was nothing to trap the heat of the previous day. Nameless
mountains hovered behind us, the lighter of two deep shades
of black. I kept looking over my shoulder as the hours passed,
watching their jagged shapes lighten to the color of a new bruise.
Aside from the yellow, dried-out clusters of low, prickly desert
shrubs, there wasn't much anything else to look for.

"What was that?" I heard Gav ask. "Is that a rattlesnake? I
heard rattling."

"That was me drinking from my canteen, dumbass," Gonzo
said. "Jesus, dude. Did you leave your balls in California?"

I shushed them, and then shushed them again when one of
the girls started complaining about having to pee.

"I told you not to drink that much water on the drive," Sarah
told her. "You never listen to me."

"Sorry I don't have the bladder of a freaking sloth."

"You mean *camel*," Sarah corrected.

"I meant *sloth*," the other girl said. "I read somewhere they only have to go once a week."

I rolled my eyes heavenward for strength, wondering if this was what Vida felt like every moment of every day.

"Status?" Cole's voice was clipped in my ear.

"Same as an hour ago," I said as I pressed my earpiece. "Nothing so far, over."

We'd taken the two SUVs down to this barren stretch of Interstate 80 and were dropped off on the side of the road; Lucy and Mike turned the cars around and drove them back to Lodi. Cole and I had mapped out the sweet spot on the highway in terms of distance from the camp. Just far enough from the camp that no one would notice the vehicles making a quick stop. But the only cover we had to hide in was the wash running along the cracked asphalt. We curved our bodies to fit its shape, and waited.

It was another ten minutes before my ears picked up on the faint hum of a distant engine. I knew I hadn't imagined it when the others began to squirm, trying to get a better look at the lip of the wash. A few seconds later, the first pinpricks of light appeared—headlights that grew in size and intensity, slicing through the darkness.

I glanced down the wash—and there it was, three bursts of light from a flashlight. Ollie had been stationed there to check the markings on the truck. It was the right one.

Zach slapped my back, the excitement bringing a grin to his face. I felt it like a jolt of electricity to my system and flashed a smile back at him as I stood.

I walked out into the middle of the road, hands shaking only a little bit as the semi-trailer truck barreled down the road. I held up my hands as the headlights blinded me—I couldn't see the details of the driver behind the windshield, but I saw the quick movement as his hand went to strike the horn. I let the invisible hands in my mind reach out blindly, feeling for his, stretching, stretching, stretching—and connecting.

The truck rolled to a stop three feet away from me.

There was a flurry of movement at my left as the makeshift tact team came scrambling up from the wash, moving toward the rear of the truck to open the trailer and jump inside.

I pushed the earpiece as I jogged around to open the passenger side door of the truck's cab. "We have our ride, over."

"Fantastic. Proceed with second phase."

The driver was frozen behind the wheel, waiting for his instructions from me. I searched through his memories and teased one up from the week before, of him making this exact ride in. I pulled that to the forefront of his mind and said one word. "Drive."

I crouched as low as I could in the cab, drawing the black ski mask down over my face. I pulled myself up to look over the dash periodically to make sure we were still heading in the right direction. The truck driver had been blasting some rap music that was angry and pounding enough to set me on edge, so I reached over and switched it off, missing the exact moment the gray, sun-bleached two-story structure and its ten-foot fence came into view.

"In sight," I said. "Everyone good at the back of the bus?"

"Peachy," was Zach's reply. *"ETA?"*

"Two minutes."

I took another steadying breath as we turned and headed off the highway onto a dirt road. The two PSFs at the gate dragged the thing open as the driver, a thick-waisted, bearded man in a short-sleeved button-down, went through the motions of turning the truck and reversing through it, his face blank. A tarp was spread out over the loading area adjacent to the main building. There were already flatbed carts out, waiting for the supplies to be unloaded. Two PSFs were sitting on them, smoking, but threw the cigarettes away and stood as the truck backed toward them. The others, having secured the gate, were hurrying back over as I took one last deep breath.

"We're in—prepare for action," I said. "Two PSFs positioned at your door, two more coming around the back."

"*Silent and fast,*" Cole reminded us. "*Ten minutes starts now.*"

A fifth approached the driver's window, calling out a, "Mornin' Frank!"

I pushed the image of Frank rolling down the window into his mind, leaned over him, and, before the PSF's eyes could so much as widen, had my gun pointed directly at his face. He was young, around Cate's age, maybe. At the sight of me, he lost the easy smile on his face. His whole body pulled back in alarm, and he reached for his rifle.

"What the fu—"

"Hands where I can see them." I couldn't control Frank and the PSF at the same time, and Gonzo and Ollie eliminated my need to. One of them cracked him on the back of his skull with the butt of his own rifle, and the other had him facedown in the dirt, gagged and secured with zip ties. He was hauled behind the truck, where four other limp forms were already propped up.

I knew some of the kids hadn't understood why we'd run through this so many times, but I think, now that we were here, they saw the answer in how smoothly we assembled into formation. The real benefit of simulations was to train your nerves to behave, to make something like this feel as normal as waking up and walking to the showers each morning. It seemed to have worked—even as we approached the door the PSFs had left open and quietly stepped inside of the building, the group felt as steady as stone to me. We certainly looked menacing enough, dressed in all black and wearing ski masks.

The hall was dark, but a stream of light spilled out of one of the rooms—the third one down on the right. I felt myself pause. The smell of bleach tinged with lemon, shoe polish, and human odor gripped me in a stranglehold. Some part of me recognized that it made sense for this camp to smell almost exactly like the Infirmary in Thurmond. Why wouldn't they use the same military-ordered cleaning supplies? But more than anything, it rubbed up against my nerves.

Gav stepped into place, kneeling down and aiming as the others crept forward. Voices trickled down the tile from the open door I'd spotted before. I waved the kids forward and crept along the wall with them until Zach grabbed my arm and pointed to the door marked CR. Control Room. That was our cue.

As we ducked out of formation, I cast one look back into the open room—four PSFs were sitting around the table, uniform jackets slung onto a nearby couch and the backs of their chairs as they laughed and smoked, dealing cards around a cramped table. As Gav and Gonzo filled the doorway I saw one look up and then look again, diving for a weapon he never reached. The Blues upended their table, threw the PSFs against the wall, and silenced them before they could gasp out a warning over their radios.

That made nine. Nico had reviewed the footage from Pat and Tommy repeatedly, counting the different faces in uniform he saw. Two camp controllers, thirteen PSFs. Fifteen targets total.

Zach and I pressed ourselves against the wall, and I reached out and knocked against the Control Room door.

"Enter," a voice called. It was a good thing we hadn't tried to charge it—the thing was locked from the inside. I heard a buzz and then a click, and Zach didn't waste a moment before pushing it open with his shoulder.

Inside there were two young women, both in black button-down shirts and slacks. The room was a wall of monitors that kissed up against a row of computers. Most of the screens were set on a series of bunks and the children sleeping in them, but they switched over to the hall, to the outside area, the recreational room across the way as we stepped inside. The one who was monitoring the screens dropped her mug of coffee down her front when she spotted what was happening across the wall. The other, standing in front of some kind of panel of switches and dials, turned and let out a small scream when she saw us. Zach had her pressed up against the ceiling with his abilities a full second after I was already in the other camp controller's mind.

An avalanche of faces, sounds, colors, landscapes streamed through my mind, thundering down over me. I searched for the relevant ones, information about how they reported in statuses, the timing of it, as Zach brought the other screaming woman down, gagged her with cloth, and zip-tied her safely away from the controls to one of the pipes running along the far-right wall.

"Done!" he called. "We have eight minutes. Erasing camera footage." Nico had shown him how to set the footage back, to loop through already recorded images, making an educated guess about the programs they used. It must have been close to reality, because Zach punched a fist in the air when he was done.

"Get the rooms unlocked upstairs," I told him, pointing to the nearest computer. "Password is capital P, capital S, capital F, one, three, nine, three, eight, exclamation mark, asterisk. Did you get that?"

"Affirmative." He relayed the next part to the rest of the team who were, hopefully, already heading up the stairs. "Unlocking doors."

I brought up the memory of the woman sitting at one of the computers, the message she'd relayed to the PSF system—exactly how I wanted her to do it now, and then again in another two hours. When I pulled back, I took away her memories of Zach and I entering. She simply nodded and went about her business, standing in front of the monitors, her eyes unseeing, her face a blank slate.

"Control is out of play, over," I said.

"Roger that," came Cole's relieved reply. *"Proceed upstairs with the others."*

Zach hit the button beside the door, unlocking it, and stepped out. I was right behind him when he jumped back, raised his gun and aimed—

"It's me," came a familiar voice. "It's me, don't shoot—"

Disbelief, dumb and mute disbelief, stole over me as I confirmed who was standing at the other end of Zach's rifle.

Liam.

"What the hell, man?" Zach shouted, throwing a furious punch toward him. "Jesus, I almost shot you!"

I hadn't moved. It didn't make sense—it wasn't him, he had gone to find Olivia. He wouldn't have come in after us, he couldn't have been so stupid, not Liam, not *Liam*—

I was so fixated on his face as I yanked my ski mask up and over mine that I didn't see the red-haired woman behind him, wild curls tumbling around her long-sleeved black shirt. She wore black jeans and boots, but I didn't get a clear image of her face until she lowered the camera that was clicking wildly, capturing everything around her.

"Who," I heard myself say in a low, furious voice, "the hell is *this?*"

"Status?" Cole asked. *"Gem—status?"*

Liam matched my stony look with one of his own. "This is Alice, from Amplify."

"Dude," Zach said, shaking his head. "Dude, this is crazy—"

Alice looked young, late twenties, maybe, but a clean face free of makeup made her appear only a few years older than the rest of us. She was taller than Liam, slender, but strong enough to haul a backpack that looked like it weighed twice as much as she did.

"Nice to meet you," she said. "Wow, this is . . . *wild.*"

Liam wasn't looking at me for my approval, just my reaction. All at once, adrenaline kicked back into my system, throwing me into action. *Accept, adapt, act.* I pressed a finger to my earpiece, cutting off Cole's request for status, and turned toward the staircase at the end of the hall.

"Liam is here," I told him. "With a reporter from Amplify."

Static trickled over the line. Zach shot me an uncomfortable look as we hit the stairs, as if he, too, were picturing Cole's reaction to this.

Finally, he answered, *"Say again."*

I repeated the information to him again as we rounded the corner of the stairs and came through the door that the team had left propped open.

The strange, familiar smell I'd breathed in on the way up finally had an explanation as we burst through the doors: the gagged and bound soldiers were secured against the same wall they'd been using to stencil and paint a message: OBEDIENCE CORRECTS DEVIANCE.

The Op team had been in the process of ushering the kids out of the five dark rooms lining the opposite wall, trying to coax them to come out. I saw the problem immediately.

"Take off your masks," I told the others. "It's all right, the cameras are off." The kids wouldn't come out until they saw that we were kids, too—that they weren't being tricked or picked up by a different set of monsters in black uniforms. One of the teen boys from the first room stuck his head out, saw the gun Gav was holding, and immediately retreated back inside. He would have slammed the door shut if Josh hadn't caught it.

Alice's camera was clicking like an insect, trying to take in the sight from every angle. I spun on my heel and knocked the camera out of her hand, wishing like hell she hadn't had the strap around her neck so it would have smashed against the tiled floor. "Do you mind?" I snapped. God—it was bad enough the kids were in here, but couldn't she at least give them a second of peace to collect themselves?

"Ruby—" Liam started, but Alice waved him off.

"It's fine, I get it." But I saw her lift her camera again anyway, this time set to record video instead. Clearly she didn't get it.

"Five minutes," Cole warned. *"Are you heading out?"*

I jogged to the nearest door, looking inside. The wooden bunks creaked as weight shifted on them, and faces squinted at me. I reached in and turned the lights on so they'd have a better view of my face. The stench of sweat rolled out, slamming into me before the whimpers and whispers of fear came. Dozens of small faces emerged from the dark, hands held up to shield their eyes.

Oh my God.

They were wearing those thin, papery uniforms, coded by whatever color they'd been classified as. I felt my stomach start to churn. One girl turned, flashing the Psi ID number someone had hastily scrawled across the back of her shirt in permanent marker. These were really kids—nine, ten, eleven, twelve, with only a few clearly older than fourteen. All of them with those hollow cheeks, carved out by hunger. Narrowed by need—if not for food, then for everything else.

"You made it!" The longer I stared at the boy that pushed his way to the door of Room Three, the harder it was for me to believe that it was Pat. They'd shaved down his dark mass of hair, stripped him down to a blue scratchy cotton T-shirt and shorts. He'd been here less than a week and already he'd let his edges bleed into the darkness of this place.

All at once, the boys in Tommy's room gasped and reached for him as he stepped into the hall, pleading him in these small voices to come back.

At night, you don't leave the cabin, one of the older girls in

Cabin 27 had told me. *You don't leave, even if it's burning down. They'll just say you were trying to escape, and that's the only reason they need to shoot you.*

None of the other kids followed Tommy and Pat out.

My mind scrambled to come up with something to avoid us having to carry them out.

"My name is Ruby," I said, quickly, "and I'm one of you. All of us here are like you, except for the woman with the camera. We're getting you out of here—taking you to somewhere safe. But we *have* to move fast. Fast as you can, without hurting yourselves or anyone around you. Follow them—" I pointed to Gonzo and Ollie. "Fast, fast, fast, okay?"

Dammit—they still weren't moving. We weren't moving, and time was ticking down so loudly in my ears, I couldn't distinguish the seconds from my heartbeat. I opened my mouth, wondering what else I could say to them. What were the words that had convinced me to take the pills Cate had offered? Or had I just realized it was my last chance of ever getting out?

For them, maybe, it was a matter of shock—we'd come charging in so quickly, they couldn't wrap their heads around the reality of it.

"Rosa?" I called. "Rosa Cruz? Is there a Rosa Cruz here?"

No one spoke or raised their hands, but I saw a small movement out of the corner of my eye—a shifting that was as subtle as someone straightening up. I took a step around Tommy, scanning the ten faces of Room Six. There was a girl at the back—nearly as tall as I was, maybe thirteen or fourteen. She must have had long, glossy curls at one point in her life, but someone had gone to town hacking it all off. I didn't see a trace of Senator Cruz in her face, aside from the warm olive tone of her skin and her dark eyes. But when she tilted her head and shifted her gaze toward me, defying her fear, just for that second—that was all her mother.

"Rosa," I said. "Your mom is waiting for you."

She flinched at the sudden attention, but after a deep breath, she stepped out of her pitch-black room like she was tearing away from the last grip of a nightmare. Rosa's hands clenched at her sides. Her breathing came hard and fast as her eyes darted around.

"Look at me," I told her, holding out my hand. "Just at me. This is really happening. I'll get you out of here. Okay?"

Okay. Her trembling, cold fingers touched the tips of mine, sliding into place. The tension bunching her shoulders didn't relax until my grip on her tightened. The other girls in her room flowed out behind her, and it was only then that the other kids lost that last bit of hesitation and followed.

"Home base," I said, pressing my earpiece. "Initiating evac."

"Two minutes," Cole said, sounding a hell of a lot more stressed than I felt. This was good. They were coming with us. They trusted us. The gratitude I felt for that small fact made my eyes prick with tears.

The others followed, lining up one by one and moving quickly. Feet slapped against the tile, smearing out the puddle of wet paint that had drifted from the forgotten can. Some of them stopped to look at the two bound PSFs, but there was no laughter, no smiles, no cheers—of course not. It must have felt like they were moving through a dream.

I guided Rosa into the line, glancing at the wall where the soldiers had been writing out that message. The kids leaned against it and used it to brace themselves as they rounded the corner down into the stairwell, smearing that same red paint, tracking their hands and fingerprints through it. Alice stood frozen in front of it, lifting her camera one last time.

It was the last clear, still image I had before the night sped up, gliding into a blur that carried us down the stairs, down the main hall, and out the very same door we had come through. The blast of cold air washed away the pounding heat from my blood. I shook the fear off, and I let myself imagine it—how good it would feel when this was Thurmond we were walking out of, when I passed through that gate one last time.

Cate may have gotten me out, but until that moment, I'm not sure I'd fully recognized that I was still a prisoner of that place. And it wasn't the cure that would give me the feeling of finally being freed from this horrible reality. It was knowing, with certainty, that I would never be forced to go back.

Zach helped Liam lift his motorbike onto the back of the truck, and gave Alice the lift she needed to get up into it. I caught his questioning look as he took her hand and nodded. She had to come back with us. She'd seen too much, was a security risk. Gonzo and Ollie were the last to climb into the truck's trailer, having dragged the PSFs we'd left outside into the interior of the camp, along with the secured truck driver.

The kids were forced to sit on the plastic-wrapped pallets and boxes, some of them clutching yellow and orange glow sticks and flashlights we'd given them so they wouldn't feel like they were being locked in total darkness. As I rolled the trailer door down, I saw Liam sitting with his back against the siding, his arms resting over his knees, watching me. I pulled the door firmly into place and secured it with the latch.

Zach was already up in the front seat, ripping the GPS out of the console. He rolled down the window and tossed it outside.

One less way for them to track us when they figured out what was happening. I was the one to run to open the gates; the fence wasn't electrified, but the PSFs had managed to secure it with a padlock. I turned to look at Zach and shook my head. He waved me back and I climbed into the cab with him.

"Brace yourself," he warned, relaying the message to me and the whole team in the back. The truck lurched forward and barreled through the gate, sending pieces flying as if they'd been made of Styrofoam. A section caught on the front hubcap and sparked against the ground, but was knocked away as we veered onto the highway, and we sped away before the sun had the chance to start rising at our backs.

SIXTEEN

WE DROVE A FULL FOUR HOURS BEFORE DITCHING THE semi-trailer truck in Reno. In an ideal world, we would have taken it straight to Lodi, only stopping once to let the kids relieve their bladders and stretch their legs, but it was marked with military insignias. Someone was bound to notice it if we kept going.

Senator Cruz had arranged for an old Greyhound bus to be brought down from Oregon and left at Reno's city limits, warning it was the only time she'd be able to put this particular contact into play as the former state governor, her college classmate, had been careful to never entangle himself too deeply in matters of the Federal Coalition and had been rewarded by Gray with the right to keep his job.

Zach and I helped each kid down, and I couldn't stop the small smile on my face at seeing the way they all seemed to want to spin around in the warm sunlight. Rosa was one of the last off, bypassing Zach's hands for mine.

"Okay?" I asked her. "How are you doing?"

She stretched her arms back and forth, swinging them around. I made sure that I kept the smile on my face so she'd know it was okay to let herself believe this would work out. Something I'd learned from Cate.

I wondered what she'd think of all this as we lifted the boxes of food and medical supplies off the truck, putting them in the undercarriage of the Greyhound bus. When I saw her again, I would make sure she knew the full magnitude of what she had done for me. I wanted to believe that if I felt all of these things, if I brought her face to mind and focused on it, she'd somehow be able to tell I was thinking about her—that I hadn't forgotten her.

That I was coming for her.

Liam walked Alice to the bus, ignoring the glances the team shared as they passed by them. After exchanging a few last quiet words with her, he got back on his motorcycle, explaining to Zach he was going to ride behind us.

I held a hand out to Rosa, who took it gratefully. Zach jumped into the driver's seat and craned his neck back, counting to make sure that everyone was on. The kids squeezed into the seats and onto the floor; after a moment of petrified uncertainty, the older kids began to play with the vents, fiddling with the lights.

"Pull your curtains all the way closed," I told them. "It's going to be another three or four hours to where we're going."

"Where is that?" one of the kids asked.

"Cali-for-nia!" Gav sang out, pounding his meaty hands down on the seat in front of him. "Let's go, already!"

"Seat belts," Zach called as he started the bus. Then, realizing there was a speaker system, repeated the order through that. "Seat belts. Welcome to Psi Bus Services. I'm Zach and I'll be your driver on this epic quest to freedom. If you look out your windows—but, obviously, don't, because Ruby just told you not to—you can give Nevada the finger as we pull away."

That, at least, made a few of them crack a smile. I gave Zach a thumbs-up and he returned it. The bus lurched forward and we were off again, really cruising. I smiled despite myself, winging along on my own cloud of happiness. I didn't come down, not for a second, until I glanced at Rosa.

She had taken the window seat, drawn her legs up to her chest to tuck under her shirt, and pressed her face into her knees.

"Rosa," I said, putting a hand on her back. The number on her shirt pocket, 9229, had been her whole identity in that place. I wanted her to hear her name. To feel human.

"You shouldn't have come, we're not ready yet. We're still broken."

"No," I said quickly, "no you're not. You're different, that's all."

"They said the good ones were the ones that died," she said, and I noticed a faint scar running down her left cheek, a narrow, spiraling pink line. What could have left a mark like that, other than someone intentionally scratching it into her skin? "That we were all wrong and we'd—we'd never get out. But they never did anything to help us. I want—I want to be fixed, we all did, we did *everything* they asked, but it wasn't enough."

"If they made you feel that way, then they were the ones who were wrong," I said. It took me a moment to realize why the words came so easily. *Clancy.* How was this any different from what he kept trying to tell me? I shifted uncomfortably, trying to think of Cate instead, how she had talked me down after I escaped Thurmond. "The most important thing you ever did was learn how to survive. Don't let anyone make you feel like you shouldn't have, or that you deserved to be in that camp."

"You were in one, too?" Rosa asked. "You got out and things got better?"

"They're getting there," I told her. "Your mom is helping us."

There. One small, trembling smile. "Has she been wearing her red suit?"

"Red suit?" I repeated.

Rosa nodded, finally sitting back against the seat. "Mom had this dark red suit she always wore when she had to go in for a big vote or debate. She said it scared the old white dudes who kept trying to shut her up or make her sit down."

"No," I said, "but you know what? I don't think she really needs it anymore."

The girl spread her fingers over her blue uniform shorts. "And you're totally . . . you're sure she wants to . . . I mean, I would understand if she didn't want to see me. I was with my Gran when they came. Mom never saw me after I got damaged—changed, I mean."

"She wants you," I said, the words spilling out from some place I hadn't dared to touch since I'd left Thurmond. "More than anything. It doesn't matter what you can do, or what any of the people at that camp told you. She's there and she's waiting for you."

They were the right words. I knew it by the pain that came with wrenching them up from where I'd buried them.

I knew it, because they were the exact words I'd fantasized about someone saying to me, just before Grams would arrive to rescue me.

She turned toward me. "Thank you for coming to get us."

I wasn't sure I could trust my voice, but I said, "You're very welcome."

"You're going to get more kids out, right?" she asked. "Not just us?"

"Everyone," I reassured her, leaning my head back against the seat and closing my eyes. It was the only way I knew of to keep from crying. It was more than just a possibility. We had done *this*. We could do it again at Thurmond. We could make this moment everyone's reality. Every single kid.

Zach brought the bus into the garage as Cole had instructed. The kids who'd stayed behind were there, opening the large, rolling door we'd kept shut and locked the whole time we'd used the space. Senator Cruz and Cole stood a way inside; the woman had her hands folded in front of her, and while she seemed otherwise serene, even from a distance, I could see the white-knuckled hold she had on herself. I pulled back the curtain and leaned away, so Rosa could see her as well. The senator must have spotted her at that exact moment, because she lost the fight she'd been waging to control herself and ran for the bus's doors, just as I stood to let Rosa pass. The girl launched herself at her mother from the top step, and nearly took them both to the ground.

The other kids looked away. We'd explained, on the drive back to California, what had happened in Los Angeles. And knowing that many of their parents had been involved in the Federal Coalition, or had simply lived in the area, hadn't sugarcoated the harsh reality.

"But we'll help you find them," I'd promised. "If Senator Cruz doesn't know for certain where they are, we'll try searching the different networks for clues."

Cole had remained where he was, nodding to the team members who came down from the bus, slapping their backs and proudly congratulating them as they spilled out and formed a cluster around him. There was a backpack at his feet, but he

318

didn't reach for it, not until Liam and Alice finally exited the bus. I knew what was about to happen, but frankly, I was too damn pissed off myself to try to prevent it.

He signaled to Senator Cruz. With Rosa still pressed against her side, she said calmly, "All right, everyone, follow me. We'll get you a nice warm shower, some new clothes, and a good meal. How does that sound?"

Liam and the Amplify reporter had their path toward us cut off as the Oasis kids streamed by, forming a line that followed the senator to the tunnel down, passing Zu, Hina, Mike, and Kylie, who'd come running to meet us. They joined the group of kids who had been left behind here, standing on the white crescent moon painted onto the cement.

The moment he was within range, Cole stooped to pick up the backpack and tossed it to Liam, who sagged under its weight as he caught it.

"I took the liberty," Cole began, his voice edged with ice, "of packing your things. You're finished here. Get on your little bike and go home."

"I'm not going anywhere." Liam's expression hardened as he shoved the bag back at his brother. "And I'm just getting started. You can't make me go."

Cole let out a derisive laugh, but I was the one to answer. The words sprang into my mind, filled my mouth like bile. "No, but I could."

I saw Zu jerk her gaze from Liam to me, her lips parting in shock. It was nothing compared to the pain of seeing Liam set his jaw and blanch, his eyes burning with a terrible, silent disappointment. How dare he act like this was the real betrayal here? He'd gone behind my back for all of this. I'd sensed he was keeping some kind of secret, but nothing of this magnitude. Nothing that risked the safety and lives of every kid here.

And why? Because he was mad Cole dismissed his idea? He didn't understand how these things worked. He'd left the League, run away. He'd checked out of training too early to understand that you fought fire with fire.

"You went behind my back," Cole said, heat pouring off the words, "and somehow contacted Amplify when I specifically told you not to. You were stupid enough to email confidential files, risking Gray's Internet crawlers picking them up and tracing them back to us. You clearly lied about going to meet that other group of kids and met with Amplify instead, wasting our gas and our time. You interrupted an Op in play and endangered *every single kid* participating in it, including yourself and the ones we rescued. And to top it off, Liam, you brought a civilian into play. I really hope it was worth it to you, because while you're getting the hell out of here, *she* is staying where we can keep her secured and locked up until this is all over."

"*Excuse me?*" Alice stepped up, brown eyes flashing. To Liam she muttered, "You said he'd be pissed, but this is . . ."

"Reality," Cole finished, holding out his hand. "Give me your camera."

She leaned away, pressing her hand against the device, which was now stowed away safely in her bag. "Listen to me when I say this," she said, "because I mean it literally—*over my dead body*. You think I'm scared of you? I survived the D.C. bombing and covered eight major city riots, including the one in Atlanta that killed my camera guy and my fiancé. So go ahead and try it, asshole."

"Okay, sweetheart," Cole said, "you can keep your camera. May the tender, glowing light from the digital screen keep you company when we lock you in your new room and throw away the key."

"That's—"

Liam held out an arm, stopping her. The woman didn't shrink back, though, and her ivory skin didn't lose its tinge of pink.

"You're right," he said. "I did go behind your back and find out how to contact Amplify. I met with Alice and her team, but only *after* I found Olivia and Brett, who I told not to come in until I was sure being here would guarantee a lower chance of getting killed than trying to survive alone in the wild. I *downloaded* files onto a flash drive to prove my story to Amplify; I never sent them. And you know why I did all of those things? Because no matter what you said in Los Angeles, this hasn't been anything that resembles a democracy, let alone a fresh start. You've ignored everyone's ideas in favor of your own and you haven't once listened to what I've tried to say, even though you know nothing about our lives and what we've been through. You like the fight, but some of us don't."

"Not your best argument," Cole said, gesturing to the team, "considering today worked out pretty damn well."

"He's telling the truth," Alice insisted. "We never would have asked him to risk sending the files digitally. He only brought us printouts, and only a few to prove his affiliation with the League. Or whatever the hell it is you're calling yourselves now."

Liam blew out a harsh breath. "We can use the footage Alice captured today, deliver a media package to their contacts to run—a package that carries an actual message. That proves something, even if it's just that people have nothing to fear from us kids. You don't *get* it. It doesn't matter if we get all the kids out of the camps and blast through every damn fence and wall between us and them. If we don't change people's minds about us, then where the hell are those kids going to go?"

Cole crossed his arms over his chest and said simply, "Bye, Liam."

I had started to turn, intending on following Cole to the tunnel, anger making my head throb, erasing every last trace of light inside my heart, when a voice piped up. "If he has to go, then so do I."

It was the Green girl I'd seen a few nights ago, the one who had painted the crescent moon on Liam's helmet. That moment, when I'd questioned who "she" was, finally made sense. The symbol was how Alice identified him during their meetings.

"For any particular reason . . . ?" Cole prompted.

"I covered for him." She tossed her dark hair back over her shoulder. "I knew he was going to meet Alice and I didn't tell anyone."

"Me too," said Lucy, wringing her hands red. "I lied about supplies he never brought in, and I don't really want to fight, I'm sorry."

"Ditto," Kylie said. "Not sorry, though."

"And me," piped up Anna, one of the Greens who'd made it out of Los Angeles. "I'm the one that showed him how to access and download the files."

Beside me, Zach scratched his head and looked up at the ceiling. "I might have showed him how he could, if he needed to, establish a contact procedure with someone."

"I'm the one who asked Senator Cruz how she contacted someone in Amplify," said another one of the Greens. "So I guess I'm out, too?"

"Me too, since—"

Cole held up a hand, interrupting Sarah. "Okay—*Christ*, I get it, Spartacus. You all made your point."

He glanced over at me. I lifted a shoulder, letting him decide this one. I didn't trust my judgment in that moment, and, truthfully, if they were all interested in sabotaging our hit on Thurmond, I wouldn't have been sorry to see them go off and live somewhere safe and away, especially if Harry delivered on his promise of trained soldiers.

"You get *one* shot," he told them. "Prove to me this works the way you want it to, and we'll adapt our plan, *but*—" His voice turned sharp as the kids behind us began to chatter excitedly. I stepped closer to him, wanting to use Cole as a shield from the now-obvious truth that most, if not all of them, had known what Liam was planning, and none of them had been inclined to let me in on it.

They probably think it serves you right, a voice whispered in my head, *for keeping them in the dark about getting rid of the agents.*

But the difference was, that had only been done to protect them. Cole was absolutely right—Liam interrupting a carefully choreographed Op and introducing an unknown variable could have ended badly for all of us, including the kids we were trying to rescue. A fresh wave of anger steamed through me.

"*But,*" he continued, "you all stay here and you cannot, for any reason, leave the Ranch without getting permission. That includes you, Carrots."

Alice colored at the nickname, absently reaching up to smooth back her red hair.

He took a step closer to her, lowering his voice. I knew that look, the way his blue eyes hooded, how the otherwise friendly smile betrayed nothing of the contempt he felt. Only his low, rough voice. "If you reveal our location to anyone at Amplify, I'll know."

Alice leaned toward Cole, her arms crossed over her chest. One brow went up in challenge. "No you won't. But I'm not in the business of getting kids killed. Unlike you."

"*Hey,*" I warned. And clearly Liam must have mentioned something about me, because she finally backed off.

"All right, everyone good? Everyone cool?" Cole nodded, motioning for the others to start nodding, too. "Great. Let's get the supplies off the bus and everything organized. Someone needs to tell me about the PSFs' faces when they saw you."

The tension broke at that, Gav busting out laughing as he relayed a story about how one of the PSFs may or may not have pissed himself when he realized what he was up against. Zu tried to catch my hand as I walked past her, but, in all honesty, I just wanted to be alone—I didn't care if it hurt her feelings, I didn't care that she was worried about me, and I didn't want to pretend that I was fine with this outcome. Losing focus was wasting time. It meant more dead kids I wouldn't be able to save.

I wanted to check in with Nico about any news of Cate and whether or not Vida and Chubs had checked in. Then I wanted to finalize the details for how I'd be taken back into Thurmond.

I burned off what extra energy I had by taking the tunnel between the Ranch and the garage at a run. The frustration drained out of me with each strike of my boots against the cement. I was through the kitchen, passing by bowls of pasta and pretzels the Oasis kids had picked up on their way, if I had to guess, to eat in the big room, when I finally heard him calling my name.

I didn't slow down, didn't let any part of me soften the armor of anger I wore. Liam ran to catch up to me. "Ruby! I want to talk to you!"

"Believe me," I told him, "you don't."

I continued down the hall until he grabbed my arm and spun me around. I stared up into his face, looking past the strain, the shadow of scruff along his jaw and cheeks, to the intensity of his eyes, and for a single instant my body confused the need to kill him with the need to kiss him.

I yanked myself away and pushed the door open to the stairwell.

"Are you mad because I didn't tell you, or because you know I'm right?" he demanded. "Because as far as I can tell, it's both."

"I think Cole gave you a pretty decent outline of the many reasons to be pissed at you," I said, turning as I reached the first landing. He was right at my heels, trying to back me into the same dark corner I'd stolen a kiss from him in. And somehow, that only made me angrier, like he was doing it on purpose.

"I'm right, Ruby," he said, taking my wrist again.

"Touch me one more time," I warned him, "and you'll regret it."

He released his hold on me and backed off. "Please, listen to me—"

"No!" I said. "I don't even want to *look* at you right now!"

Liam's smile turned mocking. "Because I dared to disagree with Cole, who could *never* be wrong, not about anything."

I whirled back on him, shoving at his chest with both hands. "Because you came within an inch of being blasted away at the wrong end of Zach's gun! Because you *could have died* and I wouldn't have been able to stop it! Because you didn't *think* and everything we've been working toward could have fallen a—!"

His eyes flashed, blue flames, as he pulled me to him.

He kissed me.

He kissed me the way I'd kissed him in the forest at the edge of the East River camp. In the darkness, the smell of damp earth and dust and leather wrapped around us. Hard—desperate—his hands fisted in my hair, mine in his jacket.

He kissed me, and I let him, because I knew it was the last time.

I pushed him away, feeling something in my chest tear wide open as the cold air filled the space between us. Liam braced himself against the wall, trying to catch his breath. I fought the stupidest urge to sit down on the stairs and cry.

He took a shaking breath. "Anna said . . . she said that Nico's been working secretly on some kind of virus. She thinks it's for the Thurmond hit. It's the kind that someone will have to go in and install before any kind of attack can happen." His voice sounded hollow. "Would you happen to know anything about that?"

I looked away.

"Jesus, Ruby," he said quietly.

He was giving me the chance to come clean about the Thurmond hit, but nothing, least of all him, was going to prevent me from doing this. I didn't need his approval.

"They will kill you," he said, anger seeping into the words. "You *know* this. They know what you are and what you can do. Are you going to sway the whole camp? Get them under your control the way Clancy did at East River? They aren't going to let you leave that camp alive, and you don't even care, do you?"

He scrubbed at his face, letting out a sound of pure aggravation. "Do I even have to ask who put this idea in your head? He's not one of us, Ruby! He's not, and you still side with him, you tell *him* the things you used to tell me. Tell me what happened, tell me how to make this right between us again. I don't understand how we broke down. I don't understand why he has this hold on you!"

"I don't have to explain myself to you." I felt a cold drop of ice spread down my spine at my own words, no matter how true they were.

"You used to want to," he said. "Do you want to know why I didn't tell you about Alice and Amplify? I came close a hundred times. I almost told you that night we were in the garage, but I stopped myself because lately . . . lately it doesn't matter *what* I say. You and Cole think it's wrong, stupid, or naïve. Dammit, I am sick to death of that word. I'm not stupid, and I'm not blind either. I can keep us fed, I can fix every damn fixture that's falling off, I can make sure all of the cars run, I can find us the one real shot we have doing some lasting good in a world that's already too violent, but it's not enough. I don't even register, do I? Not to him. Not to you, not anymore."

I said nothing. Felt nothing. Was nothing.

"I'm trying to think of what comes after—how we'll move on with our lives when this is all over. It's what we talked about before. I don't want any of these kids to live their lives stained with pain and regret and blood. I don't want that for you, either. We can do good work—we can make the whole damn world see that we're good kids in a shitty situation. *Please*—Ruby, please. Cole is going to walk you right over a cliff, and he's going to be holding your hand the entire time."

I held his gaze a moment longer, letting the words expand, filling the parts of me that were crumbling. *Think of the girls,* I thought, *Cabin 27. Sam.* All of those thousands of kids who'd been left behind as I got out. Ashley's face, the dead eyes staring up at me, the accusation I'd read in them. *Where were you? Why didn't you come sooner?*

"If I've hurt you half as bad as you're hurting me," he said, his voice ragged, "then, God, just kill me. I can't stand this. Say something. *Say something!*"

I could sacrifice this, the thing I wanted most, for them, and the trade would never balance out, not fully. I owed them more than my love. I owed each of those girls my life. They needed to know what I'd felt today as we pulled out of Oasis. We would find the cure, if it was the last thing I did on this earth, and it would be waiting for them when they got out. They would know true freedom—not because they'd be able to shed their terrible abilities, the thing that marked them as *freak*. Because they'd be able to make every choice that had been denied to them for years. They could go anywhere. Be with the people they loved.

In the end, it didn't matter what happened to me—I understood what Nico had meant now, when he talked about making amends. I couldn't go back and change the things that had happened to them, but I could sure as hell put them in charge of their own futures. It would be worth it. Losing this . . . it would feel worth it. One day.

But now, it only hurt. It felt like tearing myself into pieces. The end came with silence, and I knew Liam felt it, even if he was too stubborn to admit it to himself. There was nothing left to say. I turned and started back up the stairs.

"I'll be around," he called after me, "when you decide you want to find me."

Swallowing the painful lump in my throat, I kept my back to him and said, "Don't bother waiting."

I was at the top of the stairs, pushing the door open, when he said, "Maybe I won't."

The door swung shut behind me, clicking quietly back into place. I let my body seize up, the pain tearing through me as I went into the nearest bunk room and collapsed down onto one of the beds. I clenched my fists, released them, clenched and released, trying to work out the unbearable tightness, to set some kind of rhythm for my breathing instead of the horrible, rough gasping. Laughing voices drifted down the hall from the big room, at odds with the screaming inside of my head.

I don't know how it happened, only that my vision blurred. By the time it finally cleared, I was standing inside Alban's office with no memory of getting there. When I turned, there were two figures standing in the doorway, shoulder to shoulder, wearing mirrored expressions of concern. They seemed to communicate a whole conversation in a single look.

"So . . ." Vida began. "What did we miss?"

SEVENTEEN

"WHEN DID YOU GET IN?" THE QUESTION BOUNCED OFF the walls of the tunnel as Vida, Chubs, and a newly arrived Cole and I all walked toward the bar. "Why didn't you let us know you were so close? You do actually have Lillian, right?"

"Oh, we have her," Chubs said, his gaze drifting over to Vida. "And an explanation for not calling."

She let out a huff, crossing her arms over her chest. "It was an accident!"

"Yes, well"—he pushed his glasses up the bridge of his nose delicately—"the burner phone we had *accidentally* fell out of the car, and someone *accidentally* backed over it. Because someone was in a rush after she *accidentally* alerted some skip tracers we were nearby when she *accidentally* used her abilities to move a light pole out of the road after she had *accidentally* backed into it."

"Someone better shut their mouth before I accidentally slam my fist into their teeth." She punched his shoulder, and it was almost . . . playful.

"Shut *his* mouth, fist into *his* teeth."

"Really? A grammar lesson?"

As we climbed the ladder, I let Cole explain what had happened during the Oasis hit. I felt too newly bruised to articulate what I needed to say, and, worse, the heaviness in my skull made me feel like I was trapped underwater. I couldn't look Chubs in the eye, no matter what he did to slyly get my attention. Liam would tell him the whole story and he would side with his friend and I just couldn't. I *couldn't* with anything that didn't directly relate to Lillian Gray or Thurmond.

Vida led the four of us out of the bar's back room and into the main one. Everything had been boarded up, the useful things like plates and glasses brought down into the Ranch. The shadows were so pervasive, I almost missed the small form cowering in the far back corner booth.

She wore jeans that were clearly too big for her and a button-down shirt that must have belonged to a man. All of her blond hair was tucked up into a Braves baseball cap. She took in her surroundings with a lethal stillness, alert and assessing. The hardness in her eyes, her stance—they were all in her son, too. The sight was enough to halt my steps, turn my blood to ice. I'd always thought that Clancy physically resembled his father, but the details, the tapping of her finger against her crossed arms . . . She didn't say a word, but I heard her voice all the same, the echo of what I'd picked up in her son's mind. *Clancy, my sweet Clancy . . .*

I sucked in a sharp breath.

"They weren't keeping her inside of Kansas HQ," Vida said. "She was in one of the smaller perimeter buildings. We only knew how to find her because we picked up on radio transmissions between the agents talking about the arrangements to trade her for the agents Gray's men picked up—they kept the agents alive *specifically* to get her back. So you were wrong, asswipe," she informed Cole, "and this better be damn well worth it, because I could have had Cate back and not Looney Tunes over there."

Cole nodded and stepped forward, approaching the woman with all the care and cautiousness afforded to a spooked animal. "Hi, Dr. Gray. You're safe here."

She either didn't understand, or she didn't care—throwing his hand off her, she turned to bolt toward the door. The way she pounded her fists against the worn wood made my own hands ache. "Pale . . . ah . . . out . . . car . . . more . . . now—now—one, two, three, four, five—"

The words barely sounded like words—they were emphasized and accented strangely, the way someone would talk around a full mouth, or if their tongue was clamped between teeth.

I turned back toward Vida, who only gave a tired sigh. "For someone who can't talk or understand for shit, she is a major pain in the ass."

"She's talking, though—" I was interrupted by her guttural cry as Cole lifted her up and tried to pin her arms to her side.

"She doesn't understand anything—we tried writing, speaking slowly, different languages," Chubs said, rubbing his chin. "If there's anything left inside of her head, she can't get it out."

There's a difference between broken and ruined. With one, you can hope to piece the object back together, but the other—there's just no coming back.

I pressed my face against my hands, giving up on trying to meet Lillian Gray's dark eyes as they roved around the senior quarters we'd given her. She'd come into the Ranch yesterday afternoon terrified, and she'd spent the whole of the morning exactly that way, shaking like we'd dunked her into the Atlantic in the middle of January. It was a wonder she hadn't passed out from exhaustion yet.

Inside her mind . . . I couldn't describe it. There was actually nothing *to* describe. The first time I'd slipped into her memories, I'd immediately yanked myself back out, dizzy enough that I almost threw up. It was so cluttered, bright flashes of images flashing in no order, speeding by in a quarter of a second—too quick for me to latch onto anything. The intensity of it all was like sitting in a car that jumped from zero to a hundred. It threw me back against my seat, even as I wondered if she was doing it on purpose.

"Dr. Gray," I said sharply, trying to drag her attention back to me. "Can you tell me what your first name is?"

"Naahhmmeee," she muttered, hands cupping the rim of the baseball cap. "Don't . . . good . . . pale . . . shade . . ."

"God," Senator Cruz said, covering her face with her hands. "How can the two of you stand it? This poor woman . . ."

Cole pushed himself off of where he'd been leaning against the opposite wall. "I think that's enough for the day, Gem."

"But I haven't made any progress."

"Maybe there just isn't any progress to make," Senator Cruz offered, a hand on my back. The former First Lady had been the only thing important enough to drag her out of the senior agent quarters she'd been given, away from Rosa. I almost wished she hadn't come, because it was bad enough feeling disappointed in myself—it was gutting to think I was disappointing *her*, after all she'd done for us.

"I haven't even been trying for two full days," I insisted. "At least give me another afternoon."

Lillian Gray repositioned herself so she was lying down on the small bed, her face turned into the pillow. I could feel the frustration pouring off her, and didn't try to catch her hand as she slammed it into the plastic-covered mattress over and over.

I sighed, rubbing my forehead. "All right. We'll take a break."

"How much should we tell the others about her condition?" Senator Cruz asked.

Vida and Chubs had promised to be tight-lipped, to claim the woman was exhausted and needed rest, if pressed by any of the kids. It only bought me a little time to figure out how to help her.

Being up-front with the others wasn't an option that was in the cards for me. If they saw that Lillian Gray, their one shot at deciphering all the research and data we had about the cure, was like . . . *this* . . . it wasn't going to do anything other than swing them more firmly to Liam's side. The side that seemed like it was actually *doing* something.

From the moment we'd left Los Angeles, Cole and I had banked on having information about the cause and cure of IAAN to prove ourselves to the kids. But three weeks later, we had nothing to show that we'd delivered on our promises. Even the kids we'd pulled from Oasis spent more time in the garage than they did in the Ranch proper. The only time I saw them was when they came to the kitchen to pick up their meals, and even then they brought their food back into the garage to eat.

"I'm going to turn the door handle around so it locks from the outside," Cole said. "If we tell the kids to leave her alone, they will."

If they ever bother leaving the garage.

"I'm worried about the agents—Cate," I said. "What's the

reaction going to be when they realize that the League doesn't have her to barter with anymore?"

"The League will keep up appearances as long as humanly possible," Cole assured me. "And I told you what Harry said. He and a few others from his old Special Forces unit are going to investigate the reports of a black site prison near Tucson. Dustin' off the green berets, apparently."

How Harry had managed to find out about a black site—which by its definition didn't exist in any formal records—was beyond me. I didn't want to press Cole on it in front of Senator Cruz.

"That's promising," she said, giving me a faint smile. I shook my head. It was barely anything at all.

I removed Lillian's hat and dirty tennis shoes and tried to ease her under the blankets. Her face was gaunt as she looked up at me, but there were still traces of the rare beauty she had been.

Her eyes narrowed, and suddenly I wasn't seeing her, but her son.

"Alban would want you here with us," Cole told the woman gently. "You have friends here. *Friends. Safe.*"

"Alban?" Lillian sat straight up, her legs tangling in the blankets I'd carefully arranged for her. "John?"

Cole and I exchanged a sharp look, but, just as quickly, she fell back into muttering nonsense beneath her breath. "Hap . . . the . . . ang . . . moh . . ."

He moved to the small desk just to the right of the entrance, opening the drawer. "Dr. Gray, we have some things for you to look at after you get some rest. I'm just going to leave them here. They might be a little, uh, difficult. There's a chart—"

"Chaaaahrts." He held them up so she could see and the woman—the reaction was instant. She sat straight up and reached for them. *"Cerebellum, pineal body, thalamus, interventricular foramen—"*

The quality of her voice completely changed—it was sharp, almost aware. There was a refined edge to it, too, as if she molded each word on her tongue before she said it.

"Okaaay," Cole said, stretching the word out. "That was . . . unexpected."

And then the woman turned over on her other side, and promptly passed out.

Cole started to move toward the door, but I stayed exactly where I was, staring at her prone form. I'm not sure what made me want to try, only that I'd had enough of a chance to process what I'd seen in her head to suddenly be curious about it.

"What?" Cole asked, sounding further and further away as I slipped into her mind. The touch was as gentle as I could manage, and instead of trying to navigating the gleaming scenes that popped up behind my eyelids, I let myself be taken along their flow. I saw textbooks stacked high on a desk, young people in clothing decades out of fashion, movies flickering on screens in the dark, test grades; a bouquet of white roses that matched the dress she wore—that I wore—a younger, handsome version of the president waiting for her at the end of a long aisle strung with ropes of flowers; hospitals, machines; playgrounds, baby clothes, a child with black hair sitting at a kitchen table, his back toward me—all of these small moments of memory were cohesive, flowing as smoothly as if I had been guiding them with my own hand. It shifted, then, all of these glimpses into her life—splotches of rainbow color exploded over the scenes, and

I was falling backward through white mist, nothing above or below me.

A dream. She was deep enough in sleep now to relax both her mind and her body. When I pulled back out of her mind and away from her bed, she didn't stir at all.

"What?" Cole asked. "What did you see?"

I saw a mind that worked, that had whole, cohesive memories. And I was more confused than ever.

"I think . . ." I began, rising up from my knees, "I need to talk to Chubs."

Either anticipating the need, or just by virtue of his own curiosity, Chubs was in the computer room, sitting at one of the empty desks near the front of the room. Tall stacks of thick, intimidating books were piled around him like fortress walls. A few of the Greens had taken the laptops down into the garage to work on Liam's and Alice's projects, but Nico was still there, as he always was. He saw me before Chubs did, and by the expression on his face, I knew I needed to talk to him first.

"Three things," he said. "First, it's done."

"What we talked about?" I asked him.

He held up a plain black flash drive on a string around his neck. "All I need is to find a smaller size—one I can use to modify and work into glasses frames."

"You're the best," I said, meaning it sincerely. Cole had been right—Nico was our man, and not just because he had something to prove.

He flushed a bit, squirming at the praise, then lowered his voice drastically. "The second thing—the other thing we talked about."

"We've talked about a lot of things," I reminded him.

Nico clicked around, bringing up the now-familiar server log. "Someone sent something? Again?"

"An email, two days ago, the night before you left for Oasis—this IP is from one of the laptops, while it was still here in this room," he continued. "It went to an address that's now been deleted."

"Maybe someone was making contact with Amplify?" I asked, not bothering to hide the bitterness in my voice.

He shrugged. "Again, the simplest explanation is usually the right one."

My eyes narrowed slightly. "But you don't believe that, do you?"

"It's just . . . suspicious. Liam made it sound like they only interacted with Amplify in person, so I'm not sure who would be leaking files to them now, or why. This one only stuck out to me because it was a simple message. Do you think it could have been Cole?"

"I'll ask," I said. "I don't know how he's been contacting his stepfather."

"This is a pretty secure way of doing it," Nico said approvingly. "And Liam and the others didn't hide any of their activity when they sent the media package out last night."

"They got it together that fast?" I asked flatly. "Did any of it take with the press?"

"Well . . . that's the third thing." He clicked into a folder on the desktop, bringing up yet another new window. "All of it is offline now—Gray's censors shut the major news sites down until they stripped the story, but the photos and video have been popping up on hundreds of message boards, as well as several of the flash sites that Amplify feeds out to the net. They throw up hundreds of versions of the exact same site with different domain names and search terms embedded in the coding, so that at least one of them will pop up depending on the keywords that people are inputting. I did screenshots of everything I could find in case you wanted to see it."

He put up the screenshot of CNN's homepage as an example. The feature not only was on the main page, it took up half of it: tiled photos of the exterior of the camp, the children with their faces blurred coming out of the bunks. Our backs as we ran down the hallway in those last moments, heading for the door. The largest of the photos was of the wall, the dozens of red handprints that, if you were only scrolling by, could have been mistaken for blood. The headline under which everything fell was NO OASIS: AN INSIDE LOOK AT A 'REHABILITATION' CAMP.

"They also showed this video," Nico said. The moment it loaded, from the very first frozen screen, I knew exactly what it would be of.

I couldn't see my face—Alice had filmed it all from behind me, so that she would have a clear shot of the children coming out of the rooms. *"My name is—"* The audio recording beeped straight through my name. *"I'm one of you. All of us here are like you, except the woman with the camera. We're getting you out of here—taking you to somewhere safe. But we have to move—fast. Fast as you can, without hurting yourselves or anyone around you. Follow them—fast, fast, fast, okay?"*

I gripped the edge of the desk hard enough that Nico leaned back as he said, "I take it they didn't ask you before they used this footage?"

"They did not." And this, too, felt personal—it felt like they were throwing it back in my face. The rest of the video was shots spliced together out of order: the bound-and-gagged PSFs, a close-up of their uniforms, equipment with military decals—smart choices, to try to lend it additional authenticity.

"From the comments I read on the different message boards, it sounds like at least two major papers picked up the story. By the time I tried streaming the TV news, though, there were already government people analyzing it, pointing things out that supposedly made it fake. Did you know they released a list of kids, too? Individual photographs of them and what their parents did for the Federal Coalition?"

"I didn't," I said, gritting my teeth. "Did Cole see this?"

"Yeah, he was in here watching with me earlier," Nico said. "Look, they're probably all down there patting themselves on the back for this. But the truth is, it didn't stick. Less than twenty minutes after it went up, Gray scrubbed the web. Not only that, but a number of web hosting companies were taken offline. The comments on the forums—look, like this one?" He pointed to the timestamp. "From early this morning when the news broke."

The post read: *This is sickening—are they all like this?*

"And two hours later," Nico said, "the tone of the comments changed."

This has to be a hoax. It's too perfectly put together. I could do this in my backyard with a few actors.

The post below it read, *Then how did they get images of the kids? Old stock images? Old movies?*

Have you never heard of Photoshop?

"A lot of people don't think this is real," Nico said. "Part of the problem is that they—we, I guess—*we* don't have a name or identity as a group. We couldn't claim responsibility for this and then back it up with a history of other information dumps. Amplify is only known for boosting information that's already been released by third parties; that's where their name comes from. And even *they* haven't had enough big breaks to seem wholly credible to the general population."

"But people at least saw the images," I said. No matter how Nico spun it, that was a small victory. Because now, when others thought of the camps, these images were likely the first thing that would spring to mind.

"This isn't going to bring Thurmond down," Nico said, his dark eyes flashing. "I believe in our plan. It's the only option."

"Thanks, Nico," I said, squeezing his shoulder. "Keep me updated, okay?"

He nodded and turned back to his computer, fingers flying over the keyboard. I stood and made my way back over to Chubs. He was partially angled in the direction of Nico's computer, wearing the expression of someone who'd been pretending not to listen, even as they heard everything.

"I'm surprised you're not working in the garage," I told him, taking the empty seat next to him.

"I have no idea what you mean by that," Chubs said, though it was clear that he now had the full picture. Or, at least, Liam's half of what had happened.

"I'm sure you don't," I said, "but if that's where you want to be . . . I can understand you picking Liam's side. Everyone else did." Even Zu. *Even Zu.*

His hands came slapping down against the desk. "There is *one* side. That is the side of friendship and trust and love and that is the side that everyone should be on, and I am *refusing* to acknowledge that any other side could exist. Do you understand?"

I blinked. "Yes."

"Though," Chubs said. "I am *inclined*, being co-founder of Team Reality, to think the garage is being overly idealistic about how easily this will play out for them, as evidenced by your discussion with Nico."

"What does Vida think?" I asked.

"Vi is down in the gym right now," he said, "not in the garage. And she is, by her nature, inclined to the side that involves guns and explosions."

I nodded, then motioned toward the books, all of which, now that I was closer, seemed to be medical texts. "Are you trying to figure out what's wrong with Dr. Gray?"

"Yes," he said. "Did you make any progress on that front?"

I met his weak smile with one of my own. "It's the weirdest thing," I told him. "When I tried to look into her mind while she was awake, everything was racing—really intense colors and sounds, and images that moved so fast. But when I tried again when she was asleep, they were real memories. Coherent, whole."

"Were you able to stay in her mind for long—the first time, I mean?"

"No, it made me feel sick."

He nodded, taking that in. "Maybe that was the point. That's the only way she knows how to keep Oranges out."

"That was my thought, too."

"It makes sense. If you knew you had a son capable of coming in and making a mess of everything inside of your skull, wouldn't you try to teach yourself a few ways to block him out—protect yourself?"

Someone intelligent and determined enough to come up

with a cure for this sickness would have taken every precaution against it.

"So her memories are in there, and they're not damaged . . ." Chubs trailed off, running his finger down the side of one of the open textbooks.

"Where did you get these?" I asked, picking up the nearest brick-like book.

"A bookstore," he said, then added quickly, "after hours. Vida took them for me since I was too chickenshit to get out of the car."

"I'm glad you stopped," I said, flipping through its pages. Most of them were on anatomy, but several, including the one he was looking through now, were neuro-this and neuro-that, all with pictures of the human mind on the cover.

He looked up, an unreadable expression on his face. "Clancy can . . . he can break into a person's mind, right? What can he do once he's inside?"

I thought about it. "Influence their feelings, keep them frozen so they can't move, and . . . project images into their head so they're seeing something that's not there."

Another voice chimed in. "He can also—" Chubs and I pivoted toward Nico, who looked like he wanted nothing more than to dive back behind the wide computer monitor. "It's not just . . . it's not just that he can make them freeze up. He can move people around. Like they're toys. I saw him do it to the researchers at Thurmond a few times. He'd jump into their minds mid-conversation to listen to what others were saying. It was really hard for him to keep up. The last time he tried it, he slept a full day to recover. He would get terrible migraines so he had to stop."

Chubs gave me a look I read perfectly. *Migraines, not human decency.*

"Can he affect someone's memories?" Chubs asked. "Can he erase them . . . actually, I don't think you're erasing them, so much as suppressing them. But can he manipulate someone's memories?"

"He's can see someone's memories—" I caught myself, half-stunned by the realization that slammed into me. "He only ever saw my memories when I let him in. I don't think he could do it on his own. The real reason he tried teaching me control at East River was because he wanted to figure out how I was doing it."

"That other Orange kid you knew—what could he do?"

Martin. My skin crawled at the thought of him. "He manipulated people's feelings."

Chubs looked intrigued, flipping back through the book to a diagram each section of the brain. "That's fascinating . . . you're all using different parts of a person's mind against them. Er, sorry, that came out the wrong way."

I held up a hand. "It's fine."

"This is complicated to explain, but even though the mind has many different structures within it, they all work together in different ways. So it's not really that you're accessing different sections of the brain, but different systems within it. Like the frontal lobe plays a part in making and retaining memories, but so does the medial temporal lobe. Does that make sense?"

"Sort of. So you think I'm somehow interrupting different parts of that process depending on what I'm doing?"

"Right," he said. "My understanding is that 'memory' is many different systems, all of which function in slightly different ways—creation, for instance, or bringing one to mind, even storing." He picked up the book in front of him. "The memory of what this object is, how to lift it, how to read the pages, how I feel about it . . . all different systems. My best guess is that when you 'remove' someone's memories, you're not removing them at all, just disrupting a few of these key systems and rerouting the real memories to imagined ones . . . or disrupting the encoding process before the memory can take shape and the neurotransmitters work, so the person can't—"

"Okay, but how do you jump between different systems? Control other functions?"

"I don't know," Chubs said, "how did you do it to Clancy?"

That brought me up short.

"You froze him the same way he froze Liam and Vi. What did you do differently?"

"It was . . . the intent, I guess? I went completely still and wanted him to do the same—" The words choked off.

Mirror minds.

That's what he had told me, when I couldn't figure out how to get back out of the darkness there, sever the thread between us. Once I brought up a memory, my grip on his mind shifted back to his memories. When I went still and wanted him to do the same, he did.

I explained the theory to Chubs, who nodded. "It sort of makes sense. When you intentionally go into a person's memories, you're using the memory of how to do it rather than a memory itself. Wow, that sounded less confusing inside my head. Anyway—it involves being vulnerable to the other person having access to your memories, some sort of natural empathy on your end. I can't imagine him being willing to run the risk of releasing any part of the control he has over his mind, or that he possesses

345

a shred of empathy. Do you want to experiment with this? Maybe we can see if you can get me to move my hand—"

"No," I said, horrified. "I just want to know what system, or part of her mind, he affected to leave her like this."

Chubs sat back, his excitement still there, verging on gleeful. "It's going to take me a little time to find the answer. I'll have to go through all of these books."

"Hey, losers," Vida said from the doorway, still flushed and dripping with sweat from her workout. "I think you're going to want to see what they're working on in the garage."

EIGHTEEN

It took me a moment to even understand what I was seeing as we approached. Duct tape held up two white sheets as a backdrop behind Zu, who was perched on a folding chair. She glowed under the flood of light from four desk lamps that had all been turned and angled toward her. They'd set up a poor man's version of a studio in the corner of the room.

There were two other chairs; the one facing her, next to the camera, was for Alice, who was fiddling with the device. The other was for Liam, who sat to Zu's right, talking to her quietly.

He was the one that spotted us first, and scowled.

"What's going on?" Chubs asked, trying to take in the scene.

"Suzume's agreed to do an interview with us," Alice said, craning her neck around to look at us. She was still dressed in all black, but her hair was twisted now into a messy bun. Next to her were two different notebooks, each open to a page full of scribbles in blue ink. She had a third in her lap.

Cole said you only get one shot to prove this would work. I almost said it, but it felt petty. After only a few hours, there was

no real way to measure the full impact of the first media package they'd already released.

"Is there a problem?" Liam asked.

Vida let out a whistle, as if already predicting how this situation was going to play out. But contrary to what Liam apparently thought, I wasn't here to pick a fight.

"Zu," I said, "can I talk to you? Just for a second?"

She nodded immediately, and I felt tension release its hold on my stomach. I led her a little way away from the others.

"Are you okay doing this?" I asked. She gave me a bright nod, and held up her fingers in an "okay" sign.

"And you understand that if you do this, your face will be all over the place—they explained that, right?" I didn't want her to think I was treating her like a kid incapable of making her own decisions, and I didn't want to imply that Liam would ever purposefully trick her, but I needed the confirmation from her. My first instinct with the others, no matter what, would always be to act like a shield, positioning myself between them and the prying eyes of the world. And Zu, being Zu, seemed to understand.

She slid the small, narrow notebook out of her pocket and wrote, *I can't fight, right? Not at Oasis. Not at Thurmond?*

When I shook my head she didn't seem upset by it, just resigned. *This is the only way I can think of to do* something. *I want to help!*

"I hope you don't think I haven't noticed or appreciated all that you've done here at the Ranch so far," I said.

Zu kept writing. *What happened yesterday made me realize it's important to speak up and say your piece—what you believe in.*

"Liam has that effect on people," I said quietly.

She took my arm and moved her thumb from the corner of

the page, so I could see what else she had written. *I want to be strong like you. I want to do this to help you get what you want. I'm tired of being scared. I don't want them to win.*

The words stole the pain in my heart away, just for a little while. I managed to smile at her, and hugged her tight enough that she let out a silent, shuddering laugh.

"Okay," I said. "Liam's talking for you?"

She nodded. *I told him he could as long as he wasn't in the shot. He said it was okay, but I don't want anyone to go looking for his family because of this.*

"What about your family?"

My family is here.

I bit my lip. "You're right. We are. And, for what it's worth, I think you're going to knock 'em dead."

Zu scribbled something down in her notebook and held it up for me to see. *I will. I've been practicing. Will you stay and watch?*

"Of course."

Chubs and Vida were still standing where I'd left them, talking quietly to each other, their backs turned to Liam. They stepped away from each other as I came closer, and the quiet conversation between Liam and Alice ended the moment Zu sat back down.

I felt Liam's eyes flick to me, just for a moment, but I kept my own eyes on Zu, gave her an encouraging little smile when she glanced over one last time.

"Ready?" Liam asked.

"I have paper and a pen for her to write with," Alice said, picking up one of the bigger notebooks from the floor and holding it out to her. "She can tell me to stop at any point, and I will. She and I shook on it."

"I know. Go ahead."

Liam's jaw worked back and forth, but he said nothing. Alice waited only a moment for me to lodge another protest before she turned. From where I stood behind her, I could watch as she switched her camera over from still photos to video. Zu couldn't fix her eyes on the camera lens for long, not without a look of wariness. I watched as she adjusted her plain white shirt and jeans, folded and unfolded her hands in her lap. Crossed and uncrossed her ankles.

"Okay, sweetheart, make sure you write nice and big so Liam can easily read it. If you don't want to answer anything, just shake your head. Okay? Great—let's start off with two easy ones: can you tell me your name and age, please?"

Zu scribbled the words down, looking relieved to finally not have to stare at the camera. I thought that was the only reason she bothered writing, even though Liam clearly knew the answer to both of the questions.

"My name is Suzume," he said, "and I'm thirteen years old."

"Suzume? That's a lovely name."

"Thank you," Liam read. "My friends call me Zu."

"Can you tell us a little bit about why your friend is speaking for you?"

Zu looked away from the camera, over to where we were standing. I saw the small movement in the corner of my eye, the way Vida gave her a low, quick thumbs-up.

I've been practicing.

"Because . . . because for a long time I was too scared to say anything," Zu said. "And I didn't t-think anyone would l-listen."

Liam jumped as if she'd shot him in the chest, his face pale with shock. The world ceased to spin under my feet for that first second when her sweet, high voice emerged. It was slightly halting, edged with the nerves she wasn't letting anyone see on her face. So different, too, from the way it sounded when she had talked in her sleep—not scratchy with disuse.

"I did it," she said, almost in wonder.

"Yeah you did! Get it, girl!" Vida said, and her loud clapping was the only sound that emerged in the silence that followed. The kids who'd been watching the interview happen from where they sat fanned out on the floor to the side looked, in a word, stunned.

Chubs moved quickly, shoving past me, Vida, *and* Alice, who'd started to rise to her feet to reset the camera, and all but slammed into Zu. His face as he hugged her was a portrait of pure joy, and he didn't bother trying to hide the evidence of the tears that were beginning to track down his face.

"I'm t-trying to do an interview," Zu complained, her voice muffled by his shirt. After a moment, she relented, patting his back.

"Okay, Charlie," Vida said. "Let the girl finish before you try to drown her in tears. Come on." She carefully extracted him from the interview space, guiding him back around to where I stood, where the rest of his embrace was transferred to me. And I was more than a little glad for the excuse to look away from Zu to deal with the tears that were starting to well up behind my own lashes.

"Why is everyone acting like c-crazy people?" she said, and already her voice was getting steadier, stronger. "Can we start again?"

Liam stood up, about to drag his chair away when she grabbed his hand and said something quietly to him. I couldn't see his expression at first, not with his back to us, but I caught a glimpse of it as he pulled his chair over to the other side of the camera, and my throat ached with the pride there, the happiness. He sat back down and Zu immediately reoriented herself so she was angled toward him instead of the reporter. Her whole posture changed, relaxing enough for her to start swinging her legs back and forth.

"This okay?" Liam asked, both to her and Alice.

The reporter nodded, merely crossing the next two questions off her list.

Her next questions were about Zu's color classification and what she could do. It led naturally into a bigger question. "Were you sent to a camp by your parents, or were you picked up?"

"I made my father's car—I killed its engine by mistake. It was an accident. Up until then I had only ruined a few lamps. My alarm clock. They were talking about . . . terrorists, I think, they were saying that they thought IAAN was because of terrorists and that they should leave as soon as possible to go back to Japan. I got upset and—I didn't have a good control. I fried the engine, and cars hit us. My mom's pelvis was broken. After she got out of the hospital, she insisted I go back to school that next Monday. It was the first Collection."

The Collections were a series of pick-ups kept secret from children. If parents felt threatened by their children, or thought they were a danger to themselves or to others, they sent them to school on specific days and the PSFs picked them up.

"You mentioned you can control your abilities now. How did you learn to?"

Zu shrugged. "Practice. Not being afraid of them."

"What would you say to people who feel that letting Psi kids learn to control their abilities endangers others?"

She made her patented *Are you kidding me?* face. "Most kids only want to control them so they can feel normal. Why would I want to fry every light switch or phone I touch? Every computer? There are kids who abuse it, maybe, but most of us . . . we're more dangerous if we can't control it, and everyone can learn if you give them time."

"How did you feel when you realized you were being picked up by the Psi Special Forces at school that day?" Alice asked.

"I thought it was a mistake," she said, looking down at her hands. "Then I felt stupid and small—like trash."

The reporter's questions had clearly been designed to bleed Zu's old wounds for every last terrible detail. A question about her daily routine at Caledonia turned into how the PSFs treated them on an average day, and then on days they misbehaved. It was excruciating to try to imagine it happening to her—beyond that to hear Alice ask, "You mentioned before that you only got out of Caledonia because you escaped. Can you talk about what happened?"

Zu turned, leaning slightly so she was looking at Liam. He'd been watching with his arms crossed over his chest, struggling to keep the emotion off his face. Now he gave her a small nod, this heartbreaking little smile. *Go ahead.*

"It was planned for months by my friend—he wasn't my friend then, but he was so nice to everyone. So smart. We knew we would only have one chance to get out, and he was it. . . ." She moved into the finer details of the escape, how they had communicated the details to each other leading up to that night. "Then it was happening . . . it was working . . . it snowed the day before, and there were piles of it everywhere. It made it hard to run, but we could see that some of the older kids were already in the booth—the guard box at the electric fence's gate. They were trying to disable it—get the gate to open. I don't know what was wrong. The camp controllers must have somehow blocked them. Then we just got . . ."

Alice let her have a few moments to collect her thoughts before pressing, "You got what? How did the PSFs and camp controllers respond?"

Zu couldn't bring herself to say it. I remembered the scene so vividly and I had only seen it secondhand in her memory. To have actually experienced it . . . I snuck a glance at Liam. He hadn't moved from his rigid pose, but his skin had taken on an ashen quality.

Finally, Zu lifted her hand, made a gun using her fingers, and fired in the direction of the camera. Alice actually flinched.

Why is that surprising? I wondered. *Why would they feel any shame in mowing us down?* How had they never even considered that possibility when they'd turned their kids over to a branch of the *military*?

"Are you saying they opened fire on the escaping kids? Are you certain they were using real rounds of ammunition?"

She said in a flat voice. "The snow turned red."

Alice stared at her notebook in her lap, as if unsure of where to go next with this.

"I don't think people see us as human," Zu said. "Otherwise I don't know how they can do the things they did. You could always see that the PSFs were a little afraid, but also very angry, too. They hated having to be there. They called us all different names—'animals,' 'freaks,' 'nightmares,' bad words I'm not supposed to say. That's how they could do it. If we weren't human in their minds, they could treat us that way and not feel bad about it. That night we were like animals in a pen. Most of them shot at us from the windows of the camp's building. They'd wait until one of the kids got real close to the gate and then . . ."

I didn't realize she'd attracted a crowd until I heard someone let out a faint gasp, and found the remaining kids and Cole standing a short distance behind us. Most were focused on Zu's pale face as she explained this, but Cole was watching his brother.

"How did you escape that same fate?" Alice sounded genuinely invested—engaged.

"My friend—the one who'd planned it? They got the gate open. He came and picked me up and carried me out. I fell and couldn't force myself to get up and run. He carried me for hours. We found a car, this old minivan, and just drove for days to get away. We've been looking for safe places ever since."

"How did you survive out on the road? How did you find food and shelter?"

"We . . . I don't want to say," Zu said. When Alice sat up in surprise she added, "because there are so many kids who are still out there searching for those things, and I don't want to tell people where to look for them, or how to wait for them to show up. There were a lot of ways to do it. You just had to learn how to stay invisible—not take bad, big risks."

"By 'people looking for them,' are you talking about skip tracers?" Alice asked. "I looked up your listing in their network. The reward for 'recovering' you and returning you to PSF custody is thirty thousand dollars—did you know that?"

Zu nodded.

"Does that make you angry, knowing that someone is profiting off you that way?"

She took a long time for what should have been a very easy answer: *Yes, I'm angry, it makes me furious.*

"I don't know," she said finally. "Sometimes, yes, it makes me very upset. The price isn't a reflection of how much my life is worth—how could you calculate that? They take a flat amount, ten thousand dollars, and they increase it based on your abilities and how much potential they think you have to fight back. I think I'm okay with that price, because it shows them I won't give up and just go with them. It says I'm going to fight to protect myself."

The screen on the back of the camera showed Alice zooming in for a tighter shot of Zu's face as the girl continued.

"There are some men and women out there who live for it now, not because they need the money, but because they *like* it, or they think they're good at it. It's messed up. They act like it's hunting season. But I think . . . more of them have been forced into it. They need the money to survive. The PSFs have to do it because of the draft. I think if they stopped long enough to think about it, they would see that they're not really angry with us for what happened. Maybe they're afraid, but they're angry at the people who didn't protect them—the government, the president. They have no power to remove those things from their lives, so they transfer the blame. They act like IAAN was our fault, not something that happened to us. So the economy crashing? Us. Losing their houses? Us."

Alice started to ask another question, but Zu wasn't quite finished yet.

"I knew someone like that. He was a good person. Great person. The best. The thing is—if you want to be a skip tracer, you have to prove it. You can't get into their system or get any of their tech until you turn your first kid in," Zu explained in an avalanche of words. She twisted the notebook in her hands. "I was driving to California with a group of kids and we were being chased by these two skip tracers—real ones, the hungry ones I was talking about. They made our car flip and crash so bad that one of my friends . . . he died. They were going to take me, but another skip tracer came in and got me out of the car instead— I was trapped by the seat belt. I should have said that before. I couldn't get out and run like the others."

Liam swore loudly. I was too numb by the account to do anything other than listen.

"Was he one of the ones you mentioned before—he needed to turn one kid in to start? Can you tell us about him?"

Zu nodded. "He was old—not *old*-old, but definitely in his twenties. Maybe twenty-seven?"

Alice gave a faint laugh. "Twenty-seven's not so old."

She shrugged before continuing. "We were in Arizona . . . I think he must have been from Flagstaff or Prescott, I'm not sure. He was really angry. Something really sad happened to him, I could tell, but he didn't talk about it. He was someone who just wanted to get out of his life, but he couldn't do it without money. No matter how many times he told me he was going to turn me in, I knew he wouldn't."

"How could you tell?" Alice asked.

Yes, I thought, *how on earth could you have trusted this person?*

"I told you, he was a good person. He was . . . really struggling. It ate him up inside. No matter how many times he tried to treat me like I was a freak, he always gave in. There were two chances to turn me over to the PSFs, but he couldn't do it. Not only did he save me, but he helped save another kid and got him back to the people who were caring for him. He was the one who got me to California."

The pieces of this were coming together for me now—those people she was talking about were Liam's parents. That must have been the moment that she crossed paths with Liam's mom.

"What happened to him?"

"He . . . his name was Gabe, did I say that? His name was Gabe, and he was . . . he was really kind."

"What happened to him?" Alice asked again.

"Gabe died."

Chubs released the breath he'd been holding, and scrubbed his face with his hands. I'd known how the story ended, but it was still devastating. Seeing her face, hearing those two words . . .

"What happened to him?" Softer this time, more hesitant. Alice looked back at Liam, as if to ask if it was all right to continue to head down this path. He nodded; he understood too. She wanted to talk about this. I had a feeling she agreed to this specifically so she could talk about Gabe and what he'd done for her.

"The kids I was traveling with before? They beat us to California and were waiting at my—at the meet spot we agreed on. We didn't know that, though."

Oh, God . . .

"Gabe made me walk behind him as we looked around. It was really, really dark—we could barely see anything. When we opened the doors to—to one of the nearby buildings, the other kids were hiding in there. They saw him and recognized him from Arizona, and they thought he had followed them. One of the girls panicked and shot him."

I looked at Liam the exact moment he looked at me, absolutely stricken.

"He was a good person, and he was just trying to help—it was a mistake, but there was nothing we could do. They thought he was going to hurt them. They didn't know what I did. He died because he helped me instead of helping himself."

"That's terrible," Alice said, still looking for the right words. "That's . . ."

"Everyone is so afraid of each other," Zu continued. "I don't want to look at a grown-up and assume they're thinking of how much they can get for me. I don't want them to look at me and think of how badly I could hurt them. Too many . . . too many of my friends are in pain. They've been hurt very badly by what they've been through, but they've taken care of me. That's the other side of everything. Because there are people who are afraid, and then there are people who are so brave. We only survived being hungry and scared and hurt because we had each other."

Alice let the camera keep recording for several more seconds before finally switching it off and sitting back. "I think that'll do for today."

Zu nodded, standing up and setting the notebook down on her chair, and came straight toward Vida. "Did I do okay?"

Vida held out her fist for a bump. "You killed it, girl."

Liam was half listening to whatever Alice was saying to him, half listening to hear what was passing between Zu and Vida—he caught me watching him, and instead of looking away, he offered up a small smile. I felt myself return it, but the moment passed as quickly as it had arrived. What was important here was Zu; the small blip of happiness I'd felt at that small cease-fire was nothing compared to the joy soaring inside of me as she talked to Vida, her hands moving to emphasize her words. And as I listened to the sweet way the pitch of it rose as she got excited, a thought began to stir at the back of my mind.

I touched Chubs's arm to get his attention. "What part of the mind controls speech?"

He came out of his daze like I'd thrown a pitcher of ice water in his face. "It's a whole system, remember?"

"Right, I understand that. I guess my question is, is there something in your mind that could leave you silent or unable to process words, even if everything else seemed to be working fine?"

Now he just looked confused. "Zu didn't talk by choice."

"I meant Lillian," I said. "Like all of the lights are on in the house, but she can't get the door unlocked—she can pick up a few words here and there, but she can't understand us and we can't understand her. Have you heard of anything like that?"

He thought about it. "I can't think of the medical term, but it's been known to happen sometimes with stroke patients. My dad had someone come into his ER once who'd been in the middle of teaching a lesson on Shakespeare and then, two minutes after stroking out, couldn't communicate at all. It's . . . expressive . . . aphasia? Or is it receptive aphasia? I'm not sure, I need to double-check. One indicates damage in the Wernicke's area of the brain."

"Inglés, por favor," Vida said, catching the tail end of this. "Unfortunately, you're the only one here fluent in Geek."

He snorted. "Basically, we form what we want to say in the Wernicke's area of the brain, and then that planned speech is transferred to the Broca's area, which actually carries out the speech. I wonder . . ."

"What?" I prompted.

"Maybe Clancy managed to . . . shut down, or somehow numb those parts of her mind? Or depressed them, maybe, so they're not functioning at full capacity." He turned a shrewd look on me. "When you restored Liam's memories, what *exactly* did you do?"

"I was thinking about . . . I was remembering something that happened between us," I said. "I was—" Kissing him. "Reaching out to him somehow, it was kind of . . . instinctive. I was trying to connect to something in him." I was trying to find the old Liam I had given up.

Mirror minds.

"Oh," I said, pressing both hands to my mouth. *"Oh."*

"Share with the rest of us," Vida said, hands on Zu's shoulders. "Your half is the only half of the conversation I understand."

"I need to jumpstart her," I said.

"Excuse me?" Cole said, joining the conversation now. "Who are we giving the shock treatment to?"

"You think you can reset that system in her mind," Chubs said, understanding. "But . . . how, exactly?"

"Clancy said something to me the last time I was in his head," I said. *"Mirror minds.* I think that's what happens when I enter someone's head. I'm mirroring what's in their mind with my own. When I'm tampering with memories and searching through them, it's like I've set up a mirror between us, and all of those changes I'm imagining into existence are immediately reflected in the other mind."

"Okay?" Cole said. This was going to be nearly impossible to explain—they had no idea what any of this felt like, and I wasn't sure I knew how to articulate it.

Thank God for Chubs, though. "So you think that if you engage that part of your mind, it'll engage that part of her mind, too, and reset it?"

I held up my hands. "Worth a try?"

"More than worth a try," Cole said. "It's time we checked in on her anyway—"

There was a bang on the loading dock door—one loud sound that came like a shot through the calm that had settled over the room. Liam jumped to his feet, a grin splitting his face as he jogged to the door. It was the only reason I let myself relax as he and Kylie unhooked the padlock they'd installed there and the door rolled up, rattling like thunder as sunlight spilled in.

I counted off the eight kids as they came in, each somehow looking worse than the next; filthy, in a variety of mismatched knits. We could smell them from where we were standing, which Cole chose to note with raised brows and an expression I'd seen Liam wear a dozen times.

I recognized the new faces, but I hadn't been in Knox's camp in Nashville long enough to assign them names from memory. The kids there had been so hopeless, left with next to nothing by way of supplies because Knox and a few of the others had taken everything they brought in for themselves. Now this group only seemed to be in slightly better shape. Between them, they had a few backpacks and makeshift bags tied together from old sheets. If I hadn't known any better, I'd have thought they walked from Nashville.

Liam had reached up to start pulling the door down, but stopped, leaning out to wave the last two in. One, a tall blond girl, stopped to clasp a hand on his shoulder. The other, an even taller guy wearing a bright red-checked hunting hat, dropped his backpack and stretched.

Olivia, I thought. *Brett.*

And sure enough, Kylie and Lucy rushed forward with a cry of "Liv!"

The girl turned toward them and the other two were brought up short, actually skidding against the cement at the full sight of her face. One side of it had been burned by Mason, the Red that Knox had kept prisoner in his camp, and had scarred badly as it healed.

"Got a makeover," she said in a light voice, "as you can see. Hi, Ruby."

Brett was there in an instant, running a hand down her long braid to rest against her lower back.

I crossed the last few feet between us. Despite the fact that neither of us were particularly warm, cuddly people, I hugged her like it had been years, not a month, since we'd parted ways. "It's good to see you," I said. It really was. "You too, Brett."

"Feeling's mutual," he assured me. I stepped back, letting Kylie, Lucy, and Mike approach her, hug her, bring her more firmly into the fold. "So this is Lodi, huh?"

"This is it," Liam confirmed. "We've been busy. Did you catch the news today? We did the camp hit I mentioned to you before."

"You did it?" Olivia said, blinking. "I remember you mentioning it, but . . ."

She exchanged a confused look with Brett.

"It was all over the radio as we were coming in," Brett said. "You guys do know that the Children's League is taking credit for it . . . right?"

And just like that, the wind went completely out of Liam's sails—in fact, the air itself seemed to have been sucked completely out of the garage. It was Cole who walked over to the workstation, sending the kids standing there scattering as he switched on the radio.

We'd caught the male radio host mid-sentence. *"—we've just received the following statement made by representatives of the Children's League—"*

I looked down at my boots, hands on my hips. Senator Cruz and Rosa came rushing in from the tunnel, Nico right behind them. The woman's face was pale as she opened her mouth to call out to us. The grave voice coming through the speaker prompted her news.

"'Early yesterday morning we carried out an assault on one of Gray's rehabilitation camps located in Oasis, Nevada. We have taken the victims of his cruelty, the children interned there, and will release them only following the president's immediate resignation. Should these demands not be met, we will strike our next target.' Powerful words. If you're just tuning in, we have a breaking news update about the images and video released this morning by several noted papers . . .''

"They can't do this!" Zach shouted over the chatter buzzing around us. "They had nothing to do with it! They're making us look like terrorists—"

"Is this real?" Senator Cruz asked Cole. "Would they claim responsibility for it? Or is Gray trying to pin it on them to justify another attack on them?"

"I think they're claiming credit," I said feeling a need to inject a calm voice into the panicking fray. "Gray doesn't need another excuse to attack them, and he's been scrambling to float the theory that everything was doctored. I guess it doesn't matter, though. The League has the target on their backs now, not us."

Cole managed to wrangle his smug look—or at least dampen it somewhat. "Well, y'all have succeeded in putting another undeserved feather in their cap. But Ruby's right. This is a good thing for us."

The anchor continued, undaunted. "—fifteen Psi Special

364

Forces officers sustained mild injuries and were treated on-site. All declined to comment on the treatment of the children and the reha- bilitation camp when questioned before the arrival of ranking military officials. As of yet there has been no response from President Gray, and Washington remains silent."

The unspoken words trickled through my mind. *But not for long.*

Lillian was not only awake when we unlocked the door and came in, she was pacing the length of the room in the dark. She'd left all of the lights off, save for the one at her desk. Compared to earlier, she looked a little more presentable. Someone, likely Cole, had brought her wipes to clean off her face, a hairbrush, and a clean set of sweats. I'd seen her in press clippings wearing the cos- tume of a First Lady—suits, perfectly coiffed hair, pearls—and I'd seen her in Clancy's memory as a scientist, crisp and clinical in her white lab coat. Here, dressed like this, she could have been anyone. And that made it easier to approach her—easier to do what I had to.

"Hi, Dr. Gray," I said. "Do you remember me and Chu—Charles?"

Vida and Cole had both wanted to watch, but I'd been wor- ried about overwhelming Dr. Gray with too many people around her. I needed her calm, or at least calmer than she had been while dealing with me before.

The woman mumbled something to herself as she continued that careful stride back and forth, back and forth, not breaking pace as she glanced over at her bed and the papers strewn over it. Suddenly, she stopped and pointed at them with urgency, her mouth struggling around each sound she was trying to make. Her entire body shook with her frustration as she pressed a hand against her throat, rubbing it.

In that moment I understood. Clancy hadn't just wanted to silence her from being able to tell others about the cure. He wanted to punish her, in the exact way he knew would hurt her the worst. He'd taken her brilliant mind and trapped her inside of it.

"That's right, we want to talk about the research you did."

"Chhaaaa—" She swallowed and tried again, looking as humiliated as I'd ever seen a person. I had to fight the urge to take her hand when she raised it toward us. "Chaaaart."

"Right, the charts." I carefully took her shoulders and guided her toward the bed. I don't know if she remembered what had happened the last time I was in here with her, but she didn't struggle until I tried to force her to sit.

"Ruby," Chubs said. "Are you ready?"

Her shoulders bunched up, the muscles tightening beneath my hand. She was already preparing herself. She knew what I was.

Diving into her mind the second time was no less painful than the first. Dr. Gray turned her memories into a roaring river I couldn't cross—a stream of landscapes, homes, roads, children's toys, textbooks, flowers, silverware—anything and everything she could think of to protect the important memories.

But we were connected. That was all that mattered.

"Ruby." Chubs was standing behind me, I knew that, but it sounded like he was talking to me from outside in the hall. "Ruby, what's . . . er . . . your favorite color?"

"My favorite color," I repeated, letting the word take shape in my mind, "is green."

The shift came midway through the word. One moment I was being dragged between scenes lasting no longer than a fraction of a second. The next, it felt as if I'd been thrown against a wall of glass shards. I recoiled, physically and mentally.

"Tell me what your middle name is," Chubs said.

"It's . . ." The words brought me up closer to the pain, the sharpness of it. This part of her mind was so dark, so unbearably dark. It must have been painful for her every time she tried to speak, to use this part of her mind. He wanted her to hurt. *Hurt.*

"What's your middle name?" he repeated.

"It's Elizabeth." I felt my mouth form the words, but I couldn't hear them over the rush of blood inside my own head. *I have to push through this. This is glass. I have to break it. I have to get through it. Mirror minds.*

"Who were you named after?" Chubs's questions were keeping me in that part of her mind. Every time I had to stop and think about what he was asking, the pain became slightly more bearable.

"Grandmother," I said. "Grams."

Grams. Grams. Grams. The person who remembered me. Who I'd be able to find once this was over. *I need you. We need you.*

My grip on her tightened to the point where I'm sure my nails dug into her flesh. With one final, deep breath, I pushed against the wall as hard as I could, turning my mind into a bat and slamming against it until I felt it give with a deafening crack. I slid forward, forcing my way through, until it shattered and cut the connection to ribbons.

"Ruby, what was the name of our van? What did we call it?" Chubs must have been shouting the question to me. His voice was ragged.

"Black . . ." I mumbled, my mind in pieces—pain everywhere—agony—"Black Betty."

I didn't slide through, so much as fall past the remnants of the barrier. The world around me exploded into electric blue light—

When I came around, rising up from the murky pain, I was flat on my back on the floor, Chubs's anxious face an inch above mine.

"Okay?" he asked, taking my arm to help me sit up. "How do you feel?"

"Like I took a flaming knife to the head," I got out around gritted teeth.

"You were out for a full minute. I was starting to get worried," he said.

"What happened?" I asked, turning toward the bed. "What—"

Lillian Gray was sitting at the edge of her bed, her face hidden behind her hands. Her shoulders shook, trembling with each gasp of breath.

She's crying, I realized, rising up to my knees, *I hurt her—*

Her face was red, swollen from the force of her weeping. The air in the room had shifted, a thunderstorm of feeling had rolled back, and what was left was weightless blue sky. When she looked at me, she *saw* me. Her lips pulled back into a painful smile.

"Thank. You." She treated each word like the small miracle it was.

And then, without warning, I began to cry too. The pressure that had built in my chest gave way with the next heavy breath in, and expelled fully as I released it. I did *this*. If I did nothing else worthwhile in my life, I helped this woman. I gave her back her voice. I hadn't broken someone; I'd put them back together.

"Um . . ." Chubs began awkwardly. "Should I maybe . . . er . . ."

I stood up, swiping at my face with a laugh. "I'm going to find Cole," I said. "Can you tell her what's going on? Make sure everything is okay?"

I used the hem of my shirt to scrub my face once I was outside of the room, allowing myself a few steadying breaths before I looked in on the gym and office, then the big room, where kids were already sitting down with their plates of macaroni and cheese.

Right. Dinner. That meant . . .

I took the stairs two at a time, bounding down the hall to the kitchen. The kids serving there only shrugged and said Cole had come in and left with two plates. It would have looked too suspicious for me to wait outside of the storage room; I slipped the string I held the key on up from around my neck and glanced back and forth, making sure no one was watching as I went inside and locked it behind me. The overhead bulb swung with the movement of air, and the door behind the shelf unit groaned, not fully shut.

It was curiosity, more than anything else, that made me step into that narrow hall. It was the first time in days I'd gone to see him—Cole had simply waved me off each time I offered to do it, saying it was better for me to stay away and avoid antagonizing him when he was already furious with me. That he'd been perfectly cordial, with no evidence of trying to influence Cole's mind.

Now that she was back, I half expected Vida to be there,

watching them from the small window in the door at the other end of the hall—but no. There wasn't anyone there, making sure Clancy wasn't running wild inside Cole's mind.

If you had told me that Cole and Clancy would have been sitting facing each other on the floor eating, separated by only an inch-thick wall of bulletproof glass . . . I would have told you to keep your delusions to yourself. But there they were. The two of them, relaxing and talking with the ease of old friends.

I leaned forward, pressing my ear against the door, catching snippets of conversation.

"—wouldn't be any files on it, that's how confidential it is, the only reason I know it exists still is a PSF account—"

"—worth it if it means more boots on the ground—"

"Don't discount the propaganda they're releasing—try to use it to get your own message out there. Recruit willing soldiers—"

Ten minutes went by; fifteen. The elation I felt deflated into something that resembled dread. Not that the two of them were talking—I trusted Cole to take everything Clancy said with the largest grain of salt known to mankind—but that I was agreeing with what I heard.

"The goal should be to keep as many choices open for the kids as possible, to not let someone sweep in with regulations on how they could or should be," Clancy continued. "Is the senator even willing to stand up for their right to make decisions about their future?"

The cure is another way to control us, take decisions out of our hands.

I stepped back from the door, shaking my head. No—helping Lillian *was* giving us a choice. We couldn't make a real decision without knowing what the cure was.

Then why, all of a sudden, did the past few hours feel like such a mistake?

"—nothing else you can tell me about Sawtooth?" Cole was on his feet now, taking Clancy's empty plate from the slot in the door.

Clancy returned to his cot. There was a new, thicker blanket there now—a real pillow, too. A stack of books beside the bed stood up nearly as tall as the cot. Apparently Clancy had been a *very* good boy, if Cole had been willing to bring him all of that.

"You know everything I do. That wasn't the camp I helped set up—it was the original one in Tennessee," Clancy said. "Are you ever going to come in, Ruby?"

I leaned away from the door, but it was pointless. His eyes shifted over to the window and caught mine through the glass. With a deep breath, I unlocked the door and propped it open with my foot. Cole's hand twitched at his side as he strode toward me. I was starting to have a hard time telling his apprehension apart from his irritation.

I waited until we were back out in the hallway before opening my mouth.

"Don't," he said, holding up a hand. "I have this under control."

"Nothing is ever really under control with him," I pointed out. "As long as you're careful . . ."

"You're killing me, Gem," he said, raking his hand back through his hair. "What is it?"

"I think you have to see it to believe it."

With the others occupied by editing Zu's interviews and, at Liam's suggestion, giving their own, Cole and I were left to do the planning for an actual assault on Thurmond. We stayed up through the night rehashing the details. I would go in with the flash drive on February twenty-seventh. On March first, our team of twenty kids and Harry's forty-odd soldiers would storm the camp at approximately seven in the evening and engage and restrain the PSFs—I would need to get the program uploaded into their servers by a quarter till. The kids would then be brought to a secure location within walking distance of the camp to wait for their parents to retrieve them. Written out step by step, it almost sounded simple. The reality was stark.

The morning officially began with Cole dropping a large blanket of paper over my head, startling me awake from where I'd fallen asleep at one of the computer room desks.

"What's this?" I asked, pulling it away. At least fifteen sheets of paper had been taped together to form a whole, cohesive image of rings of cabins, shoddy brick buildings, a silver fence, and the green wilderness around it.

I jumped to my feet. "This is Thurmond. How did you get this?"

In response, he calmly passed me a silver burner phone— there was something grudging in his expression, reluctant. I took it from him, raising it slowly to my ear. "Hello?"

"Is this Ruby?"

"Speaking," I said, watching Cole's face as he watched me.

"My name is Harry Stewart—" There was static on the other end on the line, and it only made me grip the phone harder. Harry. Liam's Harry. His voice was deeper than I expected, but I could hear the smile in it. *"I wanted to let you know that last night we conducted an operation—"*

"We?" I repeated dumbly. Nico had come over to stand next to Cole, looking bewildered. I switched the phone over to speaker so that he could hear it as well.

"One you never cleared with me," Cole muttered.

"A group of old, retired army types," he said with a laugh. *"Some new friends, too, who have recently had a change of heart about serving the President. This morning at approximately oh-two-hundred hours, we conducted a raid on a suspected black site prison."*

My heart actually stopped. I felt it throb, then nothing as I held my breath.

"It was successful, and we were able to recover a number of suspected traitors and informants." He said those words—*traitors and informants*—lightly, a thread of humor in his voice. *"We've forwarded on what intel we were able to recover from the site as well as from our own sources in the government. We'll be joining you by the end of the week, but I wanted to let you know that we did get your—"*

His voice was muffled, moving away from the phone. I heard another voice, this one higher—a woman.

"Lie back down," I heard Harry say, *"I'm glad you're awake—these gentlemen will explain what happened—yes, you can speak to her in just a moment—"*

My heart was beating crazy fast, I heard it my ears, I felt it down to my toes. There was a scuffle as the phone forcibly shifted hands.

"Ruby?"

Nico let out a cry, pressing his hands against his mouth. Hearing her voice—it couldn't have been real—they—Cate was—

"Cate," I choked out, "are you okay? Where are you right now?"

"*Ruby*," she said, cutting me off, "*l-listen to me—*" Her voice was so rough my own throat ached in sympathy. "*We're okay, we're all okay, but you have to listen to me, some . . . something happened with the League, didn't it? They—*"

I heard Harry in the background saying, "*It's okay, please lie back—*"

Cole braced his hands against the desk. "Conner, what's going on?"

"*We overheard some of the . . . the guards posted there, they were taunting us, they said that Kansas HQ's going to be attacked. None of the agents—none of us can get a hold of anyone there. Can you warn them? Can you give them the message—?*"

"We'll take care of it," Cole promised her. Nico had already moved back to his computer station, his hands flying across the keyboard. "You sit tight, Harry's going to bring you guys back up here."

"*The agents want to go to Kansas,*" she said, her voice strained.

"Well, they might not have a choice," Cole said, not unkindly. "Hey, Conner, it's great to hear your voice."

"*You too. You taking care of my kids?*"

Cole gave me a small smile. "They've been taking care of me."

"*Ruby?*"

"I'm here." The words came out of me in a rush. "Are you okay? Tell me you're okay—"

"*I'm okay. I'll see you soon, under—understand? I'm sorry—the—connect—out—*"

Dial tone.

I stared at the device, letting Cole reach over and turn it off. I didn't have the strength to fight off the numb dejection that bled through me. I needed more than that. She had to know—she had to know how sorry I was.

"They're driving through the middle of nowhere," he told me. "Bad reception. Harry will call again when they get closer."

I nodded. "Do you think it's true? They're going to attack Kansas HQ?"

"Their servers are offline," Nico said. "I just tried to ping them and . . . nothing."

"I'm going to try to make telephone contact with some of the agents who are still out in the field, see if they know." Cole tucked my hair behind my ear, ran a knuckle down around my cheek. "This is a solid win. Cate's okay. We have an actual fighting force coming. Two weeks and we'll be on the other side of this. Focus on that for now. Don't let this Kansas thing trip you up. As far as I'm concerned, it doesn't matter either way."

"Of course it matters," I said. "So many people have already died—"

"I get it," he said, "I didn't mean it like that, only that the League is done either way. Claiming the hit as their own was a desperate, last gasp for relevancy. Focus on the future. The cure, now that we have Dr. Gray back in working order. Thurmond—" He tapped his fingers on the printout. "Harry went to all that trouble to track this down for us. Let's put it to good use."

He stood, taking the printout with him to tack up on the wall. I stayed where I was until he left, presumably to make good on his promise to investigate Cate's claims, and then rose, moving toward the satellite images of Thurmond's grounds, as if in a dream. My eyes traced the rings of cabins—lopsided, uneven rings, apparently. Seeing it from above, like a free bird passing overhead, smoothed out the sick feeling that had started to squirm around in my stomach.

"It's much bigger now," Nico said. I nodded, accepting the permanent markers he handed me.

He stepped back to lean against the desk and watch. The longer I worked, the more attention I seemed to attract, until I knew I had a full-fledged audience without ever needing to turn around. I labeled each of the larger structures—FACTORY and PSF BARRACKS on the two rectangular-shaped buildings to the left of the rings of cabins, GARDEN on the square of green at the northernmost point of the camp, and MESS HALL, INFIRMARY, and GATE on the right. Then I moved on to the cabins, and marked the circular CONTROL TOWER. Each ring of small cabins was outlined with either the green or blue marker to indicate its inhabitants.

I felt the focus of someone's gaze between my shoulder blades like sunlight coming through a lens, burning until I couldn't ignore the small waves of self-consciousness that began to rise. It was irrational, but it felt like I was revealing something shameful, something I had to be embarrassed about. My mood had slid so quickly from eager excitement to horror and pity that I felt myself start to prickle in self-defense.

"Are there only Greens and Blues there?" I turned around at Senator Cruz's question. She stood in the doorway, her arm looped through Dr. Gray's, who seemed to be trying to come closer. Nico took one look at her, froze, and then fled to the back of the room, almost tripping as he sat back down.

"There were Yellow, Orange, and Red children," I answered, looking back at the women, "but they were moved out of the camp about five and a half years ago. The Reds were taken into a training program, Project Jamboree. The Yellows were moved to another camp in Indiana that specializes in non-electrical containment."

"What about the Orange kids?" Dr. Gray asked.

My hand stilled, as did the air around me.

"We have no confirmed reports of their whereabouts," I said.

"Where is this?" Dr. Gray's words were still slightly halting, as if she half-expected them to start failing her again at any moment. She took a step closer, taking in the patches of wild grass and snow. If anyone looked hard enough, they would have been able to see the little dots of blue uniforms working in the Garden.

"This isn't Thurmond," she said. "Thurmond was only one building. I saw it myself."

"Once they moved the initial research programs out, they rapidly expanded the camp to house more kids," I said. "I've added a little R, O, or Y next to the cabins they used to reside in. They switched out the non-electrical locks on the Yellow cabins and never changed them back. As far as I know, the Red cabins only had additional spigots and sprinklers inside."

Senator Cruz put a hand on my shoulder and she leaned forward, inspecting my work. "Why were the Reds and Oranges in the second ring from the center, instead of in the outermost? If they were going to cause problems, it seems like they'd try to move them as far away from the Control Tower as possible."

"They surrounded them on either side with a buffer of Green cabins," I explained, "so that if they tried to attack the camp controllers, or tried to escape using their abilities, they'd have to burn down a few kids on their way."

"Did that ever stop them?"

I shook my head.

377

"Did anyone ever escape?"

I shook my head again. "The ones who tried were shot before they reached the fence. They kept at least one sniper on the roof of the Control Tower at all times—two if a group was working out in the Garden."

"Well, that kills what little faith I had left in humanity," Cole said, coming back in.

"Any luck?" I asked him.

"Nada," he said. "We'll talk later. Right now, can you walk us through a typical day? I'm sure you had some kind of a routine, right?"

"Five A.M. wake-up alarm. Five minutes later, the doors unlock. After that, it changes by month. They gave us two meals a day, so if you didn't have breakfast scheduled, you went to the Wash Rooms and worked for the next six hours until midday, when they gave you lunch. Then you had time in your cabin for about two hours before you started an evening work shift, usually some kind of cleaning, like laundry, or mucking out the terrible sewage system that always got backed up. Then dinner. Then at eight, lights out."

"My God," was Senator Cruz's only comment.

"There were over three thousand of us," I said. "They had the system down to the second. They even figured out how to accommodate for the shrinking number of PSFs, once everyone started finishing their four years for the draft."

"What would you say the ratio of kids to PSFs was?" Cole said. "Ballpark it."

I'd already given him this information in my plan, but he was asking for the benefit of the two women in front of me.

"Cate told me there were usually two hundred in the camp at

all times, plus an additional twenty bodies working in the Control
Tower. There may be fewer now that they're in the process of
closing the camp." I shook my head. "It doesn't sound like a lot,
but they're strategically placed, and they're given permission to
harass and bully the kids."

For someone who had been so involved in researching a cure
for IAAN, Dr. Gray looked sick at all of this, like it was her first
time hearing it. That seemed impossible. Certain things were
bound to be confidential, but her husband was the president—he'd
played an integral role in the development of the rehabilitation
camp program.

She looked away. ". . . You're like my son, are you not?"

"Yes," I said, "but not in the way that matters."

"Were you there at Thurmond while he was?"

"After. We didn't overlap at all. I didn't arrive at the camp
until they'd already started to expand it. Is there a reason you're
asking?"

She cocked her head to the side and I fought off the shudder
that threatened to move through me. The simple movement was
Clancy, all Clancy.

"I'm assuming that the reason I'm here is because you want to
know about my success in controlling the children's psionic abilities?" she began, straightening in her seat. "As well as Leda Corp's
final assessment as to the cause?"

"You got it," Cole said. "So, naturally, our question is what
you want in return."

It was straightforward and to the point, and still, I was some-
what shocked by it. I don't know why I had expected her—a
Gray—to do this out of the goodness of her heart. I had hoped,
I guess, that the apple *had* fallen far from the tree in that regard.

"Can we speak somewhere with a little more privacy?" she asked, glancing through the glass windows at the kids moving through the halls.

"Sure thing," Cole said. "Nico, grab us if you hear any chatter about Kansas."

We followed him upstairs, past the groups of kids moving between the rooms in the hallways, all of whom seemed oblivious to who the blond woman was. When we reached the office upstairs, Cole motioned for the two older women to sit as he walked around to the other side of the desk, and I locked the door behind us.

Dr. Gray leaned back against her chair, her dark eyes taking the small room in with one glance. "This was John's office, wasn't it?"

I'd somehow managed to forget the fact that the Grays and John Alban were once close personal friends. Alban had helped the First Lady disappear, sponsored her research trials, made a deal with her—*Oh.*

"You want us to hold up Alban's end of the bargain," I said. "You'll give us the information in exchange for being able to perform the procedure on Clancy first."

Cole let out a soft whistle. "I was under the impression it's a kind of operation. You couldn't expect to be able to perform it here. . . ."

"Of course not," she said. "You could scrub every inch of this place with bleach and it still wouldn't be clean enough for an operation. I would need you to quietly help me set up a time it can be performed at a local hospital, where I'll have trained staff."

"That's a tall order," Cole said. "There's almost no way to keep it quiet."

380

"Once the procedure is complete, the plan has always been to take Clancy and go into hiding. I want a return to a life that resembles normal, with the son I once had."

The cure is another way to control us, take decisions out of our hands. Clancy's words worked through my mind in a whisper. I listened.

"I don't . . ." I started to say. What was really my problem with this, though? Clancy had proven over and over to me that he couldn't be trusted to use his abilities in a way that wouldn't hurt others. East River . . . Jude . . . how many times did he have to show me the lengths he would go to? All to avoid becoming what he'd been at Thurmond: powerless. I'd felt his helplessness when he was strapped down on the table at Thurmond, the pain of having volts of electricity shot through his mind. I'd felt the embarrassment of losing control of my functions, the fury of being treated like an animal.

He'd save himself before a group of thousands. This time, we had to choose the thousands over him.

"Okay," I said, when it was clear Cole had been waiting for me to respond. What was it I saw flicker in his eyes—disappointment? Understanding? It was there and gone so fast, masked by his usual grim smile, I wasn't sure I had seen it at all.

"It's a deal," he said. "We'll round up the troops tonight so you can explain. Tomorrow morning, we'll start looking into viable hospital options for you."

Dr. Gray inclined her head, a silent agreement. I stood up, muttering some excuse about needing to check on Vida and the training upstairs. In truth, I couldn't seem to get the room's heavy air into my lungs—not in, not out. I was suffocating on the words left hovering inside those four walls, and I couldn't shake the feeling, not even as I wiped them frantically against my legs, that I had spilled blood on my hands.

I was alone in the computer room with Vida, telling her about the short conversation I'd had with Cate, when Zu's face suddenly appeared on the news channel livestream Nico had set up.

I'd been sitting with my knees drawn up to my chest, doing the best I could to answer her questions, all of which seemed to be a variation on, "But she's okay, right?" My eyes had stayed peeled to the screen, waiting for any late-breaking news from Kansas, and when I saw Zu I dropped my feet back to the floor so quickly that the chair rocked forward with me.

"Turn the sound back on," I said.

"—*more footage released today from sources tied to the reha-bilitation camp scandal that's rocking a newly reopened Washington. This evening, Amplify released a series of videos, purportedly of the children who were removed from Nevada. Let's take a look. . . ."*

I didn't know if it was the news network or if it had been Alice's clever mind at work with the editing, but the initial seconds of footage were of each of the ten kids who'd agreed to be interviewed, introducing themselves.

"Zach . . . I'm seventeen years old."

"My name is Kylie and I'm sixteen."

On and on until finally the video showed Zu; there was footage of her shot later, introducing herself this time. Immediately, the video launched into her describing the way her parents had dropped her off at school. Each of the kids got to tell their own version of how they had gotten away from PSFs, their parents, the world.

I pressed a hand against my mouth, looking over to gauge Vida's reaction. She took a sip from her water bottle and slammed her palm back down on the cap to close it again.

"They're fast on pulling the trigger, I'll give them that," she said. "But boo, you know I'm with you. This is great for tugging some heartstrings, but how many asses is it going to get off of couches? Where's the call to action with this? They needed our input. There's too much hope here, not enough strategy."

"They were right, though," I said, feeling strangely hollow at my center. "We did need something like this—we have to set the public up with the truth, so that when the kids *do* get out, they'll be accepted. This is *good*." Liam's instincts had been right.

"Just because they're right, it doesn't make you wrong, boo," she said, lowering the volume. "Charlie was right. You dipshits fell apart without us there to tell you what to do."

The newscaster, a perky blond woman in a deep red suit, appeared back on the screen, but almost immediately cut to a photo a program viewer had sent in. At the center of what the program had identified as New York City's Times Square, Zu's face glowed from a cluster of three billboards, a stark contrast to the dark billboards around it, the ones that hadn't been lit up for years. It was a heartbreaking photo—even without knowing the girl or the context of the interview from which the still of her had been taken, it tugged at you, demanded your attention. The words PUBLIC ENEMY, AGE 13 flashed over the image, a perfectly calibrated piece of emotional manipulation.

"Where *is* Chubs?" I asked.

Vida began to peel the label off her water bottle. "I asked Cole if our boy there could use one of the empty senior agent quarters to set up a kind of . . . medical bay, or something. First-aid station. A place to put all of the medical junk and books he's been carting around like a freaking nerd. He's in there measuring out all of his jars of cotton balls and Q-tips."

"You're going soft on me, Vi," I said. "That's almost sweet—"

The glow from the screen changed abruptly from the electric blue and white of the news station. The set flashed red, drowning out even the color of Vida's hair. "Oh, *shit*."

The structure was almost unrecognizable, but the words running below it were clear enough: CHILDREN'S LEAGUE HEADQUARTERS DESTROYED.

"*—reporting live from just outside of Colby, Kansas. Government officials have confirmed that drones were used to hit a warehouse believed to house the remnants of the Children's League. Earlier this morning, faked photographs and documents were leaked to the press, and the organization claimed to—*"

I didn't stay to hear the rest. If they had sent drones to Colby, then what we were seeing really was Kansas HQ—and all of those agents, unless they'd abandoned it earlier in the day, were gone.

Cole was in the office with the door shut, but he'd left it unlocked. I slipped inside, finding him in the chair, his hand covering most of his face. At the sound of the door shutting again, he looked up, then switched the phone over to speaker.

"*The guys said it was still burning when they got there.*" Harry. "*They picked up two survivors about a mile out of what was left of the structure, but can't get any closer. I'm going to have them pull back and meet with us in Utah.*"

"How did they escape?" I asked. How could anyone?

"Unclear. The connection was rotten and the survivors had completely lost it by the time our guys found them. The story we got was unreal."

"What makes you say that?" Cole asked.

Static filled the room, filled my brain. It was only because of the murderous look on Cole's face, the way the heat beneath his skin evaporated that last trace of softness in him, that I knew I hadn't misheard Harry.

"The survivors," Harry said. *"They claim they were attacked by a unit of kids. They said they were Reds."*

NINETEEN

"Do you believe it?" I asked. "That Reds did this?"

Cole looked up at my question. "I wish like hell I knew. It just makes me want to—"

"Want to what?" I asked.

He stood suddenly, unable to stay seated, his hand spasming the whole time. "I need to tell you something before we go in and present our plan to the other kids."

My hands twisted in my lap as I fought to keep my voice calm. "What is it?"

"I want us to go investigate and document the activities of a camp—Sawtooth, in Idaho. Clancy claims that it's one of the facilities they use to train Reds."

"And you *believe* him?" I asked, shaking my head. "Cole—"

"Yeah," he said, "I do believe him—and *not* because he's been working me over with his abilities. Because every piece of intel he's given me up until now has panned out . . . and I might have promised I'd consider letting him go if he helped. Obviously not, but still. A good motivator."

"Why, though?" I asked. "Why do we need to investigate it?"

"Senator Cruz told me she needs hard evidence of the army of Reds in order to spook the international community into action. I want to get it for her—at least *try*. If it's a dead end, so be it. But tell me I have your support on this. I promise it won't affect our Thurmond hit."

My patience finally dissolved. "If you want to do this, you have to tell the others that you're a Red. That's the only way I'll agree to support this."

He reared back in surprise. "What does that have to do with anything?"

"We've been losing the support of the kids—I can feel it. They need to know once and for all that you *do* have our best interests at heart because you're one of us." I could hear my own exhaustion in my voice. "Hasn't this gone on long enough?"

He opened his mouth, angry and clearly defensive, but closed it again, studying my face. After a long while, he said, "I'll tell Liam. Start with him tonight. Then, depending on how that goes, I'll tell the others. Is that reasonable?"

I could have cried, I was so relieved. "Yes. But you have to tell him before the meeting tonight."

He waved me off, taking a seat. "Before that, I want to run through with you how I think we should get you back into Thurmond. Figured you might want to discuss that here, rather than in front of the others?"

I nodded. "I'll tell them, but not until we're all in agreement on the strategy. Are you still thinking you want to drop me in Virginia?"

"Yes," he said. "The goal here is to get you in front of one skip tracer to start, while making sure you're not overpowered from the get-go. We'll call in a fake tip about a Green kid on the loose, and you'll have to get into the skip tracer's mind before he can run your face through the program. He'll bring you into the nearest PSF base for your reward, and you'll have him lead a PSF out to you so he can 'officially' test you and confirm you're Green. You're going to have to jump between the minds of every person you cross paths with—they can't know the truth, otherwise you'll never make it to Thurmond. The key is to control the total amount of people you come in contact with at any given time. Is that even doable?"

"Yes," I said, feeling my spine stiffen with resolve. "It is."

We assembled in the garage two hours later, sitting in a circle around the white crescent moon painted on the floor. I'd set up chairs for Cole, Senator Cruz, and Dr. Gray to sit in while we talked, but Cole walked up beside me with another, set it to the right of his, and gently pushed me down into the seat. I snuck a glance at him, trying to read how his conversation had gone, but his expression was carefully blank.

Liam, on the other hand, looked like he had just stepped off a thundercloud. I felt his eyes on me the entire time, and wasn't brave enough to try to meet his gaze.

"So as you can see, we have a new guest with us on this fine evening," Cole began, arms crossed, stance strong. "She's the scientist who conducted the research about the cure, and she's here to explain to you the cause of IAAN, as well as what the cure exactly is."

The whispers died out so quickly, I was sure we could have heard a car backfire from a hundred miles away.

Lillian brushed out invisible wrinkles in her sweatpants and started to rise from her chair, only to change her mind and sit back down. Some of the older kids must have recognized her from old news reports, but most . . . they were just looking at her in awe, totally oblivious to her last name. Alice, on the other hand, was a different story. I saw the exact moment her mind made the connection.

"Hello." With a deep breath, she turned to Cole and asked, "Where should I begin?"

"Start with the cause, end with the cure," he said.

"Ah. All right. Initially . . . when Idiopathic Adolescent Acute Neurodegeneration—IAAN—was first recognized, the common assumption was that it was some kind of virus whose manifestation was more pronounced and deadly in children than in adults. This quickly was proven to be false by the scientific community, as cases outside of the United States proved to be fairly rare or mild in comparison. After several years of research . . . Leda Corp concluded its experiments and has confirmed what some, myself included, had privately believed to be the cause."

I leaned forward in my seat, heart hammering in my chest. I bit my lip.

"Almost thirty years ago, there were attempts . . . several, actually . . . on the security of the nation. These bioterrorism attacks were launched by enemies of the United States, all involving tampering with our crops and our water supply."

Liam stood at the periphery of the group, next to Alice. He'd been watching Dr. Gray through the digital screen on the back of her camera but looked up at that, startled. I shifted impatiently, waiting for her to continue. There had been theories for years that IAAN was the result of a terrorist attack, this wasn't new information—

"The president at the time, not my—not President Gray— signed off on a confidential order to begin development on a chemical agent to counteract and nullify a number of poisons, bacteria, and drugs that could be added to a population's water supply with us none the wiser. Leda Corp developed and distributed the chemical, called Agent Ambrosia, to our country's water treatment facilities."

I rubbed a hand against my forehead, fighting the way my vision seemed to blur.

"Did they test this agent in conjunction with the usual minerals and compounds added to our water?" Senator Cruz asked, white with anger.

Dr. Gray nodded. "Yes, there was routine testing. The participants signed ironclad confidentiality agreements and were generously reimbursed for their time. They studied children, adults, animals. Even pregnant mothers, who all safely delivered their babies without complications and no defects. In truth, these researchers received so much pressure from the government to quickly implement the program that they weren't able to study the long-term effects of the agent."

They poisoned us. My lip curled back in disgust and I had to grip the sides of my chair to keep myself in it. *They poisoned us and kept us locked up for their mistake.*

Cole swung up out of his seat and began pacing, his head bowed, listening.

"Leda's recent study concluded that Agent Ambrosia is what we call a teratogen, meaning . . . meaning that women who drank the treated water unknowingly took the chemical into their bodies and it affected the brain cells of their children in vitro. My understanding of their report is that these mutations remained dormant in the children's . . . in your minds until you reached the age of puberty—around eight, nine, ten, eleven years old. The change in your hormone levels and brain chemistry triggered the mutation."

"Why did so many die?" At Cole's side, his hand gave a sharp twitch.

"Those mothers ingested higher quantities of the chemical, or there was a third, unspecified environmental factor." She said all of this so coldly and clinically, with such professional detachment, that it made me angry all over again.

This happened to you, too. Why aren't you furious? Why aren't you upset?

Olivia climbed to her feet; the sight of her scarred face made Dr. Gray flinch before she could catch herself. "How do you explain our different abilities? Why can we each do certain things?"

"The common hypothesis is that it has everything to do with genetics—individual brain chemistry, and which neural pathways are affected at the moment you transition."

"Is the chemical still in our water supply?"

Dr. Gray hesitated long enough for us to know the answer before she so much as opened her mouth. "Yes. Though now that Leda has confirmed that Agent Ambrosia is to blame, I would say it's fair to assume they're most likely planning to introduce a neutralizing chemical into the water supply, beginning with the larger cities. But seeing how many women and young children have ingested the tainted water, it may be a full generation or two before we start seeing children without this mutation."

Generation. Not just months or years. *Generation.* I pressed my face into my hands, took a deep breath.

"So if that explains what happened," Cole said, "what's your method for curing it?"

Dr. Gray shifted her posture, relaxing slightly. This was her territory, and she clearly felt more comfortable crossing into it. "The scientific community has known for some time that, essentially, your psionic abilities involve shifting the normal flow of electricity in your minds. Spiking it, really. When . . . when a child classified as Orange, for instance, is influencing someone, they're manipulating the electrical flow in the other person's brain, tampering with its usual systems and processes—not entirely different from a what a child classified as Yellow does on a larger, external scale when they control an electrical current in a machine or power line. And so on. Everything, including us, is made of particles—and those particles have electrical charges."

Regardless of whether or not any of us understood that, she continued. "The cure isn't a cure so much as a lifelong treatment. It manages, rather than cures, the affliction."

My heart ground to a stop in my chest. I could see Clancy's face as he told me exactly that, but I'd dismissed it because— because he lied all the time, because a real cure would *have* to eradicate the mutation entirely.

"It's an operation during which something called a deep brain stimulator—essentially, a kind of brain pacemaker, if you will— is implanted. Where it's implanted depends largely on abilities, but the stimulator, in all cases, releases an electrical charge of its own. It regulates the abnormal flow, shifting it into what a typical human would have."

"It neuters the abilities," Cole clarified, "rather than removes them."

"Yes, exactly."

"And this procedure can be safely performed?" Alice called. "Have you done one?"

"Yes," she said. "I have successfully treated one child."

"One isn't exactly a track record, Doc," Cole said. "One doesn't give us any sort of odds of success."

She merely raised her hands and said, "There wasn't time for more than that. I'm sorry."

"And the idea is to . . ." I almost couldn't get the question out. I felt crushed by this, choked with anger. "The idea is that every kid that's born will have to get this to prevent them from dying or changing? At what age?"

"Around age seven," Lillian said. "They may have to undergo regular maintenance, however."

That got an uneasy murmur from the kids, who finally seemed to be waking up from their shocked daze.

"What are our next steps?" Alice asked, repositioning her camera. "This is all incredible, but we have no solid proof about Agent Ambrosia being added to the water supply. Leda quickly shuttered the research program. None of the Greens have turned up any information."

"What would be proof enough for you?" Dr. Gray asked.

Alice didn't have to think about it. "Some kind of documentation that shows it as part of the treatment mixture."

"We could go to nearby treatment facilities," Liam said. "Break in, take photographs, try to find hard copy or information on their computers."

"That could work," Alice said, eyes gleaming. "I think we'd need to hit at least five or six, just in case some of them turn out to be duds. And in different states, too, so they know it wasn't limited to California. Do we have enough gas left to pull this off?"

"Wait—wait," Cole said. "Our priority now should be lying low, refining our hit on Thurmond, and waiting for reinforcements to arrive. If anyone goes out, it should be to gather more forces for the fight."

"Reinforcements?" Liam repeated, practically growling.

Cole raised his brows.

"Oh, you *bastard*," Liam snapped. "Harry? You're asking Harry to *fight*?"

"He volunteered. He and his unit of forty ex-military guys and gals are eager to do their part." Cole turned to address the kids. "Contrary to what he's been telling you, I would never have asked someone to fight who didn't want to."

"How many times do we have to drill it into your skull before you grasp the reality of this?" Alice asked. "The kids don't want *any* fight."

"Oh, they want a fight," Cole said, rounding the circle to stand directly in front of her, "but they don't want to have to wage it themselves."

"No, we want to coordinate a media blitz with the truth," Liam said. "To release the locations of camps we know about, along with the lists of the kids there. We let the American people rise up and go after them. It'll cause some chaos, but now that we have the information that IAAN isn't contagious, it increases the likelihood that foreign powers will come in as a peacekeeping force. Isn't that right, Senator Cruz?"

"It's not a guarantee . . ." she said. "But I could try to work with that."

"You're overestimating how much people care," I said, shaking my head, noting with some satisfaction that the others actually stopped to listen. "I've seen too many times that the only way we'll ever get what we want—the only way we'll ever be able to get our freedom from this—is if we get it ourselves. The camps have sophisticated security systems, and Gray has shown time and time again he'll do anything to cover his ass. What's to say the minute you release the camp information, he doesn't take it out on the kids? Use them as hostages, move them, *kill* them to bury the evidence?"

If they'd thought about that in all of their planning, it didn't show on their faces. And the fact that Dr. Gray didn't try to refute me seemed to lend some credence to the possibility.

"You absolutely *cannot* just release the information about Agent Ambrosia, I'm sorry, but no," she said. "You are severely underestimating the widespread panic it'll induce in the population."

"True," Senator Cruz said. "I'd rather not see people start tearing each other apart to get to natural water supplies. But I agree with Alice that we need evidence; not for the public, but for our foreign allies."

The buzz that moved through the room was palpable—kids were already shifting around, assigning themselves to groups to drive out to the water treatment facilities. And there was Cole, watching it all. His hand gave a painful jerk as he lifted it to rub the back of his neck, and I wondered if he felt it, too, the slow unraveling. The train that had been so clearly under our care had jumped the tracks entirely. When he looked at me, there was a silent plea in it, a desperation I had never seen in him before.

I couldn't stand it—it pushed me past furious. He'd done everything in his power to help us. To make the hard decisions. And now they were trying to push him out as leader? He was being mocked by the looks Liam and Alice exchanged? In that moment he could have backed out of the room and I wasn't sure anyone but me would have noticed.

"Well," he said finally, "I have some intel for you, if you'd like it."

Alice rolled her eyes. "I'm sure you do."

"You say you want to give the world a sense of who these kids are, but you're really just setting them up to be pitied." Cole tucked his hands in the back pockets of his jeans, his voice growing louder as the din around him faded. "What motivates people, even more than anger, is fear. Go ahead and release all that intel on Ambrosia, see where that lands this country when people start rioting over the last few fresh, untainted water sources. Or, you can show them Gray's trump card—that he's been building an army of Reds."

"What are you talking about?" Alice demanded.

"You all saw what happened at Kansas HQ today," Cole said. "But what the news didn't tell you is that there are reports that it was *Reds*, not a military unit, that attacked them."

"Oh, convenient—*reports* with nothing to back them up." Alice waved him off.

But, if nothing else, Cole now had the reins of the conversation back in his hand. He was guiding the conversation now, not letting it happen around him. "My trusted source says that there's a camp of Reds not too far from here, in a place called Sawtooth. I'd like to go and document evidence of them—their training, the camp's existence—and I'd like to give it to you for Amplify, on the condition it's used in conjunction with the actual camp hit."

"Where did this information come from?" Liam asked, his eyes narrowed in suspicion.

"A trusted source," he repeated.

His brother rolled his eyes. Alice, though—Cole had read her right. It was like a cat that had spotted a mouse creeping along the floorboards. She wanted this story, and she wasn't going to run the risk of someone else getting it first.

"Okay, what about this," she began. "We send out five teams to the water treatment facilities, and you can take a small group out to assess the situation there. Snap some photos."

"I only need one other person," he said, glancing at me.

"I'll go," Liam said, before I could. He set his jaw, daring his brother to refuse. Cole crossed his arms over his chest, eyes darting over to me, looking for a lifeline.

He doesn't want Liam to go. And it had nothing to do with how Liam may or may not have been able to handle himself, or if he trusted him. I saw that now.

"I'd still like to go," I said. "I think—"

"He just said two would be enough," Liam pressed, turning back to his brother. "Unless you think I'm going to screw everything up on your precious little mission?"

Cole snorted, his lips twisting up in a rueful smile. "All right, it's settled. Now . . . someone talk to me about our car situation. What's the gasoline level at now?"

Dr. Gray returned to her seat, finally, eyes fixed on her hands in her lap as Senator Cruz asked her something. The meeting came to a natural end as five teams formed to go out to the water treatment facilities, Alice taking the lead, dividing them up by state and choosing which one she wanted to go with.

I didn't stay around to watch the stiff conversation between Cole and Liam. I turned on my heel, vaguely aware of Chubs saying something to me as I made my way back into the tunnel, through the Ranch, back to the empty computer room. I sat back down at Nico's computer station and switched on the news livestream.

"—*obviously this is terrible if it's true and the president will have a considerable amount of explaining to do*—" This was the last one still running; the others had been switched off, one by one. A pattern had formed: a news station would show the kids' interviews, the conversation between the talking heads would swing dangerously toward the *this is true* camp, and the feed would go dark. This station seemed to be avoiding the censors by casting the guest commentator as a devil's advocate instead of a so-called expert. "—*but* what if *these children haven't been coached, and this isn't some ploy for attention or notoriety from parents? If they have been removed from their rehabilitation program, then aren't their lives in danger? Our focus should be on returning them to their camps before it's too late.*"

The host of the program arched a gray, bushy eyebrow and said, his voice deep and penetrating, "*Did you actually watch the interviews? They claim that there is no program. Based on the fact that it's been nearly a decade and we've had little to no news or progress in finding a cure, I'm inclined to agree. I don't think these children would risk exposing themselves without—*"

The video window jumped to static.

That's the end of that, I thought, rubbing my face. The room was warm, the machines humming a low song perfectly in tune with one another. The longer I listened to it, eyes shut, the easier it was to process the tidal wave of information that had come crashing down over our heads earlier in the evening; the easier it was to let the quiet anger roll through me.

What was the point of trying to keep it inside now—my fury over decisions that had been made almost twenty years ago?

And this "cure"—what a joke. Surrendering yourself to an invasive procedure that might or might not work was patching the problem over, not fixing it. I felt strangely betrayed by my own hope; I thought I'd trained myself not to bank on things that were completely out of my control. But . . . still. Still, it hurt. *What's the point in getting anyone out now if they don't have a future?* My throat ached with the thought. *At least in the camps they're protected from what they'd have to deal with out here.* How many people would really be welcoming to "freaks" out walking the streets? I fought the instinct to walk over to the satellite image of Thurmond, to tear it down off the wall and rip it between my hands, just *shred* it into a thousand fluttering pieces to match the way I was shattering inside. Why not just let those kids be taken out of the camp, let the PSFs and military raze the buildings without leaving so much as a scar on the earth?

Because if the kids are in the camps, they could be forced to get the procedure, whether they want it or not.

Because they deserve to have a choice about how they want to live their lives.

Because they haven't seen their families in years.

Because it's what's right.

I stood up and stretched my stiff limbs as I moved toward the satellite image of the camp, smoothing out a corner that was becoming unstuck from the wall. The notations I made were all still there, and I saw new ones—arrows that Cole had made, outlining the flow of the assault. He wanted us to enter through the front gate using military vehicles. We would pose, I had a feeling, as either units helping with the move or additional forces. The first drive was split between the Infirmary and the Control Tower, with smaller pairings of fighters in twos and threes moving through the rings of cabins.

I backed up to get the full scope of it all, taking a seat on one of the empty desks.

It's the right thing to do. It would just be a matter of convincing everyone else.

The door to the computer room swung open, and I turned, saying, "How did it—?"

But it wasn't Cole. It was Liam. Jaw set, blue eyes stormy. Even if I hadn't been able to feel the anger pouring off him, he was shaking with the clear effort it took to walk in and shut the door with some semblance of calm.

My whole world tilted toward him. There were so many empty spaces inside of me now, and I don't know if I'd even have recognized that until he was there to fill them. The longing turned to a dull ache; it played games with my mind. It made me think I saw it in his eyes, too, as he watched me. His anger met my desperation and the sparks from the collision crystallized, trapping us in this moment of charged silence forever.

"I'm sorry," I said finally. "I know it's too late now, but I'm sorry."

Liam cleared his throat. His voice was low. "How long have you known?"

There was no point in lying, trying to gloss over the truth. I just couldn't do it anymore. I couldn't have this guilt under my skin, cutting me to the bone each time I withheld, with each little lie. Cole had asked me to keep his secret and I had, because I felt it was his right to come to grips with his abilities on his own terms and in his own time. But I should never have let this charade go on for so long, not when it did more to tear things apart than it did to bring everyone together.

And at this point, I wasn't sure it was possible for Liam to hate me any more than he already did.

"At HQ," I said, "when he and the other agents came in to retake it, he saved my life. I saw it then."

Liam drew in a sharp breath and, in a blur of furious movement, slammed his fist into the wall next to the door, hard enough to crack the plaster.

"*Ow*—shit!" He jumped back, cradling his hand. "Christ—why did she say that would make me feel *better*?"

I was on my feet, reaching for him, before I remembered myself.

"Who—Alice?" I guessed, hating that I could hear the bitterness in my own voice.

"Yeah, 'cause some reporter is the first person I'm gonna tell after finding out my brother is a Red," he shot back. "*Vida.* When I asked her where you were."

"Oh. I'm sorry," I said. I hadn't realized until that moment, hearing those two words leave my mouth, how carefully I'd managed to balance on the tip of a needle. But it was like every ounce of strength I'd had left just . . . slipped away. I felt myself take another step, and my knees went out from under me as I dropped to the ground. I couldn't find the words I needed, couldn't put them together. I pressed my hands against my face, crying, beyond caring. "I'm sorry, I'm sorry, I'm sorry . . ."

I heard him come toward me, saw between my fingers as he lowered himself to the ground a short distance away and leaned back against the table. He rested his arms over his knees, letting his swollen right hand hang out in the air. He didn't say anything at all, waiting for me to finish, or waiting for something in himself; I didn't know.

"He said he made you swear on your life not to tell me," he said, his voice hoarse. "That I should blame him, not you."

"Yeah, but I could have told you anyway," I said quietly.

"But you didn't."

"I didn't."

He let out a sound of frustration, running his hands back through his hair. "Ruby . . . can you at least help me understand why? I'm . . . I *want* to understand. This is killing me. I don't get why no one . . . why neither of you even tried."

"It's because . . . I know what it feels like to . . ." I struggled for the right words, but every time it felt like I had a grip on them, they slipped away. "It's different for us—for him and me. The dangerous ones. I know you don't want to hear that, I'm sorry, but it's true. I saw it in the way the PSFs treated the Orange and Red kids at Thurmond, I saw it in how hard Zu struggled to learn to control her abilities, and I see it in the face of every kid I talk to. So I knew exactly why Cole didn't tell you or your parents. I lived with the fear of being found out, and so did he. First with your family, and then with the League."

"No one in the League had any idea?" Liam asked in disbelief.

"Three people knew," I said. "Alban, Cate, me. That's it."

He released a harsh breath, shaking his head.

"I wish I was better at this—at explaining. I just kept thinking about how I had to keep my own secret for so long. Six years. And then just like that, in a matter of seconds, I had to show you all what I was to get us away from that woman. It was somehow the hardest and easiest decision I've ever made, because it meant you would all be safe, but I was so sure it would be over and I'd lose the three of you because you knew."

"You . . . in the woods, after the skip tracer tried to take us in," he said, fitting the right memory together, "when you thought we were going to leave you behind."

"Yes." There was a sharp ache in my chest as I said, "But you talked to me, you told me that you all wanted me. You can't know what that feels like after . . . after being alone inside of your head for so long. It changed my life. And I know it sounds stupid, but I think part of me felt like I could be that for him. I could help him get to the point where he wasn't so damn ashamed of what he was, make him feel comfortable about being one of us so he wouldn't be so alone. It didn't seem right, you know? He's still trapped in this in-between space. Not one of us, but not one of the adults."

"That was by choice," Liam said. "He could have told us."

"Did you see how half of the kids reacted when he brought up the Red camp? Olivia? Brett? He didn't think, *Oh, but I've proven the stories wrong;* he thought, *They'll hate me, they'll be afraid of me, they'll never be able to look me in the eye again.*"

Liam looked down at his hands again. "Do you still think those things?"

"It comes and goes," I said quietly. "Sometimes. When I'm with you, I feel like I'm . . . like a beam of sunlight, you know? You chase the bad things away. With Cole, he understood the dark I could never shake. I used to think he was the kind of person that wasn't afraid of anything, but he's scared of his own shadow, Liam. I don't think I understood until tonight just how scared he was of you really seeing him."

"But that's so unfair," Liam said, his voice strained with a second wave of anger. "I know it's not right, but I hate him for thinking that me and Mom and Harry—that any of these kids who basically worship the ground he walks on—would love him less. I wish he'd trusted *us*. He could have had support in this. Nothing's changed for me."

"Nothing?"

"*Nothing,*" he repeated vehemently. "Except now I know he wasn't lighting my toys on fire with matches to be a jerk. I guess that's something."

"He couldn't control it," I said. "He still struggles with it."

Liam didn't look convinced. "By the little demonstration he gave me, you'd never know that."

"He *does,*" I insisted. "It depends on the situation." *Like when he's terrified you've been hurt, or you're dead.*

"But if you can learn control, so can he, right?"

"Learning control doesn't mean people trust you to make good choices, does it?" I felt my voice break halfway through the question, and I immediately regretted having brought it up.

"What are you . . . oh—you—" Liam's brows drew together sharply; I watched the anger deflate, and dull shock swept in to take its place. "You found . . . my note? Ruby, why didn't you say anything?"

"What could I say? You were right not to trust me. Look at where trusting me before got you."

"No! Dammit, I should never have written the stupid thing, but I was so sure he would make me leave. That he would convince you I had to leave." I pulled back, not wanting to hear the explanation, not when the pain still felt as fresh as it had that night. He didn't let me go. Liam turned to face me fully, and for the first time in what felt like years, touched me, taking my shoulder—or trying to. The moment he flexed his hand he winced. "Ow, dammit—"

"Let me see it." I took his hand carefully between mine, examining it. The touch was enough to drive my pulse back up, to spark a charge under my skin again. His eyes moved over me; I felt it like a second, sweet touch, and I wondered if he had missed this too, if he'd looked at me and felt the warmth pooling at his center. The need.

He'd broken the skin over his knuckles when he'd struck the wall, but the bleeding had already stopped, and the swelling and bruising had begun. I probed the delicate bones carefully, letting my loose braid fall over my shoulder. His other hand reached for it, took it between his fingers, and ran down its length. I caught my breath as he brushed against my collarbone. Closed my eyes. I felt the warmth around us shift as he leaned toward me, ran his finger along that ridge of exposed skin. I didn't deserve the tenderness, but it had been so long, and I wanted him too badly to care.

I raised the hand between mine and pressed my lips against the torn knuckles. He closed his eyes and shuddered.

"Not broken," I whispered against his skin. "Just bruised."

"What about us?"

The question filled me with equal parts hope and fear. "I can't forget, can you?"

"Does that matter, though?" he asked. "I don't want to forget. There's so much behind us, it's true, but does it matter if we're going the same way forward? The past few days have been hell. I see your face and it's like—I wish—I wish I had never written that stupid note. I wish I had told you about Alice. I just wanted to feel something other than useless. I wanted you to see something good in me."

"Liam—" My breath hitched. "I've never seen anything else. I want so much to have a real life. To be someone who can go home and be with her family again. I thought that I could fix myself and be the kind of person who deserves someone like you. Someone who deserves Zu, Chubs, Vida, Jude, Nico, Cate. I thought I could fix myself with the cure. That's all I've ever wanted, to be done with this. But now, I just want to be kinder to myself. I don't want anyone to implant anything in my head, or mess with who I am. When all of this *is* over, however long it takes, I won't ever have to use my abilities again. But for now I have to, and I have to trust myself to do right by everyone. Tell me what I have to do, to earn the right to have you in my life, and I'll do it—I'll do anything—"

Liam's hand slid up my hair to brush my cheek. Relief, pure and beautiful, bloomed in me as his mouth covered mine. When he pulled back, he watched my reaction carefully. When I offered a small smile, he kissed me again, and my last reservations fell away, shattering. I deepened the kiss, trying to leave him as breathless as I felt.

He pulled back, his face flushed, eyes bright. I knew the look on his face mirrored mine. My whole body was trembling, desperate to continue, to chase the fierce love I felt for him. Carefully avoiding his bad hand, Liam shifted onto his knees and started to rise from the floor, reaching down to help me do the same. He startled suddenly as he caught something at the edge of his vision.

"What is this?" he asked, taking a step closer to the printout taped up to the wall.

"That's Thurmond," I said. "Harry was able to work some contact in the government to get the image."

Liam turned toward me slowly. "That's . . . all Thurmond?"

I stepped up next to him, leaning against his shoulder. "Control Tower, Infirmary, Mess Hall, Factory . . . I labeled them, see?"

He nodded, silent. "Where did you live?"

I reached past where he was standing to one of dozens of tiny brown structures circling the imposing brick tower. "Cabin Twenty-seven, right here."

"Ruby, this is . . . all the times you told me about the camp, I knew it was big, but not like . . . *this*." He shook his head, muttering something I couldn't quite hear under his breath. When he turned to me again, Liam looked stricken.

"Do you see now?" I asked. "If we hit Thurmond, it has to be an assault. It would take hundreds of civilians to overwhelm the PSFs, and that's only if they can get through the gate. But I like what you guys are trying to do—I think we need to merge the plans. Focus the media blast on Thurmond and release the information in conjunction with the attack. We can use it as an opportunity to set up a meeting point for parents to pick up their kids once we have them out."

"But someone has to go in and install a program to disable the security system first," he said. "It's exactly what I thought. You want to go in."

"I have to," I said.

"No, you *don't*," he said sharply. "There's no way in hell I'm letting you do that! Promise me that when I get back we can sit down and talk that part of the plan through, too. Ruby, please."

He looked so devastated at just the idea of it, I heard myself agree. We could talk, but it wouldn't change anything. It had to be this way.

He squeezed my hand. "I'm such an idiot . . . I really thought he only brought Harry into this to get at me. But it's because he would actually be able to handle this kind of operation."

"He really wants to be part of it," I told him.

"Who—Harry? You talked to Harry?"

"Just for a second," I said. "He told me that they found Cate and the others and extracted them from their prison."

Liam gave a faint laugh. "Of course. Action Hero Harry. You should meet Sports Fan Harry, Master Chef Harry, and Mechanic Harry. The guy does nothing by half measures."

I leaned against his shoulder again, trying to block out the memory I'd seen in Cole's mind with something easier to stomach. "How did he and your mom even meet? I never thought to ask . . ."

"Oh, God, it's almost repulsively romantic," Liam said. "So, when Mom finally left . . . when she left her old life and took us with her, she drove straight through the night, just to put enough distance between us and the place. The car broke down in North Carolina. Harry was just coming back from his last tour of duty abroad and saw her screaming at the old Toyota, banging on the hood, everything. He pulled over and offered to take a look, and when it was clear she needed new parts, he drove us all to his mother's place, who took one look at Mom and immediately adopted her in everything but the legal sense. And we stayed with them a week. I'm pretty sure that was the slowest repair of Harry's life. He was coming home to open a mechanic garage. I didn't mention that, did I? So he was determined that she'd be his first customer, and that she should let him do it for free, as a good-luck charm for the business. Kept lying about not being able to get a part in, the rascal, just to prolong the visit enough. It gave Mom time to find a job, and a sweet little place for us to live. They didn't date until three years later. She just . . . wasn't ready to move on with that part of her life until then. And after that they were just ridiculous."

"Wow," I said. "The luck of that. If she had taken a different road, or he'd come in an hour earlier or later."

"Well . . ." Liam ducked his head a bit. "It's kind of the same for us . . . right? Maybe I've never told you this, but it was total dumb luck we were in West Virginia at all that day that we found you. I was doing everything in my power to avoid having to drive through it."

"Because of your father?" I ventured.

"Ah. So Cole told you the basics?" He waited for me to nod before continuing. "It's like the whole state has this dark cloud wrapped around it. I feel really damn lucky I don't remember life pre-Harry, because from what little Mom and Cole have told me, it was actually hell. I knew enough as a kid—a little kid, I mean—to be scared of the state and the man who lived there. That's how my mom still refers to that part of our lives. *In West Virginia* this, or *the West Virginia house* that, that kind of thing. Cole told me once when I wouldn't leave him alone that if I was bad, the man was going to come take me away." He grimaced. "I know that man is still there, and that he's alive. I had this fear, and I know it's irrational because Chubs has told me it is a million times. Right up until I turned eighteen, I had this fear that if I went back to that place, he'd find me and force me to stay."

"Why were you there, then?" I asked. Liam was a skilled enough navigator to have brought them around the state.

"Because that skip tracer, Lady Jane—she was running us to ground. I just wanted to lose her. And there was this moment I was driving along, and I saw the name of our old town, and it was just like . . . closing a circle I didn't realized we'd left open. Because that time I had the ability to get myself out of there, I knew I could fight him and win if I had to, and Mom and Cole were safe. Driving by that last time, it's like I stole back that last bit of control he had over my life. But it took going back to know that. I don't know if I ever would have believed it could be that way, if I hadn't been in that car with all of you."

He felt my hand shaking and brought it up to lay flat against his chest, where I could feel his heart thundering against his ribs. "What I'm trying to get at is, as bad as everything seems, I think, at its heart, life is good. It doesn't throw anything at us that it knows we can't handle—and, even if it takes its time, it turns everything right side up again. I want this to be over for you, so, so much. I want to go to Thurmond and get those poor kids out so you can close your own circle. If nothing else, if this explodes in our faces, then I want you to know that I love you and nothing will ever change that."

"I love you, too." I flushed at his grin, wondering at how good it felt to say the words. *I love you. I love you. I love you.*

"Yeah?" he said. "The ol' Stewart charm finally wear you down?"

I laughed. "Guess so. You had your work cut out for you."

"Don't I know it."

The door opened again, and I leaned out of his grasp, craning my neck just as Nico came in. He startled at the sight of the two of us. "Oh—I'm—you're—"

"Hey," I said.

"I . . . forgot I had something. To do, I mean," Nico said, rocking back on his heels. "But if you were going to stay I'll . . . figure it out."

"Nah," Liam said, looking at me. "I think we're done here . . . ?"

"All yours," I confirmed. "But try to get some sleep, okay?"

Nico nodded absently. I lingered a moment more in the doorway, watching as he went to his station and the light from the monitor washed him in a blue-white glow.

Liam tugged my hand toward the other hall, the stairs, the bunk rooms. I turned and tugged him in the opposite direction, toward the senior quarters and Cate's empty room. The small smile on his face made me feel a little dizzy, the good kind of dizzy. One hand began to stroke down my spine softly, sparking an entirely different feeling low in my stomach.

I stood on my toes, taking his face in my hands. Out of the corner of my eye, I saw a dark form come out of a nearby room— the little treatment room that had been set up. Liam turned toward it as the door squeaked shut and the person—Chubs— looked up, down, then back up again as his brain processed the moment.

"Oh, there you are," Liam said, clearly missing the way Chubs's nostrils flared and his eyes went wide behind his glasses. "We were wondering where you'd gotten off to."

"I was just—building some shelves, for the—uh, the supplies and books in the medical, uh, room," Chubs said, glancing between us, the door, and back over his shoulder, literally looking for an escape route.

"Did you build them all?" I asked, noticing for the first time that his shirt was buttoned incorrectly. I started toward the door, trying not to laugh as a look like death came over Chubs's face. "We're happy to help you—"

Liam finally caught on, an eyebrow slowly arching up, up, up . . .

"Nope, no—I mean, I lost a screw and had to stop—where were you going? I'll go with you—"

"Are you okay?" Liam asked. "You're acting all twitchy."

"Fine, totally." Chubs pushed the glasses Vida had made for him up the bridge of his nose, then looked down at his shirt. Without warning, he snatched my arm and started pulling me down the hall. "How are you? Are you guys okay now? Spare no details. We'll—"

The door creaked open behind us again. Chubs shrank back against the wall as Vida came strolling out, her shoulders set back, head of mussed purple hair held high—the curl of her swollen lips gave her a look of smug satisfaction. Liam stepped back, letting her by.

Vida didn't say a thing; she simply dropped Chubs's jacket over his head as she passed, letting it hang there. He waited until the sound of her boots against the tile had faded before sinking down onto the ground. Chubs kept the jacket pressed to his face, looking for all the world like he was trying to suffocate himself.

"Oh, God," he groaned. "She's going to kill me. Actually *kill me*."

"Wait . . ." Liam began, not bothering to hide the grin on his face. I put a hand on his shoulder, afraid he'd start jumping up and down in total and complete glee. "Are you . . . ?"

Chubs finally lowered the jacket. And, after a deep breath, nodded.

Well, I thought, surprised at my lack of surprise. *Well, well, well . . .*

"Wow . . . I mean, *wow.* I think my brain is going to start leaking out of my ears," Liam said, pressing the heels of his palms against his forehead. "I'm so proud of you, Chubsie, but I'm so confused, but I'm proud, but I think I need to lie down."

"How long has this been going on?" I asked. "You haven't . . . you're not . . . ?"

One look of mortification told me everything I needed to know. They had. They were. Liam choked a bit at that.

"What?" Chubs demanded. "It's a . . . it's a perfectly normal human response to—to stressors. And it's winter, you know, and when you're sleeping in a car or tent it can be freezing . . . actually, you know what? It's none of your business."

"It is if you're being stupid about it," Liam said.

"Excuse me, but I've known about contraception since I was—"

"Not what I meant," Liam said quickly, holding up his hands. "Not at all what I meant, but, uh, good to know."

I crouched down in front of Chubs, putting a hand on his arm. "I think what he was trying to say was, if this doesn't pan out, or one of you gets hurt, it'd be hard to take."

"Oh, you mean like if she erased my memory, forcing me to keep a little fact sheet of who I am in case she does it again?" The minute it left his mouth, I could tell he wanted it back inside his head, where the thought belonged. That alone eased the sting.

"Hey . . ." Liam warned.

"No, it's fair," I said. "I know you can handle it, but Vi's been . . . well, the people in her life really put her through the wringer. You'll be careful with her heart, right?"

"There are no hearts involved in this arrangement," he reassured me, which wasn't actually reassuring, let alone believable in any way. "It's . . . coping."

"Okay," I said.

"And she doesn't need anyone to protect her or fight her battles for her, got it?" he added, looking between us. The fierceness deflated somewhat. "God, she's going to kill me for blowing this. We haven't even been back for a week . . . You won't tell anyone, right?"

"Vida's the kind of person who doesn't give a rat's ass about what others think," Liam pointed out. "A quality I greatly admire in her."

"Are you saying she asked you to keep this quiet because she's embarrassed?" I said. "Embarrassed of being with you?"

"She didn't say it outright, but it's obvious, isn't it?"

"Maybe she just wants to keep it between the two of you for now because it's so new," I added. "Or because it really is no one else's business, even ours."

"You're a great catch, buddy," Liam finished. "It's not you. And she can't be *that* mad, anyway, seeing as it's only the two of us who know, and we'd only ever tell each other. And maybe a G-rated version to Zu. But, man, give yourself some credit. Obviously you've got something she likes if she's jumping your bones."

"Liam Michael Stewart, wordsmith and poet," Chubs said, shaking his head as he pushed himself up from the ground. I watched him as he fell silent, wringing his hands, trying our line of logic out. A shadow passed over his expression, one that had me wondering what he was thinking—or remembering. In the end, he shook his head. "I'm not . . . I mean, I don't have delusions of grandeur about this stuff. I know who I am and who she is, and I know it's like putting an apple next to an onion. Whatever. We have an understanding."

Liam gave his shoulder a reassuring squeeze.

"Anyway, good night," Chubs said. "Don't stay up too late. You're leaving tomorrow morning, don't forget."

Liam waited until Chubs had disappeared around the corner at the other end of the hall before turning to me, not even trying to hide his grin. "You wanna go build some shelves with me?"

I held out my hand for him to take, leading him back down toward the right door. It was almost painful, I thought, to have a heart so swollen with gratitude and what must have been pure, untainted happiness. I wanted to live inside the feeling forever.

If nothing else, this one thing—this one choice—wasn't made under pressure, or fear, or even desperation. It was something I wanted. To be as close to him as I could, with nothing standing between us. I wanted to show him the things that my words were too clumsy, too self-conscious, to really convey.

Neither of us were laughing now; the moment drew me closer to him, winding something up inside of me, making my heart feel weightless with anticipation. His eyes were dark, suddenly serious with the real question. I reached up and brushed an unruly lock of hair off his forehead before I tilted my face, brushing my lips softly against his, a question of my own. Liam let out a sweet, soft sigh, and nodded. I pulled him inside the room and managed to tear myself away long enough to lock the door behind us and take a breath.

Liam sat at the edge of the bed, his shape bright against the dark. He held out a hand and whispered, "Come here."

I swayed a little on my feet as I stepped into the circle of his waiting arms, watching his slow smile. I brushed the hair away from his face, knowing he was waiting for me. This whole time, from the moment we met, he'd been waiting for me to realize he'd known me all along, and he had never once wanted me to change.

"The you that you were then, who you are now, who you'll be," he began quietly, as if sensing my thoughts, "I love you. With my whole heart. My whole life, however long I'm lucky enough to get, nothing will change for me."

His voice sounded raw, flooded with the same searing feeling racing through me. The relief, the certainty, the overwhelming gratitude I felt that fate had given him to me, all burned my eyes, left me unable to speak again. So I kissed him and told him that way, over and over again between breaths, as he moved over me, inside of me, until there was nothing in the world beyond us and the promise of forever.

TWENTY

THE NEXT MORNING, HE WOKE ME WITH A KISS, AND then another, until the warm, lazy fog dispelled and I was forced back into reality. Liam pulled away with reluctance and reached for his clothes on the floor to start dressing. I watched him for a moment, amazed at how calm and peaceful I felt—like knowing he wanted and loved the whole me unconditionally had finally and fully brought the pieces of me back into alignment. He centered me so completely, and there was something so beautifully simple and straightforward in what I felt for him. Even something like this, something so important, had been simple for me.

Finally, seeing his amused look as he turned around, I forced myself to get up, too. I couldn't put off any longer the fact that he was leaving, but it didn't mean I didn't try as I caught him for one last, long kiss at the door.

Liam and I were the first ones to the tunnel's entrance that morning, even after he took a detour to grab food from the kitchen and shower. He had just gone back downstairs to say good-bye to Chubs and the others when Cole appeared at my left,

stepping out of Alban's old office. Just before the door shut, he caught it with his foot and held it open, looking around the room. His whole body seemed drawn with exhaustion, and there was a fresh cut on his left cheek.

I pointed to the spot on his face. "What happened here?"

"Ugh." Cole rolled his eyes, gave a small laugh. "In a move straight out of Lee's playbook, I rolled over in bed this morning and hit the dresser. Already killing it this morning."

"You actually slept?" I asked. He turned toward me, and the answer was clear enough. I knew it had to happen, that he couldn't go much longer without telling his brother the truth, but having kept secrets myself, I still felt guilty for putting him in that position last night. "Everything . . . okay?"

"Everything's okay," he said. "Felt better than I thought it would, to be honest. Liam's not the best litmus test, though—the kid would love the hell out of a one-eyed, three-legged, bald dog if it wagged its tail in his direction. Had to do my little trick for him a good five times before he believed I wasn't hiding a lighter in my palm."

Cole hefted a black duffle bag over his shoulder, its contents rattling ominously.

"Have enough guns in there?"

"Purely precautionary," he said with a wink.

"It better be. This is surveillance, not an assault, remember?"

"Aw, Gem, don't worry." Cole brought his free hand around the back of my skull, smoothing my hair down along its curve. "I'll have him back by tonight."

I pushed him away, rolling my eyes. "I mean it. Please . . . just be careful."

"You, too," he said. "Sorry to leave you to deal with the Little Prince again. If he acts up, don't be afraid to send him to bed without dinner. And double-check that the teams going to the water treatment facilities have everything they need before they head out."

"Got it."

"Harry said he'd try to check in tonight around eight. If we're not back by then, can you ask him to lock down another five pounds of C-four? Tell him I looked into hiring the buses to take everyone back east and it's a no-go."

"Got it," I said, already eager for Harry to get here at the end of the week, because it would mean finally seeing Cate. "Did you get the phone from Nico?"

Alice couldn't bear to be parted from her fancy camera, even for this, and there wasn't time to get another one. Nico had programmed a cell phone to automatically upload the photographs they snapped of the building and send them back to us.

Cole looked down at his watch, then over my head down the hall where the others had just appeared. "Taking his sweet-ass time this morning, isn't he?"

"Or someone's a little too impatient to get going," I pointed out.

"Just ready," he said. "Can we pick up the pace a little, Sunshine? It looks like a cat threw you back up."

"Better than you—you look like you came out the other end."

Cole chuckled. "Got me there."

I grabbed Liam's arm as he passed me on his way to the tunnel door, kissing his cheek. "See you later tonight."

He stepped down into the tunnel, shouldering a backpack

Cole had left for him there. When I turned to say good-bye to the other Stewart, he'd stooped, turned his cheek toward me, and was waiting. I flicked it with my finger, making him laugh again.

"You're impossible," I informed him.

"It's all part of my charm," he said, shifting the heavy bag on his shoulder. "Take care of things, Boss."

"Take care of *him*," I said, pointedly.

He gave one last mock salute before shutting the door to the tunnel. I waited until the sound of his and the others' steps faded completely before locking the door after him.

For a moment, I was tempted to go back to sleep—just showering and crashing for a few more hours sounded better than it had any right to. It already felt like a long day, and it had only just begun.

At around two in the afternoon, I realized I was being followed.

She never spoke, and she stayed well away, but Lillian Gray was there, observing from a safe distance. It made my skin crawl, the way her eyes were always assessing.

Dr. Gray was there, watching the training through the windows of the gym; hovering outside of the computer room; leaving the kitchen just as I was coming in. It took me another two hours to realize that it was likely she was trying to work up the courage to ask me something. And even then, it was only because Alice pulled me aside after harassing the woman into a short interview and told me, point-blank: "She wants to see her kid."

Seeing my expression, Alice added, "Look, I don't have any kids of my own, so I can't exactly give you insight as to how a woman's brain can get rewired to unconditionally love the same little dirtbag that scrambled her brains, but I have a feeling she'll be a lot warmer toward us if she gets her way."

"Did she give you anything you could actually use?" I asked as we walked back toward the big room.

"She's a true politician's wife," Alice said ruefully. "She talked for two hours and managed to say nothing useful. Any interest in sitting down with me for a chat, by the way?"

"Not even a word about the president?" I asked, turning the subject back to the matter at hand. That was what worried me most about this arrangement—Dr. Gray had made the arrangement with Alban to help Clancy, and she'd done it behind her husband's back. As far as we knew, they hadn't been in contact for years, but we had no sense of how she really felt toward the man. His name came up, and she shut down.

"I think she'll talk—she'll give me the smoking gun on how long, exactly, the president has known about Agent Ambrosia—but not for free. Is there any way—"

"No," I said, firmly. "It's not a good idea." Clancy had been reasonably well behaved up until now. I didn't want to tempt fate by even *hinting* his mother was nearby.

"Liam would say yes."

"Good thing he isn't here."

Alice's look of irritation morphed into one of amusement. "You're the boss, lady. I'll figure out another way to get her talking before I leave tonight."

"Are you all set for the trip?

"We should be fine. Our water treatment facility isn't too far away, otherwise we would have left early this morning like the others."

I had no idea if Alice told the other woman that I was the roadblock, but it was about an hour later that Dr. Gray found me in the kitchen, slowly and reluctantly pulling together a meal for Clancy. One look at the rapidly depleting pantry stock had taken my mind off her until, like an unwanted chill, she stepped inside the kitchen and shut the door behind her.

"If you've been following me in the hope that I'll slip up and reveal where he is, you're going to be disappointed. And," I added, "you're delaying his meal."

Her mouth tightened into a flat, bloodless line. Everything about this family was cold and distant, wasn't it? With both this woman and her son, it felt like I was constantly walking on my toes, trying to keep my balance.

"He has a mild nut allergy," she said, nodding toward the open container of peanut butter I'd scraped clean. "And he doesn't like Granny Smith apples."

Instead of being touched by this demonstration of motherly concern, I felt my expression rearrange itself into one of total and complete exasperation.

I actually bit my tongue to keep from saying, *He's lucky he gets any food at all.*

"I suppose Miss Wells told you about my request, then?"

Miss Wells . . . oh. Alice. I cut the sandwich in half and turned to walk the knife over to the sink. She was still there, watching me expectantly, when I walked back over. "Yes, she did. I'm surprised you even asked."

"Why?"

"Do I really have to remind you about what happened the last time he saw you?" I asked. "You're lucky you walked away with your life."

Finally, a crack appeared. "Clancy would never kill me. He's not capable of it. I realize how deeply troubled he is, but it's because he was never able to get the emotional help he needed after he left that camp."

"Plenty of us went into those camps," I said. "Not all of us turned out like him."

Dr. Gray held my gaze a second too long for it to feel comfortable. "Is that so?"

I felt myself straighten to my full height, ignoring the familiar stab of guilt.

"Yes," I said coldly. *She doesn't believe me. At all.*

"You should know that I have always disagreed with the rehabilitation camp program, even before it turned into what it is today," Dr. Gray said. "I have never liked my husband's foreign policy, nor can I comprehend the extreme action he took in California. But if he were to give me the facility and materials I need to perform the procedure on my son, it wouldn't even be a decision. I would go back to him in a heartbeat. I would do that, for Clancy."

I almost felt sorry for her. The simple truth was that the camps didn't damage us all in the same way. If you spent your time there feeling small and terrified, once you stepped outside of the electric fence, you didn't just stand up tall one day and resume your old life, forgetting the desperation you'd had to make yourself invisible. If you spent your time there simmering in your own anger and helplessness, that rage carried over; you took it with you into your new life.

It was disturbing to me how clearly I could see Clancy's point now. His mother really had no idea what they had done to him at Thurmond. How could someone who participated in, or at least *viewed*, the research conducted on the Psi kids have no conception of the kind of pain or humiliation he went through?

"You realize that giving him the procedure won't fix him, right?" I asked. "Not in the way that really matters to you."

"He won't be able to influence anyone," she insisted. "He'll come back to himself."

The idea was too ridiculous to even laugh at.

"Taking away his ability wouldn't take away his desire to try to control others," I said. And it sure as hell wouldn't cure him of being an asshole. "It's just going to make him angrier than he already is." *And hate you that much more.*

"I know what's best for him," she said. "He needs the treatment, Ruby—and, more than that, he needs his family. I just want to make sure that he's okay. It's not enough for me to hear he is—I need to *see* it. Please. Just for a moment. I gave you everything that you wanted last night, didn't I? Can't this be a show of good faith?"

I was willing to give her that—so far she had taken us at our word, and she had given us far more than even I'd expected. Alban, the sole person in the Children's League she'd known and trusted, wasn't around to tell her that it was okay to put her faith in us.

Nico's voice floated up to the back of my mind. *They broke something in him.* Something fundamental. Maybe she needed to see it to understand it.

"If I were to take you to see him," I began, "you couldn't give him any indication that you were there. Not a word. You'd have to do exactly what I tell you to. If he knows you're here, he'll stop cooperating and likely start figuring out how to escape. And you need to answer all of Alice's questions—for real this time."

"I can do that," she said. "I just want to see him, that he's been treated well and is strong enough to undergo the procedure. I don't need to touch him, just . . ."

Is it the mother or the scientist in you who wants to see him? I wondered, unsure which was preferable.

"All right," I said, gathering his food and a water bottle up in my arms. "Not a single word. And you stay exactly where I position you."

It didn't make sense to her until we reached the inner hallway that led to the room with the small cells. I shook my head, cutting off whatever question she was about to ask, and showed her where to stand to look through the door without Clancy being able to spot her through the small window there.

For the first time in nearly a week, Clancy Gray looked up and met my gaze as I came in. The book he'd been reading remained limp in his lap until I walked the food over to the locked metal flap on the door and held it out, waiting for him to take it. He stood, taking care to stretch his shoulders before crossing the small cell. His dark hair was nearly long enough to be tied back with a rubber band, but he kept it neatly combed and parted.

Clancy had three pairs of sweats he rotated through, and today clearly was a washing day, because he silently bent and picked up the other two sets of clothing and passed them to me through the open hatch.

"I didn't expect to see you," he said casually enough. "Did he go to Sawtooth, then?"

Did he really expect me to answer that?

No. Obviously not. "How does it feel?" he asked, placing a hand flat against the glass. "To be on that side of things? To control the flow of information?"

"About as good as knowing you'll never experience it for yourself again."

"It's incredible how things have turned out," he said. "A year ago, you were still in that camp, still behind that fence. Now look at you. Look at me."

"I am looking at you," I told him. "And all I see is someone who wasted every chance they had to really make a difference for us."

"But you understand now, don't you?" he asked, surprised. "You see why I made the choices I did. Everyone survives in their own way. When it really comes down to it, would you have changed any of the decisions you made, good or bad? Would you have stayed in Thurmond, with the opportunity to escape within reach? Would you have gone straight to Virginia Beach, not let them convince you to try to find East River? Would you have sealed off the younger Stewart's memories? You've come such a long way. It'd be a shame for our friendship to end here."

"I think there was a compliment buried in there somewhere . . . ?"

He snorted. "Just an observation. I wasn't sure you had it in you. I'd hoped, though."

"Oh, really?"

"Didn't you ever ask yourself why I wanted you to come with me after East River was attacked? It wasn't because I liked you all that much."

"Obviously not. You wanted me to show you how I messed with others' memories."

"Well, that. But also because I was trying to gather people around me who *could* step up and help me build this future. Granted, I probably wouldn't have wasted time trying with this camp strategy. I would have taken us straight to the top. I still will."

"If only you weren't trapped in this little glass cage," I said flatly.

"If only." Clancy smiled. "It'll be so easy to get rid of everyone now—if what Stewart, the elder Stewart, told me is true, you've badly hurt the government's credibility. I'll take it a step further. My father. His moronic advisors. The camp controllers. One by one, I'll tear their lives apart. The thing is, Ruby, you can stand at the head of those kids, and they'll listen, they will, if for no other reason because you're an Orange and it's the hierarchy of things. But you can't bring the world to its knees the way I will."

"The way you will, huh?" I asked, knocking against the glass. "When's that?"

One corner of Clancy's lips turned up, and I felt a cold drip of something run down my spine.

"Ruby, this is your last chance to align with the right side of history," he said. "I'm not going to offer again. We can leave now and no one will get hurt."

His gaze was as black and bottomless as it had always been, sucking me in, trying to drown me in the smooth, easy possibilities he presented.

"Enjoy your time in your box," I said and turned to go, holding his laundry out in front of me in distaste.

"One last thing," Clancy called. I didn't look back, but it hardly mattered to him. "Hello, *Mother*."

I whipped the door to the hall open, but the woman was already gone, chased out by her son's laughter.

That night I fell into a deep sleep, the kind that grips you by the ribcage and refuses to be shaken off easily. The voice in my dream, the same one that had been echoing somewhere behind me as I walked down the familiar path to Cabin 27 at Thurmond, shifted from the deep baritone of a man to a loud, almost shrill call, this time from a woman.

"—up! Ruby, *Ruby*, come on—"

The lights in the room were on again, highlighting the ashen quality of Vida's face as it hovered over mine. She shook me again, violently, until I broke free from that last bit of disorienting sleep.

"What happened?" Five minutes could have passed, or five hours—I couldn't tell. Zu hovered behind Vida, her cheeks already wet with tears. Fear ripped through me as I grabbed Vida's arm, feeling the way she trembled.

"I was in the computer lab," she began, the words pouring out of her. Was she shaking? Vida—*shaking*? "I was talking to Nico, watching the photos come in as Cole took them, and it went quiet for about an hour—I had just left to go to bed but then another photo came through and Nico ran out to get me and . . . and, Ruby . . ."

"What? Tell me what's going on!" I tried to untangle myself from the sheet, my heart hammering in my chest like I'd just sprinted ten miles.

"All he kept saying was . . ." Vida swallowed. "He kept saying one thing—*Stewart is dead.*"

TWENTY-ONE

"Liam or Cole?"

The question, the same one I'd asked her a hundred times, became more frantic as we made our way down the hall toward the computer room. The clock on the wall inside said it was two in the morning.

"Vida," I begged, *"Liam or Cole?"*

"They don't know," she said, the same answer she'd given me the first ninety-nine times I asked. "They can't tell from the photo."

"I can—" The words were out before I could think about why it would be a terrible idea. "Let me see it. I can tell them apart."

"I don't think so." She caught my arm before I could go charging into the room. I barely felt the touch. My whole body had run ice-cold. Panic made my thoughts disjointed, bursts of terrifying images interlaced with thoughts of *not him, not them, not now*—I couldn't break the pattern, I couldn't catch my breath.

"No!" That single word, a sharp bark from Chubs, brought Vida up short. "Absolutely not! Take her back to the room and stay there!"

There were a number of Greens hovering outside the window. "Get lost!" Vida barked at them. And by the force of her voice alone, they did, scrambling to get away as she opened the computer room's door and thrust me inside.

"What's going on? Did something happen?" Senator Cruz appeared in the hallway, Alice not far behind, her flaming red hair collected in a crooked ponytail, red marks from her pillow and sheets on her face. Vida must have tried to explain to them but I heard none of it. Nico looked like he'd been sick several times over, and the smell in the computer room seemed to align with that theory. He was drenched in sweat as I came toward him.

"Do you . . . do you really want to see?"

"This is a bad idea! Ruby, listen to me, you don't want to—" Chubs's pitch got higher until it finally cracked. He leaned back against the wall, his face buried in his hands.

Nico didn't move. His hands were limp in his lap, forcing me to reach over and click through the series of photos that had come through from the cell phone on Cole. There was a test shot in broad daylight—a distant mountain, Liam's back as he faced it, looking out into the distance. There were three dozen of a low, squat building, all taken after sundown. He'd captured the PSFs posted outside, a ladder up to the building's roof, a sniper in position. If there was a fence around the camp, Cole and Liam were already inside of it when they'd started snapping the photos.

"They're going in," Senator Cruz said. "I thought they were supposed to stay outside?"

They had gone inside. The images were fuzzy, lacking the brightness the full moon outside had provided. They were high up, looking down at tables below, the heads bent over them, eating. The kids wore dark red scrubs—the same uniforms we all had to wear in the camps, but the color—I hadn't seen that shade in years—

The next image was of one of those kids in uniform looking up, eyes locking on the phone. My finger hesitated over the mouse before clicking again. Nico made a small noise at the back of his throat, his hand closing over mine. "Ruby, you don't want to . . ."

I pressed my finger down.

There was a moment where my mind couldn't make sense of what it was seeing. The photos were taken inside of a dark room, the walls painted black, the lights lining the floors rather than the ceilings. The figure at the center of the room was slumped forward in a chair, the weight of his body straining against the restraints around his chest. Blond hair fell over his face, masking it. My hand gripped the desk as I clicked forward again. A metallic taste flooded my mouth when I noticed the splatters of blood on his neck and ears. The angle made it impossible to tell, I needed another photo—

Click.

"Who took these photos?" Senator Cruz demanded, though no one seemed to be able to respond.

"My guess is the people who caught . . ." Alice wasn't sure if it was a *him* or *them*. I pressed back against the question, focusing on the screen. Someone had hung a sheet of paper over his neck. Two words had been scrawled there in thick, uneven writing: TRY AGAIN.

In the corner of the shot was a sliver of deep red cloth, and even though my brain knew what was coming, knew it sure enough for the screaming to start inside of my head, I moved to the next photo.

Fire.

The image, the whole of it, was flooded with white flame.

Fire.

Fire.

A screen of gray smoke, and—

Senator Cruz tore herself away from the computer, walking to the far corner of the room, trying to escape the sight of the charred remains. "Why? Why do it? *Why?*"

The dispassionate, cold creature the Children's League had been careful to nurture in me clawed its way back up inside of me. And for a second, one single second, I was able to look at the burnt, mutilated corpse in the careful, distant way a scientist would have studied a specimen. In the small section of his face I could see, what skin remained was burnt, dark and rough, like a scab.

I moved back through the shots of the fire. The sick assholes— those goddamn sick fucks who took these pictures. I'd kill them. I knew where to find them. I would kill each and every one of them. I held onto the cold fury with everything I had because it froze out the pain, it didn't let me shut down the way I wanted to. The burn of tears was at the back of my eyes, my throat, my chest.

"I can't tell," Chubs said, edging closer and closer to full-out hysteria, "dammit—"

I scanned through the earlier photos, my stomach as tight as a fist. If I started crying, the others wouldn't be able to stop. I had to focus—I had to—I stopped on the second photo of the figure in the chair, when they'd put the sign on him. His head lolled to the left, but I saw it. I hadn't imagined it. I knew who it was.

"It's . . ." Vida leaned forward again. Her nails dug into my shoulder. "I can't . . ."

Alice had spun away from the gruesome image, overcome by her own retching. But Nico—Nico was looking at me. I felt the words leave my throat, but I didn't hear them.

"It's Cole."

"What?" Vida asked, looking between me and the screen again. "What did you say?"

"It's Cole."

A thousand needles flooded my veins, shooting toward my center. I doubled over against the desk, incapable of speech, of thoughts, of anything other than seeing the body—Cole's body, what they'd done to it. I sucked in a shallow breath, trying to push the pain down. I wanted the numb control back. My head was spiraling faster, harder than even my stomach. Because I knew what would matter to Cole, I knew what he would be asking. *Where is Liam?* If Cole was—if Cole was—

"Are you sure?" Chubs asked, when no one else seemed able to.

Out of the corner of my vision, I saw Lillian come in and, for a heart-stopping moment, thought the blond hair belonged to Cate, that somehow she and Harry were already here. I heard the murmured explanation Senator Cruz gave.

"Harry . . . we have to tell him . . . and Cate, God, *Cate* . . ."

"I will," Vida said, her voice as tight in her throat as Chubs's arm was around her shoulder. "I'll do it."

"Is Liam—" Chubs began, "is there . . . can we check to see if they took him into custody? If there's some update to the networks?"

If he'd been killed and they positively ID'd him, then they would update his profile in the PSF network and remove him from the skip tracer listings to reflect as much.

"I'm trying to get into the PSF network," Nico said, "I'm trying—it'll be faster to go in through the skip tracers'. Can you give me your login information?"

"Here, I'll put it in," Chubs said.

"Is the phone still on?" I heard myself ask as I was drawn back away from the computer, still in my chair. I didn't trust my legs to try standing. *Are we going to get more pictures?* And we would just have to *sit* there, sit and do nothing other than wait for them to come. I choked on my own rage.

"Reds?" Dr. Gray repeated. "You're sure? Can I see the photos, please?"

Nico pulled up the screen again and shifted to the computer next to him to work. Dr. Gray moved through the photos, skipping around until she found what she was looking for. The violence and horror of it registered only in her frown.

"He was dead when it happened," she said. "He would have bled out almost instantly from the gunshot to his neck."

I could have told her that. Cole would have fought to the death. He wouldn't have let them take him into their program. He would have fought until he flamed out completely.

She shook her head, turning to look at me. "This is why. This is why we need the procedure. These children shouldn't be able to do this and harm themselves and others."

My anger blew up, swallowing me in a cloud of blistering incredulity. "No, this is why no one should be fucking with our heads in the first place!"

"There's nothing on the network," Chubs said, "not yet . . . any changes to the PSF's would take an hour or two to feed into the skip tracer network."

"We—let's give him some time, he might still be trying to get away." Vida shook her head, raking her hands back through her hair. "The last photo came an hour ago. They would have sent something else if they had Liam . . . right?"

Senator Cruz looked over at me. "Where's the phone that he's been using to contact his father? I'll make the call."

"Upstairs. The office." Nico stood up so suddenly that he knocked his chair over behind him. "I'll get it. I need to . . ."

Get out of this room, my mind finished, *away from the pictures.*

He returned less than a minute later, his chest heaving as he tried to catch his breath. He held the small silver flip phone out to the senator—only to drop it when the screen lit up and it began vibrating.

For a moment, no one moved. The phone rang. It rang, it rang, it rang.

Chubs lunged for it, scooping it off the floor before it rang out completely. "Hello?"

His whole body sagged in relief. "Lee—Hey—hey, Liam, where are you? You have to—"

Senator Cruz was beside him before even I was, ripping the phone out of his grip and silencing his protests with a wave of her hand as she put the phone on speaker.

"—*took him, I couldn't do anything, I couldn't—*"

That voice I knew as intimately as my own skin, the one I'd heard laughing, pitched in fear, furious, flirting shamelessly, wasn't the one coming through the small phone. I almost didn't recognize it at all. The connection made him sound distant, at the other end of a highway, beyond our reach. The words came out of his chest so ragged, so raw, it was almost unbearable to listen to him.

"Liam, it's Senator Cruz. I need you to take a deep breath and before anything else let me know you're safe."

"I didn't—I don't know if this is okay—this was the only number I could remember, I know it's not secure, not really—"

"You did exactly the right thing," Senator Cruz said, her voice soothing. "Where are you calling from?"

"A pay phone."

Vida stepped up beside me, eyes sliding my way. I couldn't speak. An unnatural numbness settled at the center of my chest. I could say a single word.

"I couldn't get him out—we got inside, we were taking pictures, one of them saw us and we couldn't get away—they shot him. He fell down and I couldn't get him out, I tried to carry him, but they saw us and they opened fire—I didn't want to leave, I had to—have you heard anything about it on the news? Would Harry be able to find out where they're keeping him? There was so much blood—"

He didn't know.

I looked at Chubs. He looked like he had glanced up and seen a speeding car coming straight for him. I took the phone from the senator, switching it off speakerphone.

"He . . . Liam," I choked out, "he didn't make it. They sent us proof."

Until that moment, I think shock and panic for news about Liam had shut off the part of myself that would have let me think through specifics of what had happened. If Cole had been alive when they brought the Red in. If he knew what was going on, if he had been afraid, if he felt the pain. But something shattered in me at delivering the news; the flimsy door keeping the pain out bowed in and then exploded into a shower of splinters that cut through every part of me. I couldn't breathe. I had to press

ALEXANDRA BRACKEN

my hand against my mouth to keep from sobbing. My friend—
Cole—how could this—why did it have to be like this? After
everything, why did it have to end like this? We were going to do
something—for the first time, he had a real future—

Chubs stepped forward, reaching for the phone, but I tore
away from him, twisting out of his reach. I felt wild with anger
and pain, like someone had thrown acid on my skin. I had to
keep this connection to Liam. I had to stay with him. This would
destroy him—the agony of knowing that was as sharp as the loss
itself. I couldn't lose Liam, too.

"What do you mean, proof? What did they do to him?" Any
coherency was gone. Liam broke down with each word until he
was sobbing. "I couldn't get him out. . . ."

"No," I said, voice hoarse, "of course you couldn't. There was
no way and he wouldn't have wanted you to try if it meant they
got you, too. Liam, it doesn't—it doesn't feel this way now, but
you did the right thing."

The sound of him crying finally did me in, too. My grip on
the phone relaxed as my hand lost feeling, allowing Chubs to
finally pry the phone away from me.

"Buddy. Buddy, I know, I'm so sorry. Can you make it back
here? Do you need us to come get you?" He smoothed his hand
back over his hair, squeezing his eyes shut. "Okay. I want you to
tell me everything, but you have to do it in person. You have to let
us take care of you. Slow down, it's okay—"

Chubs cast a helpless look my way. I held out my hand for the
phone.

"I'm not coming back, I can't—it's—"

I interrupted him. "Liam, listen to me, I'm going to come get
you, but you have to tell me where you are. Are you hurt?"

"*Ruby*—" He sucked in a harsh breath. I could imagine him then, exactly as he must have been. Still in his Op blacks, his left forearm braced against the pay phone's aluminum shell, his face flushed and wild. It broke my heart all over again.

I gripped the phone so tightly I heard its cheap plastic shell creak. Spinning so I was facing the corner and not the gallery of faces looking at me, I dropped to a crouch in the far corner of the room. "It's going to be okay—"

"*It's not okay!*" he shouted. "*Stop saying that! It's not! I'm not coming back. I have to tell Harry and—and Mom, oh, God, Mom—*"

"Please let me come get you," I begged.

"*I can't come back to there, to you guys. . . .*" The feeling of nausea that had been growing, twisting my stomach, rose like a cresting wave. His voice seemed to click in and out. "*The line is cutting off, I don't have any more money. . . .*"

"Liam? Can you hear me?" Panic hit me like a swarm of wasps in my head.

"—*I knew this would happen. . . . dammit . . . you . . . sorry . . . Ruby . . . sorry . . .*"

I don't know when or how she'd managed to slip by so many people, or if she'd made herself so small and silent she'd been here the entire time without me noticing. Zu—she took the cell phone away, I tried to get it back, but she had it to her ear, and she was saying, over and over again, in a voice as sweet as little bells, "Don't leave, please don't leave, come back, please . . ."

I heard the dial tone. I heard that sound, saw the phone slide out of her fingers, and I knew it was over. Chubs reached for her and she clung to him, burying her face against his shoulder. "Come on, let's get some water. Some air. Some . . . thing."

"I want to go out and find him," I said.

"I'll go with her," Vida added quickly. "Nico can trace the call."

"You can't," Chubs told me gently. "You have a responsibility here."

So? I wanted to shout. I felt like tearing at my hair, my shirt— but I couldn't, I couldn't do any of those goddamn things because Cole had wrested that stupid promise out of me. *Take care of things, Boss. Take care of things.* Cate and Harry wouldn't be here for another two days. I needed to . . . I had to tell everyone.

He trusted you with this. He thought you could do it. You have to do this.

I had to. If Cole wasn't here, if Liam wasn't coming back, then I was in charge, and I had to tell the others. I had to stay here and keep it together.

"Give me a minute," I said. I only needed one. I walked briskly toward Cate's old quarters and shut the door behind me. I found the edge of the small bed in the darkness, the same one Liam and I had slept in the night before, and sat down hard. My hands reached along the coarse sheets until they found the soft fabric of the hooded sweater he'd left behind. I buried my face in the fabric, dragging in the scent of him, until finally I released it all in a silent, throat-burning scream.

Why did you have to go in? How am I supposed to do this? Why hadn't I pushed back harder, knowing where the information had come from?

And there was no answer, just the terrible silence, just the darkness pressing in.

Clancy.

He'd known this would happen—had banked on it. He'd shown Cole the camp, planted the images of it in his mind knowing that Cole was the kind of person who wouldn't be able to let it go, seeing others like him treated so damn badly. He would obsess over it, stop thinking about the odds of an actual rescue. After all, how many times had he beaten the odds?

He never had a chance.

The words blistered over my mind. I swayed with the force of the hot, singeing rush that ran from my temples to the base of my neck. My vision flashed, splitting the door in front of me into two, then four. I saw, rather than felt, my hand rise up and reach for the handle. The closer I got, the further back I seemed to be; someone dragged me back and back and back . . .

It was the last thing I remembered before the blurring dark turned to a gray static, washing over me, hooks and needles running through my veins.

When I surfaced again, there was a cold gun in my hand, and it was pointed at Lillian Gray's head.

TWENTY-TWO

"*—DOING? STOP IT, STOP—*"

"*—Ruby, wake up!*"

"*You can't do this—stop—Ruby—STOP!*"

I was floating underwater, deep enough where there was nothing but sweet, cool darkness. I didn't need to move, I couldn't speak—there was a gentle current, and it was taking me where I needed to go. It was urging me forward and I went willingly, giving myself over to the feeling. This was better than the pain.

"*—look at me! Look at me! Ruby!*"

The voices were distorted by the waves, stretched into a long, continuous drone. The words filled the spaces between heartbeats, the steady *ba-dum, ba-dum, ba-dum* in my ears. I didn't want them to find me here.

Gem. Hey, Gem.

I turned, looking for the source of the words, forcing my stiff muscles to move.

Take care of things, Boss.

There was no one there. The black currents around me were swirling harder against my freezing skin. There was nothing there.

Gem. Ruby.

441

The air burned where it was trapped in my lungs. *Where are you?*

Roo, are you okay?

I thrashed against the water, stretching my arms up and up again to drag myself to the surface. Up—there was a light, a pinprick of it, growing larger, waiting—

Come on, darlin', come on . . .

I pulled, dragged, clawed my way up—

"She's going to—"

"—do something! Stop her!"

"Ruby!"

I slammed back into my own mind. The thick, murky water drained around me as reality took shape. The static, dry smell of the computer lab. The glow of monitors reflecting against the nearby white wall. Nico's face, bloodless, hands up in front of him. My eyes shifted from the cold, heavy gun in my hand to the pale-haired woman on the floor, her arms up over her head protectively.

I jerked, looking at Nico again as the gun came down a fraction of an inch. My arm was on fire, aching like it had held the weight for hours. Comprehension dawned in his eyes, and I saw his stance relax, only to tense again as he shouted, "Vi, no!"

One minute I was vertical, the next I was on the ground, pain consuming every confused, disoriented thought. I'd been laid out flat by a hit between the shoulder blades, and what breath I had left flew out of my lungs as Vida kept me pinned to the ground.

"Wait!" Zu said. "Ruby . . . ?"

"What . . ." My mouth felt like it was full of sand.

"Ruby?" Chubs's face floated above me. "Vi, get off her—"

"She was going to shoot her—I thought she—she was going to shoot—"

"What is going *on*?" Senator Cruz cried, somewhere above us.

"I don't . . ." I started to say, the pain splitting my head in two. I felt turned around and upside down, flipped inside out. "How did I get here?"

"You don't remember?" Dr. Gray asked, sounding the calmest of anyone in the room. "You left and came back in—you shoved me to the ground. You didn't say a word."

"What?" My nails scraped against the tile. "No! I wouldn't—I don't—"

"You weren't yourself," Chubs said, gripping my shoulders. "You didn't respond to anything we said—"

"I'm sorry, shit, I'm so sorry," Vida said. "I didn't know what to do—every time we got close, you looked like you were going to shoot!"

"Nico?" I said, pressing a hand against my eyes to stop the flow of tears. There was no way to hold them in; the pain was clouding my brain, overriding my body's response. "Nico?"

"He just ran out—" Senator Cruz said. "He looked at the monitor and just took off—what is *happening*?"

Him. It was him. And through the pain, through lingering confusion clinging to my mind, I finally understood what was happening.

I clutched at Chubs's arm. "You have to—listen to me, okay?"

"Okay, Ruby, okay," he said, "just take a breath."

"No, *listen*. Go . . . you and Vida go get the others. The kids. Go get them and take them, Senator Cruz, and . . . and Dr. Gray out through the garage. Go into one of the nearby buildings. Don't let anyone leave. Understand?"

"Yes, but what are you—"

"Take what food and water you can carry, but wait in the building until you get the all clear."

The gaps in my memory, began to color themselves in. If I closed my eyes, I could see myself in the middle of a conversation I didn't remember having. Sitting down in the computer room with all the lights off. The tips of my fingers remembered each keystroke, tingled with the thought. Sleepwalking. The messages that were sent. The communications that were sent. *He can move people around. Like they're toys.* Clancy's last warning.

My thoughts spiraled, spinning together until they formed a whole, gut-wrenching realization.

He's planned an out.

They're coming.

Someone is coming to get him—and he used me to arrange the ride.

"There's been a security leak," I told them. "Me."

"What the fuck does that mean?" Vida said, helping me up from the ground.

"Nico . . . he noticed someone sending messages outside of the Ranch and trying to cover them up, delete them from the server activity log, we thought it was—" I turned toward Alice. "We thought it was you, or one of the kids working with you. But it wasn't, was it?"

"No, dammit, I told you that!" Alice said.

"I know, I'm sorry. I know that now. He's been walking me around, using me to spy on what's happening. He had me send messages for him. *Shit!*"

Escape. I let my mind work it through the way he would have. The only group that could extract him was his father's military or some kind of contractor. He hadn't known exactly where the Ranch was, likely, until I'd gone out to Oasis and he'd been able to watch through my eyes how to get back.

He'd only need the soldiers to unlock his cell, and then it'd be as easy as compelling them to leave him alone, to turn their attention to rounding up the other kids in the Ranch. All he'd have to do was slip away.

But why hadn't he just compelled me to open the cell door for him? Why wait, go such a roundabout way?

"You weren't in control of yourself?" Dr. Gray said. "Who was, then?"

I stared at her and I had my answer. Clancy wanted us to find her. To bring her here, to finish what he'd started. Only, she'd been right—he would never kill her.

He'd have me do it for him.

I looked away. She'd know soon enough that I couldn't keep our bargain.

"Lillian, let's go," Senator Cruz said, "I have to get Rosa—the others—Ruby will follow us, won't you, Ruby?"

"That's—" I could see the need to protest this in her eyes, but the senator took her arm firmly and began walking her to the door.

I ran to the board at the front of the room, wiping it clean, tearing down the satellite image of Thurmond, folding it up, and tossing it at Vida. "Please," I said to her and Chubs, "go get the kids, get them out—I need to take care of Clancy, but I'll be there soon. Guys—*please*! Pull the server and take whatever you can out of the locker."

The weapon stock would be low; the kids who'd gone out to the water treatment facilities had taken most of the handguns as a precaution. There were so few of us left in the compound—Oasis kids, mostly, who were still too wet behind the ears to go out into the field. We hadn't had time to train them for something like this.

"If you think I'm leaving you, you're out of your damn mind," Chubs said.

I doubled down on my grip, broken nails cutting into his skin. "*Go!* You have to go right now—*right now.* The Ranch's location has been compromised. You have to get the kids out. Take Senator Cruz and Dr. Gray. *Charles!* Listen to me! I'll be right behind you, but if—if you stay, no one is getting out. *Go!*"

Vida's dark eyes flashed as she took his arm and started to drag him away by force. "Right behind us?"

"Right behind you."

I ran from the computer room, shouldered my way through the double doors and stopped dead. A shiver raced through me as the unnatural silence in the hallway was punctuated by the sound of a hysterical voice. I recognized it with a terrible, sinking feeling.

I pivoted toward the storage room. The door was already unlocked, left partly open. My anxiety spiked and I couldn't tell if the low growls I heard in the distance were actual helicopters or the product of my frantic imagination.

"—you promised! You promised you wouldn't do this again!"

I bolted down the small hallway, through the open door, and into the scene already unfolding.

Nico's hands were gripped in his black hair, destroying its slicked-back shape, making it stand on end. He was pacing alongside Clancy's cell, his face bright red, as if he'd been crying. "And you did it to her! How could you hurt Ruby? *How could you?*"

Clancy sat cross-legged on his bed, looking annoyed but otherwise unfazed by the breakdown Nico was having in front of him. His eyes shifted over to me as I entered, his arms coming up to cross firmly over his chest. Nico hadn't gone into the cell, thank God, but I saw a copy of the same keys I had in my hand. *Cole's set,* I realized. We'd kept this area a secret from most everyone here at the Ranch, but Nico could have seen any one of us go inside, or found some kind of layout of the building on one of the servers. Hell, he could have just deduced it.

"Ruby—he can't keep getting away with it! He can't!" There were tears in his eyes. "You have to make him leave, just let him go, before—"

"Finally," Clancy said to me. "Can you please get him out of here? I already have enough of a migraine."

"If your head aches now, imagine how it'll feel when I rip it off your neck," I snarled.

Clancy smirked, looking me up and down. "It looks like you had an interesting night."

"Shut up! *Shut up!* Ruby, he—" Nico sucked in a breath. "It's like I told you—he can control other people's bodies. He can move them around like puppets without them realizing it. He did it all the time, to all of the researchers, I know he can do it—and he made you—he made you send those messages through the server!"

For a moment, I was sure he'd try to deny it all, brush Nico aside as being out of his mind. But Clancy didn't bother to hide the small smile tucked in the corner of his mouth.

"Really had you going there, didn't I?"

"You . . ." The idea of it was almost too much. Coming into my mind while I was asleep would keep me from sensing the tingling rush down the back of my skull that came when someone tried to force a connection between our minds. He'd walked me around like a doll—listened in on conversations, stolen whole moments of my life. I'd been his eyes and ears, and I hadn't even thought that it could be done, that there was the possibility of it.

"How long?" I demanded.

"How long have you been having those 'stress headaches'?" Clancy folded his hands in his lap. "They're the *worst*, aren't they? I'm glad I haven't been suffering through them alone. But you should know you only have yourself to blame. Every time you enter someone's mind, you form a connection with them—their memories, thoughts, will become yours. Each time you came into my mind, each time I got you while your defenses were down, you let me reinforce our bond. You're the reason I was able to do this."

"What did the messages say?" I demanded, stepping up to the glass. Nico slumped down against the wall behind me, hiding his face behind his hands. "Who were they sent to?"

"I have no idea what you're talking about," Clancy said. "You're both clearly too emotional to understand. You've been so stressed, Ruby. It's harder to control your abilities when you're so . . . frayed . . ."

. . . Isn't it?

I heard the words like they had been spoken inside of my skull and immediately threw down a black wall between the two of us, clipping the connection before it could fully form.

This was how he'd played me again—he knew the symptoms of anxiety and lack of focus, and even the headaches could be explained away by the stress of our situation.

Again, and again, and again, I thought. *Every time, I walk right into it.* We were on different levels, and I needed to stop pretending like we weren't. My mind hadn't even been twisted enough to *imagine* he'd be capable of doing this.

"That's better." Clancy gave me an approving nod. "You understand now. Your role in this is over. The Red is gone. You've set this up so well, it'll be easy to step in and finish it. You can rest now. Isn't that what you wanted?"

"You knew he'd be hurt—killed," I said, choking on the words.

"Only because you guaranteed it," Clancy said, victory making his dark eyes shine. "Who do you think sent a message to the trainers there, warning them to be on the lookout?"

There was a moment of skull-shattering pain and then I did scream. I screamed and screamed, slamming my hands against the glass until I had nothing left but a miserable, low sob to give. *My fault. My fault. My fault.*

"It's a bit tragic, isn't it? To give someone the one thing they desperately want, knowing that in the end, it only has the power to destroy them. He wanted so badly to know he wasn't the only one like him—to fit in with us. It was pathetic."

I lurched forward, vision flashing red, black, white, the invisible hands in my mind already driving toward him.

He couldn't have this.

East River, Los Angeles, Jude, the research, Cole—he had taken so much, destroyed every trace of hope just as it solidified into something real in my hands. *He can't have this.* We were too close. I was too close to finishing this.

Nico brought me up short, stepping in front of me brandishing the keys. Hands steady, expression focused, he unlocked each of the three deadbolts on the door.

"Leave!" he said, throwing the door open. "Disappear again, the way you always do! Get out of here before you ruin everything for us—call off the people you hired to get you out, just . . . disappear!"

Clancy stood up from his cot, a strange expression on his face.

"Don't you get it?" Nico said. "You haven't hurt the people

who hurt you by doing this—you never will, and you won't admit it to yourself! You can't even get close to them. The only thing you've ever done is hurt the kids who wanted to help you. We all wanted to help you!"

"Then you should have stayed out of my way."

"Why did you help the League get me out of Leda's program?" Nico asked, holding his ground as Clancy sauntered toward him. "You gave them the plan to extract me in Philadelphia, didn't you? But you were the one who left me behind at Thurmond—you left all of us, even after you told us we would get out together, we would be able to live without fear or shame or pain. Clancy . . . don't you remember the pain?" His voice dropped to a whisper. "Why couldn't you have just let me die like the others? You told me I had to live, but I wish I had just . . . I wish I had died, so you couldn't have used me."

Clancy was watching him, an expression on his face I'd never seen before.

"Why do you have to take every good thing we try to give you and break it into pieces?" Nico said. "You let them turn you into this . . ."

"This is who I am," Clancy snapped. "I won't let them change me. I won't let them touch me. Not again."

"No one is going to force you to have the procedure," Nico said, his hands up, placating. "You're free to go. You can disappear. Please . . . please . . . just call off the people who are coming. Please, Clance. *Please.*"

"I told you to stay out of this," Clancy said, his voice shaking, even as he eyed the exit, even as I could see him considering it. "Why can't you ever listen?"

"Please," Nico begged.

"It's too late," he said, hands fisted in his sweatpants. "If you weren't so *stupid*, you'd have realized that. Can't you hear it? They're on the roof. They're *here*."

"But you could get them to leave. You could make sure they go."

He's working him, I realized, half-amazed. Clancy was actually considering this, weighing Nico's words. I didn't move, too afraid I'd break the strange spell that had fallen over the room. My eyes kept darting between the two boys just outside of the cell. The tension in the room was softening, easing naturally.

"Who's here?" came a soft voice from the doorway. "Who did you call to get you?"

And just like that, Clancy hardened again, shoving past Nico. "Hello, Mother. Were you hoping I'd leave without saying good-bye?"

"Who did you call?" she repeated, her stiff posture perfectly mimicking her son's.

"Who do you think?" he said, all sweetness. "I called Dad."

"I told you to leave!" I barked at her.

"No, stay," Clancy said. "Clearly, last time didn't take. We'll have to try again, and this time Ruby won't be there to help you."

There was a beat of silence, and then the whole building rocked, shuddering under the force of some kind of explosion. Clancy looked past her, toward the door, and in that moment I was sure I had never hated him more.

The light caught the gun—my gun, the one that had been knocked out of my hands in the computer room—as Lillian Gray raised it and aimed at Clancy.

"I love you," she said, and fired.

TWENTY-THREE

A SPRAY OF BLOOD BURST FROM HIS SHOULDER, KNOCK-ing him back against the glass wall. But Lillian wasn't finished. She took another step forward, ignoring her son's scream of pain, and aimed lower, this time firing at his leg. The whole time, her face was a cold mask, as if she'd had to shut off some crucial part of herself to see this through.

Nico and I jumped with each shot. He covered his face and turned away so he wouldn't have to see it. I watched. I had to make sure he didn't get away this time.

The ceiling shook, the sound of heavy footsteps thundering over our heads. We'd have minutes, maybe, before they found us. It would need to happen fast. And wouldn't you know it? The only thing I could think of as the old, familiar calm came over me was one simple phrase: *accept, adapt, act.*

The certainty of it was more comforting than terrifying. That, too, seemed so strange—at some point, after pushing the possibility to the darkest corner of my mind, it had taken root and flourished. The old plan was gone. The new one bloomed in its place.

The string around his neck holding the flash drive had slipped clear of Nico's shirt as he stumbled away from Clancy, falling back against the cell's glass wall. I was in front of him before he could catch his breath, gripping the black piece of plastic and yanking hard enough to snap the string he'd threaded it on. And before he could react, I shoved a shell-shocked Nico back into the empty cell and slammed the door shut.

"No!"

I had the keys. I barely heard the lock as it clanged into place.

"No, no, no," he moaned, "Ruby, you know what they'll do. They'll take you back to that place, they'll kill you—they'll *kill you.*"

Dr. Gray had moved over to her son's side, dropping to her knees to apply pressure to his wounds. At that, she looked over, startled.

"I won't let them hurt me," I said, knowing what a hollow promise it was. But in that moment, I felt so sure of this plan, wanted so badly to make sure that it wasn't derailed in the aftermath of all this, that I felt confident I could, maybe, influence enough of the PSFs to keep my life.

I want to live.

"It was supposed to be me. It should be *me!*"

"Tell the others March first," I said, pressing my palm against the glass and letting the keys fall to the floor. "March first. Harry knows the plan."

"Ruby," he sobbed, "don't do this."

I leaned my forehead against the cool glass and said quietly, "I can see it now—the road Jude talked about. It's so beautiful. The rain's gone and the clouds are moving out."

I want to live.

I shouldered Dr. Gray aside and reached to take Clancy under the arms, refusing to sag under his dead weight. I dragged him through the doorway, into the short hall.

"What are you doing?" The woman trailed after me, her hands, shirt, face all stained with her son's blood. "Where are you taking him?"

"Shut the door!" I said sharply.

Nico was still pressed up against the glass, slamming his palms against it, when Dr. Gray shut the door on that last image. I looked down at Clancy's dark head as I moved, listening to his half-conscious mutterings. The coppery stench of blood filled my nose. I looked down at my hands and thought, *even now, he's staining me.*

They cut the power just as I pulled Clancy through the last door. He slid free of my hands, thumping bonelessly against the tile. I glanced back, making sure Dr. Gray had shut the last door, securing Nico safely inside. I slid the flash drive into my boot and lay down flat on my stomach, stretched out over the cold tile. I was proud of the fact that my hands didn't shake as I put them behind my head.

Breathe.

I went to that place deep inside, the one Zu had asked me about. I retreated as far as I could as the first beam of light slashed through the hallway's darkness. Fear couldn't touch me there, not even as I was hauled up by my hair and shoulder, a device flashing in my face. The dark spots in my vision blotted out the soldier's face, and I couldn't hear anything over my own steady heartbeat. When the grip on me tightened and something cold and metal pressed against the base of my skull, I knew they'd identified me.

Clancy was hidden by a circle of men in dark fatigues as Dr. Gray was dragged off to the side, clawing at the soldier who separated her from her son. One of them, a medic, stepped away long enough for me to see them lower a white plastic muzzle down over his face.

Radios buzzed, a swarm of voices flying over my head, and I heard none of it. Both of my hands were secured, the zip ties unbearable as the soldier holding me yanked them tight and flipped me over onto my back. Something jabbed into the side of my neck and I felt the pressure of the injection being forced into my bloodstream.

They are going to kill me. I wasn't even going to make it out of the building, never mind the state, if this didn't work. I should have practiced. I should have found a way to try it on a group when my life didn't rely on someone's trigger finger.

The drug they'd given me turned my limbs to powder. I felt light enough to be blown away, but it couldn't touch my mind, not yet. I fought against the drag of my eyelids, the weight that settled over them. I had one . . . I had one more thing to do . . .

I'd spent months carefully winding my gift into a tight spool, only letting it out by inches, and only when I needed it. The strain of keeping it bound up had been a steady, constant reminder that I had to work to keep the life I'd built for myself out here. It was a muscle I'd carefully toned to withstand nearly any pressure.

Letting it all go felt like shaking a bottle of soda and ripping off the cap. It fizzed and flooded and swept out of me, searching for the connections waiting to be made. I didn't guide it, and I didn't stop it—I don't know if I could have if I tried. I was the burning center of a galaxy of faces, memories, loves, heartbreaks, disappointments, and dreams. It was like living dozens of different lives. I was lifted and shattered by it, how strangely beautiful it was to feel their minds linked with my own.

The spinning inside my head slowed with the movement around me. I felt time hovering nearby, waiting to resume its usual tempo. The darkness slid into the edges of my vision, seeping through my mind like a drop of ink in water. But I was in control of the moment, and there was one last thing that I needed to say to them, one last idea to imprint in their minds.

"I'm Green."

I woke to cold water and a woman's soft voice.

The smell of bleach.

The aftertaste of vomit.

Dry throat.

Cracked, tight lips.

The metallic banging and clattering of an old radiator in the instant before it let out a warm breath of air.

"—need to run the test while subject is conscious—"

Wake up, I commanded myself, *wake up, Ruby, wake up—*

"Good. There cannot be any confusion on this, do you understand?"

I dragged myself up and out of a haze of pain and grogginess. My eyes were crusted with sleep. I tried lifting a hand up to wipe it away, to ease the tingling at the tips of my fingers. The Velcro restraint jerked but held firm, cutting into my bare wrists with a vicious bite as I tried to rise up off the freezing metal examination table.

The cold water hadn't been water at all, but sweat. It dripped down into the white plastic muzzle trapping each labored, heated breath. The black spots floating in my vision cleared, adjusting to the room's harsh artificial light. The pieces began to make sense.

The poster on the wall, the one with the color chart outlining each of the abilities, Red to Green—*Psi Classification System*, my lips formed the words on top.

High up in the corner of the room, a lidless camera eye was blinking like a heartbeat.

Calm down, Ruby. The rational part of my brain was still firing, at least. *Calm down. You're alive. Calm down. . . .*

It was sheer will and nothing else that finally brought my pulse back down. I breathed in my through my nose, out between my teeth. This was Thurmond—the Infirmary. I recognized the lemon-scented terror of it and the sounds of kids crying nearby, the rattling of carts, heavy booted footsteps, and still some part of it felt unreal to me, even as the last moments at the Ranch slammed back into me. The flash drive—my boots were still on, they hadn't taken them, thank God. I tried twisting my foot around the restraints, but I couldn't feel it against my ankle bone. I flexed and then pointed my toes, nearly crying in relief when I felt the sharp plastic corners under my heel. It must have slipped down.

You came here for a reason, I reminded myself. *The others need you to finish this. You have to finish this.*

I squeezed my eyes shut, trying to block out the images that poured in from the darkest corner of my imagination. *They wouldn't have brought you here if they were just going to kill you.* I saw the image of Ashley's pale, gray face. The way her stiff hand had fallen onto the ground, dangling into the ditch they would lower her into. Maybe this was about having an official record of where my body was buried.

And suddenly, it didn't matter what I was and what I had been through. I was ten years old all over again, waiting in terrible silence for someone to wake me back up from the nightmare I'd let myself get caught in. *Help me,* I thought, *someone help me—* Gem.

I squeezed my eyes shut against the familiar voice whispering in my ear, choked again, this time by grief. *Don't let me screw it up, please, help me,* I thought. I was alone here, I knew I would be, and somehow I had misjudged how terrifying it would be. I reached for the image of Cole's face and held it at the forefront of my mind. He wouldn't be afraid. He wouldn't leave me.

You have to walk out of here. I felt the words settle in my mind. *Not just for them, but for yourself. You have to walk out of here on your own two feet.*

The door cracked open, and the sounds from the rest of the building came flooding in. An old man's face appeared there, gray hair ringing his head like a cluster of old dust. His eyes narrowed behind his glasses, but I didn't recognize him, not until he stepped inside and I sucked in a lungful of his terrible scent— alcohol and lemon soap. Dr. Freemont, still haunting the halls of this place.

The man let out a noise of surprise. "She's awake."

Another face appeared directly behind his, a woman in gray scrubs, who was quickly pushed aside to allow two PSFs in the room. Their black uniforms were pristine, from their polished boots to the stitched red Ψ on their chests. I saw their faces and it was like living inside of a memory. The moment took on an unreal quality.

Focus.

One last person entered the room. He was middle-aged, with sandy hair that turned silver under the lights. His uniform was different than that of the soldiers, a black button-down with matching slacks. I knew this uniform, but I'd only seen it once up close. *Camp controller.* One of the men and women who worked in the Control Tower, monitoring the cameras, keeping the day's schedule.

"Ah, there you are," Dr. Freemont began. "I was just about to begin the test."

The man—his shirt was embroidered with the name O'Ryan—stepped up, sweeping a hand forward, a clear *go ahead.*

I set my jaw, fingers curling into fists. I knew better than to ask what was happening, but I read the situation quickly enough to put together a guess. The old man pulled a small, handheld White Noise machine out of his pocket and adjusted a dial on it.

All the times I'd envisioned this plan playing out, I had seen myself influencing the camp controllers and PSFs one at a time, planting the suggestion that I was really a Green, working my way through each of them as our paths crossed. But I saw now, as the doctor's finger pressed down on the device's largest button, that I didn't have to influence dozens—just four.

"This is Green," Dr. Freemont said.

The sound that came out of the device was softer than I expected, as if I was hearing it from several floors above me. The shrill pitch and blended mess of beeping and buzzing made the hair on the back of my neck stand up and my stomach tighten, but it was nothing compared to the White Noise they used over the camp's loudspeakers.

They're seeing what frequency I can hear, I thought, *shit—*

Our brains translated sounds differently than a normal human mind; if the adults in the room heard the sound, it was nothing more than a buzzing fly around their ears. There was a spectrum of pitches that affected us, each of them specially tuned to sing for each different color. I'd learned about it when Cate and the League had managed to embed the regular White Noise with tones meant for Oranges and Reds, hoping to root out those of us who might have been in hiding or posing as a different color. That sound, the thread of mind-blistering crashes and bangs, had drilled through me and left me unconscious.

I strained against the Velcro cuffs, letting my eyes bulge, letting my whole body shake and thrash, as if the sound were a knife driving repeatedly into my chest. The sounds that escaped the muzzle were low, animal moans.

O'Ryan held up a hand and the faint noise switched off. He stepped up closer to the bed, peering down at my face. I had to force my hatred into fear.

"Successful reaction," Dr. Freemont said. "Should I—"

The camp controller's face was impassive, though I saw his lip curl up in assessment. I got a good look at him now; his wide shoulders filled out his shirt and, standing over me, he seemed ten feet tall. There was something in his stance that reminded me of a knife's blade. He stood rigidly proud, his eyes cutting through every layer of control I'd built up, and I realized, a second too late, that this wasn't a normal camp controller. This was *the* camp controller.

And I was looking him in the eye.

I tore my gaze away, but the damage had been done. I'd shown too much will. He'd read it as a challenge. "Set it to Orange."

There was a lot I could withstand now, but I knew a hit of that White Noise would be like stepping in front of a speeding train. O'Ryan stood over me, staring at my face. He thought he was in control here, didn't he? That if he looked at me close enough, he'd detect me using my abilities—that if the muzzle kept me from speaking, I couldn't issue a command.

I didn't need to look at him. I didn't need to speak to him. And, in the end, I only needed to affect one person.

Dr. Freemont's mind was a swamp of faceless children and computer screens. I planted the images there in the middle of them all, a neat, tidy package based on what I could remember from my first processing through the camp, and pulled back immediately.

I pushed the image of him fiddling with the dial, pulling it back toward his chest as he turned the dial back to its original setting. He was angled away from the PSFs at the door. O'Ryan was looking at me, so smug and sure of himself, that he allowed himself a knowing smirk. I lowered my lashes, glad for the first time that there was a muzzle to keep me from returning it.

"Begin," he said.

It was easy enough to float the command to Dr. Freemont to push the button—I'd seen him do it moments ago, and could choreograph the small movement the exact way the doctor had done before. The White Noise trickled out again, running along my skin like an electric current. I let my eyes flick around, but it was harder to mime fear now. A swell of cool, careful control settled my mind.

O'Ryan looked back over his shoulder. "Turn it on."

It is on, I thought.

"It is on," Dr. Freemont said. I froze at the dull tone of his voice, risking a glance toward O'Ryan for his reaction.

The camp controller's lip pulled back. "I'm ordering one of the testing machines back from New York."

New York? Had they moved all of the big testing machines and scanners out already?

I forced the words into the doctor's mouth. *That could take weeks.*

"That could take weeks," Dr. Freemont said.

This is foolproof.

"This is foolproof."

O'Ryan's gaze was searing as it moved between the old man and me. I let my control expand, snaring the camp controller's mind. I skimmed the surface memories, the damp mornings, fog, streams of children in uniforms, but it took a forceful shove to break past them, to plant the idea. *This girl is Green. She was mistakenly identified as Orange.*

I pulled back, slipping out of both of their minds, shifting my gaze to the tiled floor.

"Fine. The Orange classification was an error." O'Ryan turned to one of the PSFs. "Get one of the Green uniforms and shoes out of the boxes. Her PID is three-two-eight-five."

"What size, sir?"

"Does it matter?" O'Ryan barked. "Go."

The doctor blinked. "Will she not stay here, then? I imagine it might be . . . disruptive to the other children if they saw her."

"One night is enough." He turned to look at me as he added, "I want them all to understand, no matter how far they run, they'll always be found. They'll always be brought back."

A whole night. Jesus—the drugs they'd given me had knocked me sideways hard enough to lose a full day. The military would have flown us back east to West Virginia—they wouldn't have risked ground transportation. Meaning . . . that would make it . . . the twenty-fifth of February. Shit. Three days to figure this out.

The doctor didn't uncuff me or remove the muzzle until the PSF was back, dropping the thin, cotton uniform and laceless white slip-on sneakers on the examination table.

"Change," O'Ryan ordered, tossing them onto my chest. "*Move.*"

The smell of black permanent marker flooded my nose as I picked them up, working my sore jaw back and forth. If it was a muscle or a joint, it hurt, but I didn't want to give them the satisfaction of limping as I stood up and moved to the corner of the room to begin stripping, aware of their eyes on my back the entire time. I began with my shoes, unlacing them quickly, tilting the right one back to pluck the black flash drive out of it. My hands felt swollen and clumsy as I slid it into my new shoe, pretending to adjust the cloth tongue. They were two sizes too big, at least, but it didn't matter to anyone watching me. My face burned with hatred as I faced the wall and stripped out of my clothes. The uniform slid over my freezing skin like the dull side of a blade. When I was finished, I turned back and kept my head bowed.

The PSF who'd gone to get the uniform, Laybrook, stepped up and gripped my arm.

"Cabin twenty-seven," O'Ryan said, the corner of his mouth twisting up in a mocking smile. "We kept your bed open for you, knowing we'd see you again. I'm sure you remember the way."

O'Ryan gave a small signal with his hand and I was hauled, literally pulled, out of the door and into the hall. Laybrook wrenched my arm again as we turned into the nearest stairwell. God, I could almost see it—all of those little kids trailing up the other direction, not knowing what was waiting for them. I saw myself in my pajamas, Sam in her coat.

The pace was impossible to keep up with. I slipped, nearly

falling onto my knees as we reached the first landing. Laybrook's expression darkened with irritation as he gripped the back of my shirt and neck, bringing me back up onto my feet.

This is how it's going to be, I thought, *with all of them. I got out, I got out and beat their system—* And now what? They had to prove to me it would never happen again? That I was just as small and powerless at seventeen as I was at ten? They wanted me to stay in that shadowy corner I'd let myself be backed into, fold myself up small, cut myself off from the others. They wanted to take everything away again, strip me down to nothing.

I snapped.

I glanced back up the steps we'd come down and shifted my gaze toward the next set, until it finally landed on the black camera watching overhead. Once we were out of its line of sight, turning the corner to start down the next flight of stairs, I bent my arm, threw my elbow up into Laybrook's throat, and held it there. I glared up through the inches that separated his stunned face from mine, and slammed into his mind. His rifle clattered against the wall, the strap sliding from his shoulder. The man had decades on me, and at least a hundred pounds, but in the end it didn't matter. We'd be going at my pace from this point on.

O'Ryan had been right about one thing, at least—I did remember the way back to Cabin 27. My fear remembered it, too, and I had to fight to keep myself from swaying as the camp spread open in front of me.

It was just that some things had changed in the months I'd been gone.

The lower level of the Infirmary had been little more than a hallway of beds and curtains, but all of those were gone now, replaced by stacked, unlabeled boxes. As we moved across the tile, the plastic in my shoe clicking with each stride, I saw PSFs bringing more up from the back rooms and offices. Their curious gazes followed us all the way outside into the pouring rain.

Gunmetal-gray skies always drew out the vibrant green of the grass and the trees surrounding the fence. The curtain of water falling around us in sheets didn't dampen the effect in the slightest, nor did it drive away the earthy smell that immediately sent my senses into an overload of visceral memory. I bit my lip and shook my head. *It's different now,* I reminded myself. *You're in control. You are getting out of here.* I tried to reach for the old, familiar numb nothing I had lived inside while in this camp, but couldn't find it.

The soggy ground shifted under my feet as I found the muddy path. I looked down, and my eyes caught on the sight of the white slip-ons on my feet. The number 3285 stared back, splattered with filthy water and wilted grass.

I took a steadying breath and forced myself forward. *You're here for a purpose. You are going to get out of here.* This was another Op. I could be hard and certain and fight here, too. There was no falling apart now. No giving into fear. Not if I was going to save the others.

Rings of cabins curved in front of me, looking darker and smaller than I remembered. I saw holes in the roofs patched over with sheets of warped plastic. The wood paneling along the sides was warping, peeling as the remnants of the last snowstorm dripped down from the roofs. The cold ran like needles over my skin, pinching and stabbing until I finally gave in and started to shiver.

The red brick Control Tower at the center of the cabins had

darkened under the rain's touch, but there were still multiple PSFs out on the upper ledge, their guns following the paths of each line of drenched kids trudging up the paths from the Garden. Their Blue uniforms clung to their shoulders, the hollows of their stomachs.

Most of the kids kept their heads down as they diverted around us, but I caught a few curious glances, all lightning-fast, under the watchful eye of their PSF escort. No—not PSF—

I spun on my heel, watching as the soldiers at the end of the line marched on, backs straight, movements choreographed and stiff. They wore crimson vests over their black fatigues.

I guided Laybrook off the path with the slightest bit of pressure on his arm, letting the next group pass by us to reach their cabins. Again, walking alongside them at the front and back of the two straight rows were the soldiers in crimson vests. No guns. No weapons of any kind. A warning trill sounded in my mind as the last group came toward us, and terrible suspicion solidified into shock.

The red vests were keeping track of the kids, devoid of any emotion. They were young, faces still round and full. My age maybe, or a few years older. They were inserted in the places where the dwindling PSF force should have been.

They were Reds.

TWENTY-FOUR

THERE WAS AN HOUR BETWEEN THE LAST WORK SHIFT, whether it was in the Garden, the Factory, or cleaning in the Mess Hall or Wash Rooms, and when they served dinner. The kids would be returned to their cabins, and each group was allotted a specific time to walk the distance between the buildings. It was a song that only worked if the camp hit each note exactly right. The kids were streams of blue and green, so deeply entrenched in playing their parts that they never stepped out, not even once, to dare interrupt the pace.

Reds. God, the others had no idea. I had no way of warning them, and the closer I came to Cabin 27, the more it felt like this was already over.

Laybrook followed me up to the cabin, unlocking the door and holding it open for me with a forced politeness. I stepped inside, my eyes meeting his pale ones for the last time. I plugged memories in over the truth, dropped in scenes of him roughing me up, dragging me around, and made him think he was as tough as he wanted to be. The door shut automatically as he turned and walked back into the rain.

467

I knew, by the silence that had greeted me when the door opened, that the girls weren't back yet. They would have switched, just recently, from Factory to Garden duty, and likely were still trudging back through the mud, or waiting at the low fence for permission to move.

The cabin—my cabin—was small enough to take in with a single turn. Brown upon brown, broken up only by the yellowing white sheets on the bunk bed. The smell of mildew mixed with a natural body odor, covering even the bland hint of sawdust from the wood. Patches of silver light streamed in through the cracks in the paneling. The wind whispered through the cabin, drawing me around the first few sets of bunks, toward the back wall.

I stared at my bunk, a familiar hopeless despair crashing over me. I bit my lip again to keep from crying.

Rain had come in through the nearby wall, slanting in to dampen the mattress. I moved toward it like I was underwater, barely feeling it as I sat down. My breath caught in my throat and stayed there as I looked up at the bottom of Sam's mattress. My fingers traced the shapes I had peeled off at night when I couldn't sleep.

You left them here. A hand rose up, pressing against my chest, making sure my heart was still beating. *You left them here, to live in this hell.*

"Stop," I whispered. *"Stop."*

There was no way I could ever make up for it. There was no way to go back and change the decision I made that night to swallow Cate's pills. The only way out was forward.

I am going to walk out of here. I am going to take every single one of them with me.

The door to the cabin popped open. They were silent as they came in, lining the narrow space between the nearby bunks.

The PSF came in, counting them off. Then, with a faint smirk, she turned and added me to the tally. The others knew better than to move before the uniform left and locked the door behind her, but nothing could have surprised me more than seeing Sam whirl around, something like hope on her face.

Her honey-blond hair had been hastily braided back, and her face was streaked with black dirt. She looked tired, pushed past the point of exhaustion; but her stance, the hands on her hips, the expectant tilt of her head—that was Sam. That was all Sam.

"Oh my God." Ellie, one of the older girls. She and Ashley had always tried the hardest to take care of the younger girls. Without her best friend standing shoulder to shoulder with her, I barely recognized her. There was a beat of stillness and then she was rushing toward me, climbing over the bunks that separated us. A good thing, too. I'm not sure I could have moved if I'd wanted to. How was it possible to be bursting with happiness at the sight of them, and still terrified about what they'd think?

"Oh my God." Those three words over and over again. Ellie crouched down in front of me, her green shirt splattered with rain. She took my face between her freezing hands, a light touch that turned into a fierce grip once she seemed to accept I was real. "Ruby?"

"I'm back," I choked out.

The other girls bottlenecked the path between the bunks, and some, Sam included, simply crawled over the mattresses and frames that stood between them and me. Vanessa, Macey, Rachel, all of them, reaching out, touching my face, the hands that were limp in my lap. Not angry. Not accusing. Not afraid.

Don't cry, I told myself, smiling even as my eyes burned behind my lashes.

"They said that you died," Ellie said, still kneeling in front of me. "That it was IAAN. What happened? They took you away that night, and you never came back—"

"I got out," I told them. "One of the nurses planned the whole thing. I met other kids like us and . . . we hid." The abbreviated truth would have to do—for now. I'd never bothered to ask Cate if the cameras could record sound in addition to video, but the sight of them gathered around me would be dangerous enough. We weren't supposed to touch each other.

"But they found you?" This from Vanessa, dark eyes still wide with disbelief. "Do you know if they took Ashley, too? Have you heard anything about her?"

"What happened?" I asked, careful to keep my tone measured.

"They pulled her in to work in the Kitchen . . . maybe two months ago?" Ellie said. That wasn't anything out of the ordinary. If there were specific, small tasks, or if they needed an additional hand somewhere like the Kitchen or the Laundry, they would pull from the older Green kids, thinking they were trustworthy, I guess. "That night, they wouldn't let us eat in the Mess. And then she just didn't come back. Do you know if someone got her out?"

They were all staring at me, and the hope in their eyes was unbearable. What would the truth do to them? I don't know if it was kindness or cowardice that made me say, "I don't know."

"What was it like?" one of them asked. "Outside?"

A faint laugh escaped my lips as I looked up. "Strange and so . . . *loud.* Terrifying, violent . . . but open, wide open and beautiful." I looked up into each of their faces, starving, desperate for something outside of the fence. "Almost ready."

"For what?" Ellie asked.

"For us."

After we ate the bread and tasteless soup they served in the Mess Hall for dinner, we made our way back to the cabin again, a Red shadowing our every step, arms swinging at his side. They'd shaved his hair down to dark fuzz beneath his uniform cap, let his tan skin go sallow. There was nothing in his eyes, not a trace of emotion in his face. During dinner, I'd had to look away to keep my heart steady and caught Sam doing the same. He'd stopped behind her at one point. She'd dropped her spoon into her bowl and stopped pretending she wanted to eat. But afterwards, I saw her look at his back, eyes devouring his shape . . . and I wondered.

Up until that moment, I had managed to clear my thoughts of what was happening to the others. What they were doing. If they were safe. Whether or not they were actually coming. I couldn't let it distract me from what needed to happen here. Just thinking of Liam out there alone, trying to find his parents to tell them what had happened . . .

As we walked, I shifted my thoughts to sweet, small memories instead. Laughter at dinner. Firelight on Zu's smiling face. Jude falling over himself and Nico when one of their handmade toy cars worked. The way Pat and Tommy had worshipped the ground Vida walked on. Seeing Chubs in North Carolina for the first time in months, and knowing he was alive. Cole's easy smile as he reached over and smoothed down my hair. Liam. Liam in the driver's seat, singing along. Liam kissing me in the dark.

I am going to walk out of here.

I am going to live.

Sam was tracking me now out of the corner of her eye; the skin tightened around her lips, pulling their corners down. There was still a hooked scar, a faint pink line curving to connect the chapped upper lip to her nose; but that, like the rest of her, had faded. And when I turned to meet her gaze, she only looked away.

I knew Sam, though. A year apart, three years since I'd blanked out every memory she had of me, and I still could read her face like it was my old, favorite book. She got braver as time went on, less uncertain about my presence. The thoughts were working behind her light-colored eyes, and she watched me from the moment the morning alarm went off at 5:00 A.M., through the entire ten minutes we were allotted to eat oatmeal in the Mess Hall, and then next to me, as we made our way through the damp, freezing morning air to begin the day's work.

I'd noticed her slight limp the night before as we moved to and from the Mess Hall, but her right leg was clearly stiffer that morning, and the movement was more pronounced.

"What happened?" I whispered, watching her catch herself on the edge of her bunk. The moment she slid over the side of her bed and down to the ground, her ankle collapsed under her. I leaned over to help her make up her bed, since no one had bothered to give me sheets to use on mine, and tried to see what had caused it.

In their typical casual cruelty, the PSF in the Infirmary had given me a summer uniform set, shorts and a shirt, but the others wore their winter ones—long-sleeved shirts and pants. The loose fabric hid whatever was it was that was bothering her.

"Snake bite," Vanessa answered as Sam pushed past me to line up. "Don't ask. She won't talk about it."

The Garden was all the way at the far end of the camp, opposite the entry gate. The electrified fence sang to you when you got this close to it; when I was younger, I used to imagine that the hum came from families of bugs that lived in the trees surrounding us. I don't know why that made it feel more bearable.

Our Red escort was the same boy we'd had the night before: hair shaved, eyes dark and almond-shaped. Beside me Sam cringed, her hands balled up tight at her sides, and limped along.

They took the life out of them, I thought, stepping through the low white fence and taking the small plastic shovel that was handed to me. I knew so little about how they had been—what had Clancy called it? Reprogrammed? Reconditioned? Mason had been shattered by what they'd done to his mind. Maybe they'd made a mistake with him, or he hadn't been strong enough to take what they'd dealt him.

How many Reds were involved in Project Jamboree? Was it possible that—no. *Stop it,* I ordered myself, *think about anything else but that.*

A PSF was passing out heavy work coats, which they allowed us to have while we were out here. He looked down at the number across my chest and skipped me completely. The ten-year-old me would have accepted the punishment, mind fixed on the cruel smile the soldier offered in exchange instead. But I didn't have to accept anything now. His mind was like glass, and all I had to do was pass through it like a ray of light. I shuffled back, taking the coat from him.

I followed my line down to the mounds of earth they'd turned up yesterday and knelt down. The dirt gave way under the soft-est touch, packing beneath my nails as I used the shovel to ease the buried potatoes up from the ground. I brushed the dark dirt away.

The shade of burnt skin.

I pressed the back of my hand against my mouth, instinctively looking up at the three red vests standing near the entrance. They stoically watched as each cabin of kids filed in and accepted their assignments.

Are they the same Reds?

My fingers flexed, tightening around the shovel. I glanced sideways, to my right. Sam was only miming work, smoothing dirt away. Still, after all this time, they forced us into alphabetical order.

"How long have they been here?" I asked in a low voice. "The Reds?"

At first, I wasn't sure she'd heard me. I pulled the next potato up and dropped into the plastic tub between us.

"Three months, maybe," was the reply, just as quiet. "I'm not sure."

I sagged slightly, blowing out a soft sigh. They weren't Sawtooth Reds. But that meant more camps, more reconditioning facilities.

"Don't you . . . don't you recognize some of them?" Sam whis-pered, leaning over as if to help me. "A few of them used to be here."

I couldn't risk another glance back to confirm this; I'm not sure I would have been able to, anyway. The Reds at Thurmond had always lived in my memory with shadowed faces. All of the dangerous ones did. But I knew for certain that I didn't recognize the Red that Sam kept searching for; every time she found him, she shuddered and oriented herself away from his gaze. But, like clockwork, she'd look up at him again.

"Do you know him?" I whispered.

She hesitated so long, I didn't think she would answer. But finally she nodded.

"From before? *Before*-before?"

Sam swallowed hard, then nodded again.

Sympathy swept through me, leaving me at a loss for what to say. I couldn't imagine. I couldn't begin to imagine what this felt like.

A PSF passed behind us, whistling without a tune, making his way up the rows between each patch of vegetation. The Garden was enormous, at least half a mile long, and required the most supervision. The handheld White Noise machine clattered against his supply belt, swaying in time to his slow steps.

I risked another glance up, realizing why my skin had crawled the moment he came into sight. This was one of the PSFs who oversaw work in the Factory—the one who liked to press himself up against the girls, hassle them to get them flustered, and then punish them for reacting in any small way. It hadn't made sense then what he was doing to me, to Sam, to the other girls, and we'd just stood there and taken it silently. Now, though—now I had a pretty good sense of what he'd really been doing, and it lit my fury. He strolled by us and Sam stiffened. I wondered if she could smell him, too—a salty, sharp tang of vinegar, mixed with cigarette smoke and aftershave.

I didn't relax until he was a good ten girls away from us.

"Ruby," Sam whispered, earning admonishing glances from the girls working the row across from us. "Something happened . . . after you left, I realized something was wrong. With me. My head."

My sight narrowed to the hole in front of me. "Nothing's wrong with you."

"I missed you," she said. "So much. But I barely know you . . . and then I get these senses, these images. They come like dreams."

I shook my head, fighting to keep my pulse steady. *Don't you dare. You can't. If anyone catches on . . . if she slips up . . .*

"You're different," Sam finished. "Aren't you? You've always been—"

Sam was ripped away, hauled back and away from my side. I whirled around. The PSF from before was back, his hand knotted in Sam's long ponytail.

"You know the rules," he snarled. "We work silently or we don't work at all."

For the first time, I saw what this past year had done to my friend. The old Sam, the one who had stood up for me countless times, would have spat back an insult, or tried to twist out of his grasp. Struggled, in some small way.

Now her dirt-stained hands went up to protect herself, without a beat of hesitation. A practiced movement. Her whole body sagged as he shoved her forward, sending her sprawling into the mud. Fury whipped through me. And then it wasn't enough for me that I would kill this man, eventually. I wanted to humiliate him.

I pushed a single image into his mind, an urge that was easy enough to suggest.

The front of his black camo pants darkened, the stain spreading down his leg. I jumped back in overblown disgust, catching the attention of another PSF just across the row of vegetation. He came back to himself with a shudder—and with slow, dawning horror, looked down.

"Shit—*shit*—"

"Tildon," the PSF who'd been watching called out, "Status?"

"*Shit*—" The man's face burned pink as he covered himself, seemingly torn between staying as he was or excusing himself to take care of the situation. Kids were sneaking glances at him, at each other. He seemed to realize it too, and rose on unsteady feet. I had just enough of a grip left on his mind to slide my right leg out to the side, and listen as his own leg mirrored the response and sent him crashing to his knees just before he reached the gate. The PSF—Tildon—he'd think he had tripped over someone. The image was the last one I planted before gently peeling back from his mind, refusing to watch as he walked briskly in the direction of the Control Tower.

Too much, I chastised myself—next time I'd have to go for something subtler. But this one, this one I wouldn't regret, no matter what. I rose unsteadily onto my feet to help Sam back onto hers, guiding her back over to our places. She was shaking, staring at me as if she knew what had really happened.

"Fix it," she whispered, "whatever you did to me. Please. I need to know."

I couldn't bring myself to look at her, knowing what sort of expression I'd see there. It had been like this with Liam, hadn't it? All of the feelings, none of the memories—that's what I'd left her with. No wonder she had seemed so confused and hostile after I'd wiped her memory. It must have been overwhelming. If she'd felt half as close to me as I did to her, the strange sense that something was wrong must have torn at her each day.

I met her pleading eyes with a plea of my own. And just like always, she understood. A spark of the old Sam surfaced. Her eyebrows drew together and she pursed her lips. This was the silent language we'd developed over the years.

The PSF who'd been gazing in our direction, hand shading his eyes to make out Tildon's distant form growing smaller and smaller, stepped over the mounds into our row. I tensed, waiting to feel his shadow cast over me. *Try it,* I thought, *try it with any of these kids, and see where it gets you.*

Instead he walked away, continuing the watch that Tildon had been forced to abandon. I held my breath and slid my hand over, under the loose dirt, to grip Sam's.

We worked through the morning into the afternoon, with only a small break to eat the apples and sandwiches they distributed for lunch. I devoured mine with dirt-stained hands, watching the changing colors of the sky.

And that night, as I lay in the bunk beneath her, I slipped into Sam's mind as soft as a breeze.

I thought of that morning I'd stepped up beside her in the Infirmary, the way her coat's tag had flipped up against her neck. The exact moment I'd taken her memories of me by mistake, the heaviness in my chest still unbearable as the moment played through.

The images were in her mind now, too, perfectly matched with mine. I was swept along with them, falling through the white, fluttering images around me. Her memories were almost too bright to watch, the wisps too thin to grasp. But I knew what I was looking for when I saw it. The black knot buried deep beneath the others. I reached out, touching it, increasing the pressure until it unraveled.

If each memory that drifted up were a star, I was standing at the center of a galaxy. Beneath vast constellations of lost smiles and quiet laughter. Whole, endless days of gray and brown and black that we'd spent with only each other to hold on to.

I'd assumed she'd been asleep the whole time; her mind had been so calm and still under my touch. But a pale arm came down over the side of the bunk, stretching down toward me. The familiar gesture stole the air from my chest, and I had to press my lips together to keep back the tears that came dangerously close to the surface. I reached up, meeting her halfway, locking my fingers around hers. A secret. A promise.

TWENTY-FIVE

MY PLAN CAME TO ME IN PIECES OVER THE NEXT TWO days. I assembled it hastily while I worked in the Garden, ignoring the blisters on the palm of my hand, and in those minutes before I passed out in exhausted sleep each night. Knowing that it would be over soon, in a matter of hours, made me feel reckless in a way I hadn't expected. Somehow it was too much time, and yet still not enough; I couldn't shake the fear that the others had changed their timing from the original plan that Cole, Nico and I had outlined. I'd told them March first, but what if it was impossible to get here in time?

What if they're not coming at all?

I shoved the thought away before it could plant itself too deeply in my heart.

At six o'clock that evening, I lay in my bunk, hands folded on my stomach. Sam's mattress shifted as she rolled onto her side, distorting the shapes I had made in the plastic. I reached up, taking a small piece of the curling plastic cover between my broken fingernails. Tugging gently, I pulled the strip off, carefully working it around, around, until it formed an even circle.

"—so the girl, after the robbers decided to take her away, she managed to steal one of their daggers and cut the rope off her hands . . ." Rachel was leading the story today, filling in the hour before we were called to dinner. Tonight, she wove the tale of yet another nameless girl, in yet another perilous situation. I closed my eyes, a faint smile on my lips. The stories hadn't gotten any better or any more original—they all followed the same plot: girl is wronged, girl struggles, girl escapes. The ultimate fantasy at Thurmond.

Physical exhaustion kept me still. As much as I had trained at the Ranch, these hours of endless work with no break, on limited food and water, were designed to drain us of the energy we'd need to muster to escape or push back. My body was a mess of quivering muscles, but I felt oddly calm, even though I knew what would happen if I made one misstep, or they figured out what I was before I could complete what I'd come here to do.

I have to walk out of here.

"Ruby?" Ellie called from her bunk at the center of the room. "It's your turn."

I shifted onto my elbows, scooting back to swing my legs off the cramped bunk. I worked out the kinks in my lower back as I thought about how I was going to finish this story. "The girl . . ." When I was younger, I would have passed it on to Sam after adding only a few words, but I could use this. I wasn't sure they would understand, but I hoped some part of them would recognize the warning when the time came.

"The girl cut herself loose from the rope and knocked the bandit off the horse in front of her. She took the reins and turned the horse around the road, heading back in the direction they had come from—back toward the castle."

There was a murmur at that. Vanessa had spent the better part of fifteen minutes describing the battle raging outside of its walls. It had provided the distraction the bandits needed to take the girl in the first place.

"She used the darkness," I explained. "She left her horse in the nearby forest and crept toward a passage she knew was hidden in the far stone wall. The fighting had stopped once the knights in black had taken the castle. They locked the white knights out, and they were unable to help the families trapped inside. But no one noticed a small, plain girl coming through the back door. She looked like a helpless servant girl, bringing a basket of food into the kitchen. For days, she stayed in the castle, watching. Waiting for the right moment. And then it came. She slipped back outside and made her way through the shadows of night, unlocking the gate for the white knights to come pouring back in."

"Why would she come back? Why didn't she just escape— hide?" Sam asked, her voice small. I blew out a soft breath, glad that, if nothing else, she understood.

"Because," I said finally, "in the end, she couldn't leave her family behind."

The girls shifted silently in their bunks, looking at each other as if wondering the same thing. No one asked the question—I don't know how many of them actually dared to hope. But three short minutes later, the electronic lock on the cabin's door popped open. The door swung in and a PSF stepped inside.

"Line up," she barked.

We hastily assembled in alphabetical order, staring straight ahead as she counted us off. She motioned for the girls at the front of the line to start moving.

I couldn't help myself. A step before we reached the door, I glanced back behind me. No matter what happened, it would be the last time I ever saw Cabin 27.

But when we walked through the door of the Mess Hall that evening, I already had to revisit a key component of my plan. Because, set up against the wall opposite of us, to the left of the window where we lined up to receive our food, was a large white screen. O'Ryan stood in front of it, his arms crossed over his chest, the blue light from a digital projector washing over him. Sam threw a nervous look my way as our PSF escort pushed her toward our table.

The last time we'd seen them use this screen had been our first week here. The camp controllers had set up the projector to scroll through the list of camp rules. *No talking during work duties. No talking after lights out. Do not speak to a Psi Special Forces officer unless spoken to first.* On and on and on.

Rather than have us line up to get food, the PSFs signaled for us to sit down and remain seated. The energy in the room was unsettling; I couldn't get a read on any of the camp controllers or PSFs.

"There have been some recent developments," O'Ryan said, his natural voice loud enough to carry through the building, "regarding your situation. Pay attention. You will only be shown this once."

The move, I thought. They were finally going to tell them about closing the camp.

O'Ryan stepped back as the lights were dimmed slightly. A computer was hooked up to the projector, giving us a glimpse of a desktop before the video window expanded and the PSF hit play.

The video wasn't about the move.

Next to me, Sam actually recoiled, her hand reaching for mine. I blinked in horrified disbelief.

It was a sight I hadn't seen in eight years: President Gray standing at a podium in front of the crest of the White House. He smiled so generously that dimples appeared on his cheeks. He waved—beckoned—to someone out of the camera's frame and, this time, the room full of reporters and cameras in front of him burst into sound as a pale-haired woman stepped up beside him, dressed in an immaculate suit. Dr. Lillian Gray.

"I've never been one to bury the lede, have I?" President Gray laughed. The First Lady disappeared into the fevered flashing of the cameras; the furious clicking of camera shutters would have put any machine gun to shame.

"It's good to be home in Washington again, to be back in this room with all of you, and with my beautiful wife. She's alive and well, contrary to wild speculation."

Nervous laughter in response.

"Her appearance here means that, at long last, I can tell you that our prayers have been answered and we now have a safe treatment that will rid American children of the psionic disorder forever," he said.

More rumblings from the press, more camera flashes. The kids around me had been trained too well to react outwardly beyond startled gasps of their own, or quick, covert glances at each other. The majority of them just sat there in disbelief.

"For years, Lillian has stayed out of the public eye so as to conduct research on this exact subject. It has remained confidential only to avoid interference from the former terrorist group, the Children's League, and other domestic enemies. While we are continuing to

seek out the cause of this tragic affliction, please rest assured that all children will be able to undergo this life-saving operation. Detailed information about the procedure is being distributed to you now."

A few reporters tried to leap in with questions, shouting Lillian's name; trying, I guess, to coax her to the microphone. Instead, she found a patch of carpet to stare at. Whoever had dolled her up had also managed to vacuum the life out of her.

"As you'll see from the footage and reports we've included, our own son, Clancy, was the first to receive this procedure."

A wave of dizziness passed over me as another form was walked out onto the stage beside them by a man in a dark suit. His head had been shaved and covered with a baseball hat decorated with the presidential seal. He kept his face turned down and out of sight, denying the cameras in front of him a shot until the president leaned away from the microphone and said something to him. His shoulders hunched, Clancy finally lifted his head. He reminded me of a horse on the ground, leg broken under it; never able to stand again, let alone run.

With all of the terrible things he'd done, and all of the terrible things I had imagined doing to him, never had this come to mind. I was shocked by the swell of emotions that rose in me, all of them too close, too wild for me to distinguish one from another. I felt sick.

He trembled, looking smaller by the moment as his parents kept their smiles plastered on their faces, giving the reporters what they wanted: a family portrait. How perfectly, I thought, have these people drawn Clancy into his own worst nightmare.

"You'll remember that he came out of the camp rehabilitation program several years ago. Unfortunately, like with any disease, there

are relapses; and this is one of the reasons why we have not felt comfortable releasing the children from these camps. We needed a more permanent solution, and we believe we have found it. There will be more information to come in regards to a timeline of when the procedure will start being performed, and a likely end date for the camp rehabilitation program. I ask you, knowing already how much you've sacrificed and suffered these long years, for more patience. For understanding. For your belief in the future we're about to enter— one that will see the reemergence of our prosperity and way of life. Thank you, and God bless the United States of America."

Before the first avalanche of questions could sweep up and knock him off his feet, President Gray hooked his arm around Lillian's shoulders, gave a friendly wave to the cameras, and guided her off the stage and out of the room before she could get a single word in.

The video ended, frozen on that last image. I felt trapped in that moment, too.

No, I thought. *Remember why you came here. Now. Do it now.*

Our PSF escort signaled for us to stand and begin re-forming our line to receive our meals, her face creased with impatience. The surprise video had put me off my original plan, but it was easy enough to pick up the pieces and reassemble them in working order. We were near the kitchen, shuffling forward, when I felt the eyes of the PSF on me.

I shoved Sam, knocking her to the ground. And if that wasn't enough to dry up every small sound around us, me shouting, "Shut up! Just—shut up!" to her did. My voice whipped through the silence, landing like a blow across her confused face.

Play along, I begged, flashing her a look. *Please.*

A small nod. She understood. I lifted my arm, as if to strike her, ignoring the way Vanessa tried to catch my wrist to prevent it. The hardest thing was not reacting to our PSF as she came toward me, crossing the distance between us in furious strides. This was more than enough to get me punished.

More than enough to get me ejected from dinner.

The girls around us kept their heads down, but their fear and confusion polluted the air around me as the woman caught me by the collar and hauled me away. O'Ryan and the other camp controllers disassembling the projector and screen didn't even look up at the scuffle.

I didn't have to suggest anything to the PSF to get her to drag me into the kitchen. The Blue kids scrubbing the pots and pans under blistering water jumped. Several that were sorting the ingredients for the next day's meals turned, momentarily distracted from their work. I searched the ceiling for the black cameras, counting them off as I went—two, three. One above the serving window; one near the large pantry; another over the long stainless-steel work table, where several of the kids were peeling the potatoes we'd only just pulled from the Garden.

The back of the Mess Hall faced the forest, providing maybe ten feet of walking space between the building and the fence. The cameras never recorded what happened there, but only pointed out into the woods. It was one of the "blind spots" we'd learned to be afraid of very quickly.

She pushed the back door open with her shoulder, and I had a second to react.

I yanked the PSF around, twisting her arm behind her to the point of snapping the bone. She let out a choked noise of surprise that cut off sharply as I entered her mind.

She unfastened her uniform, ripping off her boots, the black camo shirt and pants, the belt, the dark cap, and let them fall to the ground. I kicked off my tennis shoes, trying to match the frenzied pace I'd set in her mind. She took my uniform as I passed it to her, tugging it on with a look of blank obedience. Too calm. I floated the image of her as a young child, standing at the heart of the camp, soldiers moving around her, closing in. I only eased up when she started to cry.

The flash drive fell out of my shoe into the frostbitten grass and I quickly palmed it, squeezing it tight to reassure myself it was really there.

The swap had taken no more than two minutes. Two minutes too long, maybe. I couldn't tell—the PSFs were allowed to walk us into dark, unmonitored corners, rough us up a little bit before actually carrying out the punishment. If those missing moments had played that way to the camp controllers watching in the Control Tower, I'd be fine.

I walked the PSF toward the Garden, my breath fogging the air white with each sharp exhale. I kept my eyes on the thin chains hooked around one of the fence posts.

I wanted to say I was a good enough person not to feel some satisfaction as I sat the PSF down in the cold mud and locked her into place facing the fence, her back to the cameras on the nearby cabins and the soldiers patrolling the platform on the Tower. I wasn't. After watching so many kids left out for hours on end, simply for talking back or looking at them sideways on a bad day, I wanted at least one of them to know what it felt like. I wanted one of them to see what they had done to Sam each time they brought her out here.

It wasn't until I was walking back, passing the red vests posted along the path to the Control Tower and Mess Hall, that the first touch of nerves found me. Somehow, as I came closer to it, the brick tower had grown to be twice its original size; its crooked walls seemed to lean even more sharply up close.

This is an Op, I reminded myself. *This is no different than any other Op.* I would finish it and go home.

The PSF stationed next to the Control Tower's door peered at me through the darkness. Searchlights from the watch platform above crisscrossed in front of me, sweeping around the camp, into the dark pockets where other lights couldn't reach.

"Houghton—that you?"

I nodded, adjusting my cap down lower over my eyes, one hand straying to the rifle I'd slung over my shoulder.

"What's—" His mind unfurled in spirals of green and white and red. I needed him to tap his security badge against the black pad behind him, so he did. I needed him to step aside, so he did. He did everything I asked, even holding the door open for me as I stepped inside.

I crossed the threshold into the warm heart of the camp. The heat from the vents sank through the layers of borrowed clothes, straight to my skin and bones. As I looked down the hall, toward the stairs leading up to the platform two stories overhead, I don't know when I had ever felt so powerful in my life.

The door to my right opened, and a camp controller came out, holding a mug of coffee between his hands. The room behind him disappeared as the door slowly swung shut, but not before I saw the TV, the couches and chairs. His black button-down shirt wrinkled as he brought a hand up to yawn. The look he gave me was a friendly, *what can you do?* Half embarrassed, half unapologetic. Like the whole thing was one big joke.

I smiled, letting him pass by to get to the door propped open a

short ways down the hall. After a beat, I followed. The left half of
the building's lower level was little more than an enormous monitoring station. Screens large and small lined the far wall, each
showing a different angle of the camp. One was simply set to a satellite image of the weather; one showed a news channel on mute.

There were three rows of computers in total, though only half
of the seats seemed to be occupied. It looked as though they were
starting to pack this room up as well—working from left to right,
slowly removing the nonessential stations.

This is why they needed the Reds, I thought. The draft was up
for so many PSFs, and the ones that remained, along with the
newer recruits, were tasked with moving the files and supplies in
advance of the camp's closure.

Focus.

I stepped down to the second row, sliding into the seat. The
monitor flickered to life, waking up to reveal a basic desktop.
Blood pounded in my ears, but my hands were surprisingly steady
as I inserted the flash drive.

The folder opened and I transferred the program file over
onto the desktop; I thought I'd misread it at first, my mind half-
consumed with anxiety, but JUDE.EXE transferred quickly and
appeared on the screen's black background, next to the trash icon,
just below a black triangular outline labeled Security.

When it finished, I erased the original file from the flash
drive and dropped it to the floor, crushing the plastic shell under
the heel of my left boot. The clock on the lower right-hand corner
of the screen read 19:20.

I opened the COMMAND PROMPT window, typed START JUDE.EXE,
and the icon disappeared from the desktop.

Nothing else happened.

Shit, I thought, glancing at the small clock again. *Was that right?* *Why would*—

The blow cracked against the back of my skull so hard I was thrown halfway off the seat—caught, at the last second, by a hand that wrenched me back and slammed me against the table, hand at my throat, gun in my face.

"Here!" The PSF's face split into two. I blinked, trying to clear my vision as more shapes flooded in through the open door. "Here!"

I was pulled off the desk and shoved onto the floor, the pistol inches from my forehead, to make room for a camp controller to take my seat and begin typing. Someone had finally noticed something, then. It was over, but I'd done what I needed to.

I'd gotten this far.

I'd done this, at least.

The others in the room stood, alarmed, but backed off when O'Ryan's familiar voice barked, "Stay clear."

He typed something else, opened the COMMAND PROMPT window.

"What did you do?" he snarled.

I focused on his face, ignoring the warm trickle down the back of my neck. My line of sight solidified again and I shrugged, a smirk working its way onto my lips.

O'Ryan pushed the other soldier away, back into the ring of PSFs and camp controllers who stood nearby with their weapons drawn. My teeth clacked as he threw me back up against the wall, demanding, "What is your purpose here?"

I wiped the blood from the corner of my mouth and said nothing. There wasn't a damn thing he could do to me now that could make me feel afraid, or small, or helpless.

The camp controller turned back to another woman sitting nearby. "Key up the Calm Control."

"Group C is still in the Mess Hall," she said. "Should they be ordered back to their cabins first?"

"Key. It. Up."

She turned back to her screen and typed furiously, ending with a stroke of her pinky against the return key. "Wait—"

One by one, the monitors on the wall winked out, then each computer screen, the images blacking out with a sinister electronic hiss.

"Start the fail-safe protocol," he said.

"Sir?" she said, startled, but tried—she tried. "I'm locked out—"

"Of what?"

"*Everything!*"

"Me too—"

"—Same—"

I knew it was pointless, even as I got my feet under me, but I didn't want to admit it—I wasn't done, I wasn't ready for it to be over. The guns around me were a dozen different ways to die. I was boxed in on all sides by black uniforms. My ears rang and the ground rolled beneath my feet, but I let the invisible hands in my mind go streaming out to the minds around me, I sent them sailing in every direction like arrows seeking targets.

O'Ryan pulled his arm back and punched me in the face.

I couldn't get my hands up fast enough to block him. Couldn't get them down fast enough to catch me. I slammed into the ground, my vision bursting with static as my skull cracked against the tile. He leaned over me, unclipping a small device from his belt, holding it next to my right ear. I spit in his face and he only laughed, switching on the White Noise.

The world shattered around me. Hands seized my arms and hauled me up from the ground, dragging me through the tangle of legs and chairs. I couldn't see straight, couldn't clear my brain from the sounds polluting it. Every muscle in my body was seizing up, making me jerk, my feet thrash against the floor, and inside I was screaming, I was screaming *I'm not done,* but I couldn't hear myself think. The White Noise took me by the shoulders and shoved me down beneath the darkness, holding me there until I drowned.

TWENTY-SIX

THE SLAP WHIPPED ACROSS MY FACE, RIPPING AWAY THE shroud of unconsciousness. My vision blurred as my eyes flew open, squinting against the light. My mind felt swollen and tender, as wrung out as the rest of my body. I was half-conscious of the fact that my arms and legs were still spasming, the muscles twitching. The residual pain left me dumb and slow, and I couldn't remember why, how it had happened.

The noise blistering my mind shut off abruptly. Slowly, slowly, the room solidified around me. Tile floor. Four dark walls. One lamp. Two figures in black, moving in and out of the shadows, speaking in low tones. I heard a faint metallic clicking as one of them came closer. I smelled the mint as he smacked his gum.

"Little bitch . . ."

And just like that, memory slammed into me.

Tower.

Out.

Run.

I twisted, trying to pull out of the chair they'd put me in, but my hands and ankles were zip-tied to the metal frame. The jolt of fear-induced adrenaline cleared my mind just in time for O'Ryan to backhand me.

"Now that we have your attention . . ." he snarled, rising to his feet. Cold air bit into my shin, and I looked down to find that he'd rolled both of my pant legs up to the knee. They'd stripped the PSF uniform jacket off me, taking the knife, the weapons, anything I could have used to fight back. The boots, too, though I didn't understand why, not until O'Ryan motioned for the baton the PSF behind him carried.

The other man took that as his signal to hold up the handheld White Noise machine. I reared like a wild horse, trying to escape it, the way it blanked out my mind. *I can . . . I can do . . .* what could I do? What?

"Who sent you?" O'Ryan asked. "What was your purpose here?"

"To . . . to tell you . . ." The words didn't sound nearly as furious coming out of my mouth as they did in my head. The camp controller leaned forward, eyes narrowing into slits. "To go . . . fuck yourself."

The White Noise came on, louder, higher, a bullet that slammed through my temples. I couldn't keep the cry in. Sweat streamed down my back, my chest. It became a pattern—*on* agony, *off* pain, *on* agony, *off* pain. I couldn't catch my breath. I had to fight to keep the sweet nothing of unconsciousness away. I couldn't sleep. I couldn't leave this moment. They would kill me. I wouldn't be able to . . . I wouldn't be able to . . .

"Who sent you?"

"Fuck you!" I shouted right back in his face.

I braced myself as he swung his arm back, but it did nothing—*nothing*—to prepare me for the explosion of white-hot agony

495

that rocketed through me as his baton struck my exposed shin. I screamed, jerking against the restraints. I heard the crack, felt it inside of my head like it was my skull splitting apart. The PSF behind the camp controller only watched impassively as O'Ryan struck the broken bone again, smiling as I vomited onto the floor.

He swung again, stopping just short of my leg, a mocking smile on his face. He gave a silent wave of his hand toward the PSF, who reached for the White Noise device again.

"Not the Children's League," O'Ryan said over the hurricane of sound shredding my overloaded nerves. "It couldn't be them. So who?"

I heard the echo of it even when it switched off, white spots sparking behind my eyelids.

"Answer me, three-two-eight-five." He leaned over my face, thrusting the mangled flash drive in front of it. "What was on this? Tell me, and I promise that you'll live."

I want to live.

O'Ryan gripped my chin in his hand. "Three-two-eight-five, you should know I have no qualms about putting your kind down."

My kind.

Orange. I sucked in a sharp breath, licking the blood that had run from my nose over my busted lip. *Orange.*

He turned back toward the PSF, motioning him forward. My leg was demanding my attention, burning up my concentration, but my eyes slid over to the younger man and I reached . . . I reached . . .

O'Ryan held up the White Noise device in one hand, his service pistol in the other.

"Which would you prefer?"

I have to walk out of here.

496

The gun came up in his hand, sliding up my throat, under my chin. The White Noise device rubbed along the edge of my ear.

"It would give me no greater pleasure than to see your brains scrambled and leaking from your ears. Splattered against this floor. Tell me why you're here, three-two-eight-five, and I'll stop this. It'll all be over."

I want to live.

The building shook, throwing him back a step and rattling both the nearby table and the simple light fixture hanging over us. The pop and snarl of distant gunfire. A strange, sweet symphony of hope.

Footsteps pounded down the hall, heading out toward the exit. O'Ryan shoved himself away from me and went to the one-way window lining the wall, cupping his hands against it to try to see through it. He knocked against the mirrored surface, waiting. My line of sight was shrinking again, heading into black. The door in the corner, the one we'd come in through, had no handle. It could only be opened from the outside.

I closed my eyes, tightening my fists against a second wave of nausea.

I want to live.

I want to live.

I have to live.

"Ruby," I croaked out.

O'Ryan turned slowly. "What was that, three-two-eight-five? You ready to talk now?"

"My name," I said between clenched teeth, "is *Ruby.*"

I overturned my chair, knocking myself over onto the ground, and an aftershock of pain lanced up my leg. I played the scene out in my mind, and heard the reality on a half-second delay.

The PSF in the corner of the room lifted his gun and fired three times, missing O'Ryan on the first shot and shattering a section of the glass behind him, but hitting his mark on the second and third attempt. Chest. Head.

O'Ryan got one shot off, hitting the PSF's throat before slumping down against the wall beneath the one-way window.

I must have passed out—for a few seconds, maybe minutes. The Control Tower was eerily silent, and the only sound I heard as I surfaced back to reality was my own heart's slow, steady beat.

Move, I ordered myself. *Move, Ruby, move.*

My progress across the floor to O'Ryan's body was slow and agonizing. I needed the knife on his belt to cut the ties on my feet and hands, but it meant dragging the chair through the puddle of congealing blood beneath him. I sawed frantically, nicking my palms as I worked the knife blindly behind me.

I sucked in a harsh breath and looked down; the strange, tented skin on my shin made me gag, the sight reminding my body all over again that it was in pain. I hopped and hobbled over to the door, but I'd been right—there was no handle, and the hinges were on the other side.

I picked up O'Ryan's pistol and positioned myself against the opposite wall, using it as a brace for the gun's recoil. The reverberations raced up my arms and shoulders as the glass shards fell in waves. I switched the safety back on and went to work knocking the remaining pieces out of the window frame. Bracing my hands on the ledge, I dragged myself up and over it. The jagged teeth caught and tore at my arms and legs as I collapsed into the hallway.

The gun flew out of my hands. I reached for it through the

halo of glass around me. My fingers closed around the grip, just as the squeak of rubber against tile reached my ears.

I rolled onto my back, lifting my torso up just enough to aim at the dark figure running toward me. I fumbled with the safety, switching it off. The barrage of gunfire outside heated my blood, focusing me in the moment. I saw the black uniform and my finger curled around the trigger. I was getting out of here—I was getting out—

"Don't shoot!"

The power snapped off, throwing the building into darkness, but I'd seen his face as he pulled up his helmet. I thought at first, that I was seeing a ghost—and somehow, the reality was almost more impossible.

Liam.

"Stop doing that!" I cried, dropping my gun in terror. "I almost killed you!"

His face was so thin, practically worn down to the bone. He rushed toward me, dropping to his knees and sliding the last bit of distance between us. His hands were everywhere at once, and he was kissing me—lips, cheeks, forehead, wherever he could reach—and I was breathing him in, clinging to his sopping-wet shirt, unable to process the simple fact that he was here, that he was okay.

He shifted, jarring my leg, and I couldn't keep the scream from escaping my throat.

"Shit—shit, I'm sorry, Jesus—" Liam fumbled for the radio clipped to his jacket. "I found her—Dad, I need your help!"

It almost happened too quickly. Footsteps pounded against the ground behind me, and when Liam looked up, it was as if his helpless anger solidified, grew teeth. He reached for the gun in the holster strapped to his leg and a shudder ripped through me. I recognized the darkness in his expression; I'd seen all too many times in his brother. My hand flew out, slamming down on his, keeping his weapon in place.

Not Liam. Not now. Not ever. He wasn't a killer. Losing himself in a single moment would fracture him at his core. It would be a bone that healed crookedly inside him, until it changed his shape.

I saw the moment he came back to himself, the way his nostrils flared and his eyes cleared. When he looked up at the PSF running toward us again, this time he threw a hand out, sending the soldier crashing back into the nearest wall. Knocking him out cold.

He released a shuddering breath as he looked down at me again. Gently, with a level of care that seemed at odds with his actions only a second ago, he inspected the cuts on my arms and swore. I was trembling, but he must have mistaken the pain for cold because he ripped his jacket off and drew it around me, zipping it up my throat to trap the warmth inside. I bit back the sob welling up in my chest.

"Why did it have to be you?" he demanded. "Why did it have to be *you*?"

"Sorry," I whispered. For Cole, for making him come here, for everything, in case the darkness came back and I couldn't say it then. "Sorry, love you, love you so much . . ."

Liam kissed me again. "Can we get the hell out of here now?"

Another figure in black appeared at the head of the stairs, his shoulders heaving as he caught his breath. I scrambled for my gun, but Liam gripped my hand. "Over here—"

I saw a flash of black skin, a handsome, grizzled face as he rushed toward us. "Is she all right?"

"Not . . . really," Liam said, leaning back so his stepfather could see my leg. To me he insisted, "but you're going to be *fine*, you hear me?"

"Ouch, darlin'," Harry said, crouching down to examine it. "We're going to get you out of here, all right?"

"I have to walk out of . . . I have to walk out of here," I told him, mind fogging over with the pain. "I have to walk out of here. My own feet."

He exchanged a tense look with Liam.

"We need something to brace it with," Liam started, looking around.

"There's no time for that," Harry said. "They'll have medics at the meet point."

"I have to walk out." I didn't care how crazy it made me sound, they needed to understand. Cole would understand—would have understood. Cole was past-tense now. I squeezed my eyes shut.

When I opened them again, Harry reached over to a radio clipped onto his left shoulder. "This is Stewart. We have her. Proceeding to exit. ETA three minutes."

There was a flurry of static responses.

"Okay, darlin', I'm gonna get you up," Liam said, rising to his feet. "Put your arms around my shoulders, that's right, just like that." True to their word, once they had me up, they adjusted me so I could stand on my good leg.

I don't remember the hallway as it passed us, only how it felt each time my right leg swung forward. The frigid air on my skin as we stepped out into the night, the first touch of rain. I smelled smoke. The air hung heavy with it.

Up ahead, there was a river of green and blue moving out of the camp's front gate. The kids walked quickly, waved on by figures in black, their white bands stark against their sleeves. I was proud of how calm they were, the way they listened to the instructions they were given, even half-terrified or in shock. Thurmond, at least, had trained them to do that much.

"Reds—" I tried to say. I saw the warm glow of a fire at the far end of the camp, where the Factory was burning.

"They're secured," Harry said, giving the hand I'd hooked around his neck a gentle squeeze. "Put up one hell of a fight."

"Hurt?"

"Everyone's okay," he promised. He let out a sharp whistle, and the nearest figure in black turned around expectantly and ran toward us. She moved with a kind of animal grace, arms pumping at her side, boots spraying mud everywhere as she trampled through the puddles and thick, black mud.

I couldn't see her face through the curtain of rain, but I knew. *Vida*.

She would have crashed into us if Harry hadn't put out a strong hand to catch her.

"Careful!" Liam warned, drawing me closer to his side as Harry pulled back and untangled his grip. Vida filled in the spot he'd vacated, wrapping both arms around me.

"Holy shit," she said. "I'm going to *kill* you, I'm actually going to wring your little neck. I'm going to—to—"

"I'm going to sweep through the Mess one last time to check for stragglers," Harry said. "Mac, John, and I will bring up the rear."

"See you at the meet point," Liam said. "Ruby, let me carry you, please—"

"I have to walk." My throat ached, the words coming out in a croak. "Can you help me?"

He had already started to adjust his grip when Vida stopped him by taking the other half of my weight. "Whatever you want, as long it means getting you out of this goddamn nightmare factory. I mean, holy *shit*, boo."

Our progress was slow and awkward through the mud, but we staggered forward, drifting into the rush of kids moving out, heading toward the gate that was blown wide open.

It rained the day they brought us to Thurmond.

And it rained the day I walked out.

I knew I was in trouble when I couldn't shake the cold. Couldn't stop trembling. As we walked through the woods, following the kids ahead of us, the black uniforms with white bands at the front, my shivering made my muscles lock and limbs seize.

Vida glanced over at Liam, and our pace quickened.

"Hurts," I whispered.

"Do you want to stop? Rest?" Vida asked. "Is it your leg?"

I shook my head. "Everything."

To fill the silence, or to distract me, Liam tried to explain what had happened. "Mom gave me the number to contact Harry, to tell him . . . about . . . about Cole. She told me how to find him. They waited for me, and by then I knew I should have gone straight back, that I wanted to. But by the time we made it to the Ranch, you were long gone. Chubs was beside himself, so was Zu—all of them. Nico held it together for them until we got back."

"Fucking Clancy," Vida said. "Fucking crazy-ass Grays. They did this broadcast, him and his mom . . ."

"I saw," I said, not willing or particularly able to go into detail at that moment.

"How did you . . . never mind, it doesn't matter," Liam said. "You tell me later, when this is over and done with."

"Cole . . ." I started to say, my grip on him tightening.

His face twisted with fresh grief. "Later, okay? It's not too much farther. We had to set the meet point nearby—too many kids to drive out. I wish you could have seen it—Amplify pushed the information we gave them out everywhere. TV, the Internet, traffic signs—they bombarded the world with the truth."

"Let's see if it actually worked," Vida muttered. "If there aren't any parents waiting—"

"They'll be waiting," Liam insisted.

No matter how many steps I took, it still felt like we were falling farther and farther away from the lights filtering through the trees. I knew he was right, though, when the first helicopter appeared over us, casting a light down and kicking up the wind and rain. It was blinding—I couldn't tell if it belonged to the military or to the news.

There had been a din of noise, this faint low buzz of energy and sound I'd barely been able to detect under the shrill ringing in my ears. Now it was like I could hear the pulse of the world around me, throbbing underfoot. Up ahead, there were more lights, all pointed toward us.

The assault team, kids and adults alike, brought the huge group up short, just past the line of trees. There were buildings nearby, most likely the abandoned downtown area of Thurmond, West Virginia. Liam and Vida navigated us up through the sea of stalled bodies, shouldering our way closer to the front.

Three thousand children spread out through the trees like an avalanche, stopping up every gap between them. I knew when we were close because someone got on a bullhorn and barked out, *"Remain where you are! Any advancement will be seen as a sign of hostile aggression!"*

But if the armed forces saw us, so did the families gathered behind them.

We were moving forward again, slowly now, but at a steady pace. Finally, through the blinding field ahead of us, shapes began to form.

Two large, white tents had been set up by someone. Lights from ambulances and cop cars flashed blue, red, blue, falling over us and the double lines of soldiers that stood between us and hundreds, if not thousands, of people.

I blinked, trying to clear my thoughts. This was right—this was how it was supposed to be. Alice would have released her last blast of information during the assault, including the names of the children at Thurmond, and a location where they could be retrieved. I'd assumed that it would also give the military time to respond, and I'd been right. The soldiers, National Guard, police, and PSFs alike had assumed a defensive stance, shielded by riot gear.

"Drop your weapons, get down on the ground, and place your hands on your head," the same man ordered. *"Any further advancement will be seen as a sign of hostile aggression and we will open fire."*

We kept moving forward, toward the men and women in camouflage, toward the few in black PSF uniforms, until we were less than three hundred feet away.

The tall, clear riot shields formed an actual wall between us, but didn't mask the way the soldiers' eyes flickered over us.

The row behind them was armed and primed to do exactly as the officer had threatened; the muzzles of their guns were carefully placed in the gaps of space between the shields. They stood back-to-back with a row of FBI and uniformed police officers, who were facing the crowd of reporters and civilians. Cameras—there were cameras everywhere, flashing, recording, even as the men and women tried to block the shots or smash the devices altogether.

The helicopter's propeller announced its arrival long before it appeared in the sky. Its searchlight swept over us several times, as if scanning for one person in particular. A soldier sat at the edge of the open door, an automatic rifle in his hands as he took stock of the situation.

The officer in charge stood just left of center, behind both lines of soldiers. There was a satellite phone pressed to his ear; he kept ducking in and out of sight, as if crouching down could somehow drown out the noise of the crowd that rose behind him, breaking over all of us in a rush.

Names, I thought, forcing myself to look beyond the weapons and the gear, to the faces of regret and hope behind them. One of the kids behind me recognized one of them, clearly, because she surged forward with a shout of, "Mom—*Mom!*"

"Get down on the ground and put your hands behind your head," the officer yelled into the bullhorn. *"Do it now—now!"*

"Here!" a woman shouted back. "I'm here! Emily, I'm here!"

Watching the face of the soldier directly in front of me was like seeing a trickling creek become a river; emotion roared across his eyes, and not even the glare of the chopper's searchlight could disguise the look he cast back at the woman, who was struggling against the three FBI agents pushing her to the ground. The civilians around her pushed back, trying to drive them away from her.

The soldier was well past the point of youth; the stubble on his weathered cheeks was silver, matching the heavy brows above his pale blue eyes. He faced forward again, ignoring the uncomfortable shifting of the younger men and women to his left and right as they waited for their next order. His gaze shifted to a girl a few feet away from me. She was crying, still yelling, "Mom! Mom!" Her dark curls stuck to her wet cheeks.

The soldier shook his head. Such a slow, simple movement. He shook his head and let the riot shield fall forward into the mud. The sound somehow cut off all others. His own automatic rifle he left on the ground as he straightened up to his full height, chest out and forward, as he dodged the hand of the dumbstruck soldier next to him who'd half-heartedly put an arm out to stop him.

He stepped over his own shield, snapping the clips on his Kevlar vest and tugging it off. The helicopter's light found his path and traced it as he came toward us slowly, showing that he was unarmed. He held out his hand to her, and, after a moment of hesitation, she took it and allowed him to draw her forward to drop the vest over her head. His helmet came off next, and though it was too big for her, he clipped it on anyway, adjusting the strap tight under her chin.

The soldier picked her up and she locked her arms around his neck in complete trust. As he carried her back toward the line of soldiers, the officer in charge finally shook off his stupor enough to realize he should be shouting orders. He tried. No one, not a single one of us, listened. I heard my heart in my ears, louder and louder, and held my breath.

Holding out an arm, he pushed his way through the soldiers that tried to close the gap he'd left in the line, until, finally, the few FBI agents still standing over the woman released her. She met the soldier halfway, tearing the girl out of his arms and into hers. It wasn't until Liam reached up and lightly squeezed the arm I had around his neck that I realized the kids around me were moving again. The crack in the line of soldiers expanded as two kids followed the path they had taken through, three kids, four . . .

The officer was shouting into the megaphone, but except for a rare few, the soldiers were lifting their riot shields out of formation and turning to the side. The kids flooded through them, the same way they'd flowed through the trees; finding the openings, gathering their courage close, and passing through them.

Vida said something I couldn't hear. My head was too heavy now for my neck to support, and both of them stumbled as my left leg crumpled beneath me. Liam's hands were on my face, forcing my eyes open. It was so cold—how could I be sweating?

I was lifted up completely, carried through the crush of families. More than one had thought to make signs with their child's name, using those strange, unthinkable phrases like *welcome home* and *we love you*.

When my eyes opened again, the next face I saw was Chubs's; the word on his lips was *shock*. And Cate—there was *Cate*, her cheek bruised, tears in her eyes. She held my face between her hands and was talking to me as I was lifted off the ground.

The red, blue, red, blue, white lights stained their skin. I knew we were running, but I couldn't feel anything, even as I was lifted again, higher this time. Onto a soft surface. Unfamiliar faces. Lights flashing, snapping sounds, voices, Liam—

Ambulance. Liam tried to climb into the back with me, but he was forced out as two of the assault team members were loaded on—two men, one clutching a unnaturally limp arm, the other bleeding profusely at the brow.

"I'll come find you!" Liam was shouting as he backed out. "We'll find you!"

The EMTs strapped me down, pushing me back onto the stretcher. Liam stood a few feet away and Chubs had his arms around him, trying to talk him down, hold him in place. He saw the panic surging in him clearly as I had.

The doors slammed shut and the siren switched on.

"—tell me your name? Can you tell me your name?" The EMT was a young woman, her expression serious as she studied me. "We have a possible transverse fracture of the right tibia. Four—five—six lacerations, ranging from four centimeters to six on the upper and lower body—look at me. Can you tell me your name? Can you speak?"

I shook my head, tongue like stone.

"Are you in pain?"

I nodded.

"Blood pressure low, rapid pulse—hypovolemic shock—can you—?" One of the men on the floor was blocking the drawer she needed to get into, but pried it open with his good arm, passing her what looked like a large sheet of tinfoil. The EMT spread it over me as another put a line in my arm and began bandaging.

The strange blanket trapped in a little pocket of warmth. I began to tremble as the pain woke up again.

"What happened to your leg?" I grunted as she lifted it into some kind of brace. "Can you tell me what happened to your leg?"

"Hurts—" I choked out.

She held my face in between her hands and I felt wild, almost unhinged, as I looked into her eyes. "You're okay, you're safe. We're going to take care of you. You're safe."

One of the soldiers on the floor reached up, his blood-stained hand coming to rest softly over my wrist. "You're a good girl," he said, "you're a good, brave girl. You did a good job."

"You're safe now," the EMT repeated. "We're going to take care of you."

The wall I'd built up against the well of pain and fear and anger finally collapsed, and I began to cry. I sobbed, the way I had in the garage of my parents' house on that last morning before they took me, I bawled, because it was such a relief not to have to hold it in any longer, to have to pretend.

I didn't have to stay awake when the first pull of peaceful nothing came.

TWENTY-SEVEN

FOR DAYS, I FELT LIKE I WAS TRAPPED INSIDE MY OWN body.

There were moments, few and far between, where I could sense I was waking up, coming close to the surface of reality. Unfamiliar sounds, clicking, wheezing, beeps. Faces behind blue paper masks. Ceilings passing overhead. I had the most vivid dreams of my life, haunted by people I hadn't seen in years. I rode in the front seat of a black van, my forehead against the glass. I saw the ocean. The trees. The sky.

In the same way that the earth always hardens again after the rain, I felt myself solidify again, becoming a whole made of pieces. And one morning, I simply woke up.

To a room full of sunshine.

I blinked, body and head heavy and slow as I turned toward the source of the light. A window, the curtains framing the flowering arm of a nearby dogwood tree. The walls were painted a soothing light blue, a strange contrast to the dark gray machinery beeping and glowing around me.

Hospital.

I dragged myself up, meeting the resistance of the wires attached to the back of my hand with a few gentle tugs. Someone had draped a thin white sheet over me, and I had to use my left leg to kick it off in order to inspect the new, unexpected weight around the right. A plaster cast. A long, flannel pajama shirt. Beneath it, my arms were heavily bandaged, and I felt the pull of tape along my collarbone; I reached up to feel the gauze padding.

I let myself relax, listening just for a moment to the sound of the street below, the stream of voices on the other side of the wall. Some part of me knew that I should be afraid, but I was too exhausted to try. When I couldn't stand the sour, dry feeling of my mouth and throat any longer, I reached for the water glass on the stand nearby and downed it in one go, nearly knocking over a small vase of flowers.

There were crutches leaning against the opposite wall, under a TV mounted from the ceiling. But the moment I started to swing my feet over the side of the bed, the door cracked open.

I don't know who was more surprised—me, or the petite, steel-haired woman who stepped inside with a small tray of food. Green eyes widened.

"You're awake!" She shut the door quickly behind her, then turned back to me, absolutely glowing.

I stared at her, devouring the sight. She mistook my silence for distress—or confusion, I thought—because she quickly set the tray down and dragged a nearby chair over. "Do you know who I am?"

The word burst out of me. "Grams."

She grinned, taking my hand and holding it between her soft, paper-thin skin. For a long time, we did nothing but study each other. Her face was softer now, and she'd let her dark hair lighten

512

completely. But there was this look of mischief in her eyes that was so uniquely hers, I felt myself choke up at the sight.

"You've seen some trouble, haven't you?"

I nodded and she leaned over and kissed my forehead.

"You're here," I repeated, somehow dumbfounded by this. "You found me."

"Little girl, after they took you, we never stopped looking for you. The moment they released the list of children and the location of the camp, we were in the car speeding straight for you. It took us hours to find out which hospital you were in. You had quite the crowd guarding you, they almost didn't let me and your folks in."

I shook my head, unable to process this. "They don't remember me."

"No, they don't. It's very odd, but they . . . how do I say it? They can't drum up the details, but you've always been there. Deep down. Not here," she said, tapping her forehead. She moved her hand down to cover her chest. "Here."

I almost couldn't get the words out. "Do you know what I am?"

"Well, for starters, you're my darling, precious girl, who can do something a little peculiar with her mind," she said, her soft Southern accent stronger than ever. "You also seem to be somewhat of a media darling."

I sat back at that, suspicion working a slow path through my mind.

Grams held up a finger, walking over to retrieve a newspaper from a purse I hadn't noticed by the door. "It's been a feeding frenzy outside of the hospital for days. You have two armed guards posted outside of your room at all times, a whole wing to yourself, and still a vulture tried to sneak in and take a photo of you."

The New York Times had run with the news of the camp hit and the subsequent fallout. I spread the newspaper out over my lap, apprehension already cutting through my hard-won calm. In the time I'd been gone, Alice's original idea for an information package had changed, blossoming into the complete story of what had happened in Los Angeles, and at the Ranch. It was pages of her photographs of us, all of us—planning, playing, working. The road code. She'd written about why the deceptions had been necessary, and what editors and media bosses had worked with us to cover up the truth until the Thurmond camp hit began. There was a long profile of Cole, his face grinning up at me in black and white.

And then there was the piece about me. While she hadn't gone into any details about my abilities, Alice had deprived readers of pretty much nothing else. I was at the edge of many of her photos, just out of frame, face hidden by shadows or hair. The others—Cate, especially—must have filled her in on how I'd escaped Thurmond in the first place, what my life had been like on the run and with the League, and then, how I'd been willing to go back to the camp to help them. The paper had run photos of me being carried to the ambulance, but Liam's face was out of the shot. It might as well have been a completely different person because I didn't recognize that small, pale girl at all.

I shrank back against the pillow, feeling exposed under Grams's watchful eye.

"There's more, if you'd like to read it," she said, taking the paper away.

"Not now," I said. "Has anyone else . . ."

"Hmm?" Grams walked the paper back across the room and took up her tray of hospital food again, settling it over me. "Has anyone else, what?"

"Been by," I mumbled. "To visit."

Grams gave me a knowing smile. "A charming young woman with a mouth that could give a sailor a heart attack? A sweet little one who brought you flowers? The one who spent half a day chasing doctors and nurses around, demanding answers about your condition? *Or*, by any chance, are you referring to a very well-mannered Southern boy?"

"All of them," I whispered. "Are they here?"

"Not at the moment," Grams said. "They had to go back to the hotel—everyone's in Charleston for this fancy press conference. But they were here, and they asked me to give you this for when you woke up, so you'd know how to find them."

Grams handed me a folded piece of paper. Hotel stationery, as it turned out, with a telephone number scrawled across it. *Call as soon as you can.* Liam's handwriting.

"I missed you very much, darling girl," Grams said softly. "One day, I hope you'll talk to me about what's happened to you. I don't want to read about it; I'd much rather hear it from you."

"I missed you too," I whispered. "So, so much. I wanted to find you."

She smoothed the hair back from my face. "Do you want to see them now?"

I didn't need any clarification about who *them* meant.

"Do they . . ." I swallowed. "Do they want to see me?"

"Oh, yes," Grams said. "As long as it's all right with you."

After a moment, I nodded. When she left the room, I balanced my tray on the small table. My heart was hammering in my chest the moment I heard their footsteps.

The last time, I thought, *this is the last time I'll do this. . . .*

Grams appeared first, stepping aside to let a slight, frail woman in, followed closely by a salt-and-pepper-haired man.

It was remarkable how little I remembered about what they really looked like. Maybe the years had done damage to them the way they had to me, thinning them out, running them back and forth over life's sharp edges. It was so odd to see the shape of my nose on another person's face. My eyes. My mouth. The dimple on my chin. He wore a polo shirt tucked into slacks, she wore a dress, and I had the strange thought that they had dressed up to see me.

I wished it didn't feel so painfully uncomfortable, but I could see it in their faces. They looked at me, and all they remembered was the morning I'd been taken away, when they'd forced me out of the house in their confusion. The years stood between us, empty, aching.

So I started with the sweetness. A camping trip we had taken a very, very long time ago in the Blue Ridge Mountains; the hike down through the autumn trees, just beginning to change their colors. The air had been crisp and clear, the rolling mountains only a few shades darker than the endless blue sky above. We'd slept together, the three of us, in this little pocket of warmth in our tent, fishing for our food. I'd watched, amazed, as Dad had started the campfire.

The knotted memories released with only the slightest touch, as if they'd already begun to unravel on their own. I pulled back from each of their minds in turn, barely able to control my own feelings without the sudden flood of theirs.

"Someone please say something," Grams said, exasperated.

But I didn't need to say a word. I only needed to let them hold me as they cried.

I've heard some people say life can change in a day, completely flipping you feet over head. But they're wrong. Life doesn't need a day to change.

It needs three.

Three days for parachutes to start falling from the sky, bringing packages and soldiers in blue United Nations berets into the cities that needed them most.

For a small coalition of foreign leaders to step foot on American soil for the first time in seven years.

For Senator Cruz's story to be released, and for her to be chosen to oversee the entire country's restoration process.

For the chairman of the Joint Chiefs of Staff to resign, shrugging off the shame and collecting his pension.

For the Armed Forces to issue new orders, and to then realize the men and women who'd left their postings were never coming back.

For the President of the United States of America to disappear off the face of the earth.

For the United Nations to divide the country up into four peacekeeping zones, each overseen by a former senator of that region and a foreign power, and send in troops to oversee the policing.

For the first of nearly a hundred water riots to occur.

For Leda Corp to issue a statement denying their involvement in Agent Ambrosia, but oh-so-generously offering to supply a chemical they claimed could neutralize it.

I read about it in the papers my parents brought in. Watched it on the news. Absorbed this new reality. And that night, when visiting hours were over and two kind-but-firm nurses led my family away, I reached over for the phone on the wall. The pain-killers they'd given me were making me drowsy, but I didn't want to sleep without hearing his voice. Without making sure they were all okay.

I dialed the number and lay back down, the phone cradled between my ear and shoulder. I spun the curling phone cord around my fingers, waiting as it rang . . . and rang . . . and rang. And rang.

They're probably out. Doing . . . something. I tried not to let myself deflate as I started to reach over to hang the phone back up. I could try again in the morning.

"*Hello?*" The voice burst through the connection, breathless. "*Hello?*"

I drew the phone back and smiled as I whispered, "Hi."

Liam let out a soft breath. "*It's so good to hear your voice. How are you feeling?*"

"Better now."

"*I'm so sorry we couldn't stay. Senator Cruz asked us to come back to the hotel—there's been—it's no excuse, but it's been busy. Both Chubs and Vi said that you'd be mad at us if we didn't go.*"

"They were right." I settled back down on my side. "What's been going on? Grams said something about a press conference?"

"*Yeah, for the plan. The big plan. It's been a parade of faces coming in and out—oh, God, and get this. We have a representative in the deliberations.*"

"Who?" I asked. If it wasn't Liam, then . . . who?

"Guess who opened his big Chubsie mouth and started, in glorious detail, outlining every single thing he thought Senator Cruz should be doing the other night at dinner? It was a magnificent rant."

I closed my eyes, laughing. "No. Really?"

"Really. She told him that he had to report to the meeting room the next morning," Liam continued. *"He was either elated or irritated by the honor. Sometimes it's hard to tell with him."*

I listened to the sound of him breathing in the silence that followed. "Are you okay?"

"Yeah. Yeah, darlin', everyone's fine," he said, but there was an obvious strain in his voice. *"Mom's getting here tomorrow. She keeps saying that word, too: fine. I'm . . . I just wish you were here, is all. I'm going to come first thing tomorrow."*

"No," I said, "first thing in the morning, I'm coming to you."

"Maybe I'll just have to meet you halfway," he said, a laugh tucked into the edge of his voice.

I listened as he told me about the hundred-odd kids who were still waiting to be picked up by their parents. They'd been given free rooms at the hotel, free meals too, and a veritable army of volunteers had come in with supplies and clothes. He told me about catching Vida and Chubs getting handsy with each other in the elevator. Zu's small shrug when she was told her parents had managed to leave the country, and, until they could be contacted, she had a choice: go home and stay with her aunt, uncle, and Hina, or live with Vida, Nico, and Cate near D.C., so the latter could consult with Senator Cruz. How it hadn't even taken her a second to settle on D.C.

I told him about my parents. The way the soldiers posted outside of my door peeked in every time it opened. The way the doctor's hand shook, just a little, as he examined my cuts. And at some point, I felt myself begin to drift off to sleep.

"Hang up, go to sleep," Liam said, sounding just as tired.

"You hang up."

And in the end, neither of us did.

The next morning, clear on the other side of town, I sat sandwiched between my parents on a couch in the lobby of a Marriott hotel in Charleston, West Virginia. It was a testament to how packed it was that no one, not a single member of the press, seemed to notice me as we sat there. At about a quarter til, the crowds began to migrate toward the elevators to head up to the large conference room.

As we waited, Mom kept insisting I needed something—water, a snack, a book, some Tylenol—until finally, Dad reached over and placed a calming hand on her arm. I caught him watching me out of the corner of his eye, though, as if he needed to keep checking I was still there. This was how we were warming to each other: slowly, clumsily, earnestly.

Grams paced the floor in front of us, and it was only because she stopped that I knew someone was coming.

But it wasn't Liam or Vida—it was Cate. Her pale blond hair had been smoothed back into a neat ponytail, and she was wearing makeup, a dress. She seemed shadowed somehow, face drawn in a way that made my heart clench. I flew up to my feet, my dad reaching up to steady me as I rocked forward on my walking cast. Her pace slowed somewhat as she saw me, and I was glad when I saw the smile stretch across her face. If she had started crying, I wouldn't have trusted myself not to.

"I'm so proud of you," she whispered. "You fill me with awe. Thank you."

I hugged her as fiercely as she hugged me and I was filled, filled to the brim, with the warmth of her love. When I finally released her and introduced her to my family, it was clear they were already well aware of who she was.

She clasped my hands in hers. "Can we talk later? I need to run upstairs, but I didn't want to go another minute without seeing for myself that you were okay."

I nodded, letting her draw me into another embrace. Just as I started to pull back, she said, her voice low, "There's someone here you won't want to see."

I had a feeling I knew exactly who she was talking about, and was grateful she had given me a warning ahead of time to prepare myself.

Liam, Vida, Nico, and Zu got off the elevator that she got on. I couldn't stop the broad grin from spreading across my face. Zu was the first to reach me, a streak of pink dress cutting through the lobby to wrap her arms around my center. Nico hung back, shifting awkwardly between his feet until I urged him over. Vida had no such qualms. She gave me a hard punch to the shoulder, which I think I was supposed to read as "playful." And Liam, well aware of my parents' eyes on him, reintroduced himself to them, shaking their hands. He came toward me slowly, giving me time to get a good read on him. His hair was cut and tamed, and he was clean-shaven. If he was tired, it didn't show—but I saw a shadow of grief in his eyes. When he offered a small, shy smile, I returned it, my heart feeling like it was about to leap out of my chest.

"Hello again, ma'am," he said, perfectly polite as he shook Grams's hand. She planted a big one on his cheek and turned to me with a wink.

When he reached me, Liam simply took my arm and asked, "Everyone ready to go up?"

It was stupid to feel a pang of disappointment that I hadn't gotten a proper greeting, but my hands were practically burning with the need to run my hands through his hair, smooth the lines from his face.

When the elevator doors slid open I started forward, but he held us in place, allowing my parents, Zu, Vida, Nico, and about a half-dozen others onto the elevator. "You know what?" Liam said, waving my dad off when he reached to hold the doors open. "We'll get the next one."

And the minute the doors slammed shut, his arm slid around my waist, his other hand wove through my hair, and I was being kissed to within an inch of my life.

"Hi," he said when he finally came up for air.

"Hi," I said, now both dizzy and breathless as he leaned down to rest his forehead against mine. "Do we have to go up?"

He nodded, but it was another few moments before he actually reached over and pushed the up button.

The press conference had been set up in the hotel's ballroom space—a room that accommodated a hundred chairs, three-fourths of which were already taken by the time we got up there. When I saw that the others had saved us seats at the very back in the room, I almost cried in gratitude. Already, I was feeling eyes shift toward me, and the uncomfortable feeling would only have been compounded if we'd been in a position for the whole room to stare at the back of my head. If I couldn't make a clean escape if I needed to. Liam seemed to sense this and guided me forward, a hand on the small of my back, to an aisle seat.

No sooner had we found our spots than two men, both in military dress uniforms, moved away from us to the other side of the room. Vida gave them a little toothy smile and wave when they glanced back at us again.

The room shushed itself into silence as the first people walked out onto the stage. All were men, some military, some clearly politicians—those were the ones who remembered to turn and smile for the cameras before sitting down. I released a deep breath as Senator Cruz appeared, followed by Dr. Gray, and then, surprisingly, Cate. Liam's hand found mine as Chubs walked out, shoulders back, eyes forward. He wore a beautiful navy suit and a striped tie, finishing off the look with new, thin, wire-rimmed glasses.

"Nerd," I heard Vida mutter, but she had this pleased little smile on her face.

I glanced at Liam and found an expression as grim as mine. It was a fine package Chubs had wrapped himself in, almost enough to distract me from the look on his face. I'd seen it a dozen times—the chin jutting out, the eyes sullen. It was the look of someone who had just lost a vote.

"Damn," Liam murmured. "This is going to be bad."

And it was.

"Thank you for coming here today," Senator Cruz began, speaking without the sheet of notes someone leaned over and placed in front of her. "The last five days have been a true test of American fortitude, and I believe I speak not only for my former Congressional colleagues, but also for our foreign allies, when I thank you for your cooperation as we begin to roll out our recovery phases. The good news is, we're already eight days into the first."

Cameras *click, click, click*-ed.

"I'd like to take the time to walk you through the agreement that we signed this morning. Please save your questions until the very end, when we'll have a few moments to address them." She took a breath, shuffling her papers. "The four peacekeeping zones we established will remain in place for the next four years. Reconstruction in cities and towns that were decimated by this struggle, or by natural disasters for which the government failed to provide aid, will be handled by the peacekeeping coalition of countries in each zone, the details of which will be covered in subsequent, separate press conferences."

She let the audience absorb that before continuing. "Each zone will also be responsible for overseeing the neutralization of Agent Ambrosia in groundwater and wells found within its boundaries, as well as the destruction of any stockpiles of the chemical. Any further use of it throughout the world, as well as any use of Psi-afflicted youth as soldiers, clandestine agents, or government officials in this nation or others is explicitly forbidden by this agreement, and will be condemned."

Lillian's eyes scanned the room, almost catching mine. She sat up a little straighter, and looked pained, clearly knowing what was coming next.

"Children remaining in rehabilitation camps will be returned to their families over the course of the next month. We will be providing a searchable database to locate where each child is currently residing, but parents will not be allowed access to the camps. As part of our agreement, they will be destroyed."

Shock hit me like a blow to the face. The room began to

rumble with voices—low conversations, shouted questions, everything in between. Out of the corner of my eye, I could see Grams trying to gauge my reaction, but I couldn't bring myself to tear my eyes from the stage.

"The life-saving operation developed by Dr. Lillian Gray will be provided, free of charge, for as long as this terrible mutation exists in our society. Any Psi-afflicted person over the age of eighteen will be allowed to decide whether to opt out of the surgery, but will be required to carry special identification. Whether or not a child under the age of eighteen receives the treatment will be left to the discretion of their parents or guardians."

Lillian's eyes fell back to the table.

"We have set aside several miles of land on which to build a community for any unclaimed child, or any child who feels as though they cannot return home safely. We will require that all Psi-afflicted citizens who choose not to undergo the procedure live out the remainder of their lives in one of these communities."

I must have made some noise of disgust, because my family turned to look at me.

At that same moment someone on the stage let out a low, furious, "That is *bullshit.*"

And that someone was Chubs.

"Hold your tongue—" One of the men in uniforms was on the receiving end of a glare that would have melted a lesser man into a quivering puddle. Cate looked down at the table, biting her lip in an effort to hide her smile.

Senator Cruz coughed, shuffling her papers. Before she could begin speaking again, Chubs was already midway into his next sentence.

"Let's lay this out fully, shall we?" he began.

"Oh Jesus," Liam said, looking upward for strength.

"As an eighteen-year-old," Chubs said, "I finally have the right to choose what I want for myself, but, if I make the wrong choice, I'll still be punished for it?"

"Please save your questions for the end." But even as she said it, Senator Cruz made a small, almost imperceptible motion with her hands, as if to encourage him.

"I'm not finished," Chubs said. "If I were to choose to not have someone, potentially an incompetent someone, cut into my brain—the most important organ in my body—to 'fix' it, then I'm stuck in yet another camp, this time for the rest of my life?"

"Oh, I like him," Grams said, delighted.

"It's not a camp," one of the men in uniform said impatiently. "It's a community. Now can we move back to—"

"A community with barbed-wire fences? Armed guards? You realize that by doing this, all you're accomplishing is reinforcing in America—throughout the world—that the word *different* means *bad*, *ugly*, *dangerous*. There's no rehabilitation in that; you just want to sweep us under the rug and hope time takes care of us. I'm sorry, but that's pretty damned terrible, and clearly you *know* it's pretty damned terrible, because you've spent a total of two seconds laying out a plan that affects thousands of lives which have already been ruined by another group of people—some of them probably in this room."

"Psi-afflicted humans have abilities that are dangerous and cannot be controlled," the man reasoned. "They can be used as tools for individuals to commit crimes, gain unfair advantages, and harm others."

"Yeah? So can a pile of money. It's what a person chooses to do with their abilities that matters. By locking someone up for making a choice about their body that they have every right to make, what you're essentially saying is that, no, you don't trust us. Not to make good choices, not to treat others well. I find that incredibly insulting—and, by the way, I seem to be in pretty good control of my abilities now, wouldn't you say?"

"You believe children as young as eight, nine, ten, should be allowed to make a life-altering decision?" Senator Cruz was feeding him a counterargument to play off of—I sat back slightly, relieved my opinion of her hadn't been far off-base. She might have been overruled by the panel she sat with now, but she had found a creative way of getting her point across.

"I'm saying that the kids who've had years of their lives stolen have had time to weigh what they would choose if the opportunity came to be cured of it," Chubs said. "They've had time to think about what they would choose, and can make an educated decision. Trust me, that's all any of us ever thought about, as every hour of every day was controlled down to the minute, or when we had to struggle every day for food and water and shelter, while men and women literally hunted us. You're going to set the mark at eighteen, knowing that eighty percent of all kids previously interned at a camp can't meet that benchmark? I, at eighteen, was in a camp for a year. One of my best friends was in hers for six years, but she's only seventeen. She has to subject herself to a decision made by the same people who sent her away in the first place?"

I grimaced, fighting not to look over at my parents. I didn't need them feeling any guiltier than they already did.

"We need to move on from this topic," another one of the men said, "otherwise we won't be able to take questions—"

"I agree," Dr. Gray said suddenly, then clarified. "With the young gentleman. Unless they've committed a crime, or the psychological toll of their experiences has impacted their decision-making abilities, or they've harmed someone, I believe the children we take out of the camps should be able to choose. However, parents of children who haven't reached the life-or-manifest threshold should be allowed to make the decision and will need to do so before their child's seventh birthday."

Her voice was strained to the point of fraying, beyond tired. The reporters ate up every single word she offered, jumping to their feet to launch a volley of questions at her, all of which could be summed up as: *Where is President Gray?*

Senator Cruz stared at her notes, then asked casually, "Do you believe you could figure out a better system, given what we have to work with?"

"Yes," Chubs said without a hint of arrogance. "And I think if you proceed with this option, you'll not only be ignoring the mental and emotional health needs of the children coming out of the camps, but you'll be condemning them to a life of fear and shame. And if it's going to be that way, then you might as well have left them in the camps."

"Good," Senator Cruz said, "We'll reconvene our discussion on this point following the conclusion of this panel. Should any other Psi-afflicted youth like to join us, please speak to me."

In the midst of all of this, someone had disappeared from the front row of seats—a young man in a baseball cap. He'd faded to the outer edge of the room, and was moving quickly toward the exit. With his face turned down and his arms crossed over his chest, he could have been anyone.

But I knew exactly who he was.

I slipped away, waving off Liam's and Vida's questioning eyes, and held up a single finger. I had a feeling this was going to take far longer than a minute, but with Senator Cruz talking again, this time about future congressional and presidential elections, their attention was drawn back to her.

The hall outside was ten degrees cooler than the stuffy sweat-box the ballroom was becoming. I had a feeling he had come out here for the silence, though, more than the cool air. He'd walked nearly to the end of the long hall, and taken a seat across from a window overlooking the hotel's parking lot.

"Come to laugh, have you?" Clancy asked, his voice hoarse. He never turned his head, only kept his eyes trained on the window. "Enjoy it."

"I'm not here to laugh," I said.

He snorted, but said nothing. Eventually, his hands tightened in his lap, clenching and releasing. "I keep losing feeling in my right fingers. They said they'd never seen the complication before."

I bit back the reflexive *I'm sorry.* I wasn't.

"I told you this would happen, didn't I?" Clancy said. "That the choice all of you were stupidly chasing ended up in the hands of the people who put you away in the first place. It didn't have to be this way."

"No," I said pointedly. "It didn't have to."

For the first time, he turned and looked directly at me. The recovery from the surgery had drained some of the meat from his bones and the color from his skin. I had a feeling that if I were to lift off the baseball cap, I'd find a newly shaved head and fresh scars hidden there. "What happened to Nico?"

Well. I hadn't expected that. "He's here. Didn't you see him?"

His shoulders rose and fell with the next deep breath he took in.

"Did you want to talk to him about something?" I prompted. "Maybe about something you *regret*?"

"I only regret losing control of the situation. But . . . it doesn't matter. I can figure a way around this, how to deactivate the device she planted there. How to get everything back. I can do it. I'm closer to the right people than ever. I can find my father, wherever he's hiding. *I* can do it."

And, somehow, I'd known that would be his answer. Because this is who Clancy was at his core: someone who'd always had everything, and still needed more. Still wanted the one thing he'd never, ever be able to achieve.

But when he looked at me, his dark eyes sunken back into his skull, it told me something else—that maybe what he really wanted, what he couldn't admit out loud, was the exact same thing his mother had wished for all these years. Pride played a dangerous game in his heart, warring with exhaustion. I felt myself hesitate, fingers curling into fists as I thought of all of the lives he'd played with so callously, the good ones that had been lost, so that he could find ways to survive.

And there, too, at the back of my mind was the boy on the examination table, scared and alone and boiling with helpless hatred.

The one with the sweet smile that now lived only in his mother's memory.

I knew what he would have done if our situations had been reversed, and I couldn't deny the small voice telling me to do exactly that—walk away, let the pain and humiliation grow in him like a cancer until they devoured him. And that alone was a reason to reconsider. Because no matter how many times he'd tried, he'd never successfully molded me in his image. And now he never would.

It wasn't to free him of his guilt.

It wasn't to punish him.

It wasn't anything other than an act of mercy.

There were no barriers between us, no blocks. His life spilled through my mind, whirling in colors and sounds I'd never been allowed to see, I'd never been strong enough to find. I took what I could and replaced it with something better. He had never been tested on, never been an Orange, never at East River, or in California. There were things I saw, secrets so horrible, I'd never wish to inflict on another person by sharing them. I focused on the brightness. I left him with only that—the simple story that he had been with his mother this entire time, that he had helped her all of these years, that the love he still felt for her was a good, pure thing to hold on to.

And when I turned to go, releasing his mind for the last time, he looked out the window again at the blackbirds diving and rolling around each other, fluttering across the blue sky, and he smiled.

I started back down the hall again, eyes down, thoughts a mess. I didn't see the woman coming out of the ladies' room until I collided with her, and ended up with a mouthful of her bright red curls.

"I'm sorry," I said, untangling myself. "I'm sorry—I wasn't paying attention."

"Lucky for me," the woman said, her voice low and smooth. "I've been trying to track you down for days. How's the leg, kid?"

At that I looked up, finally realizing who this was. Alice. She'd pulled herself together today, traded the scrubby jeans and coat I'd seen her in at the meeting point for a full suit that didn't quite fit her. Her hair was a loose, wild mane around her shoulders, held back by a pair of thick-framed glasses and a pen she'd probably stuck there and forgot about.

"It's been better," I said, eyeing her warily.

Seeing that I didn't return her smile, she sighed. "Look, kid, if this is about me running your story, I'm not going to apologize. I have a duty to report the facts, the truth . . . and the truth here is that it's a hell of a story. There are a few pieces of information you could fill in for me, if you have a second . . ."

"I don't."

Alice shifted uncomfortably, as if just remembering what I was and what I could do. She lowered her voice and glanced around to make sure that no one was listening. "I got a tip that Senator Cruz spoke to you and a few others about some kind of program—top-secret stuff. Ballsy of her, considering she just told that whole room that every nation is banned from using you all in any kind of military or clandestine services."

I schooled my reaction, keeping it neutral. Not yet. But I didn't doubt that the conversation was coming.

I stepped to the side, and she followed me, blocking the way again. If I hadn't been in the mood for this before, I was even less so now. "I have to warn you. I *really* don't respond well to being cornered."

Alice held up her hands. "All right, all right." Her hand disappeared into the purse looped over her arm, fishing around for something—a business card.

"If you ever want to talk," she said, "you call me any time. I'm all ears."

I waited until she disappeared back into the ballroom, then ripped the card in two and let the pieces flutter to the floor. I turned back to the ballroom just in time to see Zu and Vida come dashing out, holding hands as they ran toward the elevators. A moment later, Liam and a harried-looking Chubs appeared.

"Ah!" Chubs started to come toward me, his expression narrow. "You should be resting that leg—"

Liam released his shoulder and grabbed my hand. "Let's go, let's go—"

"What's happening?" I asked glancing into the ballroom as we passed it. Someone was up at the podium making a speech, but the room was otherwise exactly as I'd left it.

"Jail break," Liam said, his eyes bright as the elevator opened and he drew us inside. "Trust me."

Fear released its grip on my throat as we rode the elevator all the way down to the underground garage, Liam bouncing on his heels the entire time. Chubs eyed him warily as we were dragged back out.

Liam freed a set of keys from his pocket and held the black plastic fob up, listening for the sound of the lock. Vida and Zu appeared from behind one of the rows of cars and ran toward the beeping, flashing, dust-splattered SUV with Arizona plates.

"You are ridiculous," Chubs informed him as he walked toward the car, loosening his tie; but he went anyway, the smallest hint of a smile on his face.

I caught Liam's arm, hating the way his expression fell when he saw mine. "What's this about?"

I knew what denial looked like, and this had shades of it—the stubborn unwillingness to acknowledge that something was wrong. Something had overturned inside of him that could never be fully righted.

"It's about . . ." He ran a hand back through his hair. "It's about how everything will be different going forward. You'll go back to Virginia with your family, and I'll go back to North Carolina with mine. And if we want to see each other, I need permission to take the car. You'll need to run it by your parents to get their okay. We'll be living with a set of rules we haven't had in years, and while there's something a little wonderful in that, I just want this . . . I want to forget for a little while. Outrun the hurt. This one last time, I just want to go somewhere no one else can find us."

I smiled, taking his arm when he offered it. He walked us slowly, carefully, around the back of the car. He opened the door and helped me up into the front passenger seat, arranging my awkwardly bulky walking cast with care. He leaned in to buckle my seat belt, using it as an excuse to kiss me again.

"Where are we going?" Chubs shouted at him as Liam ran around the back of the car to the driver's-side door.

"Quiet, dear," Vida said mildly, resting a hand on his leg.

"Yes, dear," Chubs grumbled back.

Next to them, Zu beamed.

I was still smiling when Liam buckled himself in and turned to address the group. "Okay, team. Where to? I figure we have about an hour before the conference ends and, for once, we've got gas to burn."

"Is this how you got around before?" Vida wondered aloud. "It is a miracle you dumbasses survived."

534

"Told you," Chubs mumbled. I reached back and smacked his arm. "Fine. Okay. Where does everyone want to go?"

"Beach, beach, beach, beach," Zu chanted.

"Uh, not sure there's one nearby, so we'll have to take a rain check on that one. Anyone else?" Liam asked. "Vote?"

"I don't care," I said, leaning my head back against the seat. "Can we just get lost and see where that lands us?"

"Darlin', that is the best damn idea I've heard in a long time. You're navigator. Tell me when and where to turn." He turned the keys in the ignition, letting out a "Yes!" as an Allman Brothers song came pouring out of the speakers. By the time we rolled up the ramp and out of the parking garage, even Chubs's groans had turned to laughter.

We drove, winding through the city streets until we found green, tree-lined roads, making our way toward the lazy lines of the river that ran along the curved spine of the city. Liam glanced over at me, taking a break from his off-key crooning. Lit by the warm afternoon sunlight, his fingers entwined with mine over the center console. Zu rocked in time to the music, chattering excitedly about each and every sign we passed. Chubs slid a book out of the backseat pocket in front of him, examining the cover for a moment before flipping it open. His fingers absently tapped the cracked spine to the beat as Vida leaned against his shoulder and closed her eyes.

I brought my window down, letting my free hand drift out to catch the wind.

And the open road rolled out in front of us.

ACKNOWLEDGMENTS

It is a wonderful, bittersweet moment to arrive at this page and realize I've reached the end of a series that has been responsible for so many amazing memories—and for bringing some truly incredible people into my life.

I would again like to start by thanking the editorial geniuses I've been lucky enough to have in my corner: my editor, Emily Meehan, for seeing the potential in a story about superpowered teens roaming Virginia in a beat-up minivan, for her incredible eye for teasing out the heart of each book, and for not drop-kicking me out a window every time I turned in a 600-page draft (seriously); Laura Schreiber, for reading the story first, loving the characters in all the right ways, and working so hard on each draft from the very beginning; and Jess Harriton for the masterful behind-the-scenes work that kept us all on the same page.

To all of the heroes, fairy godmothers, wise guides, and wizards alike who make the magic happen at Hyperion every single day: working with you has brought this journey to a true happily-ever-after. Thanks much to Suzanne Murphy, Stephanie Lurie, Dina Sherman, Simon Tasker, Joann Hill, Marci Senders, Elke Villa, Seale Ballenger, Jamie Baker, Andrew Sansone—everyone!

This series would still be nothing more than a document on my computer if not for the guidance, encouragement, and care given to me by my amazing agent, Merrilee Heifetz. I'm also incredibly grateful to Sarah Nagel and Chelsey Heller for their support and savviness over the years. Thank you, Team Writers House!

Heaps of love to my critique partners and their smart, beautiful minds: Anna Jarzab, who has always seemed to know the story and characters better than I do, and has been both an invaluable sounding board and a champion, and Sarah Maas, who inspires me to be braver and dig deeper with each draft and for getting it—all of it!

I owe everything to my family—to my mom, queen of perseverance and unwavering love, for inspiring me to take risks; to Daniel for reading all those early drafts and giving me awesome feedback; and to Steph for never steering me wrong with her PR advice.

And to you, dear reader, for following Ruby and her friends to the end. I hope that when you have the chance to crack your world open wide with new possibilities, to meet new people, and to take a turn down an unexpected, new road, you do just one thing: carpe the hell out of that diem.